Oberst

Oberst

A NOVEL BY

WILLIAM HARRINGTON

DONALD I. FINE, INC.
NEW YORK

Library of Congress Catalogue Card Number: 86-82177

ISBN: 1-55611-014-6
Manufactured in the United States of America

10   9   8   7   6   5   4   3   2   1

To Diana With Love

I

WEDNESDAY, JUNE 14, 1944

SORRY, Sir, but you *are* a bit late, and your orders were to proceed on schedule, even if you were not here."

"But not the Kraut, Captain," said Colonel Sir Henry Harding.

"Oh no, Sir. Not him, not without your specific order. So far just the Irish lad. We're ready for Margaret Simon now. If you'd care to step in . . ."

Sir Henry glanced at the ashen face of the captain. He was sorry he couldn't have been a bit later himself, but of course it would not do to ask Captain Berkey and his crew to do what you were not willing even to witness yourself. Sir Henry set his shoulders and accompanied the captain into the execution chamber.

Wapping Special Prison was a red brick warehouse, separated from the Thames by a couple of acres of burned-out ruins. The dock that fed goods into this warehouse had been bombed to rubble in 1941, and in 1943 the building was taken over and converted into a temporary prison to house a limited number of special prisoners: spies and saboteurs and British men and women guilty of treason. Two special courts met within the walls: a civilian court that tried the treason cases and a military court that dealt with Axis spies and saboteurs.

Executions were necessarily carried out from time to time. At first, German

7

officers convicted of spying were shot by a firing squad, but the sound of the volleys had escaped the building and alarmed the neighborhood. Since the autumn of 1943, all executions were performed by hanging. The room into which Captain Berkey now led Colonel Sir Henry Harding was the room that housed the gallows.

Three army sergeants acted as executioners, each one a wounded veteran: one shot through the foot before he could be evacuated from Dunkirk, one with a left arm shattered on Crete, one riddled with forty-two identified pieces of shrapnel at El Alamein. They bustled about the big, high-ceilinged room in the center of the building, barking orders at the three frightened privates who had volunteered to assist.

As Colonel Sir Henry Harding and Captain Berkey entered, one of the sergeants was on a ladder above the gallows platform, knotting another thick hemp rope to the structural beam. The hangman's noose was already tied, with the traditional thirteen loops. Following orders, one of the privates seized the rope and climbed it a few feet; it stretched a little. It was right.

Sir Henry's eyes fastened on a stretcher that lay to one side of the gallows. A body wrapped tightly in a gray blanket lay there.

"The Irish lad," said Captain Berkey. "Terrence Kilbane. I swear, Sir, he was unconscious. They had to hold him up to put the noose around and—"

"Just as well," Sir Henry said brusquely. "We'll proceed with Mrs. Simon. Bring her in when you are ready."

The captain went to the telephone on the wall and gave the order to bring in Margaret Simon.

Colonel Sir Henry Harding smoothed his bristly white mustache with the index finger of his right hand and sat down at the small square table just inside the door. He was small and florid, the very caricature of a peppery guards colonel, a bit myopic but too vain to wear his glasses. He wore civilian clothes —a tight gray single-breasted suit, striped shirt, a guards tie.

Captain Berkey returned. "I'll say something, Sir. It may be a bit out of line, but it doesn't go well with the lads, and it doesn't with me, that we hang Terrence Kilbane and Margaret Simon but maybe not the German colonel." Captain Berkey took off his steel-rimmed glasses and wiped them with a handkerchief from his pocket. "After all, Sir, he's the chief offender. He is the one who recruited them."

"Colonel Heinrici is a German officer serving his country," Sir Henry said stiffly. "After all, we have chaps in the field serving like Heinrici. Terrence Kilbane was a traitor. So is Margaret Simon."

"Still—"

"Terrence Kilbane and Margaret Simon betrayed our country," Sir Henry continued sharply, "and their treason cost us dear. It may have cost the lives of hundreds of good men. What sort of people would we be, Captain, if we lost the courage to hang our traitors?"

"Very well, Sir."

Sir Henry turned his eyes to the six executioners, who were waiting for Margaret Simon. "Keep them here. Let them be ready," he said. "We may yet hang Colonel Heinrici."

Two young soldiers opened the door through which Sir Henry and Captain Berkey had entered, and two burly uniformed prison matrons led Margaret Simon into the chamber. A thickset, forty-year-old woman, she was dressed in gray coveralls, many sizes too big for her and rolled up halfway to her knees. Her hands were handcuffed behind her, and a wide leather belt circled her body, tightly pinning her arms. Pushed forward, she trudged barefoot toward the gallows, her steps shortened by the shackles around her ankles. When she caught sight of the scaffold and the noose, she moaned and stumbled. The matrons nearly lost her.

Sir Henry knew her. She had been in her time a communist, an anarchist, and a fascist; she had lived all her life in bitter protest, never certain—so far as Sir Henry could tell from his review of her thick file—just what it was she really supported.

It seemed that Margaret Simon had but one purpose in her life: to destroy, so that what she destroyed could be replaced with something better. But nowhere in her record was there any suggestion of what she thought would be better. She was the daughter of a Welsh coal miner, the wife of a London machinist, the mother of a son who was fighting in Burma.

She had recruited Terrence Kilbane to work with her in Heinrici's employ, and the testimony of the Kilbane boy was emphatic that the forty-year-old woman had made a carnal plaything of him. However, Terrence, toward the end, had been more deeply concerned about how he would explain to God his sins with Margaret Simon than how he would explain his crime of treason. In any event, the evidence was clear beyond any question: Margaret Simon had worked for Heinrici, helping him to gather information and operating what was known on the Continent as Radio Heinrici.

She was weeping, and when she saw the gray-wrapped body lying on the stretcher, she screamed. Her eyes darted around the room, stopping for an instant on Colonel Sir Henry Harding, long her interrogator; but the noose that waited for her on the scaffold drew her eyes irresistibly, and her focus locked on it.

The matrons pushed her up the steps of the scaffold. She was pushed, whimpering, to the center, where she stood on the trapdoor. One of the sergeants quickly circled her legs just below the knees with a belt and buckled it tightly. The chaplain stepped forward and spoke to her. She gawked dumbly at him.

As one of the sergeants put the noose over her head and tightened it on her throat, her long hair caught in the noose. Almost gently, he pulled it out. The sergeant held up the black hood, and she shook her head violently.

Now the sergeant stepped away, and the chaplain remained alone with her. They spoke urgently until the sergeant stepped forward and touched the chaplain's arm. The chaplain moved back.

Left alone on the trap door, Margaret Simon screamed—"NO! NO! OH, MY GOD!"

The sergeant shoved the lever over, and the trapdoor fell away from under her. The rope snapped taut. It jerked to and fro for a quarter of a minute, from her last convulsive kicks, then hung straight and silent.

Colonel Sir Henry Harding asked Captain Baldwin to pour the whiskey. He did not want to risk showing a trembling hand to the captain. Even more, he did not want Miss Adriana Kip to see his hands shake. He had been a soldier since 1917, but never before had he actually witnessed an execution.

Captain Baldwin left his cane leaning against his chair as he stepped to the table, opened Sir Henry's leather-covered traveling bar, and took out the whiskey and three silver cups. He could walk a few steps without the aid of a stick—hobble, actually. His left leg was beyond supporting his weight for more than a moment.

Adriana Kip watched him. Sir Henry studied her reaction to the captain's swaying progress from chair to table. Her pale blue eyes were intent and sympathetic, yet oddly detached. He had heard of her that she could be ruthless.

"I've not shown either of you the file," Sir Henry said. "It's a very confidential one. If you elect not to proceed with the mission—or refuse to work with him—I don't want you to know anything about this man. We may find another use for him, and I don't want the word out anywhere that we have him. You'll see why as we go into the matter."

Sir Henry accepted the shot of whiskey from Captain Baldwin, tossed it down, and handed the cup back for another shot.

"The question is," he went on, "do either of you reject the idea of going to Paris as two members of a mission of three—the other member being a German Abwehr colonel?"

"On what basis would we trust him?" asked Baldwin. "What prevents his betraying us the moment we are on the Continent?"

"I'd rather not say for now," said Sir Henry. "You will hear shortly, if you agree to work with him."

"How can we agree to work with him when we don't know the answer to that question?" asked Adriana Kip.

"I ask you only as a matter of principle," said Sir Henry. "If either of you would refuse to work with him in *any* circumstance, then there is no point in going further with the conversation."

"Do we retain the right to refuse once we have the facts on which we can judge the matter?" asked Adriana Kip.

Sir Henry nodded.

"Very well, then," she said. She raised her cup and swallowed her whiskey.

Adriana Kip was flawlessly beautiful. So everyone said, and Sir Henry, now that he had finally met her, understood what they meant. Her long hair was platinum blonde. Her eyes were icy blue. She had been a swimmer for the Dutch team at the 1936 Olympics in Berlin, and she retained the body of an Olympic athlete, even though she had borne a child in 1939. She was dressed tonight in dark blue coveralls, tightly belted at the waist and unzipped for coolness on this summer night—showing a hint of decolletage.

"Yes," said Sir Henry. "The German officer is an Abwehr colonel. Both of you understand, of course, that the Abwehr is the traditional German military intelligence organization, not one of the new Nazi organizations. Our colonel is not, in other words, a fanatic Nazi—or, at least not necessarily. To the contrary, he's a well-educated man, rather sophisticated, in fact. A linguist. You'll find his English flawless. His French is just as good."

"And you have him in custody here?" Adriana asked.

"Yes. He has been in England for some time. A spy. A very effective one, indeed. Fortunately, we got onto him eventually. Tonight—in fact only a few minutes ago—we hanged the two British traitors who were his confederates. In a little while we will offer him a chance to save his own life. If he doesn't take it, we will hang him immediately."

Adriana Kip lifted her cup. She frowned skeptically at Sir Henry. "The Germans don't know you've caught him," she said as she took a sip of whiskey.

"Uh . . . Yes, that's right. Perceptive of you, Miss Kip."

"And your control over him has something to do with that fact," she said.

"Precisely. So—shall we have him brought in?"

She shrugged, and Captain Baldwin nodded.

"Before we do, let me explain that the colonel has been the subject of a rather thorough psychiatric evaluation. We've learned that he's touchy on a point or two. One of them is his name. It is Heinrici—pronounced Hine-REEKY. He will bristle if you use any other pronounciation. He insists on the point that he is a soldier, serving his country. He was most distressed to learn that he would be hanged, not shot by a firing squad. He told us he expected to be put to death as a spy—accepted that risk when he volunteered—but that he expected an honorable death, shooting, not a shameful one."

"Sticky fellow," Baldwin said.

"If you agree to work with him, both of you will be given the complete file on him, including the psychiatrists' report. When you see the file you will see the recommendation that he be interrogated naked. We've followed that recommendation—to good effect, I think. But this evening, since you are here, Miss Kip, we will bring him in dressed."

"Don't make any concessions for me, Colonel," she said.

Colonel Sir Henry Harding smiled nervously. "Well, uh . . . You will discover that we are working with an exceptionally strong personality, and, uh, the technique *has* given us something of an advantage over him. If you are really sure you don't mind, Miss Kip . . ."

They had an exaggerated sense of drama, the English. No one had such a capacity for turning tragedy into farce. And they were playing out this one for all—no, more than—it was worth.

They had put him in a cell where he could hear the bang of the gallows. He had heard it twice, and he was supposed to believe they had hanged Terrence Kilbane and Margaret Simon. Maybe they had. Maybe not. He guessed there was another scene to be played before they led him to the gallows—for which they were staging elaborate preparations.

He sat on a wooden bench in a tiny, brick-walled cell: chained hand and foot, wearing gray coveralls so ludicrously small that he could not button them. If in fact they hanged him tonight, it was their intention, apparently, to be sure he went to the gallows without dignity. And dignity had always been important to him.

His mind went back to a spring morning in 1940. . . . He had stood that morning in a group of officers, beside a railroad track running through an undamaged Belgian village. The morning was sunny but pleasantly cool; a light breeze bore earthy odors from the fields. Belgian farmers trudging past hardly glanced at the knot of German officers. He recalled his thought: *Mensch und Ubermensch*, man and superman: his reaction to the contrast between the lumpy Belgian peasants and the proud young lions of the conquering army. *Mensch und Ubermensch*.

Then the Führer's train had arrived, early. A hundred guards scrambled out, forming a cordon, and two offensive SS officers examined the officers' sidearms to be sure they had all complied with their orders to carry them unloaded. Next came the dog, led from the train to relieve herself on the grass. Finally, the Führer, unmistakable in the light, wrinkled military raincoat, the cap, the well-known black trousers. He glanced around, took the dog's leash, and walked toward the knot of officers.

When Heinrici's turn came. He saluted the Führer and shook his hand, thinking that this was the man his father dismissed as a *strassenkind,* a street urchin. His father had mocked the toothbrush mustache, the posturing, the voice . . .

"You are the son of Generalleutnant Friederich Heinrici. I remember him from the Great War."

"Long since retired, Mein Führer. A schoolmaster for many years now. In Speyer."

Hitler nodded, then Heinrici's commanding officer told him briefly of Heinrici's services: "Very thorough work, Mein Führer. Because of what Major Heinrici did over the past two years, our paratroops and glider-borne engineers were able to save many bridges that otherwise would have been demolished by the Dutch. He provided exact charts, showing the placement of demolition charges, location of communications wires, where the nearest garrisons were, and so forth."

"You speak Dutch, Herr Major?" Hitler asked.

Heinrici grinned. "The Dutch seemed to think so, Mein Fürher."

The Führer was still chuckling as he hung around Heinrici's neck the Iron Cross, First Class. Heinrici had been told he would be awarded the medal, but he did not expect what happened next. As if on impulse—though Heinrici could not believe it happened that way—the Führer promoted him to the rank of oberst. Suddenly, at thirty-three he was the youngest colonel in the Wehrmacht. . . .

"All right, Heinrici. On your feet."

Captain Berkey unlocked the door and entered the cell, backed by two big sergeants.

"Is this, uh—"

"Not quite yet, apparently—and unfortunately," Berkey said. "You seem to be scheduled for further interrogation." One sergeant squatted to unlock the shackles; the other seized his wrists and unlocked the manacles. "Strip down, old boy. Usual routine."

"Sir Henry Harding must be a queer," muttered Heinrici as he shoved the coveralls down around his feet.

The sergeants relocked the manacles and shackles. Grabbing Heinrici by the arms, they led him out of the cell and along the brick-paved corridor toward Captain Berkey's office, where he had already been interrogated two dozen times. As usual, he could not keep their pace in his shackles; he stumbled, and they jerked him forward.

This was the sixth or seventh time they had forced him to strip naked before they took him in to confront Colonel Sir Henry Harding. Each time he had protested. Each time he had been furiously angry. This time—well, this time he was not so angry. He was scheduled to be hanged tonight, and this meant they were not going to hang him. Not tonight, anyway.

Adriana had prepared herself for the sight of a naked man; but when the prisoner was led in she was startled and discomfited just the same. He was not an ugly brute of a Nazi; he was a tall, slender and hard-muscled handsome man, with brown hair, a sensual mouth, and hazel eyes that were right now flashing anger. He was heavily chained, hand and foot. She could not but stare for a moment at his genitals: big, thick penis and bulging brownish scrotum. Seeing her, and seeing where her eyes went, he jerked his arms free of the two sergeants and cupped his hands over his crotch.

"Sit down, Heinrici," Sir Henry said.

"This is *outrageous*, Colonel," Heinrici said. "A woman—"

"A brave and competent agent of Special Operations Executive," Sir Henry interrupted. "Miss Adriana Kip. *Sit down, Heinrici.*"

As the two sergeants pushed Heinrici down on a wooden straight chair, he spoke directly to her. "It is an *indecency,* Miss Kip that either of us should be subjected to this."

"If I can endure it, Herr Oberst, I am sure that you can," Adriana said. "I have seen a naked man before."

"Nevertheless—"

"And Captain William Baldwin," interjected Sir Henry. "They know a bit about you, Heinrici. Let me tell you a little about them. You are going to need to know a bit about them."

Adriana watched the German officer struggle to regain his composure. He glanced at her and subdued some impulse to speak.

"You will forgive us, Captain Berkey," said Sir Henry. He waited for the captain and the two sergeants to leave the room and close the door. "Now, Henirici—"

"First, I want some of that whiskey," Heinrici said.

That was an interesting ploy, Adriana thought. A test of wills. The German would learn something by whether or not Sir Henry let him have a drink of whiskey.

"Why not?" said Sir Henry. "You're going to cooperate or you're going to hang. Either way—"

To Adriana's surprise, Sir Henry went to his leather-covered traveling bar and poured whiskey into another of the silver cups. He handed it to the German, who had to raise his hands from his crotch to accept it.

"Miss Kip," said Sir Henry, "is actually Mrs. Dirk Ter Horst. Her husband was a Dutch javelin thrower at the 1936 Olympics. She was on the Dutch Olympic team too, a swimmer. They were married. He studied medicine. They had a child, who was killed in the bombing of Rotterdam. Her husband has been missing and is presumed dead since his unit was overrun by German troops while trying to defend a bridge on the River Maas."

"You are telling me she has reason to hate Germans," Heinrici said quietly.

"I do, indeed, Herr Oberst," Adriana said.

"Some Dutch soldiers brought her with them when they crossed the North Sea in a small fishing boat," said Sir Henry. "In this country she was recruited first to serve as a swimming instructor for recruits. She wanted more important duties, however, and we were glad to accept her as a volunteer for SOE. She took full SOE training and has returned to the Continent three times, each time accomplishing a more important mission for us. I called her brave and competent. You may be sure she is both. She is quite capable of killing. She has done so on two of her missions."

"Spying is a risky business, Miss Kip," said the German. "As you can see."

"Captain William Baldwin was seriously wounded in the Dieppe raid," Sir Henry continued. "He was a commando, a volunteer for extremely hazardous duty. It being impossible for him to return to his commando duties, he volunteered again—for SOE duty. He is well qualified in every way, and he speaks fluent, unaccented French and German. If you agree to accompany him and Miss Kip on a mission I will describe in a moment, he will be the commanding officer."

"I anticipated some sort of proposition," Heinrici said.

"Shut up and listen," said Sir Henry. "You spent some years in Paris, Heinrici. So tell me, are you familiar with a store on boulevard Haussmann, called Mercier?"

Heinrici nodded. "Yes. I have bought shirts there."

"The store was established by a French Jew named Adolphe Mercier in 1876. His grandson Henri Mercier owns it today. About four weeks ago, Henri Mercier, together with his wife and son and daughter were arrested and lodged in Gestapo prisons in Paris. They were arrested because the son, Charles Mercier, foolishly carried a pistol on his person while riding his bicycle to deliver messages for certain underground groups. He was stopped for some sort of minor check—we don't know why—and the pistol was discovered. He was taken to Fort Vincennes, and an order was issued for the arrest of the remainder of his family. Then it was discovered the family are Jews—"

"Zionists," said Heinrici. "You government is under pressure to rescue a family of Zionists."

Sir Henry glanced first at Baldwin, then at Adriana, and she saw irritation with the way the German's perception and logic ran so fast. The German, she concluded, was every bit the formidable personality Sir Henry had described. His kind had killed her child and almost certainly her husband. And no wonder. The toy soldiers the French and British had sent against the Germans had been no match for them. She wondered if anyone in this room was a match for the keen mind of this man.

Sir Henry sighed loudly. "Charles Mercier, the lad on the bicycle who caused it all, was shot in the cellars at Fort Vincennes two days after he was arrested. Narcisse Mercier—the mother—has already been shipped to Ravensbrück, the concentration camp for women in East Prussia. Jeanne, the daughter, is being kept in Paris for the time being. It seems the nobility of the SS and SD enjoy abusing young Jewish women. As for Henri Mercier, the clever operatives of the Gestapo and SD have not yet discovered who they have in their prison at

Fresnes. Henri Mercier has saved scores of Jews—maybe hundreds—from death in concentration camps and prisons. Yes, Heinrici, he is a Zionist. But your clever friends of the Gestapo haven't figured that out yet."

"I am astounded at how much you know, Sir Henry," said Heinrici. "I mean about what the Gestapo knows, in what prisons people are held, and who has been shot and transported. Are you sure of these facts?"

Colonel Sir Henry Harding smiled. "You have operated within our security for a long time, Heinrici. Does it surprise you that *we* know something of what *you* are doing?"

"The world is full of traitors," said Heinrici.

"We have your frequencies, your schedules, and your codes," said Sir Henry. *"Alte Kameraden. Fräulein Koeppfel. Aus den letzen Tag.* Hmm, Herr Oberst?"

Adriana saw the German stiffen.

"We broadcast weekly," said Sir Henry. "Radio Heinrici identifies itself for General Hausser. We give him information we want him to have—just enough of it accurate to keep him on the hook. Come now, Heinrici. Did you expect us to do otherwise?"

"Ich gratuliere," Heinrich muttered bitterly.

She studied him. He was tugging on his chains, unconsciously, as if he could not believe they were locked on him. His pale and muscular body glistened, though the room was not hot enough to make him sweat. The compulsion to cover his crotch with his hands had abated, and he exposed his genitals as he brought his arms up to wipe his forehead on his wrists. The psychiatrists were right, she suspected; nakedness diminished him. God knew how strong the man would be when he was clothed and free of chains.

"If we hang you," sair Sir Henry, "we can keep radio Heinrici alive indefinitely. General Hausser will come to understand eventually, of course, but the war may be over before the Abwehr determines that Oberst Heinrici has been caught and that Radio Heinrici has been sending disinformation."

"Very clever," said Heinrici.

"We have options," said Sir Henry. "We can send disinformation they are *bound* to discover. We can create the impression that Oberst Heinrici has changed sides. That would create something of an embarrassment for your father in Speyer."

"So you suggest," said Heinrici bitterly, "that I betray my country to save my father."

"No," said Colonel Sir Henry Harding. "There would be little profit for us in that. If on the other hand, you betrayed your country to save your own life—"

"Very clever," Heinrici said.

"If you go to Paris with Captain Baldwin and Miss Kip—"

"We will have total control over you, Herr Oberst," Adriana interrupted, her thoughts racing ahead of Sir Henry's words. "At the slightest sign of betrayal—"

"—we broadcast," said Sir Henry, "the disinformation that sends you to a Gestapo prison, to a death more horrible than hanging in a British prison."

Heinrici's glance traveled from face to face, stopping only for a judgmental instant on each. "You want to try to rescue these Jews?" he asked. "Are they that important?"

"A matter of humanity, Heinrici," said Adriana. "An alien concept to you, I'm sure."

II

THURSDAY, JUNE 15, 1944

IN her Chelsea flat—a billet, actually, provided by the British government—
Adriana lay on her bed in the dark. Sleepless, she stared at the images her mind
projected on the deep black field between her eyes and the ceiling. But for the
murmur of traffic on the street and the muffled rush of the outgoing tide in the
Thames, she might have ascended into that field and into those images; those
small sounds were her anchor to reality.

What a coincidence she had found in that file that Colonel Harding had so
ingenuously offered. . . .

Adriana Kip. The crowds had chanted it once. *Adriana! Adriana!* She had
done many things well—a bit of piano, a little dancing, a little science, a little
literature, some language study: all the things the schools required, plus most of
the things a proud parent might ask. But in the canal, in the river, finally in the
natatorium . . . it was her swimming that generated the acclaim.

She knew that her quick appeal hadn't lay solely in her accomplishments.
The crowds had cheered for the swimming, yes, but also for the show of her
ripe young body in tight swimming suits. Her photograph appeared everywhere.
It was said for a few months that she was second only to Queen Wilhelmina as a
recognized public figure. When she returned from Berlin without a medal, she

18

remained a heroine, only now with a handsome young man at her side and rumors of marriage whispered everywhere.

Dirk, too, came home without a medal. One of the newspapers said he had returned from Berlin with something better—the adoration of "the princess of the pool." It was true: He was three years older than she, an intense, sober-minded young man who was studying medicine at Leyden. When her mother died in the winter of 1937, it was Dirk's love and care that made the ordeal endurable. Adriana returned with him to Leyden and enrolled in courses in art and literature.

Their public romance had fascinated Holland. If they had not married, said one newspaper, a million people would have been disappointed. But they did not disappoint. In the spring of 1939 they were married, and in time the adulation began to dwindle, to be submerged in grim anxiety over the sinister menace that abruptly gripped everyone's attention.

As Europe slipped toward war, Dirk and Adriana lived in a small flat adjacent to his father's clinic in Rotterdam. Dirk's plan was to join him eventually in his small practice. That was the life he and Adriana planned: the quiet, prosperous, satisfying life of middle-class Hollanders. She became pregnant. Her life revolved around furnishing the flat, then around the baby that was coming. The cheering was over, and it was a wonderful memory. A new satisfaction was to replace it.

The baby was born in January 1940, and they called her Wilhelmina.

Dirk was, by necessity, an officer in an army-reserve unit; duty meant spending three days a week with his army battalion, assigned to defend a bridge on the River Maas, about sixty kilometers from Rotterdam. It was supposed that if the Germans tried to pass through The Netherlands on their way to France, Bridge 34 would be important to them. Therefore, their orders were to blow it up if necessary.

It was very likely, Adriana knew now from the file the English let her see, that Colonel—then Major—Konrad Heinrici had prowled around Bridge 34, examining the Dutch defense arrangements, spotting the explosive charges, chatting in Dutch with the villagers, learning just how Bridge 34 was defended. When German paratroops descended on Bridge 34, they would know every detail of the disposition of the defending force, plus the exact location of the detonators and charges.

Dirk's battalion was fully mobilized on May 8. He left home that Wednesday morning, promising to return on the weekend—unless the Germans actually invaded. He did not return on the weekend. The Germans invaded on Friday.

By noon Dirk was dead or a prisoner. She didn't know; the news had been totally confusing. The Germans were in the outskirts of Rotterdam. The Germans had been driven back. The French had advanced fifty kilometers into Germany. The Dutch government had flown to Berlin to confer with Hitler. The

Dutch government had surrendered. Rotterdam was an open city. Rotterdam would be defended by the British Expeditionary Force. General So-and-so was here. General Somebody-else was there. She dined with Dirk's parents every evening, and all they could discuss were rumors.

On Tuesday, Adriana decided she could no longer sit in the flat with the baby, waiting for news. She needed to buy food. There were rumors of developing shortages. She carried Wilhelmina down the street a few doors and left her with Dirk's mother. That was the last time she saw Wilhelmina: in her grandmother's arms, crying and reaching after Adriana as Adriana hurried away to do her shopping.

The bombers came over while she was in the vegetable market. Hundreds of them, it seemed. As she and thousands of others stared in open-mouthed horror, bombs began to drop from the bellies of the airplanes. She stood in helpless terror and saw hundreds of tons of explosives dropped into the center of a crowded city. The vegetable market seemed to be just outside their target area. Later she would say she wished it had not been.

The Ter Horst Clinic was in the target area. Their homes were in the target area. She watched the bombs fall into their neighborhood, saw the debris of homes hurled upward through fiery black smoke. While the bombs still fell she ran back into her neighborhood—already certain it was pointless, already stricken with knowledge that did not need to be confirmed.

The houses were gone. The clinic was gone. The baby and her grandparents . . . they were gone, too—beyond the slightest doubt.

Adriana remained for an hour at the end of the street. She sat on the pavement with a bag of vegetables cradled in her arms like the child she had lost, and she rocked and wept—and so many had suffered so much that hardly anyone noticed; no one tried to comfort her.

As she sat there in stunned confusion the idea came to her that Dirk must not be told by strangers. What was more, she needed him. She had no one else, and she needed her husband. She set out walking.

"Adriana! Adriana Kip!" People still recognized her, and they helped her. She walked out of the city of Rotterdam that afternoon, and in the eveing she was taken in hand by a family who operated a hatchery. They gave her a bed for the night and the next morning took her on their pony cart as far as they dared. Although begged not to go, she insisted on walking on, to find her husband at Bridge 34.

Soon she was walking among German soldiers. They let her pass. Not one attempted to touch her. The victors, she saw, could be as staggered and fatigued and dirty as the defeated. She saw their bodies lying on the roadsides and in fields. Somehow, she saw no Dutch bodies—probably because the Dutch went out as soon as they could and dragged their dead away for decent burial. The

German bodies just lay there, covered with buzzing black flies. And their horses—the dead horses, grotesque masses of bloody flesh stiffening in the ditches—symbolized war as nothing else did.

She reached Bridge 34. It was intact. No one knew what had become of the defenders. There had been a sharp, quick fight just before dawn. When the villagers ventured out, the Germans controlled the bridge, and German tanks were crossing it. Six Dutch bodies were found. No, Lieutenant Ter Horst was not among them.

"Adriana Kip!"

Five rough men. They would not leave Adriana Kip to be taken to Berlin as a trophy. The battalion detailed to defend the bridge? It had been overrun. Some had been quick to surrender. Her husband? Wherever he was, she would not find him by wandering around in a daze in the middle of this hopeless war. The five men would hear no argument. They took her with them. Three days later she was with them on a boat, bobbing in the North Sea, on her way to England.

The quiet, settled life of a once-heroine had come to a brutally abrupt end.

Now . . . a Zionist. His daughter. Was saving two Jews the best contribution she could make to undermining the German war effort? She stared into the darkness and wondered. Killing Germans . . . saving Jews. Saving lives, any lives. Saving . . . She hadn't thought in those terms for a long time. Destroy . . .

Adriana rubbed the tears from her eyes.

"We understand each other clearly, Prime Minister," said Colonel Sir Henry Harding. "Do we not?"

Sir Henry had a cup of coffee and a snifter of brandy, and he stood marveling at the bank of telephones with which Winston Churchill's little underground study—one of his command centers—was equipped.

"If we do not understand now, we never shall," said the prime minister.

"These people are not expendable," Sir Henry said grimly.

"No one is. No one of ours."

Sir Henry continued determinedly. "But their chances of success are not good."

"That is understood," Churchill said. "They are people capable of carrying out the mission, are they not?"

"Beyond doubt," said Sir Henry. "Exceedingly capable people. Each one is, however . . ."

"Eccentric," said Churchill.

"Very well, sir. Eccentric."

"Baldwin's eccentricity should, in the circumstances, prove no problem."

"I cannot see how it could interfere, Prime Minister. Particularly if the other two don't discover it."

* * *

"Ah, Lenny, Lenny . . . ye *weel* be sleek again. Ye weel. Anyway, what difference to us? I love ye just the same."

David Auchinleck bent over Captain William Leonard Baldwin and fondly kissed his flaccid penis.

David was a big, bluff man: muscular, broad-shouldered, with thick black hair and eyebrows and a coarse, pitted face. He was the only man Baldwin had ever made love with, and he could not imagine ever doing it with any other. He had made love with women too, and in the physical sense had enjoyed it more, but no woman had ever been the friend that David was. Baldwin had long since rationalized that it was almost inevitable that a friendship like theirs would lead to love. Had there been no sexual involvement he would have enjoyed the friendship anyway, but David had wanted his body, and Baldwin had been unable to find any overpowering reason to deny him.

Before the war, life for William Leonard Baldwin had been centered on cold laboratories and warm cathedrals. Professionally he was a chemist, emotionally a medievalist. His fondest memories were of damp silent mornings at Cambridge, riding his bicycle along the river in fog or light rain, on his way to the laboratory or the library. He would often cross King's Bridge and step inside King's College Chapel, not because he was particularly religious but because it enriched his day to begin it by standing just inside the entrance and reminding himself once more of what marvels mankind could achieve. At a young age he was already known for his innovative work in the electrochemistry of the ganglia, but he counted all such achievement nothing against the achievement represented by the time-worn stone of the chapel's soaring vault.

That he associated the subtle complexities of organic chemistry with the subtle complexities of medieval architecture was the basis of his reputation as an eccentric. Organic molecules were bound by no unyielding compulsion to arrange themselves in stultifying symmetry, no more than medieval architects had felt compelled to build rigidly straight and parallel. He had written to that effect—causing tolerant smiles among his senior colleagues. A romantic chemist! Well . . . He *was*, after all, they acknowledged, a supremely competent, effective scientist.

David Auchinleck was an artist, whose specialty was heroic sculpture. Sir Henry Harding, whose specialty was knowing everything, did not know that two heroic male nudes, one facing Park Lane in Hyde Park and one in Russell Square, were of William Leonard Baldwin—though the likeness was exact and there for anyone to see. Baldwin had posed hour after hour, weekend after weekend, over a period of two years. While he posed they had talked of art and literature and philosophy, sipping wine, munching on bits of cheese, enjoying a thousand little jokes, building a robust friendship while David created the brawny bronze nudes that would win the world's admiration. They had won Baldwin's long before.

Wounded at Dieppe, in the dark, in the water, Baldwin had felt the clutches of death. He had dropped his pistol, dropped his knife. He fell headlong in the surf. No one noticed. Others were falling around him, and no one noticed that Lieutenant Baldwin was down. He crawled out of the water and lay on the sand with the waves rushing up around him, threatening to suck him back into the sea. He found he could not rise, could not walk, could not even crawl. He screamed, but others were screaming too. The blood pouring out felt like hot gravy spilled on his leg. He tore off his shirt and tied it around his leg like a tourniquet.

Why had he survived at Dieppe, when others hadn't? Because he yelled louder? Someone had dragged him into a pitching boat, where he lay screaming long into the night. He had heard them talking of amputating his leg—whether this took place in the hospital in England or on the boat he would never know. Anyway, it wasn't amputated. Sent home for Christmas, Baldwin stayed there, at Budleigh Salterton, for a few days, anguished by his hero status—he knew he wasn't. Then, lying about how long his leave was, he went to Chelsea, to David, and stayed with him until he had to return to the hospital.

The prime minister lit a long cigar. "The key," he said, "is the German, Heinrici."

"It is indeed, Prime Minister."

"We place much trust in him. Can we be confident his countrymen continue to trust him even as much as we do?"

"We have been conservative with Radio Heinrici," said Colonel Sir Henry Harding. "Before D-Day we used it to send a bit of disinformation that suggested the invasion would fall on the Pas de Calais. Apart from that, we have sent the Abwehr only bits and snips of genuine intelligence—no further disinformation. It has been our thought from the beginning that we could use Heinrici—"

"For some special operation," Churchill muttered, nodding.

Sir Henry sipped cognac. "Yes. Some urged that we send major disinformation, as though Heinrici had achieved an intelligence triumph. Or that we use Radio Heinrici to send disinformation suggesting the invasion had been postponed until July." He shook his head. "They would not have believed it, and even if the Abwehr had, the SD would not. Since the Abwehr has now been consolidated in the RSHA—the Reich Main Security Office—nothing communicated to the Abwehr fails to come to the attention of Himmler."

"The Reich Main Security Office was not supposed to have a foreign intelligence function," said Churchill.

"The Nazis are drawing every intelligence function closer and closer to themselves," said Sir Henry. "Hitler doesn't trust the military anymore. He places more confidence in information he gets from Nazi organizations like the RSHA."

"How will Colonel Heinrici's return to the Continent be understood?"

"We will send a message on Radio Heinrici, saying he has been experiencing a heart murmur—so identified by a London physician. He feels he should return to the Continent, at least briefly, for examination by Wehrmacht doctors. Before he is put aboard a boat for his return to the Belgian coast, he will be overdosed with dihydroergotamine." Sir Henry smiled. "If he is examined within seventy-two hours, the Wehrmacht doctors will find heart irregularities. Of that we may be certain."

"If he survives."

Sir Henry nodded. "If he survives. I am assured he will. Adriana Kip will carry a supply of the drug and will give it to him again whenever the Wehrmacht doctors schedule another examination."

"He is well connected, is he not?" Churchill asked.

"Yes. He has friends in Paris—both French and German. In high places."

"As he did in London," Churchill said. He shook his head. "Victoria Lady Dunforth."

Sir Henry smiled wryly. "The notorious Lady Vicky."

Heinrici remained in his cell, still chained hand and foot. Someone said the gallows was being dismantled. The soldiers used the execution chamber to play an American game they had learned from American troops in England. Basketball. The big room where the gallows had stood was a good room for it, they said. Tomorrow night—tonight, actually, since it was now well past midnight —some Americans from an airfield in Kent would be in London and would play basketball in the room where Margaret Simon and Terrence Kilbane had been hanged. No one would tell them.

They were dismantling the gallows without performing the third execution because he had accepted the proposition offered by Colonel Sir Henry Harding. What else could he have done? If he hadn't, he would be dead—right now, before the dawn of another day. Death before dishonor. Who'd said that? Whoever it was, had he been facing the gallows within a quarter of an hour? Who was he, soldier or philosopher? Talk is cheap, the English were fond of saying. To live was the point. Dishonor might be temporary. Death was permanent. Back to the Continent . . .

He tugged on his chains. Damn! They had put them on tight this time. The sergeants resented his reprieve.

Anyway . . . Captain Baldwin and Adriana Kip. Back in Paris he would not be naked and in chains.

Adriana . . . In a way, she reminded him of Vicky.

Vicky knew he had been arrested. He had managed to reach her by telephone at the very last moment, when he knew he could not escape. She had not dared, of course, attempt any intervention on his behalf, but he wondered if she knew anything of what had happened to him—especially that tonight he had been spared the gallows. In that final, breathless telephone call he had assured her he would never mention her name, no matter what, but still she must have lived in terror.

He had met her in August of 1935. Posing as a young Belgian printer named Philippe Valence, he had taken his vacation from employment with the Paris firm of Galien et Fils and moved into a modest pension in Juan-les-Pins. He could afford only a single room, some blocks from the best streets, yet, was able to spend three August weeks in what had been then a less-than-fashionable but comfortable town on the Riviera. And, dressed well, fluent in French, German, Italian, and English, he had expected to enjoy—at least peripherally —the glories of a summer holiday on the Mediterranean coast of France, the fabled Riviera.

Or so he meant it should appear. He was, of course, an Abwehr agent.

In another pension half a block from Heinrici's quarters, a handsome young Briton was lodging with a pretty young English girl. Overdressed in linen suits, carrying a stick, wearing a broad-brimmed Panama hat, Robert Benton-Holmesby was a slight, bright, affected figure who strolled the streets of Juan-les-Pins with his plump blonde mistress. He drank too much, laughed too readily, and attracted too much attention in bars and restaurants.

Well he should. He was in fact Victoria Lady Dunsforth, the wife of Alan Lord Dunsforth. Her companion that summer in Juan-les-Pins has, her impassioned lover, Pamela Huddleston. An essayist and historian, Pamela Huddleston would in future years publish the definitive biography of General Braddock. Victoria Lady Dunsforth was a published poet. After years of resistance, Lord Dunsforth and Charles Huddleston had finally surrendered and consented to their wives' whims, and the two women, both in their late twenties, were spending the summer on the Continent in the roles to which they aspired.

Their husbands had been the subject of sneering contempt at Abwehr head-quarters in Berlin—husbands who would allow their wives to spend a summer vacationing in an unnatural relationship. Huddleston, Heinrici was told, was nothing. But Alan Lord Dunsforth was a career man at the Foreign Office, and vulnerable to any scandalous publicity his wife's shameful aberration might produce. Heinrici was to try to gain influence over her, and then over her husband who might one day be the source of useful intelligence. It was a small, speculative investment of agent time by the Abwehr. If Heinrici could establish something in three weeks, fine; if not, he would enjoy a vacation and return to work unrewarded, but without blame for a failure.

In spite of all her pretense and posturing, Vicky was in private an enticing woman, excitingly feminine, strong-willed, opinionated, and brilliant in conversation. Pamela, though equally strong-willed, was soft-spoken and slow to laugh.

Valence-Heinrici insinuated himself into the company of the two women with interest and enthusiasm. It was nothing difficult. He was young, handsome, conspicuously virile, and as ready with a quip or a laugh as either of them. Able to join in their conversation, speaking French, he never let them see that he understood everything they said to each other in English. He created for this assignment a deferential, ingenuous, nonthreatening persona.

Pamela Huddleston, oddly, readily accepted him as a third member of their group; it was she, not Victoria, who confessed to him what he already knew very well: that Robert was a woman.

He never saw them make love—though they talked about it quite openly, once they judged him their friend. ("It's quite nice, actually, Philippe, and you should not pretend to judge what you don't know.") He watched as Victoria switched Pamela's bare legs with a branch of willow, leaving thin red welts, actually drawing blood from the soft flesh just at the edge of her bathing suit— And he watched as Pamela knelt before Victoria and licked her feet. It was the kind of thing he had been told to expect of the English.

He had sent the required reports. Lady Victoria and Mrs. Huddleston, he told Berlin, were lesbian lovers. Obtain photographs, Berlin responded. Substitute yourself for either one of them in the other's affections.

Carrying an expensive camera, pretending to be an ardent amateur photographer, he took many photographs of Vicky and Pamela, none scandalous—unless Berline considered it scandalous to see pictures of two women kissing—and it was easy and natural to develop an affectionate—even an erotic—relationship with Vicky. They did not go to bed together that summer, but before they parted—he back to Paris to resume his job as a Belgian printer in a French shop that printed government documents, she to London as the charming wife of a career Foreign Office administrator—they had progressed beyond ordinary summer affection. Oddly, Pamela had been amused, not jealous, and the three of them had separated reluctantly, even painfully.

"I never really believed you were a Belgian printer, or that your name was Philippe Valence," she said to him in 1943 on Oxford Street, where he had been alarmed to encounter her. "You are German, aren't you? What the hell are you doing in London?"

He didn't tell her he was now Edward Townsend-Markham, once again a printer, this time for Barrington Brothers in Jermyn Street, printers and engravers by appointment to King George VI. He did tell her he was in London for only a few hours and would be leaving with his regiment aboard a ship waiting beyond the Tower. No, she said, he was a German spy, and she didn't care; she wanted to see him again.

Correct procedure under those circumstances would have been to kill her. But she still was as she had been: slight and boyish—cropped hair, tight-fitting trousers, shirt, jacket and necktie—still a scandalous figure and still irresistibly exciting. She had demanded he visit her in her flat in Bloomsbury, and he had gone there the next evening.

Radio Heinrici never reported that the oberst, head of the Heinrici mission, had reestablished contact with Victoria, Lady Dunforth, wife of the Third Secretary, Foreign Office. When he called her to tell her he was about to be arrested, it was only to assure her he would not disclose their relationship, no matter what happened.

Colonel Sir Henry Harding, puffing on one of Churchill's fine big cigars, waited impatiently. Their conversation had been interrupted by a telephone call reporting to the prime minister new progress by the 59th Division in the encirclement of Caen.

"It's not a matter of gratitude," the prime minister said as he put down the telephone, picking up the discussion as if nothing said on the line had engaged his attention at all. "Though God knows we owe the man a debt of gratitude."

"Four agents," said Sir Henry.

"Yes. Four lives saved for us by Henri Mercier. One cannot say he has been less than generous in *our* cause, with *all* his resources." The prime minister nodded emphatically, shaking his jowels. "Money . . . Courage . . ."

"Gilchrist is angry that we won't send him," said Sir Henry. "He owes his life to Henri Mericer, he says.

"He may not go back," said the prime minister tersely.

"No. He is too experienced an intelligence agent to think we would even consider sending him. He knows that gratitude has no place in this kind of work."

"And what of Jade Amicol? Has he been informed?"

Jade Amicol, code name for Colonel Claude Ollivier, was the chief of all British intelligence operations in France. Sir Henry nodded. "Jade Amicol knows of the mission, but our three agents don't know of him. We trust no one with his identity."

"It is to be understood," said Churchill, "that if our agents cannot rescue Henri Mercier, they are to—"

"—kill him," said Sir Henry, sparing the prime minister the need to say the words. "If they can. It may be too late already."

"It is inconceivable to me that the Gestapo don't know who they have in custody."

"They could be laying a trap," said Sir Henry. "However—what little information we have been able to obtain suggests very clearly that Henri Mercier is in the hands of middle-rank Gestapo agents whose sole concern is with ordinary Paris security and that they do not suspect who he is."

"Or what they could torture out of him."

Sir Henry nodded. "Or what they could torture out of him. When he was arrested, two SOE groups moved and changed codes—three Resistance groups disbanded. Henri Mercier has paid immense bribes to both German and French officials who remain in office, and I suspect *they* don't even know he's in custody—or they would have him killed. That, of course, is how we know he hasn't talked yet. When and if he does, some highly placed collaborators and some money-hungry Nazi officers are going to disappear into Gestapo cellars. As long as they are in their offices, Henri Mercier has not talked."

"And, obviously, they have not tortured him yet."

"Quite so, Prime Minister. And there could be no reason except that they don't know who he is."

"Do our three agents know about the gold?"

"Only Baldwin and Miss Kip," said Sir Henry. "Heinrici does not know, of course. In no circumstance is Heinrici to know. God knows what he might do if he saw a chance to get his hands on hundreds of thousands of pounds in gold."

"Have you any further information as to how much Mericier may have had or where it is hidden?"

"Nothing. No one knows exactly how much gold he had accumulated. During the late thirties, scores of French Jewish families converted part of their assets into gold, in the hope it might some way help them if . . . if—"

"—if fate should ever turn as cruel as it has in fact turned," said the prime minister.

Sir Henry nodded. "They created a humanitarian fund. It was administered originally by a committee, but within a short time Henri Mercier was the only survivor of the committee and therefore in sole charge of the fund. Our Zionist contacts believe he has disbursed many millions of francs, mostly in bribes and other payments to German and French collaborationist officials, to obtain the release of scores of Jews. What makes his arrest even more tragic is that they believe that just before his work was interrupted he was negotiating to delay the mass deportation of French Jews to Germany—a delay he hoped would last until the Allied armies liberate Paris. If that is true—and our contacts say they are almost certain of it—then he must have tens of millions of francs left in the fund."

"But you don't know where or with whom he was talking," said the prime minister. "And that is what makes his rescue so critical. Even if others know where the gold is, Henri Mercier alone knows how to make the best use of it. The lives of hundreds may be at stake."

"Against a very slim chance we can do anything about it," said Colonel Sir Henry Harding.

"The agents we are sending—?"

"As a group they possess the best qualifications we can bring to the task. Not to mention that Baldwin and Miss Kip have their own personal motivations."

"Especially Colonel Heinrici," Churchill said. "As we said, he is the key."

"Trusting him is a grave risk, but in the short time we have, there is no alternative. If he indeed commits his special skills to our mission, it has some small chance of success. If he betrays us—" Sir Henry shrugged.

"In that case, I trust that Miss Kip or Captain Baldwin will kill him."

"They are authorized to do so," said Sir Henry, "at the first sign of betrayal —and, at their discretion, at any time when he is no longer valuable to them. Considering how very much both of them hate Germans, I shall be very surprised indeed if Colonel Heinrici survives his visit to Paris."

III

JUNE 22, 1944

HEINRICI returned to the Continent aboard a fast German patrol boat that had picked him up in an East Anglian inlet. The boat dashed across the North Sea, straining its engines to obtain the highest possible speed, the young naval lieutenant in command terrified of the Spitfires he was sure would dive out of the western sky at the first light of dawn to riddle his boat with machine-gun fire. The boat pitched and leaped, its steel hull slamming against the North Sea chop.

Heinrici lay alone on a bunk belowdecks. He was not seasick, but nonetheless nauseous and suffering from a headache and pains in the chest—the result of the pills the British had given him just before he left. He wasn't sure they hadn't done something *too* convincing.

The June night was too short for the boat to cross and recross in darkness, and full daylight found it thirty miles off the Dutch coast, exposed. Fortunately, a storm was blowing in and the chop had grown to swells. Even so, the lieutenant continued to force maximum performance from his engines, and the boat began to climb and plunge, shoving its sharp bow into waves and cutting through, submerging the decks under crashing salt water. The foaming water exploded through every crack, spraying Heinrici's bunk and adding to his misery.

He couldn't tell the young fool on the bridge that an attack on this boat was the last thing the British had in mind. They had tracked him meticulously as he came from Holland to East Anglia, and they were tracking him now. He could have rowed across unmolested.

At long last, when he had begun to doubt he would survive the voyage, he heard the engines slow, then drop to a low rumble, and shortly he heard shouting and thumping as the boat was moored at a stone quay.

"Willkommen, Herr Oberst!"

The major who had greeted him was followed by an army surgeon who subjected him to a quick preliminary examination and ordered a litter brought. He was carried ashore and driven by ambulance to a hospital in Rotterdam, some thirty minutes away. The doctor and the major, riding in the rear of the ambulance, helped him out of his wet clothes and wrapped him in scratchy wool blankets. The doctor checked his pulse and blood pressure repeatedly.

"We will examine you quite thoroughly at the hospital," he said, "but I doubt you have suffered a heart attack. You seem to have developed a murmur, together with elevated blood pressure. A course of medication, with some bed rest in the hospital—"

"Not for long, I hope," said the major. "Your orders, Herr Oberst, are to report to General Hausser in Paris as soon as you are able to travel."

Heinrici nodded and closed his eyes. How would Colonel Sir Henry Harding's plans have developed if General Hausser's orders had been to report as soon as possible to *Berlin?*

Three days later, on Sunday, he boarded a train for Paris. The doctor released him reluctantly, but Heinrici insisted on going; he had been assured by the British physician that the symptoms would diminish and disappear within a week. Heinrici promised he would check into a Paris hospital immediately upon arrival, but he promised himself too that he would take a small additional dose of the drug before he let another doctor examine him. Adriana Kip was supposed to be carrying the drug, and he hoped she had reached Paris and was waiting for him.

The stubby, high-winged, black Lysander was one of ugliest airplanes ever built—and one of the most valuable and effective. Its landing wheels were enclosed in huge fairings, with big headlights mounted in the front of each. Its oversized auxiliary fuel tank hung between the wheel fairings like a great fat bomb. The squadron that flew them was known as the Moon Squadron, and over the years it had made hundreds of successful drops and pickups in occupied France.

The Lysander carrying Adriana Kip effected a rendezvous over the Channel with twenty B-25s on their way to bomb a rail junction near Beauvais. Though the Lysander flew slower and soon fell behind the formation, it remained just below the bombers long enough to confuse German radar observers, who in any event would concentrate on the twenty bombers and likely not even notice a single blip separating from the squadron. Over the town of Forges-les-Eaux, the Lysander dropped rapidly to a lower altitude and headed for a field south and east of the village of Chaumont-en-Vexin. It was due over that field at 0300 hours.

Adriana had jumped six times in training, once before over northern France. Seated in the glass-enclosed rear cockpit of the Lysander, she peered down, looking for the earth. Never before had she jumped into a void, into darkness or fog, toward an objective that was wholly out of sight. She could not believe they would ask her to do so.

She wore black coveralls and a hard leather helmet. A commando knife, compass, map of the drop zone and surrounding roads and villages, first-aid kit, and rations of chocolate and tinned meat were stuffed into the pockets of the coveralls. In a belt at her waist she carried a Wembley revolver. All of this would be disposed of, once she had made contact with the Résistance group that was expecting her. In her clothes under the coveralls she carried only the forged documents identifying her as Janine Lechevalier, a few thousand francs, and a tiny bottle of the pills she was supposed to give Heinrici if he needed to reinforce his pretense of illness. The nylon cups of her brassìere were printed with SOE identification codes — in an ink that was invisible until soaked in urine.

She could survive a perfunctory check but not a thorough investigation. A label on the little bottle listed a St. Denis pharmacy and the doctor who had prescribed them. The pharmacy and doctor were real, but neither of them had ever heard of Janine Lechevalier. The trick of printing complex identification codes on items of clothing had been used before; a knowledgeable counterintelligence officer would know how to check for them. And she knew that eighty per cent of the SOE operatives dropped into Europe since the beginning of the war had died in German prisons. She doubted that Baldwin knew this. He seemed innocent in some ways.

Even with the ground in sight, she was terrified of the jump, far more than the hazards of the work she was undertaking. At least once she was on the ground, what happened to her would be partly a matter of how shrewd she was, how brave — and she had little doubt on those scores. But during the drop she would have no control, and that prospect unnerved her. She gripped the nylon webbing of her parachute harness with sweaty palms.

"Two minutes, Miss. Ready?"

The cockpits of the Lysander were separated, and the pilot could speak to her only through his microphone and her earphones.

"Ready," she said weakly.

"Push back your canopy, Miss."

She pushed it back and felt the rush of damp-smelling air of the cool night. She leaned over and looked down. Nothing but mist.

The aircraft engines was all but silent, throttled back as the pilot—navigating God knew how—descended toward a field.

"There's a fog over the field, Miss. You might not be able to see the field from back there. But I won't tell you to jump till *I've* seen it. And I'll recognize it, don't worry. I've dropped agents here before. If we don't get a look first time round, we'll come round again. If we don't see it second time, we'll go for the alternate field. But jump when I tell you. I won't yell go till I've had a good look."

"Okay," she said, and for an instant her tension was slightly relieved by amusement with herself for having used the ubiquitous American word.

"Roight."

Except for the wind rushing through the open cockpit, the night was utterly silent. If there was a moon, she could not see it. She unbuckled the seatbelt and stood up to have a better look over the side. Nothing. They were flying over a void of gray mist.

"I see the signal light, Miss! Be ready."

Adriana looked down again. Her breath stopped. Could she force herself—

"Go! Go, now!"

Shuddering, gasping for the breath that seemed beyond reach, she threw one leg over the edge, then the other, and launched herself into gray nothingness.

Out in the void, she clutched at the parachute ring and jerked at it. As always—miracle—the parachute tore noisily out of its pack and flowered above her. The harness snapped her upward, and she hung on the shrouds and the canopy, trembling and gasping and searching desperately for the ground.

It was there, rushing upward, threatening. She extended her legs, and in a moment she thudded onto a field not yet harvested—still green and moist.

"Janine!"

They were there. My God! so fast. In seconds, they were around her, three of them, efficiently cutting her loose from the parachute—and pulling away the Wembley revolver and searching her for extra ammunition.

"Pour nous, n'est-ce pas?" a male voice grunted.

"Oui, Monsieur, pour vous. Et—"

"Je m'appelle Le Concombre, Mademoiselle."

His name, as a Résistant, was The Cucumber. He explained that he was a Parisian and would take her to Paris.

Not daring the roads before curfew ended, they walked through the fields for an hour as the sun rose and the mist evaporated. She gave the Frenchmen the chocolate and tinned meat, which they accepted gratefully and ate hungrily.

When the sun was high and white they recovered two bicycles hidden beneath some brush and leaves on the bank of a stream.

In mid-morning Adriana and Le Concombre rode through Pontoise. In mid-afternoon they crossed the Seine in Nanterre, and by 1700 hours they were riding down the Champs Elyseés.

Le Concombre knew every element of the way. Their papers satisfied the police, and the German soldiers at the five checkpoints they passed during the ride accepted their explanation that Mademoiselle Lechevalier was returning to Paris after spending a week visiting a farm family near Chaumont-au-Vexin. The only problem was that the young blonde in the short skirt, her fair skin pink from riding all day in the sun, was too pretty. Soldiers invited her to stay and visit with *them*. But it was in good humor, and they were not delayed. Well before curfew they reached the flat in the Eleventh Arrondissement, where Le Concombre left her with a French family who had volunteered to hide her for a few days.

Two minutes on the surface. Two minutes, no more, and the submarine would submerge, sink noisily into the Mediterranean waters, leaving him alone on the surface in a rubber boat to make his way somehow to shore. The sailors were solicitous, lifting him down from the cold wet deck to the bobbing little boat. They mumbled words—good luck, that sort of thing—then disappeared down round holes in the deck, leaving the submarine looking like a big dark abandoned hulk.

Baldwin put a small sealed can overboard and let it float away on fifty yards of string. It contained the forged papers he would need when he was ashore, and if he happened to blunder into a German patrol at the edge of the surf, he could release the string and let the compromising forgeries float out to sea. Then he dipped the paddle in the water and pushed away from the dark hull of the submarine. Squinting at the dark shoreline, he began to paddle. The submarine sank behind him.

The French were waiting, as he had been promised—not the goddamn Krauts, thank God, but two Résistants: middle-aged men in civilian suits.

"Bienvenue, Capitaine."

He came ashore just outside the fishing town of Sète, about halfway between Marseilles and the Spanish border, just west of Montpellier. He wore the uniform of a British army captain and carried identification as Captain William Leonard Baldwin. If Germans had been waiting here for him, he was a British officer, not a spy.

"Oder...," the man knee-deep in the surf continued, adopting a German accent, *"Hauptmann von Wetten, nicht wahr?"*

Yes, he was from now on Hauptmann—Captain—Gerhard von Wetten, wounded veteran of the Afrika Korps, newly released from a rehabilitation center in Montpellier and carrying travel orders for Paris, where he was to report to Abwehr headquarters for an assignment to confidential intelligence work.

He would be Hauptmann von Wetten for a day or two only, but he had been thoroughly briefed about the man—who was actually a prisoner of war in the States. The French would provide a uniform. His papers—identity card, pay-book, ration cards, letters ostensibly from his father and a girl in Mannheim, and his travel orders—had been prepared in the SOE laboratories and were in the can floating behind the rubber boat.

His false identity was incomplete, Colonel Harding had pointed out to him, sufficient for the two days he had to maintain it, but he must avoid anything that would inspire any inquiry beyond the routine. A telephone call to Mannheim would undo him. When he arrived in Paris, he would be provided by Heinrici with a different identity, one much better supported.

There on the beach they outfitted him in the khaki uniform of the Afrika Korps, complete with a pistol in a stubby holster. They told him to tuck his pants into his desert boots, to settle his battered khaki forage cap squarely on his head, to wear his pistol far forward on his left hip. They had been told he would need a cane, and they provided one: an antique French walking stick with a thin glass flask for brandy in its hollowed-out head—the kind of thing a wounded German officer might have picked up as a souvenir. They provided also a small leather valise containing underwear and socks and an extra shirt.

The group waited for dawn, then set out for Marseilles in a strange small automobile that was powered by burning wood in a large vessel attached to the rear.

Traveling by automobile was at the same time evidence of status and cause for suspicion. Fortunately they reached Montpellier before encountering their first police check; it would have been difficult to explain what Hauptmann von Wetten was doing west of Montpellier. Between Montpellier and Arles they were stopped three times, each time questioned by hostile Vichy police agents.

At Arles his Résistants turned him over to a Catholic monsignor and a nun, who would drive him to Marseilles. The monsignor was real; the nun, a Résistant, heavily armed beneath her habit.

War was not apparent on the face of France. The roadsides were colorful with flowers, as they had been painted by Van Gogh, Monet and a thousand others. The country was lush, windswept, and fresh. But the visage of war was reflected in the face of the girl in the nun's habit. She was sallow and gaunt, suffering from malnutrition. It was difficult to relate hunger to the warming green maritime fields, but there it was. He realized he had shown too little appreciation when the first pair gave him a hardboiled egg for breakfast.

He saw no Germans—at least not any he could identify as such—until they entered Marseilles. There, they were on the streets: men of the Wehrmacht in field gray, a few Afrika Korps men in khaki, and altogether too many in the dreadful black uniform of the SS, strolling casually in the streets with grotesque silver skulls on their caps. The sight was chilling.

The Résistants dropped him off a block from the railroad station, wished him godspeed, and drove away. He was alone in Europe.

The station was noisy: a madhouse of jostling officers in long queues, complaining, arguing, demanding. All had their travel orders, and all wanted accommodation on northbound trains. Men with rank as low as captain, he was brusquely told, would be fortunate to get places at all, much less comfort. But as he watched, Baldwin observed that being wounded seemed as good as rank; there was a special queue for wounded men. He exaggerated his limp and mimed pain and shortly found himself on a priority list. Even so, he spent the entire day sitting in the station, waiting to be called; it was mid-evening before he boarded a train. A major named Clauberg, who had been severely wounded by shrapnel in Italy, shared his small compartment. Clauberg's left arm was gone from the elbow down; the left side of his face was a mass of shiny red and white scars.

The major was tired, in pain, and not interested in conversation. As the train crept north, stopping, it seemed, at every station, Baldwin slept or feigned sleep to avoid what little talk the major did want to make. It was his first chance to sleep in thirty-six hours.

Military policemen and Vichy functionaries wandered constantly through the cars, making frequent demands for papers. The third time Major Clauberg was wakened—this time by a shabby Frenchman with a rude demand for his papers —he drew his sidearm and coldly ordered the man out of the compartment.

At Lyon, where a half-hour stop was announced, officers who were awake left the train to get a bite to eat in the station. It would have been suspicious to pretend he was not hungry, so Baldwin left the compartment with Major Clauberg and climbed down onto a dark and silent platform in a blacked-out city.

An aged Algerian kept open the ruin of what had once been a station restaurant, and they went in through a door that opened directly onto the platform. Food was sold over a counter in a large smoky room dimly lit by a few weak yellowish bulbs. For an exorbitant price they bought a small loaf of bread, a bit of crumbly cheese, and a jug of harsh red wine. Baldwin and the major, together with a few other officers, sat on benches at bare wooden tables and hurriedly wolfed their food.

The French functionary the major had driven from the compartment entered the restaurant, accompanied by an SS officer and a man wearing a raincoat. The Frenchman nodded at Major Clauberg, then left the room. The man in the raincoat approached them.

Herr Major. Herr Hauptmann. Ich bin Kurt Wiesel, Kriminalrat, Geheime Staatspolizei." He nodded at the SS officer. *"Hauptsturmführer Brenner. Kann Ich Ihren Papiere sehen, bitte?"*

Wiesel was a nondescript man, vaguely middle-aged. His face was pitted with acne scars, and his pale blue eyes were sleepy and expressionless. He glanced over Major Clauberg's identity card, paybook and travel orders, then over Baldwin's.

"Herr Major, bitte," he said wearily, gesturing to the major to get up and follow him.

The major rose and followed. Baldwin, trying to appear unconcerned, concentrated on his wine and cheese but saw that the Gestapo agent was taking the major only to a small room just off the restaurant.

The SS man sat down at the major's place and began to eat his bread and cheese. "Why is the major reluctant to show his papers?" he asked.

"Only because he had shown them several times already," said Baldwin. "In any event, he did not want to show them to a French official."

The hauptsturmführer shrugged. "How long have you known him?"

"Since we found ourselves assigned the same compartment on the train."

"He has a short tempter, does he not?"

"He has been in combat," said Baldwin. "And wounded. That can cost a man his patience, even sometimes his good judgment."

The hauptsturmführer finished the major's bread and cheese, then drank his wine. He chewed loudly, ran his tongue around his mouth to clear the cheese, and said no more.

Major Clauberg returned, conspicuously shaken. He sat down weakly and offered no objection to the fact that the hauptsturmführer had eaten his food.

Wiesel now beckoned Baldwin to accompany him. Baldwin, went, steadying his nervous steps with his walking stick. They went inside the little room, furnished only with a square table and one straight wooden chair, lighted by a solitary bulb in a gooseneck lamp. A telephone sat on the table. The window was boarded over. Kriminalrat Wiesel closed the door and sat down, leaving Baldwin standing.

"Papiere," he said curtly.

Baldwin could not control the trembling of his hands as he laid his collection of forgeries on the bare table. He tried to feign weariness and boredom, but he doubted he was successful. The German's glance flicked up to Baldwin's face, then back to the papers, then again to his face. His examination of the documents was careful, a slow scan that was taking too long.

Baldwin moved to the side of the table and leaned against it as if he needed its support. He crossed his arms and slipped his right hand up his left sleeve. His probing index finger found a tiny wooden handle.

Kriminalrat Wiesel shot one last hard glance at Baldwin, then reached for the telephone.

Baldwin whipped eighteen inches of fine steel wire out of his sleeve and, with a practiced movement, dropped it over the German's head, and jerked it hard into his throat. The ends were tightly looped around short wooden dowels, making it possible for Baldwin to pull on the sharp wire with all his force. The wire did not strangle the Gestapo agent; it cut his throat. He slumped to the floor, gurgling, horrified, clutching feebly at his throat, and died as the shiny red stain of his blood spread over his raincoat.

Baldwin opened the door. "Herr Hauptsturmführer," he said, beckoning.

The SS officer died the same way.

Baldwin switched off the gooseneck lamp. He turned the button on the lock, so the door would lock behind him. He told Major Clauberg everything was all right, and they returned to the train.

He knew of course he could not stay aboard. The bodies would be found, the alarm would issue, and the train would be stopped. The next stop was Chalon. The major was asleep, and Baldwin left the train. He waited in the station until the train pulled out, then complained loudly that he was a wounded officer with orders to report to Abwehr headquarters in Berlin, and the train had left without him! The stationmaster examined Baldwin's orders and told him that he could put him on a slow local train for Paris if he did not mind traveling that way. Baldwin sat in a coach crowded with hostile French civilians and arrived at the Gare de Lyon in the middle of the morning.

Reporting to the officer's billeting office, Heinrici found he was expected and that General Hausser had left orders that he was to be billeted in the Royal Monceau Hotel, a fine luxury hotel on avenue Hoche, overlooking the Arc de Triomphe, which loomed above the green trees that shaded the avenue. The general had ordered a tailor to attend him immediately on his arrival and to fit him with the correct uniform, insignia, and decorations. The general had left for him, too, a note, telling him to secure his medical examination, rest for a day or two, and then call for an appointment.

On Wednesday, wearing a field gray tunic, breeches, fine soft leather boots, and a peaked officer's cap, with the Iron Cross at his throat—wearing in fact what he had rarely worn during all the years of his service—Oberst Konrad Heinrici left the Royal Monceau and set out for a rendezvous with Hauptmann Gerhard von Wetten.

It had been arranged before they left London that each day at noon Baldwin would go to Les Invalides and spend a quarter of an hour leaning on the marble balustrade above the Tomb of Napoleon. Nearly every German officer went there to muse at the tomb, and his presence would attract no notice. He had been there Saturday, Sunday, Monday, Tuesday, and now Wednesday.

"Guten Tag, Herr Hauptmann."

Baldwin started and jerked around to face Heinrici. For a moment he didn't recognize the tall, handsomely uniformed, comfortably self-confident officer. *"Guten Tag, Herr Oberst,"* he mumbled, then remembered to salute.

"Es tut mir leid, Sie warten zu lassen," said Heinrici. Sorry to have kept you waiting. He tipped his head to the left, indicating the way out. *"Ich kenne ein gutes Restaurant."*

When they were outside, walking apart from the crowds of soldiers and civilians that surrounded the tomb, Baldwin began to speak urgently in English. Heinrici cut him short and told him to speak German.

Baldwin continued, "Tomorrow Adriana Kip would have been at the tomb. I cannot continue to walk the streets of Paris in this Afrika Korps uniform."

"I expected to have you transferred into field gray and assigned to me," said Heinrici. "Where are you billeted?"

"I don't dare go near a billeting office, or any other army office," Baldwin said miserably. "I . . ." He paused as if he were about to refuse to say why he would not go to a billeting office. "Hauptmann von Wetten is a murderer. My forged documents didn't pass examination. I had to kill a Gestapo agent and an SS officer in the Lyon railroad station. I couldn't help it, I had no choice. I'm lucky to be here."

"Ah," Heinrici said, dismayed to hear that two Germans had already been killed for this mission. He feigned insouciance. "So. The documents supplied by Colonel Harding did not even suffice to get you to Paris. Well . . . anyway, you're here. Assuming you had no alternative, you've done good work. Where are you sleeping?"

Baldwin sighed. "On a pallet under the roof in a third-rate flat in a fourth-rate neighborhood. Arranged by Miss Kip's friends of the Résistance."

"And where is she?"

"Hiding in a flat. She has a bed at least."

"Am I to understand," Heinrici asked crisply, "that you have not established your British contact in Paris?"

Baldwin filled with breath and drew himself erect. "Of course I have a contact. More than one. But they are not experts at forging identification, nor do they have wardrobes of German uniforms."

"So I will provide you new identification."

"Isn't that part of your commitment?" asked Baldwin. "We are in *your* city, are we not?

"You will have new papers, as agreed, though I had not expected there would be so urgent a need for them. What is more important, Herr Hauptmann, do you have the means of contacting Colonel Harding?"

Baldwin nodded. "We do. And the means of advising him as to whether or not we have your complete cooperation."

"Of course. Very well. I will make some arrangements. And whether you like them or not, you and Miss Kip will have to accept them. It was stupid of your Colonel Harding to send you here with such fragile identities, even if they were only temporary. May I assume Special Operations Executive will supply what Colonel Harding promised? I am thinking of money—French francs—and weapons."

"They can do that. I can requisition what we need."

"Very well . . . Return to your pallet and stay there until I can work on your problem. Let Miss Kip make the next contact with me. Let's say on Friday. At noon, once again. On the parvis before Notre Dame. If I am not there, then the next noon and the next. Tell her to be sure to bring the pills. I cannot permanently avoid a medical examination."

Baldwin nodded. Sensing that Heinrici was about to walk away from him, he spoke quickly. "The restaurant you mentioned . . . I haven't had a decent meal since I've been here."

Heinrici smiled. "It's not so easy. However . . . We are German officers. We should be able to find something."

They ate a simple but filling meal in a small restaurant on rue Odinot. When they were finished, Heinrici summoned a vélo-taxi for Baldwin, since he was unable to walk all the way back to his quarters. Pedaled by a young woman with strong legs, the vélo-taxi sped away toward the Concorde bridge and the Right Bank—Baldwin slumped glumly in the seat, the picture of dejection and resentment.

IV

WEDNESDAY, JUNE 28, 1944

HEINRICI'S appointment with General Hausser was scheduled for 1400 hours. The Hotel Lutétia—taken over by the Abwehr as its Paris headquarters—was only a few blocks from the restaurant where he had just lunched with Baldwin, and he walked there.

General Karl Hausser rose behind his desk, received and returned Heinrici's salute, then extended his hand. "Welcome to Paris, Heinrici! Please, sit down. Let me call for a nice cognac."

The general's office had been the sitting room of the best suite in the hotel. His Louis XV desk sat under a crystal chandelier, on an oriental carpet covering a parquet floor. The general was ten years older than Heinrici, his face all jowls and chins. He was known in the army as a highly effective administrator and in the Abwehr as a capable intelligence officer.

"The excellence of your work in England has earned you another Iron Cross," said the general. "I recommended it, and the Führer himself, who remembers you, personally approved. My congratulations!"

"Thank you, Herr General." Heinrici said.

"And now—your medical examination. What are the doctors saying?"

"I have not been to the hospital here in Paris, Herr General. There is no need. I am not ill."

"The doctors in Rotterdam think you are ill. Their report—"

"I was ill in Rotterdam, Herr General, but not as they thought. I was given a drug in England, to cause an irregularity of the heart."

"Given? *Given by whom?*"

"By Colonel Sir Henry Harding of the SOE. I am sorry to have to report, Herr General, that I was captured by the British about six weeks ago. The English and Irish members of my operation were hanged. I was about to be, but they offered me my life if I would return to the Continent and work for them. I accepted in order to be able to come back and—"

"*Six weeks!* But . . . my God! Your radio transmissions!"

"They moved in so suddenly they captured my codes with my radio operator."

General Hausser rose from behind his desk and stalked to the window. He clasped his hands behind his back and stared down at the street. "Your transmissions have been . . . counterfeit since—since when, Heinrici?" he asked quietly.

"Since May 16, Sir."

"Even the operator's touch on the key . . . ," muttered the general.

"They recorded the transmissions over a period of time and then let another operator practice until he could duplicate the touch." Heinrici shrugged. "We have done the same thing."

"So everything since . . ."

"I am in Paris as part of an SOE team," Heinrici said. "On a mission they think important. If I do not cooperate, they will transmit disinformation suggesting that I am a traitor. If I cooperate"— he shrugged—"they say they will release me from any obligation to them."

"Do you believe that?"

"Of course not. All I can say is, I have gained time. And I've gotten back here to report the situation to you."

"They control you," Hausser said glumly.

"They think they do. The threat to transmit disinformation is their supposed control over me. They suppose I will be put in a Gestapo prison if—"

"*And so you will!*" shouted General Hausser. "So you will, and so will I! Do you suppose that only the Abwehr listens to Radio Heinrici? No! It is monitored, its every signal recorded, by the Sicherheitsdienst. On the slightest *suspicion* that you . . . Heinrici—" He stopped.

"Herr General?"

"Heinrici . . . while you have been in England— No. I was about to tell you things have changed. Actually, nothing has changed. You are not naïve. You know that not all of us work toward the same ends. The Party organizations—

SS, SD, Gestapo—have objectives very different from those of the army, and we have been subordinated to them."

"Herr General—"

"Listen to me, Heinrici." The general returned to his chair. "I will have to review the files of what came in on Radio Heinrici in the last days before the June 6 invasion. I am afraid I remember what some of the transmissions were —disinformation about the invasion, more suggestions that it was to fall on the Pas de Calais. Rather shrewd. Rather clever of the British. I passed it all along to the OKW, of course. If the SD suspected—even *suspected*, Heinrici—from that moment your life would be short and painful. And so would mine. The whole Abwehr is under suspicion already. Admiral Canaris has been demoted. He is now 'Chief of the Economics Warfare Department.' If it should be learned that one of our principal—"

"Herr General," Heinrici said indignantly. "No betrayal was involved. I was powerless to—"

"You are naïve if you think that makes any difference, Heinrici."

"It *makes* a difference, Herr General!"

"To *you* it does. To *me* it does. But not to the gentlemen of the Sicherheitsdienst." The General opened a handsome box and took out a long Cuban cigar. He cut off the tip with a small knife, lit it, and shoved the box, knife, and lighter toward Heinrici. "Radio Heinrici fell silent when it broadcast the message that you were ill and needed to be picked up and returned home. But this Colonel Harding has your codes and could broadcast again at any time. We are at his mercy, Heinrici. What does he demand of us?"

"Not very much, actually," said Heinrici. He ran the cigar under his nose, sniffing the unique aroma of its tobacco before he cut and lit it. "The release of a family of imprisoned Jews. Could that be so difficult to arrange?"

"That's all he wants? We arrange the release of these Jews and he . . . *What* Jews?"

"A family named Mercier," said Heinrici. "Henri Mercier—"

"Mercier," grunted General Hausser. "So. Your English colonel has chosen his Jews with care. I know what he wants."

"Zionists."

"No, Heinrici, not Zionists. Not Zionists at all. Ten fortunes in *gold* is what he wants. I would be surprised if he has even told Mr. Churchill what he's doing. A hundred million francs. Probably more. Five million marks. In gold."

"Herr General?"

"Jews, Heinrici. Jews. Does it surprise you that they have money? This Mercier is a broker in Jews. He buys them from the SS and pays for them with gold."

"I'm afraid I don't understand, Herr General."

"Don't you know what we are doing with the Jews?"

Heinrici nodded. "Suppressing them."

General Hausser put his cigar aside in an ashtray, picked up his telephone, and ordered the cognac. "You have been in England for some time," he said to Heinrici in a lowered voice. "What is your opinion about who is winning the war?"

"The English claim they are," said Heinrici.

"And we claim we are. But who *is?* Who do you think?"

Heinrici shrugged. "I . . ."

"You are unwilling to say. Well, let me tell you. Three weeks ago, the English and the Americans invaded Normandy. We failed to stop them on the beaches, they consolidated their forces, and today they are fifteen and twenty kilometers inland along a two-hundred-kilometer front. They are landing reinforcements by the tens of thousands, plus all the supplies they need. Heinrici—" he paused and glanced around the room as if someone might hear—"we may have to withdraw from Paris before the end of summer."

"Surely, Herr General—"

"Surely I am exaggerating. No, I am not exaggerating. Now, as to Jews. What are we going to do about the French Jews if we are compelled to withdraw from large parts of France? Let me tell you, Heinrici, what we are going to do. *We are going to take them with us."*

"How many?" asked Heinrici.

"How many Jews? *All* the Jews, Heinrici. All of them. No matter if we have to transport hundreds of thousands. All the Jews in France, in Belgium, in the Netherlands—all are to be transported to Poland and European Russia for resettlement. That is the policy."

"Whose policy?"

General Hausser picked up his cigar. "The Führer's policy," he said somberly.

Heinrici had stiffened and sat forward on his chair. "The transport alone . . . It has to be an intolerable burden. How can we afford to divert men and equipment to ship thousands of Jews from western Europe to the east?"

"The trains go every week."

"English propaganda has it—"

"—that they die en route. I have no doubt that many of them do. We ship them in freight cars. Some die on the way. I have no doubt of it."

"What happens to the rest of them?"

"I suggest you do not pursue the question," said General Hausser. "I suspect that some die in transport—they are jammed into freight cars without sanitary facilities, without food, without even enough water. When they arrive in camps in the east, I suppose more of them die, for like reasons. Some are probably put to death for resisting or trying to escape. And I suspect some may die of the abuse practiced on them by the race fanatics of the SS."

"Still . . ."

"Still that leaves many thousands." The general shook his head. "To speak truthfully, Heinrici, I don't want to know. I am afraid of what the answer may be. And, if you will take my advice, you will not inquire further."

"Slave labor," Heinrici murmured. "Making munitions."

General Hausser sighed. "Let us hope so," he said. "The truth could be worse."

"Worse?"

"You had better turn your thoughts to Mercier," the general said crisply. "Well before the war, the Jews began to collect money to facilitate the emigration of Jews from Germany. At that point the fund was used literally to buy German Jews, to bring them to Paris and pass them on to resettlement, a few of them in Palestine. When I say buy them, I mean that bribes were paid—some to German officials, some to French and Belgian and Swiss officials—to let *specific* Jews cross the borders."

He was interrupted by a deferential rap on the door, followed by the entrance of a blitzmädchen, a handsome German girl in gray uniform, bringing the cognac. He waited until she had put down her tray and hurried out before continuing.

"When we occupied France and the SS began the deportation of Jews, the bribe-paying continued, simply on a new basis. Whether we win or lose this war, there are some SS officers who will go home quite wealthy."

"But Mercier?" said Heinrici. "I remember his store from my years in Paris in the thirties. I was not aware he is a Jew."

General Hausser was pouring cognac now, and he glanced at Heinrici and smiled. "No. Not very many were aware of it. When the order went out for all Jews to register, the Mercier family did not comply, and no one denounced them. The Gestapo didn't know he was a Jew until they had him in custody and took his pants down."

"They why did the Jews entrust their money to him?"

"For the very reason that we didn't knew he was a Jew. He could move about the city and make his arrangements much more freely than could a man wearing a yellow star on his coat. Before the war the Jews of Paris regarded him as a traitor. After 1940 they regarded him as the most useful and effective Jew in France. The irony here, Heinrici, is that Mercier, who cared nothing for his Jewishness before the war, became a shrewd and competent agent of the Zionists. We made him that, Heinrici. Our race policy made a Zionist of Henri Mercier."

The general handed Heinrici a snifter of cognac, saluted silently with it, then sipped.

"Are you telling me," asked Heinrici, "that the Gestapo still does not know who they have in custody?"

General Hausser nodded. "Apparently."

"But we know. That is, the Abwehr knows."

"Why not? Does it surprise you that we know and the Gestapo does not? Or does it surprise you that we and the Gestapo—and, for that matter, the SD—do not share information? We don't share with them. They don't share with us."

Heinrici sipped cognac. He frowned and pondered for a moment. "Is it possible to secure the release of Henri Mercier? Is it in *any way* possible?"

The general shrugged. "By some kind of deception, maybe. By an armed attack at the prison. Certainly not by an Abwehr request that they turn him over to us."

Heinrici drew and released a deep breath. "At the very least I have to convince the other two members of the team—and through them Colonel Harding—that I am doing all I can to secure the release—"

"—or to effect an escape," the general said.

"Or to effect an escape. Otherwise—"

"Yes, otherwise Radio Heinrici transmits a fatal message. Perhaps the simplest thing would be to tell the English that Mercier has already been executed. They couldn't blame you if he was dead before you arrived in Paris."

Heinrici shook his head. "I'm afraid we can't solve the problem so simply, Herr General. The English have sources of information. They know what prison Mercier is in. They know what prison his daughter is in. They know whether or not Henri Mercier is still alive."

"And they know about the gold, too," said General Hausser. "I entertain no doubt about that. At least Colonel Harding knows about it, and I would imagine your SOE team knows. That's why you are here, really, don't you see? They want the gold. I doubt they have much interst in the Jew—except to question him and learn where the gold is hidden."

Heinrici put the cognac aside for a moment and picked up his cigar. "Are we in fact losing the war, Herr General?" he asked.

"Besides the invasion of Normandy, we have been driven out of Rome," said General Hausser. "There is hard fighting in Poland. Our cities are being bombed unmercifully. Judge for yourself."

Heinrici drew on his cigar and then stared thoughtfully at the smoke he exhaled. "Five million marks in gold could solve a myriad of problems."

"And create as many more, Heinrici. If we manage to get our hands on the gold, it must be put at the disposal of the Abwehr. We do not turn ourselves into—" The general hesitated.

"—Nazi pigs," Heinrici said. "Nonetheless, we may make, I think, a distinction between looting Europe to make ourselves rich, on the one hand, and seizing an opportunity to escape the Götterdämmerung. May we not, Herr General?"

"Götterdämmerung . . ." mused General Hausser.

"Personal *or* national."

"You will regard yourself, Heinrici, as under strict orders to surrender into my personal custody, for Abwehr use, any assets that come into your hands. Gold or anything else. *Understood?*"

"Understood, Herr General."

"I can't help you much," said the general. "I assume your SOE confederates expect to effect this rescue otherwise than with Abwehr assistance. I assume they have Résistance contacts. I will want full reports on that—who their contacts are, how they work, and so on. I want detailed reports on every aspect of your developing scheme to wrench Mercier from Gestapo custody. I may be able to give you minor help from time to time."

"You can help me now, Herr General," said Heinrici. "I need identity documents for two English agents. Whatever a Parisian needs these days. I need them by Friday morning."

General Hausser nodded and raised his glass again. "You will have them, Heinrici. And whatever else I can provide. And from you I expect the name and location of every SOE agent your two people contact. When this is over, we may move in on the SOE so effectively that the gold will seem a minor issue."

"They don't trust me sufficiently to give me any information about their SOE contacts," said Heinrici.

"Work on it," the general said with a little smile. "Let us see what a clever fellow you are. Incidentally, I will need photographs of the two English agents. For the *cartes d'identité*."

Heinrici returned the smile and nodded. "I will get them Friday or Saturday. Then the cards will be ready—?"

"Sunday," said the general. "With ration books."

"I will do all I can to achieve our purposes, Herr General," Heinrici said solemnly.

"I assume that," said General Hausser. "But, you understand, I reserve the right to—"

"—to order my death if dire necessity requires it."

"I am glad you understand."

By vélo-taxi and on foot, Heinrici spent Thursday reacquainting himself with Paris. The streets were strangely quiet; only the German forces and a few privileged Frenchmen drove motor vehicles of any kind. Bicycles and vélo-taxis comprised the bulk of traffic. The city was without electricity most of the day and much of the night. Even the ceiling of his luxurious hotel suite was black from the sooty smoke of candles.

The French—their diet and the necessity of pedaling and walking had slimmed them. Besides being shabby, many men's clothes were too large, hanging loose on their diminished bodies. Parisian women, though, somehow kept their special flair, looking stylish in their imposed slenderness. They wore shoes with wooden soles, patched and faded clothes, and their complexions betrayed their privations; yet, they pedaled through the streets with long hair flying, showing shapely legs as skirts flew. They still touched their lips with lip rouge, their cheeks with cosmetic blush, and somehow in that summer of 1944 many of them still found flowers to wear in their hair or on their blouses.

The military occupation was oppressively in evidence. The swastika banner hung everywhere: from the Eiffel Tower, from a hundred public buildings, from hotels . . . everywhere. German signs spoke on every corner, pointing the way to offices such as those of the Miltärbefehlshaber in Frankreich, the Hauptver-kehrsdirektion Paris, and the General der Luftwaffe Paris. Field gray uniforms were ubiquitous. Even now, Paris remained a favorite goal for soldiers on leave, many taking what they feared might be their one lifetime opportunity to see it.

For the benefit of the officers, especially high-ranking officers, the dining rooms of the best hotels and a few of the best restaurants remained open, serving what they could. A few of the best nightclubs still operated, as did a few of the best bordellos.

For soldiers, entertainment in Paris consisted of gawking at the monuments —followed, perhaps, by a thin meal and a cheap strip show featuring a listless performance by an emaciated dancer.

Heinrici stopped by the flat in rue Cardinet. Yvette's name was no longer on the doorbell, and the concierge said no one by that name had ever lived there. Obviously the old woman was unwilling to give any information to a German officer. So . . . he would not find Yvette—for he couldn't give the concierge the name Phillippe Valence, and Yvette had never heard the name Konrad Heinrici. A shame. He had known few girls as sensual.

He was one of the lowest-ranking officers billeted in the Royal Monceau, but someone had passed the word as to who he was, and general officers greeted him with respect in the halls and lifts; and a small group of them invited him to dinner Thursday evening. He soaked from six until eight in his mammoth tub. The bruises on his wrists and ankles were a grim reminder that he still was, in effect, a prisoner of the English—a fact that was difficult to remember when he sat down to dinner with Generalmajor Hans Wicke of the Wehrmacht, General-leutnant Friederich Karl of the Luftwaffe, and Gruppenführer SS Heinz Schenck.

"Were you still in London when the victory weapons began to fall?" Schenck asked.

Heinrici knew he meant the flying bombs—the put-putting little bombs that fell indiscriminately over London and the suburbs. "Yes, I was, Herr Gruppen-führer—when the first of them fell."

"And the English were panicked?"

"Well . . . Not as yet, Herr Gruppenführer. The bombs fell somewhat at random, landing in fields, in the river—"

"Ineffectively?"

"No, no, of course not," Heinrici hastened to say. "But as adjustments in the aiming mechanisms are made, they will gain more effectiveness, Herr Gruppenführer."

The SS general smiled. "The first. It is only the first of the Führer's special weapons. Within six months the English will surrender, gentlemen. I have that word directly from the Führer's war headquarters in East Prussia."

The entire party lifted their glasses of champagne. *"Sieg Heil,"* muttered Heinrici.

"And the Russians?" asked Generalmajor Wicke.

The SS general put down his glass. "Once the English and Americans have sued for peace, the Russians will collapse."

"Then," ventured Heinrici, "there is no question of our victory?"

"None, of course," said Gruppenführer Schenck. "Why would you ask such a question?"

"I was in England for a long time," Heinrici said, "constantly subjected to their propaganda. I did not believe it, of course, but I am grateful to you, Herr Gruppenführer, for your assurance."

Schenck, a gaunt, pallid man with a nervous tic that snapped his right eye shut after almost every word, put his hand firmly on Heinrici's. "Herr Oberst," he said heartily. "Served by men like you, and by thousands of others almost as brave, how could the Fatherland lose a war?"

Heinrici laughed and lifted his champagne. "It could not," he said. "And will not. To the Führer!"

"To the Führer!" echoed the others.

At noon on Friday, Heinrici strolled onto the Place du Parvis de Notre Dame, the large public square in front of the famous cathedral. He anticipated no difficulty in spotting Adriana Kip, and indeed he didn't—she was a striking, exceptionally beautiful blonde. As it was, his approach to her intimidated a kriegsmarine lieutenant who was trying to make a date with her.

Mon Dieu!" she exclaimed. *"La croix de fer! Est-elle nouvelle, mon colonel? Pour votre service en Angleterre?"*

Heinrici ignored the sarcasm. "A German officer of my rank," he said in French, "will be served in one of the cafés on rue du Cloitre."

She shrugged. "On this visit to Paris I would be a fool to decline nourishment."

"You need not worry about that," he said as he led her toward a café on the narrow street to the left of the cathedral. "You will be living from now on in a suite in the Royal Monceau."

"Indeed? By whose orders?"

"It is not a question of orders," he said. "It is a question of doing what he we have to do. I have a suite. You can sleep in the sitting room. I will provide a new identity for you, with papers immeasurably superior to those provided by Colonel Harding. Your identification makes you a young woman who knew me in the 1930s. You have now gladly taken up residence in my hotel suite—to renew the old relationship perhaps, or more importantly to enjoy the comfort of my quarters. In any event, it places us together, where we can cooperate more efficiently. It is impossibly awkward to have to meet you in public places."

She grimaced, then slowly nodded. "Very well, *Herr Oberst*. And Baldwin?"

"I will obtain papers for him. He was with the French Ninth Army, was wounded at Gembloux on May 14, 1940, was captured, and repatriated through the efforts of Pierre Laval. Because he is crippled, he is exempt from labor service. He is, in fact, assuming the identity of a Frenchman who was not actually repatriated, but it will suffice. You know, I suppose, that he compromised the identity Colonel Harding furnished?"

"It wasn't his fault," she said. "The papers were inadequate."

Heinrici ordered soup, bread, cheese, and wine—ignoring the hostility of the waiter who served them in this bleak room of vacant tables.

"Fault is not in question," Heinrici said. "The new papers will not be forgeries. They will be authentic, from the Kommandantur. I will need your photographs, however—Today. Tomorrow. I will meet you on the parvis again tomorrow at, let us say, eleven in the morning. The photographs will be put on your documents, and I will have them for you Sunday."

"Very well," she said. "But now—what are we going to do? I mean about Henri Mercier and his daughter."

He glanced around the room. "Henri Mercier," he said, "is still in Fresnes Prison, though I can't believe they will keep him there much longer. The daughter is still in Romainville. I would judge we have very little time. I cannot arrange a release. We have to think in terms of an escape."

She nodded. "Expected."

"The daughter. Is the mission a failure if we don't get her out, too?"

"It may be a failure when he learns his wife and son cannot be saved," Adriana said. "The daughter . . . think of her as essential."

Heinrici sighed and shook his head. "I can provide some forged papers," he said. "Perhaps some uniforms and a few weapons. But what we most need is *personnel*. Men. I assume you have contacts?"

"How many men?"

He shrugged. "I don't know yet. I'm not sure what we will have to do. Probably a half dozen men at least. Two fast vehicles, stolen, most likely—and at the last minute. We need men who are intelligent and brave."

"Or women," she said.

He nodded. "Or women."

"I am not sure what the Résistance will be willing to provide," she said. "The unit I am dealing with is not enthusiastic about this mission."

"Will they meet with me?"

"Yes. I think so. On their own ground. On their own terms."

"Have you been provided with adequate money?" he asked.

"Adequate for what?"

"To buy things we may have to buy. Guns perhaps. We may have to buy our weapons. I assumed Colonel Harding provided—"

"Baldwin has access to funds."

"Draw twenty thousand francs or so," Heinrici said. "Tomorrow we must buy you some clothes. When you move into the Royal Monceau, you must be well dressed."

"I'll buy—"

"No. Not alone. With me. It is only my nationality and rank that will make it possible for you to buy suitable clothes in Paris today."

"Oh, yes. The Teutonic lords of creation! You're about to be knocked off that little pedestal, you know."

The waiter slammed a carafe of thin-looking red wine on the table. Heinrici sniffed it and wrinkled his nose. "Maybe we are," he said to Adriana, leaning closer to her and speaking directly into her face. "For the moment, however, my rank and nationality are important advantages to us. We have little enough chance of succeeding with—and damned little chance of surviving—this impossible mission we've been sent on through the stupidity of the English, who are no better friends of yours than of mine. I suggest you subdue your hostility for the next two or three weeks and *exploit* my unfair privileges."

He poured wine into her glass, then into his. "I assume you are as much interested in survival as I am. Let us make that our first priority, Miss Kip. When we have survived, then you can hate me all you want. In the meantime, it is a dangerous indulgence."

She sighed. "Very well, Herr Oberst," she said grimly. She raised her glass. "A truce. For as long as necessary."

"Then you can kill me," Heinrici said. "Or I'll kill you. We will see."

"I look forward to that, Herr Oberst."

U

SUNDAY, JULY 2, 1944

ADRIANA lay in a tub of hot, soapy water in Heinrici's bathroom in the Royal
Monceau. She had enjoyed nothing like it in more than four years. Certainly
you couldn't in wartime England—nor, in fact, in Paris, unless you were a
German officer or his mistress—and it was in that role that she was now in-
stalled in Heinrici's suite. The papers issued to her by the Kommandantur identified her as Jacqueline Clement, a dancer at the Moulin Rouge.

She and Heinrici had bought clothes for her yesterday. Even with his nationality and rank it had not been easy. Everything was scarce in Paris, and they had
discovered that shopkeepers wanted German marks, not francs. They had spent
four hours selecting two outfits for her—a light blue dress suitable for dining in
the hotel, with a long black jacket to wear over it when they went out in the
evening; and one of the tailored gray suits that was the height of fashion in Paris
that summer.

Tonight they would dine in the hotel. Pretending to speak only French, she
would sit at a table with an SS officer—perhaps even with an agent of the
SD—and listen to their talk. It was important, Heinrici said, to pick up their
peculiar modes of speech: their slang, their neologisms; otherwise she might

betray the fact that she had not spent the last four years in Paris.

Heinrici was thorough and methodical. Weren't they all? She had never known a German, really, until 1936, when she went to Berlin Olympics. It had been a revelation, not only of their politics but of something in the German character that the Nazis had surely not planted there: an antecedent rigidity coupled with a stern self-imposed discipline. She had been astonished by the humorless German athletes, grimly determined to demonstrate the superiority of their new system. But not just their new system. Themselves. Their race. Their *volk,* as they put it.

Her chief competitor in the 100-meter freestyle had been an eighteen-year-old girl from Dresden named Erika Wessel, as pretty a girl as Adriana had ever seen. But her competitiveness extended beyond swimming, to everything she thought about or did. Also, she was unconsciously arbitrary.

"What symphony do you think is the greatest?" she would ask, wearing a smile that was almost a sneer, waiting with a superior air for an answer she confidently expected to demolish with her own better knowledge. "But it is Beethoven's Ninth," she would say when answered. "That is known. Everyone *knows* that." Her opinions were absolutes. Adriana had wondered what kind of education the Germans got—and if Erika's assured pronouncements were the product of the Nazi system of education, which after all had only been in place three years, or of something pre-existing.

Upon winning the bronze medal, Erika apparently considered it permissible to turn some of her competitive spirit toward the handsome Dutch javelin thrower who was involved in a burgeoning romance with the swimmer she had just defeated. Her method was direct. She offered Dirk Ter Horst what Adriana Kip had not yet considered offering him—what in fact *he* had not yet considered suggesting. Erika didn't win that competition. And she was no more graceful in defeat than she had been in victory.

They were not graceful, the Germans. None of them. Adriana saw something of Erika in Konrad Heinrici.

And something different, too. It was difficult to think that Heinrici would ever commit himself to anything—the way Erika committed herself to whatever cause was put before her. Erika was a *believer;* Heinrici was a disbeliever. He did not believe in Nazism, or in Germany. He did not believe in God or in justice or in humanity—and certainly not in this mission on which they had been sent. If he believed in anything, it was in himself: in nothing, it seemed, beyond himself.

Well . . . neither, for that matter, did she—not anymore. And the difference between them was that she regretted it. She regretted her isolation and cynicism. Heinrici seemed focused on the present and the future, not at all on the past. It was as if he had none. He was like a machine: impersonally effective.

But it did make him a good ally for this dangerous work.

Heinrici had gone out, saying he would be back in plenty of time for dinner. When asked where, he had turned on his heels and walked out.

"Herr Oberst?" The SS guard, though deferential to Heinrici's uniform and rank, raised his machine pistol and pointed the muzzle at Heinrici's belly.

"Wo ist Standartenführer Bayer?" Heinrici asked, inquiring after a nonexistent SS colonel.

"Bayer? Standartenführer Bayer? Ich ihm weiss nicht, Herr Oberst." He didn't know him.

"Uhmmm . . ." Heinrici murmured with a small frown. He glanced around the Pantin freight station adjoining the stockyards. *"Juden?"* he asked casually.

"Ja, Herr Oberst."

Heinrici turned and looked. *"Juden . . ."*

Cattle cars were drawn up along the tracks in the freight station, some of them already full. Faces peered out through the barbed wire nailed across their air openings. He watched the officers herd others along—men, women, children—and force them to climb into the cars. Several hundred people in two ragged lines, one for men and boys, one for women and girls.

SS men with machine pistols formed a guard rank to make certain that no one broke away, while others with truncheons kept the lines moving. Officers yelled for all to strip to their underclothes; the trackside was littered with clothing. Prodded with truncheons, the people took off their clothes and tossed them down: the men all but their underpants, women all but panties and brassières, except those who showed that they had nothing under their slips and were allowed to keep those. Many—both men and women—had shaven heads.

There were only a few children, but they were treated the same. Half-naked little boys, tottering on their thin legs, were bullied away from their mothers and forced to join the men's line. Mothers shrieked. Children wailed.

People reached down from the doors of the train cars and helped the others climb up—except in two of the most overcrowded cars, where they tried to push them away. Guards beat people back into the cars as other guards forced the doors shut. People within the closed cars screamed and moaned. Each small breath of wind carried a sickening stench.

"Standartenführer Bayer?" An SS officer had spoken to the guard and now spoke to Heinrici. *"Sind Sie sicher, Herr Oberst?"*

"Ein freund," Heinrici said quietly. *"Nicht hier?"*

The officer shook his head. *"Nicht hier."* He said firmly.

"Es macht nicht aus," Heinrici said with studied casualness. *"Danke."*

As he walked away he glanced back one more time. He had not believed it. *Gott mit uns,* it said on the belt buckle of his uniform—of all German uniforms. God with us. He had always sneered at the pious, meaningless little slogan. But now God had better be with us. All mankind will hate us.

Thank God he was a linguist. Thank God he knew how to live in Paris. With the money he would wrest from Henri Mercier, he could escape the vengeance that was going to fall on Germans.

"Incroyable!"

Heinrici had just handed his old friend a bottle of Chateau Lafitte, and he was not sure if it was that which "Papa" Marcel Ange found incredible or the sight of him—as Philippe Valence—in the uniform of a German officer.

"Will you invite me in, Papa, or must I stand here in the street?"

"Come in, for God's sake!" Papa growled, grabbing him by the arm and yanking him through the doorway. "If you stand in my door and people see . . . Why the squarehead uniform, Philippe? They'll shoot you for putting on that suit!"

Papa Ange drew him into his house. Heinrici glanced around. Nothing had changed. The little parlor was as it had always been. The maroon plush couch still sat before the window on the street, no more worn than before. It was where Marie and guests sat. The master's chair—overstuffed and rose-colored —faced it. Papa's smoking stand sat by his chair, filled with half-burned pipe tobacco, burned matches, and two pipes. The little house was heavy as always with the mixed aromas of pipe smoke and of onions steaming in the kitchen.

"Philippe! Cheri!"

Somehow, Marie had not lost weight. She was still the plump, comfortable, late-middle-aged woman she had been when last he saw her, in 1938.

"Mama! Here. Open this. It should breathe a little before we drink it."

"Ahh! He still knows how to live! But—but why are you wearing the uniform of a squarehead colonel?"

"There might be two reasons," said Heinrici as he sat down on the couch. "One might be that I always was a German officer, a spy. And the other might be that I have discovered a way to get my hands on a hundred million gold francs. Maybe both reasons are true. If you and Papa are interested in a share of the gold, then maybe you don't care about the uniform and why I am wearing it. Hmm?"

Marcel Ange was not as old as he looked, and he looked fifty. He wore a soft wool cap, which he almost never took off, indoors or out, a threadbare white shirt buttoned to his throat, dark blue wool pants. He had hung a gray jacket on a peg by the door, because it was a hot day. His skin was lined, his hair gray. He wore a walrus mustache.

Marie went to the kitchen to open the wine—from where she could hear the conversation and interject comments.

"You *are* German," said Papa. "I used to wonder. Belgian, you said you were." He shook his head. "The Belgians are not so clever."

"I am talking about a hundred million gold francs, Papa," Heinrici said soberly.

"Uhmm. The war makes poor men of most of us, rich men of a few, dead men of many." He shrugged. "This gold is not just lying somewhere to be picked up."

"No. Not lying, *waiting* to be picked up. The Jews have it. The Germans want it. The English want it. And I'm sure, once the Resistance learns of it, some of them will want it. But I may have a way to get it away from all of them."

Papa smiled under his bushy mustache. "The Jews have it? Have you ever tried to pry money out of the hands of a Jew?"

Heinrici shook his head almost convulsively. "Have you seen what they're doing at Pantin Station?" he asked.

"Oh, yes," said Papa. "I haven't seen, but I know. Mama! Let's serve the wine in the Jew cups."

"If you're not afraid of a curse," she said from the kitchen.

"You feel sorry for the Jews now, huh?" asked Papa. "That's a change, isn't it?"

"Not sorry enough." Heinrici laughed, then called into the kitchen, "Mama, could you find some use for maybe twenty million in gold?"

"No! What would I buy? A new house?"

"The war has not made me poor," said Papa.

"It will be over soon," said Heinrici. "What then?"

Papa shrugged. *Plus ça change, plus c'est la même chose.*

"Twenty million, Papa! Listen to Philippe!"

Papa shrugged again—a great Gallic shrug. "I listen."

"I am going to need guns," said Heinrici.

Papa shook his head. "No guns. I have no supply of guns. Unless you want to shoot birds."

"And automobiles. Two fast automobiles. Stolen shortly before they are turned over to me."

"No. There are automobiles in storage. There is no petrol, so people store them. We can get them out for a price. And we can get the petrol for a price."

"What about men?" Heinrici asked.

Marie returned from the kitchen, bearing the bottle of wine and three silver cups on a silver tray.

"Jew cups," Papa said, picking one up and admiring it in the light from the window. "Solid silver. Feel the weight. Solid silver. They use them in some kind of ritual—like the way the priest does, I imagine."

"Where did you get them?" Heinrici asked.

"Well, I did a Jew a favor, and he gave them to me." Papa looked smug.

Heinrici hefted one of the cups. "An important favor, I should judge."

Papa nodded. "It was important to *him*."

Heinrici poured a little of the wine into each of the three cups. He lifted his. "To old times," he said. "And new."

"To the gold," Marie said. "Tell us more about this gold."

"Men," Heinrici said. "I still need to know what men you can provide."

Papa shrugged again. "It is not so easy, you know. What are these men to do? And from whose share are they paid?"

Heinrici chuckled. "Let us hold that question until we need an answer. In the meantime, you could perhaps identify a man or two. If we need them—"

Papa ticked off on his fingers. "Guns, which I can't get. Two automobiles, which I can. Two men. You propose to pay me twenty million for *that?*"

Heinrici shook his head. "For the most important part. Within a few months —maybe within a few weeks—the whole damned world is going to come apart, Papa. I can't go to Belgium. I can't go to Germany. I can't stay in France. I need—"

"—a new identity!" Papa began to laugh heartily. "If you are willing to pay twenty million francs in gold for it, you will have it, my friend! You could have had it for two hundred thousand."

"I don't want it for two hundred thousand, Papa. You know what I want, and I want the very best in every way. I want to live another forty years. Here in Paris, probably. That is why I offer you twenty million—which may be a large part of my share."

"Who gets the other shares?" asked Papa bluntly.

Heinrici drew in a breath. "Maybe no one," he said. "I don't know yet. And I don't know exactly how much there is. I'll amend my offer, Papa. *One third* of whatever I can get. Expenses . . . we share."

"The squareheads are no fools, Philippe," Marie warned. "They have made Paris—"

"They will be gone soon," Heinrici said flatly.

"Ha!" She sneered. " 'Avant que ne tombent les feuilles,' n'est ce pas?" she said, referring to a Churchill speech in the summer of 19943, in which he was supposed to have promised the liberation of France "before the leaves fall"—or so millions of German propaganda posters had it. She nodded. "Again this year?"

"Ah, Mama," said Papa. "They are ashore in Normandy."

"It is a long way from Normandy to Paris," she said. She tossed back her wine and reached for the bottle. "As it was a long way from the Marne in 1914."

"Right now, Papa," Heinrici said, "I have some simple needs and no money to pay for them. I ask you to make an investment."

"An advance against your share," said Papa. "All right. But with interest."

"No. An advance with no interest. Simple needs."

"Which are?"

"A room. Better still, a small flat. Somewhere around here. Unknown to anyone but us. Civilian clothes. Civilian identity papers."

"Unknown to—?"

"Unknown to everyone but the three of us."

"Is this all you wish, Philippe?" Papa said sarcastically. "Just that? On credit?"

"There are others I could have approached with the proposition that we share millions in gold."

"Then why did you come to me?"

Heinrici smiled. "Do you remember when I printed counterfeit import licenses for you, Papa? I could have done that for someone else, too. And maybe you could have gotten the documents from someone else. We chose each other because we were the *best*. We are again, Papa." He raised his silver cup. "Having discovered a beautiful business proposition, one that requires a man of imagination and courage, I came to you. Who else?"

Papa chuckled and saluted Heinrici with his cup. "Who else?" he said.

Baldwin sat on the seat of a vélo-taxi, watching the billowing full skirt of the girl who was pedaling him through the streets toward Les Halles. She had taken a succession of narrow streets—rue de Quatre Filles, rue des Haudriettes, rue Michel-Le Comte, rue Grenier–St. Lazare and now, as they approached boulevard de Sebastopol, she grimaced over her shoulder.

"*Merde*," she muttered. "*Les bittes*."

She had used a vulgar term for the Germans. Baldwin had learned that German soldiers were often called *bitte*—from their own word for "please" and their habit of saying "*Das, bitte*" and "*Dieser, bitte*," as they grabbed for whatever they wanted. In wartime Paris many a Frenchman had adopted *bitte* as a slang term for the male organ—and for the German soldier.

The girl had pedaled into a police check, one they could easily have avoided if she had turned a block or two back, circled the Eglise St. Merri, and approached Les Halles from the Rivoli side. Now the vélo-taxi had been seen. There was no alternative but to get in line and pass through.

Only two *bittes* were working the check: two ordinary soldiers in field gray, carrying rifles, standing back and watching the French examine identity cards. Ahead in line were two automobiles—one of them a gazogène that was powered by a cylinder of natural gas—one small lorry, six other vélo-taxis, and a score of bicycles. Everyone was showing identification. Everyone was being questioned.

Baldwin pulled out his card. It identified him as Henri Foulard, a wounded

French veteran of the battles of 1940. By occupation he was a printer. He lived in the Eleventh Arrondissement, on rue de Lappe, and was employed part-time by Galien et Fils, printers and engravers.

Heinrici had sent the card, together with a ration book and a demobilization certificate, so presumably they had originated with the Kommandantur itself and had all the right stamps, the right watermarks, and so on. The stamps on the card indicated it had been issued early in 1943 and revalidated twice since then. It was bent and dog-eared, as if he had been carrying it around for a long time.

"Vos fiches, Monsieur," said the tall, mustached French policeman.

Baldwin handed over the card: the only document he was carrying. The policeman studied it. Then he studied Baldwin for a moment, as if he found something interesting in Baldwin's ill-fitting, shabby workingman's clothes.

"Blessé?" he asked, nodding at the stout walking stick the Résistants had provided. Wounded?

"Oui. Coup de fusil. 1940." A gunshot wound.

The policeman nodded. *"Le blessure, est-il évident?"*

He wanted to see the scar, to see if the wound was real. Very well, Baldwin would show him. He pulled up his trouser leg, exposing the deep and grotesque scar that traced the path of a spinning, tumbling bullet through yielding flesh and bone.

"Je le regrette, Monsieur. Passez."

The girl pedaled on. *"Imbécile,"* she muttered when they were a few meters on.

She turned into a street facing Les Halles, the great Paris market and, in quick turns through tiny narrow streets, brought him to the door of Brasserie du Vinaigre. He paid her and hobbled to the door.

The brasserie was a mean, ill-lighted large room, peopled by weary, resentful French men and women sitting at rough wooden tables, nibbling on spare servings of tough, sawdust-augmented bread that they dipped in yellowish oil. Some also had dollops of grayish beans. At a table in a corner, two German soldiers, armed with machine pistols, ignored the hostile stares and dully swilled pots of red wine.

Baldwin sat down, and a waiter approached, a big, burly old man with unkempt gray hair and unshaved gray whiskers. *"Monsieur?"*

"Je voudrais quelque chose . . . uh . . . Peut-étre une botteille de Volnay."

The old man glared at him at first, as if too suggest he must be insane to ask for Volnay in such a place at such a time; then, abruptly his face and voice softened, and he asked, *"Quelqu' an?"* What year?

Baldwin shrugged. *Uh . . . 1939 est un bon an, n'est ce-pas?"*

"Oui, Monsieur. Un très bon an."

Ten minutes later Baldwin sat at a table in a flat above another brasserie, two blocks away. Here he was offered wine from a bottle, a good red vintage, with a bit of white cheese and a slice of white bread. He sat facing two Frenchmen. One called himself Le Concombre, the other Le Docteur.

Le Concombre had been imaginatively named. Tall, pallid, and bald, he did indeed suggest a peeled cucumber. Le Docteur, a tall thin man with slicked-back hair, was dressed in a well-worn black suit, dark blue shirt, and flowered necktie. The speech of Le Concombre suggested an industrial worker; that of Le Docteur, a member of the prewar underworld. Le Docteur did most of the talking.

It was disconcerting to discover how much they knew—who Colonel Sir Henry Harding was, who Oberst der Abwehr Konrad Heinrici was, who Captain William Leonard Baldwin was, who Adriana Kip was, and why they were in Paris. They knew how Baldwin had used the name von Wetten and that he had killed two Germans in Lyon. While Le Docteur spoke, Le Concombre examined Baldwin's identity card.

"It would be a grave and dangerous error to trust this German colonel too far," said Le Docteur. "The Abwehr is our most dangerous enemy—followed by the SD, the Gestapo, and the SS in that order. Abwehr agents are usually smart, not burdened with ideology. They are professionals. They are cynical. They have hurt us."

"What we have been asked to do is worth the risk," Baldwin said. "It isn't simply a matter, you understand, of rescuing the two Merciers. Personally, I wouldn't risk my life for them, and I wouldn't suggest you do. But what Mercier can do . . . The number of lives he can save—"

"Still—" Le Concombre interrupted. "Do you trust this German?"

Baldwin shook his head. "No. Of course not. We trust him as far as we must, because we must, and no more. And at the first sign of betrayal, we will kill him. That is understood."

"God grant we will have the opportunity," said Le Docteur.

"Will you meet him?" Baldwin asked.

"When *we* say and where *we* say."

Baldwin smiled. "I wouldn't want it otherwise."

Adriana entered the dining room on Heinrici's arm—conscious that she was going in to dinner with a man who had been directly or indirectly responsible for the death of her husband. She wore the light blue dress they had bought yesterday. Heinrici was resplendent in a uniform far more competently tailored than anything worn by most officers. Though the Iron Cross at his throat looked ugly to her, he wore it with silver leaves that said he had earned it more than once, and it won for him the respect, even the awe, of other officers.

"Herr Oberst!"

"I warned you," Heinrici whispered to Adriana. "The SS . . ."

Although Gruppenführer Heinz Schenck wore tonight the field gray of the army, his insignia were those of the SS—silver lightning slashes on his collar, the Party Badge of the National Socialist German Workers Party.

"Please join us, Herr Oberst," said Schenck. "You and your most charming lady."

"We cannot do otherwise," Heinrici muttered to Adriana.

Adriana smiled as she approached the SS general and the woman who sat with him at his table. Schenck was an oddly emaciated man, not one of the inflated Germans she saw so often on the streets of Paris, and he seemed to have suffered some kind of facial injury that had produced a nervous tic in his right eye. The woman with him was slender and erect—slender by election not deprivation—and wore a long black tailored skirt, white silk blouse, and black turban wound around her head.

"Let me present my friend Fräulein Martine Paul," said Gruppenführer Schenck. "You may know her name already. She models for Schiaparelli."

Heinrici kissed her hand. "And allow me to present my friend Fräulein Jacqueline Clement," he said.

"Do you speak German, Fräulein?" Schenck asked.

Adriana smiled and shook her head.

"Neither of them," said Schenck to Heinrici. Then he switched to clumsily accented French and said, "Well, then, we shall speak the language of the ladies."

Schenck summoned a waiter and ordered two more wineglasses and two more plates of the paté he and Martine Paul were eating as an appetizer.

"How fortunate you are, Heinrici, to have found so beautiful a young lady in the few days you have been in Paris."

"I served here before the war, Herr Gruppenführer—as you know. I met Jacqueline then."

"And what do you do, Mademoiselle? Are you employed?"

"Part of the time," said Adriana. "I am a dancer."

"You may have seen her at the Moulin Rouge," said Heinrici.

"Ahh! And"—Schenck made gestures to suggest nudity—"do you . . . ?"

Adriana smiled and nodded.

"Ahh! I must come and see you."

"I am not working now," she said. "I am staying with Konrad for as long as he is in Paris."

A bland conversation continued for some time. The Schiaparelli model seemed vacant-headed but sensitive enough to be embarrassed by her association with an officer of the SS. She seemed to find a guileless pleasure in associating with another Frenchwoman who was living with a German officer. Schenck ordered dinner for all of them—fish and vegetables and white wine.

Heinrici watched Adriana. He was sharply conscious that he was sitting at this table with an extraordinarily beautiful woman. Schenck assumed—every-

one who saw them assumed—that they slept together. God, how he wished
they did! She was nearly perfect—maybe altogether perfect. He wondered if,
undressed, her body would reveal a defect that was beyond imagination now.

"Oberst Heinrici has been in London," said Schenck. "He is skeptical of the
effectiveness of our victory weapons, so he will be interested to know that
forty-five of them landed in London today. The Americans and English have
been driven back toward the sea in Normandy. I think we may expect the war to
be successfully concluded before the end of the year."

"May I ask you a question, Herr Gruppenführer?" Heinrici said.

"Of course!"

"I wanted to speak a few words with an old friend of mine, an officer of the
SS, and I was told he was in command of some kind of operation at the Pantin
Station. I went out there this morning, and he wasn't there—"

"I can find him for you," said Schenck. "What's his name?"

"Hans Bayer," said Heinrici. "But my question is, what sort of operation is
being carried out at Pantin Station? I saw a lot of people being loaded in freight
cars. Jews, I suppose—"

"Yes, Heinrici, Jews," said Schenck crisply. He glanced uncertainly at
Adriana and the model. "Well . . . I suppose it's nothing our two charming
friends should not hear. But it is not, ladies, a subject for idle gossip around the
city."

Adriana smiled affably. Martine Paul frowned and stared at her plate.

"We are resettling the Jews," Schenck said. "They are being moved to farm
communities that are being built for them in Poland and Russia. It is the
Führer's policy to establish for the Jews a state of their own, which is of course
something they have always wanted. We cannot move them to Palestine, so we
are moving them to a new state in the East."

"I was concerned," said Heinrici, "about the use of transportation resources
to move Jews, when we need all such resources so urgently for military purposes."

"You are correct to be concerned," said Schenck smoothly. "We are moving
only a few of them at present. The ones you saw being loaded this morning are
malcontents and saboteurs. That is why they were being put in freight cars."

"I saw children among them," said Heinrici.

Schenck turned up his palms. "Of course. We resettle them as *families*."

"I see," said Heinrici.

"I used to have Jewish friends," Martine Paul said quietly. She shook her
head. "I don't know . . . I never saw—"

"Of course you didn't," Schenck interrupted, smiling. "You never saw one of
them manipulating international finance to make Jews rich by impoverishing
millions of Germans or French. You never saw one of them steal a little business from a Christian by some infamous swindle. You never saw one of them

defile a Christian girl." His smile broadened. "I never did, either. But we know it happened. *I* had Jew friends, too, years ago. Two or three of them. I never caught one of them in a criminal act. It's stylish today to say that you used to know a Jew and never saw him commit a Jew crime." He chuckled. "Since none of us ever knew a Jew that acted like a Jew, one has to wonder where all the real Jews were hiding."

"Are any exceptions made?" Martine Paul asked as she lifted a small bite of the filet toward her mouth. "I mean, are any Jews exempted from resettlement? If one had a particular talent that we needed in a business—"

"Simplest thing in the world," said Schenck. "All it requires is a stamp on the identity card. The exemption is available to any Jew who performs skilled work for a non-Jew business."

"And their families?" asked Adriana.

"Of course. We do not separate families."

"I have never had a Jewish friend," Adriana said offhandedly, as if the matter were of none but casual interest. She tipped her head and smiled coquettishly. "But I have heard the men are marvelous lovers."

"Not their women," said Schenck. "I know men who have tried them. They say they're cold, unresponsive." He laughed. "No wonder their men are obsessed with seducing Christian girls."

"They are all so—so clannish," Martine said. "I said I used to have Jew friends, but when I think about it, I never really did. They always hold back something. Do you know?"

"That was my experience," said Heinrici. "I knew many of them at the university in the twenties. All very intense, very busy, very competitive."

"They were preparing to take over the world." Schenck laughed. "Fortunately, *we* moved faster."

In his office on the rue des Saussaies, Kriminalinspektor Hans Gebel worked late on Sunday evening. He sensed that his transfer back to Berlin might come soon, and he wanted to close as many files as possible, lest an accumulation of unresolved matters work to delay his return home. Fifty-three years old and a career police officer, he had been a detective with the Prussian State Police until 1933, when he moved to the Secret State Police—the Geheime Staatspolizei, the Gestapo. He was sent to Paris in 1941, very much against his wishes: the transfer separated him from his wife and teenaged children in Potsdam. So far as Kriminalinspektor Gebel was concerned, service in Paris was a hardship. In his three years in Paris he had acquired a taste for only one thing French, Gauloise cigarettes, and even they had become almost impossible to obtain. He resented the French criminals who made it necessary to maintain a large security force in Paris, who filled his office with files.

Wearily he opened still another folder. Ah. This one he could close. A young

Parisian, Charles Mercier by name, had been caught with a weapon. Stupid boy, riding a bicycle, carrying a pistol. The police who stopped him had only wanted to see his identity card, but he had panicked and tried to flee; the resultant search disclosed the pistol. Under interrogation the Mercier boy had implicated Alain Duplessis, Georges Meunier, and Nicolette Armand. When they were in turn interrogated, they implicated four others, and so a small, Communist-oriented cell of the Résistance had been eliminated.

On Friday, June 2, an execution team had shot Charles Mercier, Alain Duplessis, Georges Meunier, and Nicolette Armand. Three days later they shot the remaining four.

The file would have been closed then, except for the fact that Charles Mercier had been an unregistered Jew—and so, as it turned out, were all his family: father, mother, and sister. What was more, Henri Mercier was the owner of a well-known store, was prosperous, and probably had a fortune hidden somewhere. The standing orders in such cases were to interrogate the subject and to locate, if possible, any hidden money; it was subject to confiscation for state use.

The wife and daughter were of no particular interest. He had transferred them to the custody of the SS, for deportation. For a month now he had kept Henri Mercier at Fresnes, going out to interrogate him when he had the time. Either the man was amazingly tough, or his fortune in fact did consist of only the store and its stock, plus his home and its furnishings. Gebel disliked subjecting a prisoner to the full rigors of torture unless he was a threat to the state, and Mercier was no threat—just a possible source of a bit of money. Anyway, this was a file that could be closed. Gebel turned to the typewriter on the table behind his desk and typed an order releasing the Jew Mercier from Gestapo custody and making him available for deportation.

The order arrived Monday afternoon on the desk of Obersturmführer Heinrich Schubert, in SS headquarters on Avenue Foch. Schubert was twenty-four years old, a wounded veteran of tank action in Russia, where he had served in a Waffen SS panzer brigade. He had been posted to Paris as compensation of sorts for the shattered hip joint that condemned him to crutches or a wheelchair for the rest of his life. He lived with a French girl, with whom he was deeply in love, and enjoyed his life in Paris. The news of an Allied invasion of Normandy was disturbing; he had been thinking of settling permanently in Paris after the war.

In the office he rolled around in a wheelchair, which was more convenient than hobbling on crutches from his desk to a file cabinet and back. He remembered seeing a file for this Henri Mercier the Gestapo had now released, and he wheeled over, pulled it out, and studied it.

—Henri Mercier, 50 years old, unregistered Jew, imprisoned at Fresnes pending interrogation concerning secreted assets, now available for deportation.

—Narcisse Mercier, 45 years old, unregistered Jewess, deported to the concentration camp for women at Ravensbrück in East Prussia.

—Charles Mercier, 21 years old, unregistered Jew, executed for possession of a prohibited weapon and membership in a Communist cell of the Résistance.

—Jeanne Mercier, 19 years old, unregistered Jewess, imprisoned at Romainville, available for deportation.

Attached to the sheet for Jeanne Mercier, a handwritten note from Oberführer Erhard Franck ordered indefinite postponement of her deportation. Though his order was entirely incorrect, it was not to be questioned. Herr Franck was a high-ranking officer of the Sicherheitsdienst and an honorary oberführer of the SS—a rank roughly equivalent to brigadier general. For whatever reason, the girl would stay at Romainville.

As to the father . . . there was no option but to put him on a list for transport.

Obersturmführer Schubert hated this work. He knew that the papers he shuffled and stamped sent Jews to their death. They were enemies of the state, enemies of the new order, enemies of mankind probably; still, he had heard rumors of what happened to them when they reached the East, and he suspected the rumors were true. It was too horrible to contemplate. He was glad his own role was only clerical, that he would never have to decide who went and who didn't. He would consider refusing even to sort and stamp the papers—except that he knew someone else would do it if he didn't. Besides, if he refused this work they would send him away from Paris.

He laid the Henri Mercier document on his green desk blotter, pressed a large rubber stamp on a red ink pad, then stamped the document: the deportation order. With his fountain pen he wrote the date on the stamped order—04/7/44 —and added his initial. Henri Mercier would be put on the first train with available space.

VI

WEDNESDAY, JULY 5, 1944

ADRIANA stood at the dusty window, staring intently down at the rue St. Vincent on the north slope of Montmartre. A young Englishwoman sat on the dirty attic floor and tapped the key of a small radio transmitter plugged into an outlet. This was the morning period when Paris had electricity. It would have it again for four hours this evening.

The antenna wire was strung around the attic, draped over broken furniture. Though the girl at the key was young and pretty, she had an undernourished drabness about her, and she worked the key with a nervous, staccato touch that was probably well known to listeners in London. She listened intently, copying the incoming message, then tapped a reply, listened again, transmitted again.

Le Concombre stood apart, grimly watching, puffing on a cigarette.

"Christ!" Suddenly the girl scrambled to her feet, yanking at the antenna wire, and rushed to repack the radio in its case.

Le Concombre pointed to the bulb in the stairway light. It had gone out. "A German trick," he said to Adriana. "They identify a block or two where they suspect a transmitter is working, then they listen and cut the power while a transmission is going out. If the transmission stops, they know there's a transmitter in the neighborhood. We never transmit long enough to let them locate us with direction finders, so this is their rough-and-ready way of finding us. They'll make a house-to-house search now."

The English girl handed Adriana the paper on which she had been copying the transmissions from London. "I suggest you read that and get rid of it right away," she said.

Le Concombre lifted two floorboards, and the girl slipped the radio into the hole.

"You can leave," he said to Adriana. "You're well dressed. You have good papers—and if necessary you can have them call the Royal Monceau and confirm you live with Heinrici." He glanced at the English girl, who now had turned even paler than before. "Sybil and I must stay in the house."

"If they break in," the girl said soberly, "they will find him and me in bed. But how would we explain your being here?"

Adriana nodded. She read the message and tore it up, and on her way down she stopped at the water closet and flushed down the bits of the paper. When she reached the street door, she could hear the grinding engines of lorries coming up the hill, but the Germans were not yet in this street. She stepped out and started up the hill, in the direction of Sacré Coeur.

Half a dozen Germans in field gray, rifles in their hands, came around the corner just ahead of her. *"Fräulein! Halt!"*

She stopped. They advanced toward her, and one stepped ahead of the others. *"Papiere!"* he barked. *"Carte d' identité."*

She was carrying a small purse that Heinrici had bought for her Saturday. Taking out the identity card he had given her, she handed it to the German.

"Wohin gehen Sie?" he muttered as he scowled at the card. Where are you going?

She smiled wanly and turned up her palms. *"Ich . . . uh, sprecht . . . nicht."*

The German blew a sigh. *"Ou allez vous?"*

She pointed at the basilica at the top of the hill. *"A l' éeglise,"* she said. To the church.

He glanced almost involuntarily at the white dome of Sacré Coeur at the top of Montmartre. For a moment he regarded her suspiciously. Then he glanced at the men waiting for him to decide what to do about this handsome young woman. *"Eh bien,"* he said irritably. *"Passez."*

She walked on up the steep incline of the street, struggling to keep calm, not to appear frightened or hurried. Then she heard shots. She stopped and looked back. She saw no Germans. A few Frenchmen stepped out of doorways and stared down the hill, in the direction from which the sound had come. There was no way to know what had happened. She drew herself erect, steadied herself, and walked on.

*   *   *

Paris buses were still running, and she was able to find one and ride down from the basilica to rue de Rivoli, from where she walked to Les Halles.

She was accosted almost immediately by a handsome young German officer who offered her ten thousand francs to accompany him to his hotel. She told him in German that she was living in the Royal Monceau with an officer who substantially outranked him, and who would not be pleased. He saluted and hurried away. As he walked toward the Palais Royal, she saw him also salute a Frenchman in a blue suit, who now walked purposefully toward her.

"Madame Orange?" he asked.

"Non, je suis Madame Haricot."

It was a prearranged exchange of signals, and she accompanied the Frenchman, who said he was called Le Rasoir—The Razor—through a tangle of streets and finally into a tobacconist's shop. They entered the back room and from there climbed narrow stairs to a tiny, neatly furnished flat.

Le Docteur was there, sitting at the window, watching the street. He wore black trousers held up by red and blue braces, a white shirt with no necktie, and held in the corner of his mouth the diminishing butt of a foul-smelling cigarette.

"Le Concombre?" asked Le Docteur.

"The Germans were listening," said Adriana. "They cut off the electricity, then sent what must have been a hundred men into the neighborhood. He sent me out. I was stopped but not detained. I heard shots. I don't know if—"

"They wouldn't have sent a hundred of them if they had known where the transmitter is. It's a bluff. Nothing new. They'll search—"

"They'll find Le Concombre in bed with Sybil," Adriana said with a nervous smile.

"Lucky fellow," Le Docteur said dryly. "But did they complete the transmission to London?"

"Most of it. Colonel Harding knows what we are doing, anyway. His message to us was 'Press forward. Time is of the essence.' He reminded us we have been in Paris two weeks."

Le Docteur summoned Le Rasoir to take his place at the window, then moved to a chair at a round table covered with a red-and-white checked cloth. "Before the German colonel arrives," he said, "I want to say something to you, Mademoiselle Kip. Your Colonel Harding sends you to Paris to undertake a damned hazardous operation, which is going to cost some people their lives, we may be sure, and he sends *three* of you. You are Dutch, so maybe you don't know there is a long-standing suspicion in France that the English like to risk French lives in the hard operations. Colonel Harding sends three of you—only one of you English, in fact—and seems to expect *us* to supply the men who must stand up to the German gunfire. A typical SOE operation."

"Our orders are to do it without loss of life," said Adriana.

"Oh? And how is that to be done?"

"I don't know," she said. "That's the point of having Heinrici with us. We thought he might simply be able to persuade someone to give an order freeing the Merciers. Apparently he hasn't been—"

"Mercier," interrupted Le Docteur. "No one has ever explained why we should take such trouble and risk to free this Jew. Do you understand it, Mademoiselle Kip?"

"Only that Henri Mercier is a very brave man who has risked his life to save the lives of others," she said.

"Others? What others?"

"Jews . . ."

"Yes. Jews. Saving each other. And for them, too, we French are supposed to stand up in the line of fire."

"The Jews he has saved are Frenchmen, Monsieur," said Adriana.

"Oh? Are they, or are they Jews? Which are they?"

"French Jews," she said firmly.

"Ah. French Jews. I see."

Le Rasoir, who had been standing at the window, watching the street, turned and said, "The German colonel is coming. As to the Jews, let me say something, Robert. When my mother was suffering horribly in her last illness, the doctor who attended her was a Jew. He was a caring man, more than any other doctor I ever knew. When the Germans came they made a law that no Jewish doctor could attend Christian patients, and people were deprived of his care. Now I hear he has been sent to Poland, where he is to work in a quarry. If I am going to risk my life—which frankly I am not anxious to do—I would as soon risk it for a man like him as for one of the Frenchmen who spat at him and drove him away from food lines when he was forced to wear a yellow star on his coat."

"Quite a speech, Raymond," said Le Docteur. "I—"

"Colonel Heinrici," Le Rasoir said as Heinrici appeared at the top of the stairs.

Heinrici was in uniform and was followed by the young German captain who had approached Adriana on the street. The captain grinned broadly when he saw her.

"You have met Le Capitaine already, Mademoiselle," said Le Rasoir with a smile. "Because of his blue eyes and blond hair, we make him cut his hair very short and go out occasionally as a German officer."

"Well," said Le Docteur. "Colonel Heinrici. Be seated. I'm sorry I can't offer you wine. All the good wine has been taken for your countrymen."

"I would have brought you some if I'd known it," said Heinrici aloofly. He sat down and faced Le Docteur across the table, observing the shabby, proletarian condition of the Frenchmen. "What else can I supply? Cigarettes?"

"Explanations," said Le Docteur. He sat down opposite Heinrici. "Assurances."

"Such as I have," said Heinrici blandly. "Where is Foulard?"

"You mean Captain Baldwin? He is out doing some reconnoitering. An independent sort of fellow, now that he has papers."

"He'll get himself killed," said Heinrici.

"I'm sure he won't," said Le Docteur. "He'll leave getting killed to us. Now as to explanations and assurances—I want to be assured that this operations is worth the risk we are being asked to take. Why should we help you?"

Heinrici shrugged. "If for no other reason, because General Koenig has ordered you to help us," he said.

Adriana was startled by his statement. General Pierre Koenig was chief of the FFI, Forces Français de l'Intérieur, a deputy of General deGaulle. Colonel Harding had given no intimation to her or to Baldwin that General Koenig had ordered any of the varied units of the Résistance to aid this mission. To the contrary, the SOE orders were to be diplomatic, to attempt to *persuade* the Résistance to take a role in the operation. Her anger rose. Heinrici was trying a dangerous ruse, on his own authority.

"I have seen no such orders," said Le Docteur.

Heinrici shrugged again. "I cannot help what you have seen or not seen," he said calmly—a calmness he did not feel, testing these people. "This mission is as important to France as it is to England, and General Koenig transmitted the orders. Did he not, Mademoiselle Kip?"

Damn him! He knew she couldn't say no. "Yes," she said quietly.

"Even though your leaders went to some lengths in their attempt to unite all French forces under the joint command of the FFI, I realize that communication is sometimes difficult," Heinrici said in a tone she feared was too contemptuous.

Le Docteur shifted his eyes from Heinrici to Adriana, then to Le Rasoir and Le Capitaine. He sighed, acquiescing, at least for the moment. "How many are to die in this attempt to rescue a Jew from a Gestapo prison?" he asked.

"Two Jews are to be rescued," Heinrici said. "Father and daughter. From two different prisons—Fresnes and Romainville. And I very much hope that no one dies. If we work together, and if we are careful and smart, we may be able to carry off the two rescues simultaneously and with no loss. If we can't do what we have to do without trying to shoot our way in and out, then we can't do it at all."

"Let that be clearly understood, Colonel," said Le Docteur. "If we had the strength to assault Fresnes or Romainville and free prisoners, there are people we would free before we'd free your two Jews. I don't care what General Koenig orders—we will not send men into those places to die, just to rescue this man Mercier and his daughter."

"I have no intention of committing suicide myself," said Heinrici.

"Just what is your part in this operation?" Le Rasoir asked.

"I will lead the group that goes to Fresnes," said Heinrici. "Baldwin will lead the group that goes to Romainville. Each group will need two or three other men. Obviously, it would be well if they are men who can speak German, or at least understand it. They must be outfitted with German weapons and dressed in German uniforms. I suppose you can supply the guns and uniforms."

Le Docteur nodded. "We can."

"I think they will have to be SS uniforms," said Heinrici.

Le Docteur nodded again.

"We will need two automobiles with petrol. I think I can supply those. Beyond that we will need forged documents. May I assume you have skilled forgers available?"

"Who forged the identity cards you supplied to Captain Baldwin and Mademoiselle Kip?"

"I have exhausted that resource," Heinrici said. "The identity cards, incidentally, are not forgeries—they are real. The stamps are genuine. But the people who provided them cannot provide forged documents ordering the release of the Merciers. We will have to make those ourselves."

"There will be difficulties," said Le Capitaine. "Identity cards are easy enough. The documents carried by German officers are printed on special paper that is watermarked and embossed. There is a faint design laid into the blank paper, always visible under the printing. They examine those things when the documents are presented. The paper is quite resistant to attempts to make changes. It tears at the touch of an eraser. It dissolves if you use chemicals on it. We have SS identity books that we've taken from dead SS men, but"—he shook his head—"I don't think we can make changes in them."

"You could if you had the right paper," said Heinrici. "I may be able to supply that."

"And there is another problem," Le Capitaine continued. "We have never seen an order transferring custody of a prisoner. What kind of paper is that printed on? What stamps does it require? What signatures?"

"We will have to get one and examine it," said Heinrici.

"You will have to get one, Colonel," said Le Docteur. "It is your friends who produce them."

"I will need some information," Heinrici said. "Who issues the orders for the deportation of Jews? How are those orders delivered to the governors of prisons? Is there a regular delivery? What time is it made? I can probably find out all this if necessary, but I have no apparent reason to ask, and if I ask such questions, it will raise suspicion. There is probably someone in the Résistance who already knows all the answers. See if you can find out for me."

"That should be easy enough," said Le Capitaine.

As Adriana watched, the Résistants' hostility to the mission slowly dissipated. It had originated mostly with Le Docteur anyway; Le Rasoir had not been hostile and neither had Le Capitaine. Le Concombre wasn't either, and she hoped the gunfire on Montmartre had not been aimed at him and Sybil. Le Docteur—Robert—would probably cease to be a problem, too. He was a blusterer, anxious to maintain his leadership over men who seemed less than pleased to accept it.

"Do you speak German?" Heinrici asked Le Docteur.

Le Docteur shook his head.

Heinrici turned to Le Capitaine. "But you do. And well, too."

"I will go with you to Fresnes," said Le Capitaine. "Or to Romainville with Baldwin."

"Good," said Heinrici.

"So, Théo is a volunteer," Le Docteur said cynically.

"I need a volunteer for tonight," said Heinrici.

"For what?" Le Docteur asked.

"For a burglary. One man, to go with me. Armed. It should not be too dangerous."

"I will go," said Adriana.

"One of the men," said Heinrici.

"*Nein, Herr Oberst,*" she said firmly. "*Ich will fahren. Verstehen Sie?*" I will go. Do you understand? She had closed the question.

He stared at her for a moment, then abruptly nodded.

They could do nothing until after dark, Heinrici said, so they dined in the hotel. They were alone this time, and she complained to him about using the name of General Koenig to the French when in fact General Koenig had sent no orders of any kind.

"You or Baldwin can take care of that," he said. "Send word to Colonel Harding. General Koenig can repair the deficiency, even now. Anyway, I wouldn't worry about it. The Résistance is so splintered that urgent word from deGaulle himself only reaches half of them. They don't govern France, you know—though some of them seem to think they do."

She dropped the subject. "When are we to be briefed—I mean, Baldwin and I—on precisely how this operation is to be carried out?"

"When I know myself," said Heinrici. "You can see what I have in mind. Do you have a better plan?"

"No. But you must keep Baldwin and me fully informed of everything you are doing. I don't want any repeats of this afternoon," she said icily.

"You have seen everything so far," said Heinrici. "And tonight . . . You shouldn't have insisted on this, incidentally."

"I'm better trained than any of the Frenchmen," she said.

"Let's hope you don't have to prove it."

They left the Royal Monceau a little after nine, dropping the comment to a friendly officer in the lobby that they were going to take in the show at the Moulin Rouge. He was in uniform. She wore her dinner dress. They had themselves pedaled to the Moulin Rouge in a vélo-taxi, but they did not go in. Instead, they followed directions Le Rasoir had given them and walked west three blocks, then up the slope of Montmartre on the western edge of the cemetary. They reached an address Le Rasoir had given them, knocked on the door, and were admitted by Le Concombre.

"Oh God! I was afraid—"

"No," said Le Concombre. "Just shooting their guns in the air. Poor Sybil trembled. Come in! Colonel Heinrici."

Adriana had described Le Concombre as the kind of man who would not refuse to shake the hand of a German officer, even if he decided later to kill him, so Heinrici extended his hand, and Le Concombre took it.

"We all use code names, as you've heard," said Le Concombre. "You can call me Claude if you wish. I have ready what you need. Really, I should go with you."

"I suppose you follow the same rule I do," said Heinrici. "Only risk as many people as you absolutely have to. And Mademoiselle Kip insists on going."

"So," said Le Concombre.

They changed their clothes. Le Concombre had been asked to provide workingman's coveralls—*bleu de travail*—for Heinrici and a drab blue dress for Adriana, with wooden soled shoes for both of them. They smiled over the ill fit. Heinrici had worn his sidearm, a Walther PK-38 pistol, which he now tucked into one of the deep pockets of the coveralls. A small electric torch went in another pocket. Le Concombre offered Adriana a small Spanish automatic, which she accepted and dropped into a little cloth bag with her identity card.

"*Bonne chance,*" Le Concombre said at the door. "I will be here all night."

They set out on foot, a long walk ahead of them. After making their way down the north slope of Montmartre, they reached rue Ordener and turned east. The streets were lively. The Métro ran until midnight, and people were drinking whatever they could get in the bars or shopping in the sparsely stocked stores. Many people just strolled. Heinrici set a fast pace, and Adriana kept up with him without complaint.

They walked into the area of freight stations, where the streets were almost dark, and on into the quarter called La Villette—a distance of almost four kilometers. By the time they reached the canal basin—Bassin de la Villette—the last Métro trains were pulling out of the stations all over Paris; the city would soon fall under the midnight curfew. What was more, the electricity would be shut off, and the city would be dark.

He slowed a little now—whether because he had tired or because he did not want to seem quite so purposeful, she did not know. They followed the Quai de la Seine northeast and passed the church of St. Christopher; then they turned north along the Canal de St. Denis. Shortly he turned northwest, into one of the streets of La Villette. After two more turns, he brought her to the main entrance of a large brick building.

She read the sign:

GALIEN ET FILS
IMPRIMEURS ET GRAVURES
1886

Heinrici glanced up and down the gloomy, deserted street. He beckoned to Adriana, and she followed him along the front of the building and around a corner, into a short alley that led to a loading dock at the rear. He stopped in the alley, knelt, and began to examine the bricks along the foundation. Presently he found what he was looking for: a loose brick. He tugged at it. It resisted. He tugged again, and the brick came out in his hand. He reached into the hole and groped in the dark. Grunting, he pulled out a key and held it up to her.

"Now, if they haven't changed the lock," he whispered.

He led her back to the main entrance door, inserted the key in the big brass lock, and turned. The old lock rasped and thumped. Heinrici seized the handle, pressed down the latch tab, and pushed the door open. He pulled Adriana inside and closed the door.

"How . . . ?"

"I worked here in the 1930s. I needed to enter at night sometimes, so I hid a key." He shook his head as he locked the door from the inside. Glancing around in the almost totally dark entrance hall, he said, "Let's hope nothing else has changed either."

"You were a spy," she said.

"Yes."

"But a printing company? Why?"

Heinrici shrugged. "I had to work somewhere. I knew a little something about the printing trade. Sometimes I came in at night—for special reasons."

She didn't need to know everything right now—for one thing, that Galien et Fils had been printers for French military intelligence, the Deuxième Bureau. In a special department in this building they had counterfeited the official documents of every government in Europe. Passports, police passes, driver's licenses, residence permits, work permits, health certificates, export and import licenses, diplomatic and military documents . . . everything. Every document carried by every French spy had been printed here, by Galien et Fils. Of course, they also printed legitimate documents of all kinds.

His assignment had been to steal samples of what they printed. Their false documents were sent to Berlin, and tiny, very subtle changes were made in the genuine documents—creating differences an examining German officer could be alerted to look for but which, as the Abwehr hoped, the Deuxième Bureau would not notice. It had worked very effectively. French agents entering Germany were detected the first time they showed their documents. And the Abwehr had let them go ahead and function—under constant surveillance.

What he wanted tonight was the paper. French agents had bought or stolen the special kinds of paper the company needed. In 1938, when Heinrici left here, Galien et Fils could print any document a French agent needed to establish himself as an agent of the Gestapo, an agent of the Sicherheitsdienst, an SS officer, an Abwehr officer . . . anybody.

"Are you, then, a printer?"

"An engraver," he said. "I volunteered for this work and was thoroughly trained. But"—he sighed—"we have no time for reminiscence. I don't think there's a watchman in this building but we should go as far as we can without using the electric torch. Keep a hand on me. I know where I'm going."

He led her into the main pressroom, just behind the entrance hall. It was a huge room; a little gray moonlight filtered through a skylight. The great presses were well-maintained, and the dim moonlight gleamed off their polished surfaces. Heinrici stopped before a big bin.

"Look," he said. "Here's what they're printing now."

She squinted over a handful of spoiled documents from the trash bin—wall posters in French, one announcing an execution, posters in German, garish, multi-colored propaganda posters, advertising posters for motion pictures and exhibitions. From the floor beside a smaller press Heinrici picked up a spoiled sheet of ration coupons.

There was no locked door between the main pressroom and the rooms where the secret work for the Deuxième Bureau was done. There never had been. The employees of Galien et Fils were the sons and grandsons of other men who had worked there, and they knew their place; none of them would think of venturing into a room where they were not permitted. Heinrici turned the knob on the green door and walked into the department where he had worked ten years before. These rooms had no windows. In the center of the building, the department was accessible only through other rooms, and it had never been otherwise protected.

When the door was shut, the three rooms of the secret department were absolutely dark. Heinrici switched on his little electric torch and glanced around. Everything was in its place: the special press for precision printing, bin after bin of type, the linotype, the cutting and binding machines that could assemble counterfeit passports, the vats in which engravings were etched, the machine that made rubber stamps, and, behind a glass partition, the workbenches where the engravers worked. Everything was dusty. Apparently Galien et Fils had no new contract for counterfeit documents.

"You should stay outside," Heinrici said to Adriana. "If there is a watchman, you'll hear him, see him."

She nodded and returned through the green door into the main press room.

Lighting his way with the electric torch, Heinrici hurried through the secret pressroom and into the storeroom: his real objective for the night. Flashing the beam around the shelves, he was surprised again at how little anything had changed. The shelves were still heavy with cartons of paper, naively labeled *Service de Sécurité Allemagne, Police Secret d'Etat, Allemagne,* and so forth.

He opened the box labeled *Abwehr* and pulled out a sheet. The paper matched that on which his own Abwehr identity card was printed. Even the stiff cover material, in which the document was bound, was the same. For the Abwehr, at least, the document game had ended in 1940. Even if it hadn't, he doubted anyone would still be scrutinizing documents for the extremely fine distinctions that had meant so much five years ago.

He pulled out a box of SS paper and a box of SD—it was exquisite. Not only was the paper underprinted with a faint design; it was marked also with a pattern of colored fibers. Only money was printed on paper so fine. Looking around, he found cover material, and searching further, he even found the dyes for embossing seals on papers and photographs—painstakingly forged by the engravers. He emptied a box and began to pack his treasures.

"Hsst!"

He switched off the light. He heard the green door close quietly.

Heinrici turned the little torch on again, to give her light to find her way to him.

"Watchman!'" she whispered. "Or somebody. With a torch. Only one man, I think."

"You stay here in the storeroom," he said. "I know where to watch out in the pressroom."

He trotted across the pressroom, crouched behind the linotype, and switched the torch off again.

They waited. Soon they heard footsteps outside. The green door opened. A *bitte*—Heinrici, too, now used the word—stood in the doorway, a big electric torch in hand, lighting himself as well as the room with its strong beam. He was armed with a machine pistol but wore a forage cap instead of a helmet. For a moment he stood in the doorway, flashing the beam around, and then he closed the door and walked away.

Heinrici slipped back into the storeroom. "Take this," he said to Adriana, handing her the box of paper and other supplies. "I need one or two more items."

She could not see what he was doing, because in the pinpoint of light from his tiny torch only he could see into the shelved boxes. He remembered . . . Ah! Here they were. He pulled out Swiss, British, and American passport blanks and stuffed them in the pockets of his coveralls. On further impulse he pulled out blanks for Brazil, Argentina, and Mexico. In yet another box he found assorted driver's license blanks, for Britain, Switzerland, and several American states. He stuffed some of those in his pockets. If they proved to have no other use, they would be a good gift for Papa Ange.

"All right," he said to Adriana. "We can go."

When they opened the green door, the main pressroom was dark and silent. The German guard was in another part of the building, maybe even outside the building. Anyway, walking around with his huge torch lighted, he was easily avoided. Heinrici led Adriana back to the front door. As they left, they locked it behind them, and then returned the key to the hidey-hole behind the brick.

"You realize, I hope," he said to Adriana as they stood in the darkness of the alley, "that what we've done so far has been easy compared to what comes now. We are on the streets after curfew, and we have four kilometers to cover. We can't go back by rue Riquet and rue Ordener."

"Do you know the city well enough to find a way through the back streets?" she asked.

"I wouldn't have brought us here if I didn't," he said. "But first step away from me a little. I have to relieve myself."

She stood with her back to him as he stepped away a few paces and urinated. "It would be a good idea," she said to him, "if we walk a little separated. If the one walking ahead is stopped, the other may be able to help."

"Good," he said. "I'll lead. Let me carry the box. Just don't lose sight of me."

He walked toward the canal, and immediately they found that the clack of their wooden soled shoes echoed through the silent streets. They had to stop and take them off. Fortunately, they were wearing heavy socks, which they knew would wear through before they had walked four kilometers on rough pavements, but that was a problem for later.

Heinrici led, working his way west through the lesser streets, avoiding the main streets. The silence was oppressive. It was the sullen quiet of a captive city, wholly alien to Paris. They crossed the rue d'Aubervilles without seeing a patrol. In the shadow of the freight stations they hurried south and turned west on the rue de Départment. Heinrici had no doubt there were sentries all around the stations, so he detoured south on rue Caillé to a street he would have liked to avoid but could not—the broad boulevard de la Chapelle.

The tracks to the great railroad stations, Gare de l'Est and Gare du Nord passed under the boulevard, and, as Heinrici had feared, he had no sooner turned into the boulevard then he heard hobnailed boots hammering the pavement. Backing into rue Caillé, he stopped Adriana, and they retreated into a doorway.

The patrol marched past and turned north on rue d'Aubervilles. Heinrici gestured, and Adriana trotted along beside him. Unfortunately, they had to cover two hundred meters in the open before they could turn north into the tangle of dark, narrow streets behind St. Bernard's church. They sprinted over the rough pavement, bruising their feet. As they reached Place de la Chappelle, they heard a shout from the boulevard to the west. Heinrici ran even faster, and Adriana kept pace with him, until they reached the refuge of the neighborhood.

No one followed. The shout had come from a *bitte,* beyond question, but he had probably taken them for nothing but curfew breakers and had seen no reason to set a whole squad to looking for them.

"That's the worst of it," Heinrici whispered. "From here we can keep to small streets, climb Montmartre, and go down the other side to your friend's house. It's a big city. They can't patrol everywhere."

Adriana sat down on a doorstep. She had already worn holes in the heels of her socks; she pulled them off, turned them over, and put the knit fabric between her feet and and the streets. Heinrici followed her example.

Heinrici still leading, they moved north and west and began to climb the Montmartre slope. After sprinting across one more boulevard, they entered a neighborhood where long flights of stone steps connected lower streets to higher. The white dome of Sacré Coeur stood above. This neighborhood that had epitomized the old gaiety of Paris was eerily quiet.

At one point they heard the footfalls of a patrol. It was foolish, Heinrici noted, for patrols to walk the streets in hobnailed boots. They could be heard for blocks.

He kept twenty meters or so ahead of Adriana, as she had suggested. He glanced back often to be sure she was keeping up. The socks were in shreds now, and his feet had painful blisters. Hers had to be at least as bad; but she did not slacken her pace or ask for rest, though when he glanced back he sometimes saw her limping. The basilica was to their left now. They were three quarters of the way back to the house where the Résistant Le Concombre waited.

"'Alt!"

Heinrici stiffened. His hand went to the pistol in his pocket. He could not see the man who had spoken.

"Well, Fräulein. Where might you be going in the middle of the night?"

Heinrici stared. The two Germans had rounded a corner after he had passed and apparently had not noticed him. He pressed his back to a wall. They were intent on Adriana and were not looking around.

"Hold your hands above your head, Fräulein."

The one who was talking was not in uniform. He was in civilian clothes—

dark suit, slouch hat—likely a Gestapo agent. His French was all but incomprehensible. The other man was an SS soldier in black uniform, armed with a rifle.

Heinrici put down the box he had carried from Galien et Fils. He slid along the wall, wanting to close the distance as much as possible before he struck. The one in civilian clothes was the more dangerous, he judged. The soldier would need a second or two to comprehend and lower the muzzle of his rifle.

The civilian began to search Adriana, patting her down with both hands. Good. That meant he was not holding a pistol aimed toward her.

"Aha! What is this?" He had found the Spanish pistol in Adriana's pocket.

Heinrici drove his fist into the base of the man's skull, crunching bone and tissue, and the man dropped to his knees. Heinrici turned to the soldier and threw the same fist at his chin. The soldier staggered back, lowering the barrel of the rifle, and Heinrici struck him again, square in the center of his face, breaking his nose and knocking him off his feet. Heinrici grabbed the rifle away, lest the man fire a shot that would rouse every patrol in the arrondissement.

Still on his knees, the stunned civilian clutched at his jacket, tearing it open and grabbing at his pistol. Adriana had a knife in her hand, and with a quick, smooth movement she stabbed him through the throat. Good. Necessary. But before Heinrici could react or stop her, she scrambled to the fallen, half-conscious SS soldier and thrust the knife into *his* throat.

Heinrici watched, momentarily stupefied, as she calmly wiped her knife clean on the soldier's uniform. My God! Who had she thought that young soldier was? She pulled open his tunic and took his papers from his pocket. Then she crawled back to the body of the civilian and methodically pulled out his pistol and his papers, handing everything up to Heinrici with a gesture that suggested he find a place for it all in the copious pockets of his coveralls.

"Adriana . . ." he mumbled.

She tipped her hand in the direction they had been going when she was stopped, and walked off.

He hurried after her and fell in step beside her. "I suggest we don't tell your French friends about those two," he said. "You realize . . . the SS will shoot hostages in the morning. For every German killed—"

She looked up into his face. "Maybe I—"

"We had to do it," he said. "Left there alive, they would have raised the alarm. Anyway, hostages would have been shot for two Germans knocked unconscious, the same as if they had been killed. All I am saying is, Le Docteur might—"

"I won't tell them," she said.

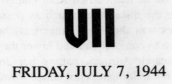

VII

FRIDAY, JULY 7, 1944

THEIR print shop was in the cellar of a rundown neighborhood cinema in Montparnasse. Since there was no power in the afternoons, during the matinee the projector was run with electricity from a bicycle-powered generator. Half a dozen young men and women sat on benches in a room behind the projection booth and waited their turn on the pedals. Although the theater was compelled to show a certain quota of propaganda films, it attracted crowds in need of diversion by running mindless musicals and light comedies from the thirties, bland films to which the German censors could not object.

The constant traffic in and out of the theater was useful to the Résistants: it made their comings and goings less apparent. The booming of the loudspeakers behind the screen masked the sound of the hand press below.

Baldwin had hobbled down the steep wooden stairway into the cellar, and now he sat gratefully on a sagging theater seat that had been retired many years ago. Théo, Le Capitaine, was with him and he had insisted they come by bus, not by vélo-taxi; too much riding in vélo-taxis, he said, suggested more money than a wounded and labor-exempt veteran in shabby clothes should have. Baldwin's leg hurt him, and he was all but exhausted. Still, he was determined not to complain, and he accepted with a smile a splash of the fiery calvados offered by the forger.

With wry simplicity, they called the forger Le Faussaire. He was a late-middle-aged, chainsmoker who had somehow managed to keep a paunch, loose jowls, and a ruddy complexion—perhaps by forging ration coupons. He sat at his workbench and used a big magnifying glass to examine the paper Heinrici had handed over to Baldwin yesterday afternoon.

"Excellent!" he said, laughing. "Les Boches themselves couldn't detect—"

"Because it's genuine," Baldwin interrupted. "It's the real paper."

"The stamps are not so good," said Le Faussaire. "Not Paris."

"You can take care of that, can you not, Faussaire?" asked Le Capitaine.

"Anyway," Baldwin interjected, "it might be well for the highest-ranking officer in the group to have papers stamped in Berlin. That might avoid a question or two."

Le Faussaire pressed one of the rubber stamps on an inkpad and stamped a piece of paper. He stared at the imprint. "The date is wrong," he said. "But that's easily changed. Berlin . . ."

"We will provide photographs," Baldwin said. "Names. Ranks. Units. We will want five sets of SS identification documents, one of SD."

"SD!" exclaimed Faussaire. He stared at the paper. "Why not papers to identify someone as Adolf Hitler himself?"

"Can you produce the documents?" Baldwin asked.

Le Faussaire grinned. "Of course! Why not?"

Marcel Ange thumbed through the blank passports Heinrici brought him. Though he tried to conceal his reaction, his enthusiasm was evident.

"Are these good?" he asked.

"They were good in 1940," Heinrici said. "They are good except for changes made since then."

"Uhmmm . . ." The old man frowned. "What is your price for these, Philippe?"

"No price," Heinrici said. "They are yours. A token of my friendship. With three exceptions. I want a Swiss passport, a Spanish passport, and an American passport put on three of those blanks by your best forger. The rest of the blanks are yours."

Papa Ange nodded gravely. "An acceptable gift."

"A token." said Heinrici.

"Swiss, Spanish, American . . . A man must have his alternatives, no?"

"Yes. And the cars? What about the cars, Papa?"

"I have found a fine Mercedes," said Papa. "That would be good, wouldn't it? And a Citroen. With petrol."

"Excellent."

"They will be costly. From your share of the gold, Philippe."

"How costly?"

"I am not sure yet. But these cars must be ones that cannot be identified with any living owner. And after you have finished with them, they are useless. You may as well wreck them or drive them into the river—they will be no good anymore."

"Keep them reasonable, Papa."

"What is reasonable? But"—he gestured toward the box of passport blanks—"we are friends. And I have something else for you, at no cost whatever. The room you wanted—your own place. And the clothes. But the *carte d'identité?*" He shrugged. "No. I figured you are in the business of supplying those."

"Where is this room?"

"Not far from here. It's modest, you understand. But unknown to anyone but me. I have a suit of clothes for you here. You must not go near that room dressed like a squarehead. Change, and I will show you where it is."

A few minutes later Heinrici walked along a narrow street with Papa. They looked alike, a pair of French workingmen in cheap suits and flat caps. Heinrici carried his uniform in a wrinkled brown paper bag. Papa did not accompany him as far as the room but handed him the key at a street corner, pointed out the door, and ambled away.

The room was above an all-but-abandoned butcher shop: a single room, not quite so small as Heinrici had expected, a clean, sunny room furnished with a big old brass bed, an easy chair, a straight chair and table, an armoire. It could have been a room in any one of a hundred small hotels in Paris. It was one of three rooms on the floor, with shared access to a water closet and a bath. The doors to the other two rooms were locked. Heinrici guessed that their occupants would take no notice of him, as he would take no notice of them. Papa would surely have chosen a room where the neighbors were at least circumspect.

He hung his uniform inside the armoire. He could not return to the Royal Monceau wearing the suit Papa had provided, and he could not leave this room dressed as a colonel of the Abwehr, so he was going to have to change somewhere, maybe in a public rest room. In the future he would come here in civilian clothes—but in a suit he could wear on returning to the hotel.

For the moment he stretched out on the brass bed. His mind began to explore the possibilities. He could use a Swiss passport and go to neutral Switzerland. Spain, though, might be more open after the war, less likely to be looking for German officers taking refuge. He had heard, too, that America was a wide-open country, a country where identity documents were never asked for, where an English-speaking man could lose himself. Granted, the Americans spoke an odd, flat kind of English, but if there was one talent on which he prided himself, it was his talent for picking up languages and dialects and soon speaking them like a native. He had an ear for nuances and a flair for mimicry. A few weeks in America and—

Someone rapped on his door. Heinrici rolled off the bed and grabbed the pistol out of his holster in the armoire. He opened the door cautiously, standing back to keep out of sight.

"Philippe?"

"*Sidonie!*" he gasped.

She pushed the door wide open and came in. "A gift to us both," she said. "From Papa." She glanced calmly at his pistol and then ignored it as he put it back in the armoire.

In six years she was but little changed. She was still the girl with the open, smiling face, wide mouth, narrow eyes, dark, prominent brows, and short brown hair brushed flat against her head. As always she wore a little straw hat—this one blue, with a yellow hatband tied in a big bow in front like an exaggerated bow tie—tipped jauntily to one side.

She threw her arms around him, and her kiss was hard and wet—this, too, like before.

"Ah, Sidonie! Papa—"

"He told me you had come back to Paris. How long would it have been before I saw you?"

He held her close in his arms. "Look in the armoire, Sidonie."

She glanced at the field gray uniform. "Yes. Papa told me about that. That's dangerous, Philippe."

He stroked the back of her neck. "It's real," he said.

"I never thought you were a Belgian printer. Not after I got to know you. Philippe Valence . . . What is your real name, then?"

Heinrici smiled. "It depends on when you ask. And who you ask. Do you have a suggestion? I'm looking for a new name."

She began to take off her clothes. She was wearing a mannish jacket, what every stylish woman in Paris seemed to be wearing this year, with a thin cotton sweater underneath. "How about Woodrow Wilson?" she suggested. "That was popular after the last war. Oh, no . . . this time—Franklin Roosevelt. That will be popular. That will be well thought of."

Heinrici began to take off his own clothes. Papa had sent her here with the word that Philippe had not been with a woman since he returned to Paris and would surely want her. He did. He had not been with a woman in months, not since he picked up a WREN on Regent Street and shared dinner and the night with her in . . . in March, maybe in February.

Sidonie was naked now and lay back on the bed. She was full-breasted. That was what made her . . . He wanted to put the thought out of mind, but it was what made her a successful high-priced whore. That was what she had been six years ago, anyway—a girl who had worked the lobbies of grand hotels.

"What's happened to you since we last met?" he asked as he pulled down his trousers. "Anything different?"

She shrugged. "I'm thirty years old now. You can see . . . Things are not as well arranged as they were." She lifted her big breasts in her hands, and it was true—they were not as firm as they had been. "We've had bad years, Philippe. The *bittes*—is it true you're one of them?"

"Sometimes," he said.

"I got married," she said.

"Really?"

"No, not really. You know what I mean. He wanted me to stay away from other men. He rented a flat for me. It wasn't bad. Then . . . Well, you know. I think he may be in England. Or . . . We hear there are French divisions in the Allied armies in Normandy."

"He may be coming back," Heinrici suggested.

She shrugged again. "He has a wife, of course. And a child. That is, he has if the *bittes* haven't done something to them."

"My countrymen won't be around much longer," Heinrici said.

"Thank God for that." She beckoned him to lie down with her. She reached for her little handbag and drew out and lit a cigarette. Apparently she wanted to talk a while. She lifted his penis in her hand. "Looks the same," she said. "Six years hasn't changed you much."

"More than you can see," he said.

"I wondered what happened to you. You didn't owe me a call, but—"

"You'd have gotten one," he said, "except that I had to leave very quickly."

"The cops?"

He nodded. "One little deal too many."

What he told her was true. He had lived well in Paris his last two years there, on the proceeds of business he had done with Papa and others. The skills the Abwehr had taught him, plus the facilities of Galien et Fils, had allowed him to earn money and live far better than either an engraver or an agent of the Abwehr could do on the wages paid.

"Not money," she said. "You didn't start counterfeiting banknotes?"

"Oh, no. Just documents."

"Papa said you were the best engraver he ever met. You could go back to that work, even honestly, if you wanted to."

"I'm afraid they'll be looking for a skilled engraver."

"Who'll be looking? Are you one of those who could be hanged . . . Or shot?"

"It's been threatened."

"By . . . ?"

"By the English."

Sidonie laughed. "They don't count. They or the Americans. I mean, does anybody *real* want to hang you?"

"Some might find reason."

She frowned and dragged on her cigarette. "Politics . . . ," she muttered. "Do you have a woman?"

"Not really. I live with one, but we don't sleep together. Cold as a blue diamond."

"Why don't you throw her out?"

"I can't. A matter of business."

Sidonie stared distastefully at her cigarette, then crushed it in the ashtray on the table by the bed. "You know, if you decide to stay in Paris . . . Well, you know."

"I hope to be able to stay in Paris," Heinrici said. "Or at least to be able to return."

She rolled toward him and threw an arm and leg across him. He clasped her well-remembered body to his. It was always pleasant to make love with Sidonie.

After Heinrici went out, Adriana ordered lunch for two brought to their suite. Choices were few, even in the Royal Monceau, but in twenty minutes two waiters arrived with a wheeled table, bringing a lunch of sliced meat, cheese, bread, a salad, and a bottle of white wine. Adriana wrapped the food in newspapers, packed it in Heinrici's leather briefcase, and scattered a few crumbs on the plates to make it appear they had eaten everything. Then she went out, carrying the briefcase.

She walked east on avenue Hoche, toward Parc Monceau, but shortly turned north into the Seventeenth Arrondissement. Watching the street signs carefully in this neighborhood she did not know, she found her way to an address not far from the Church of St. Francis de Sales. She knocked at the door and was admitted.

"My name is Jacqueline Clement," she said to the dour woman who answered the door. "I was sent by Monsieur le Concombre."

The woman nodded, stepped back from the door, and nodded to one side. With a gesture, she guided Adriana through a door to the right, into a comfortably furnished sunlit parlor where half a dozen canaries fluttered in cages. Potted flowers lined the windowsills.

Only when Adriana was seated did the woman speak. "Le Concombre sent word that you were coming. You are, he said, Dutch. He told me no more than that."

Adriana opened the briefcase. "I brought you some things from the hotel where I live. I know what shortages you live with in Paris today, and—"

"It wasn't necessary," the woman said, but she could not conceal her enthusiasm or her gratitude. "Uh . . . as Le Concombre probably told you, my name is Henriette Boulanger."

"Yes. He said you might be able to help me locate my husband."

"How much did he explain?"

"Only that you had sources of information."

"It is very simple," said Madame Boulanger. "No magic. Many prisoners of war have been repatriated. Many thousands have not. Whenever a French prisoner arrives home we question him about other men he saw in the prisons and camps. So we have created a large index of names. The Germans know we do this—it is no secret. I have already checked the index for the name Dirk Ter Horst. I am sorry . . . but it is not in the index."

Adriana closed her eyes. She held her breath for a moment.

"Mademoiselle . . . I am sorry. Our system is informal. Anyway, he is Dutch. He could very well be alive . . . "

"Our child was killed in the bombing of Rotterdam," Adriana whispered. "She was with his parents. They were killed, too."

"I am very sorry, Mademoiselle," said Madame Boulanger.

"Maybe you could—maybe you could make further inquiry," Adriana suggested weakly. "He may be remembered for who he was. Dirk Ter Horst was a member of the Dutch Olympic team in 1936. A javelin thrower. Someone might remember that."

Madame Boulanger nodded. "Someone might."

"And he might be remembered for being married to me. I am Adriana Kip."

"You are . . . My God! Yes, I can see that you are, now that you tell me. I remember you. My God, don't the Boches recognize you?"

Adriana shook her head. "So far, none has."

"I will initiate an inquiry," said Madame Boulanger. "I will ask if anyone has any news of the husband of Adriana Kip. That will make a very big difference. It will stimulate people's memory."

"I will not give up trying to find him," said Adriana.

"No," Madame Boulanger said quietly. "We never give up. I've had no word of *my* husband either."

"I shall be grateful, Madame, for any help you can give me."

General Hausser returned Heinrici's salute, then shook his hand. He pointed to a chair, and Heinrici sat down.

"Have you anything of significance to report?" the general asked.

"Not really," said Heinrici. "Except that things are going well."

"Have you learned anything about the Résistance that would justify any action?"

"Herr General," Heinrici said, "I have learned nothing that would justify our moving against any Résistance unit, even if Colonel Sir Henry Harding weren't threatening us with difficulties."

"I try not to think about that."

"Are you making contingency plans, Herr General?"

"My contingency plan is for you to keep your English friends satisfied that you are making progress toward achieving the rescue of Henri Mercier. And I must tell you, time is running out for you. He has been transferred from the custody of the Gestapo to the custody of the SS. That means he is available for deportation."

"How soon would he go, then?"

"Assuming they see nothing special about him," the general said, "he might be put on a train next week. There was a time when they were sending out a trainload of Jews every day. Today there aren't so many Jews left—besides, transport has become more difficult. There is a train scheduled for next Friday, July fourteenth."

"Bastille Day," said Heinrici. "A fine irony."

"It is by no means certain he will go on the July fourteenth train," the general continued. "Or for that matter that he will go on the next or the next. At this point, the question seems to lie with the governor of the prison. But you have little time, Heinrici."

"The daughter?"

"She has been available for deportation for a month. I suspect there is some reason she is being held at Romainville. Maybe someone finds her attractive."

"I am grateful for the information," said Heinrici. "I am still without a final plan, but I have taken important preliminary steps. I can report the details if you wish."

General Hausser shook his head. He took out a cigar and offered the box to Heinrici. "I understand you have dined twice with Gruppenführer Schenck," he said. "Once in the company of the charming Martine Paul."

Heinrici took a cigar. "He likes the Royal Monceau dining room."

"Who was the woman with you?"

"A member of the SOE team," said Heinrici. "Her name is Adriana Kip. She's Dutch."

"Effective?" the general asked skeptically as he lit his cigar.

"I would call her very effective, Herr General."

"Does she speak German?"

"Fluently."

"But she pretended not to when she dined with Gruppenführer Schenck."

Heinrici smiled. "Your sources of information are—"

"Martine Paul works for *us*," said General Hausser.

"Ah. So even in his bed, he—"

"We have made her a promise," said the general. "I may ask for your help in redeeming it. There may come a time, not long from now, when she will need to escape, first from Schenck, then from the righteous vengeance the French will probably visit on any woman who has conspicuously cooperated with the German authorities. She appears to have cooperated with the SS, which will probably inspire a particularly violent wrath. If she tells them she spied on the SS for the Abwehr—" He shrugged, smiled. "Well, it's hardly going to help her."

"May I ask you, Herr General, for some help with a matter that involves Fräulein Kip?"

"I've told you my participation in this operation of yours must be limited. But . . . What is it you want?"

"Adriana Kip was married to a Dutch officer named Dirk Ter Horst. Ter Horst was either killed or captured trying to defend a bridge on the River Maas. The Dutch called it Bridge Thirty-four. Can you make an inquiry as to whether or not this Ter Horst is alive?"

"What good would that do?"

"If he is alive, it's possible she would abandon the SOE mission to go looking for him."

"If that is so, why not simply tell her Ter Horst is alive, whether he is or not? At the appropriate time."

Heinrici frowned. "I would rather not do that, Herr General."

"Why not?"

Heinrici drew a deep breath. "She has sources of information. It would be disadvantageous for information from us to contradict what she has learned from someone else."

"Martine Paul reports that she is exceptionally beautiful. Long blonde hair. Pale blue eyes . . ." He grinned.

"She is extraordinarily beautiful," said Heinrici stiffly.

General Hausser laughed. "Beware, Heinrici! Beware."

"She also hates Germans and is quite capable of killing," Heinrici said.

The general turned over the papers in a pile to the right side of his desk. "Two Germans were killed on the Butte de Montmartre early yesterday morning," he said. "An agent of the Gestapo and an SS soldier. They were killed with a knife, and their papers were stolen. Could your SOE group have had anything to do with that?"

"I am sure they did not, Herr General," said Heinrici. "Fräulein Kip was with me all night, and the other member is a crippled English officer. He does not move far on foot."

"The SS shot ten French hostages yesterday because of the murder of the two Germans on Montmartre. If you encounter the people who killed those two Germans, you might tell them they are directly responsible for the deaths of ten Frenchmen."

"These hostages, Herr General. They are—"

"No one in particular," said General Hausser. "Curfew violators are usually taken to the nearest police headquarters, where they spend the rest of the night blacking boots, cleaning toilets, and the like. If their papers are in order, they are released in the morning. If they are unfortunate enough to have been picked up on a night when a German was murdered in Paris, then they are hostages. Of the ten shot yesterday, four were in custody for illegal trade in rationed goods, and six were curfew violators. For the SS, it was a matter of simple convenience. They had those prisoners already in custody."

Heinrici nodded. "I see."

"You can understand why Mademoiselle Paul is so anxious to accompany us if we are forced to withdraw from Paris," said General Hausser. "And understand this also, Heinrici—that I myself have formed my plans for a quick departure. I suggest you think of what you will do. I would not want to be in Paris the day our authority crumbles."

"I assume your plans are confidential," Heinrici said. "I hear that planning a retreat is strictly forbidden."

"My plans," the general said, "are for an orderly transfer of this headquarters from Paris to another city."

"I hope to accompany you, Herr General," said Heinrici.

"I hope you do, Heinrici. Either that, or return to London."

Heinrici descended into the Métro station and caught the train for the Concorde station. It was his intention to walk up the Champs-Elysées toward the Royal Monceau, stopping for a glass of beer in one of the sidewalk cafés, where Adriana was to join him at six.

He did not notice that he was followed.

Oberleutnant Dietrich Krueger had been waiting in the lobby as Oberst Heinrici came down from the general's office, and he had disposed of his cigarette and set out after Heinrici. He followed him to the café on the Champs-Elysées. There he sat down, pretended to read a newspaper, drank a cup of wretched ersatz coffee, and remained until the striking blonde came along and sat down with the Oberst.

Oberleutnant Krueger disliked this assignment, but he would, of course, carry it out as meticulously and thoroughly as he could. He was one of two officers assigned to watch Heinrici. His partner, Leutnant Hals, had lost the oberst and his companion two nights ago when they left their hotel on their way to a show at the Moulin Rouge. Leutnant Hals had lacked money for a vélo-taxi and took the Métro to the Moulin Rouge. They never arrived. What is more, they did not return to the hotel before mid-morning. Except for that twelve-hour gap in the surveillance, Hals and Krueger had managed to keep good track of Oberst Heinrici.

They reported directly to General Hausser. The assignment was absolutely confidential. The general emphasized strongly that the oberst was almost certainly an honest man, faithfully serving the Reich. What was more, the oberst was working on a difficult and secret assignment.

It must be an interesting assignment, the oberleutnant speculated. This morning the oberst had gone to a home on Montmartre, changed into shabby civilian clothes for an assignment in a nearby room, left the room with the woman while still dressed in those clothes, and changed back into uniform in the men's room of a Métro station. It appeared the oberst had contact with the Résistance.

While in General Hausser's office, Oberleutnant Krueger learned something he was not supposed to know. His eye had stopped for a moment on a copy of one of his own reports to the general, one of the many that had to be laboriously written out in duplicate. He had only wanted to see if the general had written any favorable or unfavorable comment on it. What he saw was a note in the general's own handwriting. He was forwarding the reports to Admiral Canaris in Berlin. To the long-time commanding officer of the Abwehr, now in disgrace and demoted to a minor office!

TUESDAY, JULY 11, 1944

ERGEANT Willi Weibel pulled his goggles down over his eyes as he stomped on the starter pedal of his motorcycle. As a dispatch rider, he wore a steel helmet, a rubberized coat, breeches, and boots. He was a square-jawed Bavarian, forty years old and proud of his assignment as dispatch rider in Paris. It was his reward, probably, for his years of service to the Party before he joined the army. Willi Weibel had joined the Brown Shirts in 1924 and, as a member of the SA, had never wavered in his loyalty to the Führer, through the worst of years and now the best. He had served four years in an infantry unit, fought in Belgium and France, then in Sicily and Italy, and finally was ordered to Paris. He carried documents among the various headquarters, speeding through the streets on his roaring, unmuffled cycle. He took pride in the way he had learned the streets of this city in a few months.

Settling himself on his seat, he checked the straps of his dispatch bags one more time. Then he twisted his throttle and sped away from Place des Saussaies, from the old French Ministry of the Interior that had been taken over as headquarters for the SS and Gestapo. He roared through the short street to the Madeleine, right down the rue Royale to the Place de la Concorde, left into the rue de Rivoli and to the Hotel Meurice, headquarters of the Militärbefehel-

shaber Gross Paris—the commanding general. The sergeant in the first-floor
message center always gave him a cup of the morning coffee—the best in
Paris—so he was inside the Meurice ten minutes. When he came out, he settled
himself comfortably on his motorcycle once again and set out on the next leg of
his long ride to deliver the documents dispatched this morning by the SS and
Gestapo.

His next stop was Fresnes Prison. He enjoyed the ride to Fresnes. He enjoyed
it so much he did not even take the most direct route but rode instead along the
river quays, crossing at the Pont Sully, and riding west along the quays of the
left bank for a view of the great cathedral before he turned south at last on
boulevard St. Michel and headed for the Porte d'Orleans.

Though goods were scarce in Paris, Sergeant Weibel had managed to send
home packages of things that pleased his wife: a stylish hat, a necklace, a bottle
of French scent. Paris was a beautiful city. As soon as the war was over—as
soon, really, as the English and Americans were driven out of Normandy—he
would arrange somehow to bring his wife to Paris.

"There you are, Monsieur," said the tobacconist to Heinrici—not guessing
that the tall French-speaking civilian at his counter was a German. "Every
morning. You could set clocks by him. He rides by here every morning at the
same hour."

"Where is he going?" Heinrici asked, as if only casually interested in the
dispatch rider.

"To the prison, Monsieur. He brings the orders from the rue des Saussaies—
who is to be shot, who tortured, and who loaded on the buses for Pantin."

"Pantin?"

"Pantin Station, Monsieur. When people are deported to Germany, they are
taken from here to Pantin Station and loaded on trains."

Heinrici nodded. "So . . . ," he said. He was wearing a well-cut gray suit, a
gray hat, and carried a walking stick.

"You understand it is none of my business, Monsieur," said the tobacconist.
"I neither approve nor disapprove of anything the government does. But, being
here, I observe."

"I understand," said Heinrici. "So, thank you, Monsieur." He put the pack of
cigarettes he had bought into his pocket. "Bonjour, Monsieur."

On the street outside, Le Concombre had also watched the dispatch rider. The
avenue de la République led directly to the main gate in the gray stone wall of
the prison.

"Look at the place," grumbled Le Concombre. "You'd need tanks to break in
there."

"Obviously we can't break in," said Heinrici.

Baldwin stood to one side, leaning uncomfortably on his cane, pretending he was not with Heinrici and Le Concombre and that he did not know them.

"The dispatch rider arrives every morning at this hour," said Heinrici, glancing at his watch. It was 10:30. "Obviously he comes on Highway Twenty. I believe you see what we have to do."

"If we kill him, they'll shoot hostages," said Le Concombre.

"Then we must not kill him," said Heinrici. "Did you copy the number off his cycle?"

"Yes. WH 91558."

"Good. How well do you know these streets?"

"I don't know them," said Le Concombre.

"Then we must learn them. When we leave here with Henri Mercier in our automobile, we must return to Paris by a different route than Highway Twenty and Porte d'Orleans."

Le Concombre nodded. "We can drive about."

They had come to Fresnes in an automobile. It was the Mercedes promised by Marcel Ange, taken from a garage early this morning and delivered to Heinrici at the Royal Monceau. The permit was forged.

Although Heinrici was wearing civilian clothes, he was carrying his genuine papers as Konrad Heinrici, Oberst, Abwehr. Le Concombre was driving as his chauffeur.

As they drove away from the tobacconist's shop, Baldwin hobbled off toward the prison and around the wall to his left. He was making his way along the street faced by the wall when the Mercedes, having circled the prison, stopped and picked him up.

In his handwritten report to General Hausser, Oberleutnant Krueger said, "Oberst Heinrici left the Royal Monceau at 0830 hours in a licensed Mercedes automobile bearing what appeared to be correct permits. He was dressed in civilian clothes. The automobile seemed to have been left on the street, since Oberst Heinrici himself drove it and appeared to be alone. Having no means of pursuing an automobile, I am unable to report where Oberst Heinrici went. He returned to the hotel without the automobile at 1600 hours."

"It is an error," said Heinrici, "for all three of us to be together." He glanced first at Adriana, then at Baldwin. "Hereafter, we must avoid such meetings. If the SD caught us now, they would have the whole mission."

They were in the flat near Les Halles with Le Concombre, Le Docteur, and Le Capitaine.

"We have little time," said Heinrici. "Which is now my chief concern. A train will leave Pantin Friday. If Mercier is on it, we have lost. As of now, we cannot send men to Fresnes with a forged order to turn him over because we don't know the appearance of such an order. That is why we must intercept the dispatch rider and get access to his dispatch bags. We cannot simply kill him on the road, since hostages would be shot in reprisal. We *must* have the bags, we *must* see the orders, we *must* forge similar orders, and we *must* do it all tomorrow. Otherwise, we cannot make the effort at Fresnes on Thursday."

"And how do you plan to do all this in one day?" asked Le Docteur.

"I can think of only one way," Heinrici said. "It involves risk, but"—he shrugged—"what doesn't?"

"What do you have in mind?" asked Adriana.

Heinrici drew a deep breath. "You said you can provide SS uniforms. What is the highest rank you can provide?"

Le Capitaine drew a finger down over his mouth. "Uh, I think we have the uniform of what they call a standartenführer, an SS colonel."

"Very well," said Heinrici. "All I want are the insignia. All the insignia. Don't overlook the collar patches—they are essential. Also, I could use a Nazi Party badge. I will wear my own uniform, with SS insignia. And I will need identity documents—your forger can use the materials we obtained for him last week. My appearance will have to be altered somehow. An eye patch is probably too obvious. Maybe we could darken my hair—using something that can be easily washed out. And eyeglasses, eyeglasses with ordinary glass, not lenses. I must by photographed for my documents."

"By when?" Baldwin asked. "How soon do you need all this?"

"By tomorrow morning, very early."

"Just what are we going to do?" Adriana asked.

"I am going to get the documents we need to look at," said Heinrici. "Alone. Once you have provided what I've just mentioned, I'll need no more help. No one *could* help. It is a job for one man."

He arrived at the former Ministère de l'Intérieur on rue des Saussaies at 0930 hours—Standartenführer Klaus Brunner, SS. He walked about in front for a moment before he went in, looking for the cycle numbered WH 91558. It was not one of the three motorcycles standing on the street before the building. He went inside.

If the dispatch rider reached Fresnes regularly at 1020 hours, then he had to leave the rue des Saussaies between 0945 and 1000 hours—a man on a motorcycle, riding through streets almost void of motor traffic, would not take more than half an hour to reach Fresnes. Heinrici would have liked to come here half an hour earlier, but he doubted he could walk around SS headquarters, looking busy and doing nothing, for three quarters of an hour without arousing suspicion.

A crisply uniformed untersturmführer examined his identification, saluted, and admitted him to the building. Inside, SS headquarters was what he had expected: a hive of officious men—and a very few women—all hurrying from room to room, floor to floor. He noted a few of the offices listed on the directory board—HSPF, Höherer SS und Polizeiführer, who was of course General Karl Oberg; BdS, Befehlshaber der Sicherheitspolizei, commander of security police, his dinner companion General Schenck; SD, Sicherheitsdienst; and RUSA, Rasse und Siedlungsamt, the Race and Settlement Office.

"Can I help you find anything, Herr Standartenführer?"

He turned from the directory and found himself facing a stout young woman in the gray uniform of a blitzmädchen.

"Uh, no. I was just looking for the RUSA. I think I may have a friend working there. A Standartenführer Bayer."

"Recently transferred, Herr Standartenführer?"

"Yes, both of us. I was at Caen."

"I don't believe I know the officer, sir. The RUSA is on the second floor. You've found your own office all right?"

"Oh, yes. I've been here a week."

She nodded and walked away. He wondered if he only imagined that she was suspicious.

Heinrici found a cloakroom. He put his cap on a shelf, opened his briefcase and took out a folder of papers, and put the briefcase on the shelf by his cap. Without a cap and with papers in hand, he looked like an officer working in the headquarters.

He began to look for the way the dispatch rider would enter and leave the building.

Likely there was a dispatch room, a station where dispatch riders picked up and delivered documents. Likely it would be on the ground floor. He found it: a bare, green-painted room where a clerk stationed behind a screened window handed leather dispatch cases to the riders. The riders were given receipts for cases they delivered and signed receipts for the ones they took. Leaving the window, they went down a narrow hallway to a guarded door that opened directly onto the street where their cycles waited. There was a toilet just inside that door, Heinrici noticed. Some of them went in there as soon as they arrived.

Heinrici squared his shoulders and walked up to the screen window.

"Herr Standartenführer?"

"The dispatch rider who takes the morning delivery to Fresnes Prison," said Heinrici. "Has he come in yet?"

The SS sergeant behind the window glanced at his watch. "Oh, yes, sir. And gone again. Ten minutes ago."

Heinrici felt his stomach tighten, and his mind turned with the implications of this news. "Uh . . . Is there another delivery there today?"

"Not ordinarily, Herr Standartenführer. I can arrange a special delivery."

"Not necessary. At what time will he go tomorrow?"

"That's Sergeant Weibel, sir. A very punctual man, very methodical. He

leaves here at 0930 hours every morning. He makes a stop at the Hotel Meurice
before he goes out to Fresnes."

Heinrici nodded. "Tomorrow will be soon enough," he said.

"It is my own fault," Heinrici said. He was in the bathroom, washing the
darkener out of his hair. In the living room of the flat, Le Capitaine and Adriana
were at work on his uniform, removing the SS insignia and reattaching the
Abwehr insignia. "I should have known it was possible the dispatch rider did
not go directly from rue des Saussaies to Fresnes."

"You're lucky you got in and out of that place," said Adriana. "You could not
have gone any earlier and stood around waiting for the man without arousing
suspicion. I think you took all the risk you could."

"We could have shot the rider," said Le Capitaine. "Somewhere outside
Fresnes, along the highway."

"And lost five French citizens in reprisal?" Heinrici said through the water
that dribbled down his face.

"We will just have to signal Colonel Harding," said Adriana, "that it has not
been possible to effect the rescue before—"

"What then?" asked Heinrici. He swung around to face her. "And then—"

"Radio Heinrici?" she said. "No. Not necessarily. In the first place, we have
no reason to believe Henri Mercier or his daughter are going on that Friday
train. And if they do—well, I will signal Colonel Harding that we did our best.
I'll be honest about you, Heinrici, and I'm sure Len Baldwin will be. The deal
was that you would help us as much as you could and not betray us. So far as I
can see, there is no reason for Radio Heinrici to transmit."

"So we just wait and see if the Merciers go on the Friday train," Heinrici
said. He shook his head. "I don't like that. There *is* an alternative."

"What alternative?"

He came out of the bathroom, rubbing his hair with a towel. He sat down at
the round table, facing Adriana. "Suppose the Friday train doesn't go," he said.

"Who could prevent it?" asked Le Capitaine.

"Every train going east out of Pantin has to cross the Canal d'Ourcq, on the
bridge just outside the yard. If—"

Le Capitaine shook his head. "Blow it up? It is guarded. You talk about their
shooting hostages—"

"Théo," Heinrici interrupted, using the name he had heard some of the others
call Le Capitaine. "Who will be on that train?"

"Jews," said Théo.

"And who else?"

Le Capitaine glanced uncertainly at Adriana. "You are suggesting—"

"Résistants, Théo," said Heinrici. "The SS is deporting Jews, yes. The cars
will be full of them. But the Gestapo and SD are deporting prisoners too—Ré-

sistants, real and suspected. In the rue des Saussaies they are not so deluded as to ignore what is happening in Normandy. They think they may soon have to withdraw from Paris. Those of them who are realistic *know* they will. So they are emptying the prisons."

"What prevents them from taking the train around by another route?" Adriana asked.

"The other route takes it through the city," Heinrici said. "I doubt they would risk that—exposing cattle cars full of human beings to tens of thousands of people, including thousands who are armed and ready to rise. Too great a provocation. It is German policy to keep order in Paris as long as possible."

"They will rebuild the bridge," said Le Capitaine. "In a few days—"

"Who knows what will happen in a few days?" Heinrici said. "The armies are fighting hard in Normandy. If there is a breakthrough, the situation could change as quickly as it did in 1940. And I can tell you, there will be a breakthrough before much longer. Germany has lost the war."

Le Capitaine frowned. "I will have to discuss it with the others. And they with still others."

"Tomorrow night, Théo," said Heinrici. "It must be tomorrow night."

"What role will *you* play?" asked Le Capitaine.

"*All* the role, if necessary," Heinrici snapped. "Get me the explosives, and I'll blow up the damned bridge by myself—if there's no Frenchman who wants to go along."

Oberleutnant Krueger and Leutnant Hals stood at attention before General Hausser in his headquarters in the Hotel Lutétia.

"Again," General Hausser said. "Again you've lost him."

"He entered a tobacconist's shop near Les Halles, Herr General," Leutnant Hals said miserably. "He did not come out again. I waited four hours."

"And then—only then—did you go in to find out if there was a way out the rear of the shop."

"Yes, sir."

General Hausser smiled. "Obviously, he had discovered that you were tailing him and decided to lose you. And that may have been your good fortune, Leutnant. He might have decided to kill you. I warned both of you that this man is a skilled professional. It appears he can lose you whenever he wants—which doesn't surprise me. And since he wants to so often, he must have spotted you."

"Yes, Herr General. He must have," Leutnant Hals agreed apologetically.

"Well, then," said General Hausser. "I will change your assignments. Go to your billet and rest, Hals. I will have a different job for you tomorrow. That will be all for now."

When Hals was gone, the general spoke to Krueger alone. "When Heinrici reports here again, I will introduce him to you. Then I will assign you to him, to assist him in what he is doing in Paris. It's a very touchy mission, Krueger. I am placing a great deal of trust in you. It will be your duty to help Heinrici in any way he wants. But besides that, I want you to watch for any sign that he is moving off on an independent course."

Oberleutnant Krueger nodded. "He is a mysterious man, Herr General."

In their suite in the Royal Monceau, Heinrici had ordered dinner brought up for him and Adriana. Admittedly tired, he was soaking in the tub.

"This city," he said to her through the open bathroom door. "Almost untouched. Never bombed. There's still hot water here—"

"For us," she interrupted. "For *you,* actually. Do you know how ordinary Parisians heat water? By burning wads of newspaper in little stoves they have made for it. They've learned to sprinkle a little water on the newspaper to keep it from burning too fast. They say they can bring a liter of water to boil with one big sheet of newspaper."

"Ah. Well. I suppose," he amended. "Still, Paris has not been bombed. Except once. And what they hit that time was Sacré Coeur."

They spoke English, a language with which both of them were comfortable. Heinrici had spent so much time in England that he found he thought in English most of the time. So did she.

She was sitting in her parlor, reading a propaganda newspaper, waiting to receive the waiter with the dinner. During the afternoon she had supplemented her meager Paris wardrobe with a white blouse and a black skirt, which she now wore. She could see the steam rising from the tub, fogging the bathroom mirror.

"It's Paris, not Rome, that's eternal," he continued. "It's indestructible. Berlin is gone, I am told—simply gone. It will never be the same. And you saw London."

"I saw Rotterdam," she said sharply.

"Adriana . . . I'm sorry. For all the good it does, I am sorry."

"You are right that your apology does no good," she said quietly.

"It's worse than that, you know," he said. "My work in Holland before the war may have had something to do with what happened to your husband."

"I know that."

"I won't apologize for that. I am a soldier. He was a soldier. Our countries were at war, and he would have killed me if he could. But I do apologize for the bombing of Rotterdam. We have already suffered a horrible punishment. In kind. In kind, Adriana. Our cities . . ."

"Your file in London said you have no family except your aged father," she said.

"My mother died in 1939," he said. "My father is a retired schoolmaster, living in Speyer. He was once a general, as you heard Colonel Harding say. I have no brothers or sisters. I am not married. I have no children."

"Unless my husband somehow survived, I have no family either," she said. "A half brother I haven't heard from since 1938." She shrugged. "No family."

"It makes what we have to do easier," Heinrici said. "It makes every other aspect of life harder."

"Are you expressing philosophy or sentiment?"

"I—"

The waiter rapped on the door. While Adriana received the meal and watched the waiter lay it out, Heinrici dried himself and put on a heavy white terrycloth robe furnished by the hotel. He sat down across the table from her. They had veal and red wine.

"Sentiment," he said, smiling.

"According to the psychiatric evaluation done on you in London, you are incapable of sentiment," she said.

Heinrici smiled. "Adriana," he said. "You and I are intelligent people. Either of us is entirely capable of generating any kind of psychiatric evaluation we want. Those fellows aren't clever."

She laughed under her breath. "No. First they told us you were incapable of emotion—then they recommended we interview you naked, giving you a chance to demonstrate some very strong emotions."

"Bastards," he muttered.

"You are an odd man, Heinrici," she said. "I don't begin to understand you."

"Adriana . . . my name is Konrad."

Her eyes flared. The *bitte*—the *bitte* was watching her, appraising her reaction. She drew a breath and sighed. "You—"

"We killed your child. We Germans. And probably your husband," he said. "I didn't, but my country did. Because you're Dutch, you don't bear much of that kind of responsibility. But don't suppose we Germans bear it all. The British sank the French navy. The Americans and British are bombarding Caen this very hour—mercilessly. Their planes have bombed Belgian cities, and Dutch. And this is not to mention the constant bombing of German cities . . . including homes, schools, hospitals, everything. I served my country as a spy in Holland. But I never hated the Dutch. I didn't hate the English who proposed to hang me."

"You are going to say that this is what war does to us, that war justifies—"

"No. War justifies nothing. It makes us do things we hate. I'm a creature of war, Adriana—the last war, which established the circumstances in which I grew up, and this war, which, in its own way, has consumed my whole adult life."

"You're terribly ready to risk your life," she said. "You amaze the French. They don't understand you."

"I take Colonel Harding's threat very seriously."

"Yes, and so you should. He could do what he threatened."

Heinrici poured wine for them. "Your health, Adriana," he said, lifting his glass.

"And yours . . . Konrad."

"I don't know why I was sent on this mission," Baldwin said bitterly. "It is ridiculous. I am a burden, that's all. I am nothing but a burden."

They sat in Baldwin's room on the rue de Lappe, sharing the breakfast Heinrici had carried from the hotel. Baldwin heated the coffee over a small tabletop stove in which he burned wadded newspaper to heat the coffee—just as Adriana had described. The little room was hot in the July sunshine, and Baldwin sat in his undershorts, showing his badly scarred leg. Heinrici had removed his tunic.

"Your limitations were well understood by Colonel Harding, I am sure," said Heinrici. "And your abilities. They were understood by Adriana and me."

"Claude—Le Concombre—is the only one willing to go," Baldwin said angrily. "Théo would, but he is a member of a Résistance cell at the Sorbonne, and his leader has ordered him to carry a dispatch to Soissons, and he won't be back in time. That means *she* will have to go. She. A woman. Because the goddamned cowardly French—"

"Do you still wonder why we defeated them so easily in 1940?" Heinrici aksed as he put ersatz butter on a bit of tough bread.

"They hate each other as much as they hate the Germans," said Baldwin. "Resistants come in—in *flavors*. Communists—"

"They are obsessed already with how they are going to govern France after you and the Americans liberate it for them," said Heinrici.

"But *goddamn!* You and Adriana . . . I can't go. She—"

"William Baldwin," Heinrici interrupted gently. "What are you called? Bill?"

"It's William Leonard Baldwin, and I'm called Len."

"Let me tell you something, Len. I don't know if she told you, but she was not to tell the French. The night we went out to steal the paper—the paper you delivered to the forger—she killed two Germans."

"I know," said Baldwin. "She told me."

"Ten French hostages were shot."

Baldwin nodded. "Yes. She knows that, too. She cried over it."

"She had no choice," said Heinrici. "The mission would have been over if she hadn't done it. My point is that she is capable of it. She went after them like a tiger—efficient and utterly cold."

"She has killed before," Baldwin said. "Colonel Harding warned me she . . . He warned me that—"

"I know what you mean," said Heinrici. "But, woman or not, she will do her part tonight. I'd hate to be the man who blocks her way."

Baldwin nodded. "Even so, you can see how I feel," he said quietly.

"The weapons," said Heinrici. "You are sure you can get the weapons?"

Baldwin nodded. "I seem to have rank—if nothing else."

Heinrici paused, coffee mug in hand, to study for a brief moment the sober, nervous face of the English officer. It was odd, he thought, that this aloof, sullen young man should reveal himself this way. "Len . . . ," he said tentatively.

"Konrad," Baldwin said impulsively. "Don't get yourselves killed tonight. I wouldn't want to be left here alone."

Adriana put her hand under the cloth covering the bread basket and poked her finger into the doughy mass of a kilo package of plastique. She nodded and replaced the cloth.

Heinrici, who knew very little about how to use explosives, watched apprehensively. She said she had been trained to set charges and detonate them. Baldwin, who had skeptically questioned her on the subject, agreed that she knew what she was talking about.

Heinrici and Adriana had come out on the Métro, to the Lilas station, and had walked from there to the meeting place suggested by Le Concombre: a tiny working-class café two short blocks from Fort Romainville. Heinrici had wanted to see it, had wanted Adriana to see it, since it was possible she would have to be a part of the team that came for Mercier's daughter.

The gray stone fort, like that at Fresnes, had once been a part of the defense system surrounding Paris. Now, unlike the fort at Fresnes, it was dilapidated. A barbed wire fence supplemented the stone walls. According to General Hausser, more than two hundred women were imprisoned there, most of them Résistants.

Le Concombre had brought the plastique in a bread basket, tucked under half a dozen loaves of bread that were covered by a white cloth. He brought four kilos—enough, he said, to destroy four bridges. Riding a bicycle, he had come to a skidding halt in front of the café. The detonators and wire were strung around his neck inside his shirt. The batteries that would fire the detonators were inside what looked like a small bicycle tire pump.

Le Concombre sat down with Heinrici and Adriana, saluting them casually, as though he saw them there every day. He was dressed as usual, in working-man's clothes: a soft wool cap on his bald head, a rumpled white shirt under a brown jacket. Heinrici, dressed in the same way, was carrying papers identifying him as Philippe Valence. Adriana wore her black skirt and white blouse.

It was Heinrici's plan to do their work and return to their quarters before curfew. He saw no reason to risk another encounter like the one last week. On the other hand, they could not go near the canal bridge until after dark. Though the sun had now set, a long red twilight persisted, and they sat in the café, Claude smoking a strong, foul cigarette, all of them drinking the bitter coffee substitute that was all the café could provide.

"You are confident of the explosive, I suppose," Heinrici said under his breath to Claude.

"Compliments of the English. I've never used it, though I've been thoroughly instructed about how to set it and fire it. The same kind of stuff has been used by the Maquis. They say it's good."

"It's powerful," Adriana said. "I've never used it either, but I've seen it used. There is enough. You may be sure of that."

"Do you have a pistol, Claude?" Heinrici asked.

Le Concombre nodded. "Under the plastique. Two of them. One for you."

"One for Adriana," said Heinrici. "I have my own, under my jacket."

"I intend to throw mine away as soon as we have done our job," said Le Concombre. "It is extremely dangerous to carry weapons."

"Agreed," said Heinrici.

They fell silent for a long moment, during which a young German soldier stepped into the doorway and looked around, as if searching for a familiar face. Then, uncertain and receiving no welcome, he withdrew and passed from their sight on the street. He had looked no older than eighteen and was unarmed.

"We have a bit of a walk," Heinrici said. "I wouldn't mind seeing the area before it is entirely dark."

With glances back at the prison they would be revisiting in a few more days, they set out northeast, through the shabby neighborhood that bordered the Paris cattle market and slaughterhouses—facilities that were all but abandoned that summer. The red sky turned purple then gray. It was still twilight when they reached the avenue de Metz and the canal bridges.

There were two railroad bridges, actually: one carried the track that ran east through the yards from Pantin station; the other ran south from Le Bourget. Beyond the two bridges the two tracks ran parallel to the east. Neither Claude nor Adriana knew which bridge carried the Pantin track. Heinrici, who had frequented this area ten years before, knew, but he wanted, just the same, to refresh his memory before dark.

The canal was not much wider than a street. It was not dug deep into the flat land; only low barges could navigate it, passing under its many bridges. The two steel bridges spanned from stone wall to stone wall; they did not stand on tall piers. Built in the nineteenth century, their structural components were supplemented with ornamental tracery.

So far as guards were concerned, there didn't seem to be any. The neighborhood on both sides of the canal was built up with commercial buildings; lights burned in most of them. A dim lamp burned at each end of the two bridges.

Le Concombre found a utility pole to which he could chain his bicycle, some two hundred meters west of the bridges. He returned, carrying the bread basket.

"How do we do this?" asked Le Concombre.

Heinrici looked at Adriana.

She nodded. "I know a little about it. Usually what you try to do is knock the bridge off its piers. We could try to blow away the foundation from under either end, but I'm not sure that would work. It sits on stone and earth. I think we're going to have to break it in the middle."

"We can't just walk out on it," said Heinrici. "We'll have to climb underneath and go out under the tracks."

"Impossible," grunted Le Concombre.

"Not impossible," Heinrici said. "Tell me something. Is that stuff waterproof?"

"Absolutely," said Adriana.

"And the detonators?"

"It's all waterproof," she said. "Saltwater-proof."

"Then I'll go in the water," said Heinrici. "I'll swim along the wall until I'm under the bridge, then find a way to climb up."

"I'll go with you," she said. "It will need two of us. Claude can stand guard."

"No," he said. "No. I can—"

"I was an Olympic swimmer."

"Even so—"

"I am coming with you, Colonel Heinrici," she said. "It reduces the risk of failure."

A darkened building stood at canalside, and in its shadow, on the narrow stone path between its brick face and the canal wall, Heinrici undressed. Le Concombre tied the cloth from the bread basket into a sling and tied the packages of plastique into it, using a bit of the detonator wire. Heinrici could sling the package around his neck. Adriana, Le Concombre whispered, could wind the detonator wire, with the detonators, around her neck and shoulders.

"If I see or hear anything," Le Concombre said softly, "I will toss a stone in the water."

Not having anticipated he would have to go into the canal water, Heinrici had worn no underclothes under the heavy wool suit the Résistants had provided. He could not set out through the streets after the explosion in a soaked suit of clothes, so when he slipped over the wall and was ready to drop the two meters into the water of the canal, he was naked; he had no choice about that. Adriana retained her panties and a brassière. He dropped first. The splash seemed immensely loud. Then Adriana dropped beside him. It was difficult to believe they hadn't alerted a score of men by their noisy splashes.

The water was cold and about two meters deep. They kept close to the wall and paddled quietly toward the bridge, some fifty meters away. The packages of plastique were surprisingly heavy. The dim lights on the bridge seemed now like giant floodlights glaring on the water. A truck passed by on the avenue de Metz, its lights for a brief moment illuminating the bridges.

They reached the bridge abutment. As Adriana had said, the bridge simply sat on reinforced segments of the canal walls. In the shadows beneath they began to examine the wall, looking for the hold that would allow them to climb to the bottom of the steel structure. Though the wall was not smooth, they found no protrusion that offered sufficient purchase to let them climb.

Adriana set out ahead of him and swam quietly to the opposite wall. By the time he arrived, she had found a small handhold and had lifted herself out of the water. Spread-eagled on the wall, clinging to cracks between the stones, she dug her toes into other cracks. The bridge was still beyond her reach. He stared upward, and in the dim gray light he could see her face. She was gasping, and she shook her head.

He gestured to her to let herself down. She dropped quietly.

Putting his mouth to her ear, he told her what he would do—leaving the plastique with her, he would swim along the canal to a boat that was tied to the wall. If he stood up in the boat, he could reach the top of the wall and climb up; then he would return to help her. She shook her head, but he unslung the plastique from around his neck, handed it to her, and swam away in the shadow of the wall.

When he reached it, he discovered the boat was half-submerged. As he climbed into it, it slipped beneath the surface. Even so, it was a wooden boat, and though waterlogged still buoyant, and it afforded him the base he needed for a thrust up the wall. It sank deeper as he pressed down with his feet, but it allowed him to reach the top. He clung to the stones there and, after taking a breath, scrambled over.

He crouched. He had skinned his knees and his hips, and the abrasions stung. He was aware, too, now that he was out of water and exposed on the stone walkway, that he was stark naked. Keeping in his crouch, he trotted back to the bridge, cursing the light burning above. As quickly as he could, he slipped over the edge of the wall again, this time where he could reach the steel, and in a moment he was in the roughly corroded understructure and out of sight from above.

Adriana was watching. He could make her out in the gloom below; he could hear her treading water. He found a handhold in the steel at the point where the bridge met the wall, and he hung there and extended his feet toward her. She grunted as she rose as far as she could. She reached his feet, and he felt wet cloth hung over his foot. He understood what she had done, and he thrust his leg out and lifted the bundle of plastique upward. In a moment he could reach it with his hand. He shoved it into a cache in the steelwork, pushing it back until he was confident it was secure.

He gripped a beam firmly and extended his feet as far down as he could. She seized his ankles and climbed the wall. Feet against the stones, her arms circling his legs, then his hips, she worked her way up. After a minute her arms clapsed his body, and she was able to reach for the steel. She loosed herself from him and for a moment hung under the bridge as he did; then she swung her legs up, found a purchase in the understructure, and raised herself into the tangle of beams under the tracks. She reached out for him and helped him climb up beside her.

They lay there for a long moment on the cold, hard steel, catching their breath and taking time to survey the canal and canalsides. It remained quiet. He saw tiny specks of light in her eyes: the reflections of reflections off the canal.

"We could set the charges here," she whispered. "But better in the middle."

He nodded. Slinging the bundle of plastique once more around his neck, he began to work his way toward the center of the bridge, hanging, crawling, pressing between beams, progressing slowly. She followed. The wire and detonators still hung in loops around her neck. They knocked off birds' nests as they crawled. The understructure was crusted with decades of dust and grime that came off on their wet bodies, until they were splotched with black.

They reached the center. She pointed to the angles where the beams were riveted to elements of the truss. Leaving her with two packages of plastique to push into those angles, he carried the other two packages to the opposite beam and began to mold the doughy material into a joint. It was pliable and conformed itself to the angles of the joint, adhering readily. In a couple of minutes he had pressed a huge mass of the plastique into place—two kilos—and crawled back to Adriana.

She, too, had pressed two packages of the dough into an angle and was already shoving a cylindrical detonator—a little object that looked like a small copper pencil—into the explosive. It was attached to the two insulated wires, and she brought those back and knotted them around a bolt so that tension on the wire would not pull the detonator out of the plastique. He took two detonators and returned to his charge. He shoved them in the plastique, tied the wires, and returned again to find that she was finished.

Still they were not done. She was wrapping bare ends of the detonator wires around bare ends of one of the coils that hung over her shoulders. He took one of the coils and, surprised by its heavy weight, returned to his charge. They should have brought pliers, he thought. He knotted the wires around bolts, then twisted them together.

"So . . . ," she whispered.

Heinrici nodded. He pointed to the end of the bridge where they had not been able to climb up, the side of the canal where Le Concombre waited in the darkness. Unrolling their coils of wire, they made their way across the understructure, bruising and chafing themselves on the corroded steel, until they were at the wall once again.

The question now was, should they drop into the water once more and swim along the canal, or take the chance of hurrying along the path? He pointed to the path. She nodded. They slipped out of the understructure and crouched in the shadows on the stone path, the top of the canal wall.

Plop! They had no taken more than two steps before a stone plopped in the water. They scrambled back under the bridge. Huddling there, painfully alert, they heard the footsteps. Hobnailed boots. Two pairs. And the soldiers came, two Germans carrying stubby submachine guns. They came from the direction where Le Concombre was hiding, so obviously they had passed by him without seeing him.

They were talking, in crude Bavarian accents, of their sexual experiences with French women. Both sounded very young, but they were capable of shooting, just the same, or at the very least of raising an alarm. Adriana pressed hard against Heinrici, trying to retreat more into the angle where they hid. Her flesh was cold. Her panties and brassière were clammy. He circled her with his arm and pulled her back as far as he could.

The two soldiers walked to the second bridge, crossed it on the tracks, and walked west on the far side of the canal.

Heinrici patted Adriana on the shoulder. She slipped out of their hiding place and started along the top of the canal wall, drawing her wire out of its loops and laying it behind her. He followed. By the time they reached Le Concombre they had run out of wire.

"It's not enough!" she whispered.

"No. Not enough," Le Concombre agreed.

"The explosion . . . ," Adriana said. "We'll be too close. We must go back, cut loose one wire, and splice it to the other one. One charge is enough to bring the bridge down."

Heinrici shook his head fiercely. "Go back? No! You two go around the corner of the building. I'll go down in the canal water and fire it from there. I'll be far enough away."

"No," Adriana said urgently. "You have no idea how powerful the stuff is."

"Attach the wires to the batteries, Claude," whispered Heinrici. "And Adriana, as soon as it goes off, come back and help me up over the wall. Take my clothes back there with you. We'll have a minute or two before anybody recovers wits enough to look for us."

She shook her head, but she gathered up his clothes and hers from the ground behind the path—where the two soldiers fortunately had not seen them. Le Concombre handed Heinrici the battery case.

Heinrici slipped over the wall and once more dropped into the water.

"Ho! Wer ist?"

The splash had alerted the two soldiers, who were across the canal and not twenty meters west. They began to sweep the area with sharp, strong beams from their electric torches.

Heinrici held the battery case above his head and shoved the handle down.

A brilliant white flash lit the bridge for a brief instant before turning into an angry, boiling, yellow-red glow that rushed out in every direction. Deadly chunks of steel came hurtling through the air. Heinrici ducked under the water, aware that he really had underestimated how powerful the plastique was, just as Adriana had said. Under water he could hear the impact of debris on the surface. When he could no longer hold his breath, he broke through the surface and shook the water from his eyes. What he saw was unwordly.

The bridge was gone—not broken, gone. Debris was still falling, splashing into the water, clanging onto the canalside, crunching through roofs. There was no fire. There was no smoke, except for a white haze that hung over the canal where the bridge had been. Trees were gone. Buildings had collapsed or were collapsing. The canal seemed almost to boil with the splashes of small bits of debris that still fell.

"Heinrici!"

He looked up. Le Concombre was above, reaching down for him. He thrust up and grabbed the extended hand. In a moment he was on the wall again, following Le Concombre into the shadow behind the corner of the brick building.

Adriana stood there, naked. She had discarded her wet underclothes and was pulling on her skirt and blouse. Heinrici gathered up his own clothes and began to dress as fast as he could. He found his hands difficult to control, and he dressed clumsily.

"The two—" he gasped.

"The two Boches," said Le Concombre. "Cut in two by flying steel. Look at the building—all the windows. The other bridge—I think the other bridge is knocked off at one end. We have a little time. Only a little. I threw the pistols in the canal. I say adieu for now. Better we go separate. *Bonne chance, mes amis.*"

Le Concombre trotted around the corner of the building and across the avenue de Metz.

Adriana trembled. "Too damned much of the stuff," she murmured hoarsely. "We used too much. I was sure you were dead. Claude thought so." She choked, sobbed twice, then stiffened and drew a deep breath. "Let's move," she said.

IX

FRIDAY, JULY 14, 1944

I T was after midnight when Heinrici and Adriana returned to the Royal Monceau, but the curfew did not apply to a uniformed oberst and his lady. He had changed into his uniform and she into her dinner dress in the flat near Les Halles, and midnight came as they walked up the Champs Elysées. The lights went out, and they walked in the moonlight. Half a dozen times police or military police approached them, and half a dozen times Heinrici received a respectful salute. Twice they were offered rides to the hotel. Twice they declined and walked on.

Adriana's thought as they walked silently together, exhausted, bruised, their arms and legs abraded and raw, was that this city was the most beautiful she had ever seen and that when the war was over she would find some way to live here. Why not? Unless Dirk proved to be alive—and realistically she could hardly believe he was—nothing drew her back to Rotterdam: no family, no home, maybe by now not even any particular friends. An American in London had suggested she come to the United States after the war. But America, known to her only through films and books and the talk of Americans she had met, had always seemed a strange, cold, alien place. She was not sure she could ever like it there.

England. She had been told she would be welcome there. But it was almost the same. The English were so preoccupied with themselves that she could not imagine they would ever accommodate a Dutch woman.

The great arch loomed ahead of them—under normal circumstances proudly lighted, tonight gloomy and dark, as much a symbol of France's agony and shame now as it had been of Napoleon's triumphs.

Heinrici took her arm. She stiffened at first, then she accepted the friendly gesture. He was an enigma: shrewd and brave, obviously enough—but what more?

In their dark hotel suite—there was no electricity after midnight—they groped for the shutters and opened the window to get at least the night glow into the rooms. He lighted one candle and put it in the bathroom. Both of them had been surprised by the amount of light a single candle cast into a three-room suite, warmly relieving the horrible black dark and the cold gray moonlight.

Adriana sat down on the couch in the parlor. Suddenly, little as she liked it, however much she did not want to, she slumped and began to shake with shallow, gentle sobs.

Heinrici sat down beside her. "I could cry, too," he said gently. "When you've been so *very* afraid—"

Her eyes were closed, and she slumped weakly. "Do you know what we've just *done?*" she asked. "Before we went out to do it, it seemed so *damned* reasonable."

"The train won't go tomorrow," he said.

Adriana looked up into his eyes, where reflections of the candle glinted as tiny points of yellow light. She sighed and closed her eyes.

"Or the day after," he whispered.

She nodded.

He put a hand on hers, in her lap. She opened her eyes and found them focused on his collar tabs and Iron Cross, the insignia and decoration of a German officer. Her breath stopped for an instant. She looked up and found his solemn gaze meeting hers.

"Adriana . . ." He lowered his chin and touched her lips with his; gently and only for an instant.

She allowed it. She let him kiss her. Then she jerked her head around, turning her face away from him.

"Adriana," he said, "you know, we're going to pull this off—we're going to rescue Henri Mercier and his daughter. Then there will be other things to think about."

"What other things?"

"The war is almost over," he said. "We have to think about life afterward."

Adriana closed her eyes and nodded. "Yes. We have to think about that," she said quietly. "Sometime."

"You won't have to hate me then."

She shrugged. "I don't hate you now, Heinrici. Not anymore. It's pointless. Anyway. . ."

"Anyway?"

She looked up into his face. "I guess you're not what I supposed. Not altogether."

He smiled. "Not altogether evil?"

She tipped her head aside and let him brush her cheek with his dry mouth. "No. Not altogether anything. Much more complex." . . . She rose before he could kiss her again and walked into the bathroom.

"Sergeant Weibel!"

Sergeant Willi Weibel, about to stomp down on the starter pedal of his motorcycle, was perplexed by the sight of the officer who had come trotting out and now called his name.

"Jahwohl, Herr Standartenführer."

The officer puffed. "Ah! I'm glad I caught you, Sergeant. The orders for the governor at Fresnes Prison, please. We may have made an error."

"Herr Standartenführer . . . ?"

"Standartenführer Brunner, Sergeant. You are Sergeant Willi Weibel, aren't you? You have the envelope of orders for Fresnes, haven't you? Hand them over, Sergeant."

The standartenführer was not asking for the package of orders; he was *demanding* them. He looked and sounded like a man about to lose his temper. Very well, he would hand them over, and after that he would return and make sure this Standartenführer Brunner had the authority to demand them.

Opening his dispatch bag, Sergeant Weibel flipped through the brown envelopes of orders until he found the thick envelope for Fresnes. He handed it over.

The standartenführer scanned the papers briskly, glancing only for an instant at each one, obviously looking for one specific order. "Ah," he said. "Here. An error, Sergeant. A stupid error! There is a man inside who will wish he had been more careful." The standartenführer handed back the big brown envelope. "Thank you, Sergeant. That is all. You may go."

Sergeant Weibel returned the envelope to his bag. He raised his arm. *"Heil Hitler, Herr Standartenführer,"* he said.

The officer returned his salute. His attention was fixed on the order with the mistake in it. Sergeant Weibel was grateful that the error was not his. He stomped his starter and sped off toward the rue de Rivoli. As to returning and questioning the standartenführer's authority—well, that could wait for another time. The officer knew his name, and if he heard that Sergeant Weibel had returned to inquire . . . Well, discretion suggested that was a kind of trouble Willi Weibel did not need.

Baldwin scrutinized the document, the order to the governor of Fresnes Prison to transfer the prisoner Alain Delacorte from close confinement to ordinary regimen, and to clothe him suitably for deportation.

"Rather ordinary, I should think," Baldwin said.

"The paper is entirely ordinary," said Heinrici. "Nothing special. But look at the stamps and signatures. Can Le Faussaire duplicate those? If he can't, I can. But I will need access to his shop."

"I'm sure he can do it," Baldwin said. "I'm not altogether experienced in this sort of thing, you know, but it's my distinct impression the man can do just about anything in the way of forgery."

"Our lives will depend on it," said Heinrici.

Just after noon Heinrici kept his appointment with Genreal Hausser, this time not in his headquarters in the Hotel Lutétia but in the dining room of the Hotel George V. A lower-ranking officer was sitting at the table with the general when Heinrici arrived—a young officer, patently ill at ease.

"Ah, Heinrici," said General Hausser. "We were early. You are on time. Let me introduce Oberleutnant Dietrich Krueger."

The lieutenant stood and bowed stiffly from the waist. "It is an honor, Herr Oberst," he said. "I have heard your name often."

Heinrici nodded and sat down.

"Oberleutnant Krueger," said the general, "is assigned to my headquarters. I have confided in him something of the nature of your present assignment in Paris."

Heinrici nodded again to the lieutenant. "An awkward assignment," he muttered.

"I have decided," said General Hausser, "to place Oberleutnant Krueger at your disposal. He can be of substantial help to you. You can rely entirely on his discretion, Heinrici."

"Thank you, Herr General," said Heinrici. "I am not sure exactly what assistance I will require, Herr Oberleutnant, but I am certain we will work well together."

He had no illusions. General Hausser had just hung a tail on him. Constantly eluding the lieutenant would add another level of complexity and difficulty to the work ahead.

"Are you aware of what day this is?" the general asked.

"It is Bastille Day," said Heinrici. "An important holiday for the French."

"They used to celebrate with fireworks, did they not?" the general asked.

"Yes. Well, they celebrated with fireworks last night. An immense explosion. It destroyed a railroad bridge near the Pantin Station. Killed two German soldiers.

It has impeded temporarily the deportation of two trainloads of Résistants and Jews, who were to have gone today."

Heinrici kept silent while a waiter lifted a bottle of white wine from the ice bucket by the table and filled his glass.

"On the general's orders," Krueger said quietly, "I examined the deportation list. The Merciers, father and daughter, were not on it."

"The destruction of the bridge will delay deportations for a few days," the general said. "Then they will resume."

"The Merciers were not on today's list," said the lieutenant, picking up his narration where the general had interrupted him, "but their deportation has been authorized. We must anticipate that it will occur very shortly."

"You have little time, Heinrici," said General Hausser.

"I am well aware of that, Herr General."

"Tell me . . . very frankly. Do you really think you can succeed with this scheme?"

Heinrici sipped wine. "I have not as yet encountered an insuperable obstruction," he said simply.

The general smiled. "Like a bridge."

"A fortunate coincidence," said Heinrici.

"Well," General Hausser said, drawing a deep breath. "Oberleutnant Krueger can be of great help to you. I suggest you take full advantage of his assistance."

"Thank you, Herr General. I will have orders for him shortly."

Adriana returned to the house in the Seventeenth Arrondissement, where again she was received in the sunlit parlor where canaries sang. She had returned with dread, afflicted with a sense that she was going to hear something final. Madame Boulanger had had a week to circulate the question through her network of returned prisoners of war—had anyone seen the Dutch Olympic javelin thrower, Dirk Ter Horst, husband of the Olympic swimmer Adriana Kip? Madame Boulanger offered her calvados, and Adriana accepted a generous splash of the fiery apple brandy.

"A man—you will forgive me if I don't tell you his name—was wounded and captured at Charleville, when his regiment broke and fled. Panzers, you know. He was hauled by lorry to Sedan and then by train to Gelsenkirchen, where he entered a hospital for prisoners of war. He was in a large ward with twenty or thirty other prisoners. A few of them were Belgian, a few Dutch."

"My husband?" Adriana asked quietly.

Madame Boulanger sighed and nodded. "He says so. Dirk Ter Horst. I am terribly sorry, Mademoiselle Kip, but according to this man your husband died of his wounds. The man insists it was in fact Dirk Ter Horst. He says he had heard of him, and of you. He says he could not be wrong."

Adriana closed her eyes for a moment. "It is . . . as I expected," she whispered. She sipped the strong, stimulating calvados. "I am grateful to you. It is better to know."

Madame Boulanger nodded. "Yes. Many of us have learned that. It is better to know."

Adriana rose. "Thank you. I will . . . go now."

She walked. At first aimless, half numb, little conscious of the summer day, she walked south to Parc Monceau, then southeast, heading generally in the direction of Les Halles and the flat where she might find Le Concombre, maybe Baldwin, maybe even Heinrici. She crossed boulevard Haussmann and wandered into boulevard Malesherbes, and a few minutes later she found herself on the Place de la Madeleine, facing the Church of the Madeleine.

A constant stream of people, both French and German, ascended and descended the steps. A nun—probably a novice from her costume—started up the steps, and Adriana was moved to follow her.

Adriana sat down inside. The great church breathed with the hushed murmur of two hundred people, most of them praying. She was not strongly moved by religious feeling, but she sensed vaguely that if anywhere there was anything left of Dirk, she would know it here. A few images came: of the best moments of their lives—of their heady days as Olympic athletes, of winter nights skating on a frozen river, of sunlit days playing with their baby in an open field, of their small warm house in Rotterdam . . . But she was an alien in these memories. She did not belong in them.

And as of today, she was free from them.

Adriana stood and walked out of the church. She walked between two of the huge Corinthian columns and down the steps, pressing her way through the throng coming up. She wept, but she walked steadily—east toward Les Halles.

In the flat above the tobacconist's, just off Les Halles, Le Concombre was waiting nervously. Heinrici arrived alone, dressed in his Abwehr uniform, carrying a bottle of wine he had bought from a reluctant wine steward at the Hotel George V. Le Concombre sat at the table, puffing on a harsh, foul-smelling cigarette.

"Mon ami," Heinrici said, handing over the bottle of wine.

"Where is Adriana? Do you know?" Le Concombre accepted the wine without a glance at the bottle.

"She should be here shortly," Heinrici said, glancing at his watch.

"We cannot stay here," said Claude. "We must try to intercept Adriana on the street."

"Why? What is wrong?"

"The Gestapo has arrested the English radio operator," said Le Concombre. "Someone has betrayed us. It must be. They could not have done it otherwise."

"Who do you suspect?"

Le Concombre shook his head. "The others suspect *you*. That is why I am here alone. I waited for you. Le Docteur and Le Rasoir were not willing. They expect a Gestapo raid on this place."

Heinrici stepped to the window and looked down the street. "I don't know where Adriana has been or from what direction she'll come," he said. "We should separate. You wait for her around Les Halles. I'll walk around the Palais Royal and meet you before the Church of St. Merri in half an hour."

It was Le Concombre who encountered Adriana. She had come west on the rue de Rivoli and did not turn north until she came to the rue du Louvre. He took her to the church, where they were fifteen minutes early.

They stood just inside the doors of the church, ignored by a priest who hurried by.

"The others suspect the colonel," Le Concombre told her. "But I—" He shook his head firmly. "What he did last night . . . He risked his life. That was no charade. A man playing a game with us would not risk himself like that. He's a Boche, but—"

"But Sybil?" she asked him. "How did it happen?"

"The Gestapo," he said. "They came and got her, at the house in rue St. Vincent. It must have been about the time we were blowing up the bridge. I was going to rue St. Vincent afterward, not to my own place. The Gestapo pigs knew I was coming. After they took her and tore the place apart and found the radio, they waited for me. But a neighbor took the risk of going out and calling our friends. Le Docteur, Le Rasoir, and Le Capitaine were waiting for me on different streets. It was Le Capitaine who stopped me. In three more minutes I would have ridden the bicycle up to the door and . . ." He shrugged.

"They took her? You are sure?"

"Yes. The neighbor saw her dragged away. Then the pigs went to work with wrecking tools and tore the house apart. They found the radio. They came out with that eventually and put it in a car. And after that they waited."

"They tracked the radio signals," said Adriana.

"No. She had no message to send last night. No. She was betrayed. I was betrayed."

"We were all betrayed, then," she said.

They stepped outside the doors and saw Heinrici just as he rounded the corner. He hurried toward them.

"I have a key for you," he said immediately. "A private room. A place of mine. Both of you should go there. Don't leave the room until you hear from me. I may be safe yet. Also, I may be able to find out what has happened."

He handed them the key to the room Papa had arranged for him.

Oberleutnant Krueger put down the telephone. Frowning, licking his lips, he pondered for a moment on the orders he had just received from Oberst Heinrici. He wondered if he should discuss the orders with General Hausser before attempting to carry them out. Actually, the general had ordered him to consider himself under Heinrici's command—save only if the oberst showed a sign of betraying his mission or the Fatherland. Indeed, he was not even to report what Heinrici did unless it was suspicious. Krueger decided. He picked up his cap and left the headquarters.

Half an hour later—it was by now late in the afternoon—he sat across a desk from Hauptsturmführer Werner Ernst in the SS and Gestapo headquarters in rue des Saussaies. Though wearing the black uniform of the SS and holding an SS rank one grade higher than Krueger, Ernst was anything but prepossessing. His small brown eyes darted about nervously, and his little mouth was pinched into a permanent half-smile. He seemed the perfect professional file clerk: likely meticulous, likely unimaginative. Krueger was unsure as to why he had been referred to Hauptsturmführer Ernst. Did his man have authority?

"It is a question of coordination, Herr Hauptsturmführer," said Krueger, reciting the speech he had mentally rehearsed on his way from the Hotel Lutétia. Heinrici had outlined the ideas for him and left it to him to find the words. "I do not complain of the matter. Indeed, in some sense I congratulate the officers who accomplished the arrest. But we do think the Gestapo should know this arrest interfered with an Abwehr operation of some importance."

Hauptsturmführer Ernst scratched away with a fountain pen on a sheet of paper on his desk blotter. "Noted," he said. "And specifically, how?"

"We had identified the woman as an English radio operator," said Krueger. "We had established contact with her. It was our intention to use her to transmit significant disinformation to the English. A useful intelligence ploy, as I am sure you know."

Hauptsturmführer Ernst did not look up from his writing but said, "You could have notified us of this."

"We accept our share of responsibility, Herr Hauptsturmführer, and, as I said, I have not come to convey a complaint. We should have notified you. You should have notified us. The matter dramatizes the necessity for better coordination. My superior, Oberst Heinrici, who as you may know has only recently returned from several years of honored service as an intelligence agent in London, is anxious to achieve better coordination. He has instructed me to say that he has been surprised to learn that a certain attitude of . . . rivalry seems to have developed between our services. For his part, he forbids his officers to consider themselves in any way competitors of the SD, SS, and Gestapo."

The hauptsturmführer's pen scratched away faster with this. "I see," he said.

"I am ordered also to inquire if we might have a representative present during the interrogation of the Englishwoman? If not, may we submit questions to be put to her?"

Hauptsturmführer Ernst raised his eyes at last. "I am afraid that will not be possible," he said. "The Englishwoman was carrying poison, and she swallowed it."

"She is dead?"

The hauptsturmführer nodded.

Krueger was unsure as to how Heinrici would receive that news. His anxiety about the Englishwoman had almost suggested he had a relationship with her. Well . . . He wanted to know something more.

"Herr Hauptsturmführer. As you can imagine, the Abwehr identified this woman by penetrating a unit of the Résistance. We hope to be able to profit further from that penetration. If, on the other hand, what we have done is penetrate a unit with members who also report to you . . . ? Well, you see."

"Tell me the names of the members of your unit, and we will be careful not to interfere," Hauptsturmführer Ernst said blandly. "That will be very effective coordination."

"I have not been given the names, Herr Hauptsturmführer," said Krueger. "They have been revealed only to those of us who absolutely must know."

The hauptsturmführer's fixed little smile flickered broader for an instant. "Herr Oberst Heinrici can establish his good faith by giving us these names."

Krueger had anticipated this turn in the conversation and was ready for it. He leaned back, smiled. "As of the moment, Herr Hauptsturmführer, you are one ahead of us. Last night someone from rue des Saussaies—quite accidentally, of course—terminated an intelligence operation we expected to be highly advantageous. Now we are offering to do all we can to avoid returning the favor. There is no question of good faith, I think."

Hauptsturmführer Ernst regarded Krueger with a blank face. "Perhaps not."

Now Krueger used a ploy Heinrici had counseled. "Oberst Heinrici hopes we—that is, you and I—may initiate the cooperation he is hoping for, so it may be quietly done, without reference to officers of higher rank."

The SS man opened a file that lay to one side, the only file on his bleakly tidy desk. He eyed it for a moment, feigning offhandedness. "Robert Masse," he said. "A paid informer."

Adriana and Le Concombre waited disconsolately in the near darkness of the room where Heinrici had sent them. Uncertain as to whether the room was supposed to be occupied and as to whether or not a light there would be viewed suspiciously by the neighbors, they had not switched on the light when the evening hours of electicity began. Le Concombre, who had stood for the past hour watching the sunlight fade and darkness fill the narrow street, now sat down wearily on the edge of the bed. Adriana rose and took his place at the window.

The street had been quiet. Occasionally someone came and tried the locked door of the butcher shop on the ground floor. A crying child ran past. A patrol of four German soldiers marched by. Now, as Adriana watched, a man in a shabby gray suit and a flat cap, carrying a walking stick and poking idly at the pavement as he came, shuffled along the sidewalk opposite, pausing occasionally to look up at the windows on this side of the street. He walked with shoulders hunched. Stopping before the door directly opposite, he squinted up —Adriana could swear directly at the window where she stood watching him. Then he crossed the street, and she could hear the door open below.

She drew the pistol from her handbag: a 7.65 mm Belgian automatic equipped with a silencer—one of two weapons handed to Baldwin by their SOE contact. Le Concombre was startled to see she was carrying a weapon, and he rolled off the bed and moved toward the door. She gestured to him to be quiet and wait.

Two knocks. "Adriana! Claude! *Ouvrez la porte!*"

Adriana nodded, and Le Concombre opened the door. The shuffling old man from the street stepped into the room and closed the door behind him.

"Robert Masse," Heinrici spat.

"Le Docteur! *Merde!*" swore Claude.

"And . . . ," Heinrici said quietly. "Sybil is dead. She took poison."

"Sybil . . . ," whispered Le Concombre, dropping on the bed.

Adriana whipped around and faced the window and the street as her eyes filled with tears; she wiped them with the back of her hand.

"How?" muttered Le Concombre.

"I haven't been able to find out very much," said Heinrici. "Only the name. I didn't even know that was Le Docteur, though I'd heard him called Robert. He is a paid informer."

Le Concombre's chin jerked up. "My God! That explains—but how much did he tell them? I mean, has he betrayed us all, compromised the Mercier operation?"

"I can't think so," said Heinrici. "Otherwise—"

"Otherwise we would all be in a Gestapo prison," Adriana said.

"If he is playing Judas," Heinrici said, "then he probably sells information a little at a time, pretending to be discovering it for the purpose of selling it. Being a paid informer is a delicate business. His own arrest is always imminent. In fact, that may be all he's paid—his own freedom."

"Robert," Le Concombre said bitterly, "is a professional criminal. Before the war he was a pimp, among other things. Even now, he trades in the black market."

"Why did you accept him to work with you?" Adriana asked.

"God knows. We received orders. You know, we do have ranks. We were ordered to accept Robert Masse as a leader. He has been useful—his kind always are. He knows how to get things."

"But why Sybil?" Adriana asked. "Why would he tell them about Sybil?"

"SOE radio operators are highly valued, both by London and Berlin," Heinrici said. "Betraying her may be the best thing Le Docteur has done for his Gestapo friends."

Le Concombre shook his head. "I have a different idea," he said. "Robert may have wanted only to betray me. He knew where I would be last night. He did not know how long it would take us to complete our mission at Pantin. He told the Gestapo I could be found at the place in Rue St. Vincent last night. But they went too soon. Or maybe . . . maybe he just gave them poor Sybil as a sweetner."

"Why would he betray you?"

"Because I stand between him and the leadership of our group." He sighed. "I hope you are not so naive as to suppose we are unified. We are Gaullists, Communists, Christian Democrats, Catholics . . . and more. Then there are personalities. When there is no law, no leadership that can impose its rule, then men contest the leadership. We were ordered to accept Robert, but some of us disliked him—Le Capitaine, Le Rasoir . . . I myself, of course. And he dislikes me."

"I can think of a score of objections to that explanation," said Heinrici. "I am more concerned about what he does next. He sold you to the Gestapo, Claude. And they did not get you—though Sybil may have pleased them more. I would guess they would put him under severe pressure now."

"Yes," Adriana said. "Suppose they didn't know about Sybil. But they got Sybil. Through Le Docteur. Maybe he impresses them now as a more valuable informant than they had thought."

Heinrici glanced again at his watch. "I have an appointment," he said. "I sent word to Baldwin to met me at Gare St. Lazare. He too must be warned."

"It is reasonably safe for us to go on the streets, I think," said Le Concombre.

"Yes. Le Docteur may have betrayed you, but the Gestapo doesn't know where you are. Don't venture anywhere near your usual haunts."

"The hotel?" asked Adriana.

"I am going back there tonight," Heinrici said. "You, Claude, can use this room if you wish."

Le Concombre nodded. "I have other places," he said.

Heinrici kept his appointment with Baldwin at Gare St. Lazare. Inside the big railroad station, where hundreds of people circulated in mid-evening, Baldwin sat on a bench and waited. Heinrici had changed from civilian clothes to uniform under the eyes of Marie Ange, who had not ceased to chatter and complain during the ten minutes he was in her house. Baldwin, shabby in the clothes of a printer, sat with his walking stick between his legs. Heinrici sat down beside him, and they talked as though their meeting were a casual encounter.

"Sybil is dead. She was betrayed. She took her poison. The traitor is Le Docteur."

"Then it's all over," Baldwin said quietly.

"Maybe not. They haven't struck yet. They've not come for me, or for Adriana—or, for that matter, for some of the others, like Le Capitaine and Le Rasoir. How about the forger?"

"When I last saw him, he was all right," Baldwin said.

"The situation has become far more dangerous," said Heinrici. "Maybe you should get out. If you want to withdraw . . . withdraw. You have the means of getting out, haven't you?"

Baldwin nodded. "And Adriana?"

Heinrici shook his head. "Not yet. For now, she insists on staying. I'll do everything I can to get word to you if—"

Baldwin shook his head. "If Adriana is staying, then I am staying."

"Then get back to the forger tomorrow, Len. Don't tell him what's happened. But be sure he's got the documents ready as soon as possible."

Rue de Tiquetonne. Two blocks from Les Halles. A vaulted cellar, once a wine cellar but now empty. By the light of two candles, five men and a woman engaged in angry argument.

"It was *not* the German," grunted Le Concombre between clenched teeth.

"Oh, of course." Le Docteur sneered. He wore a white shirt and black pants held up with red braces, and the butt of a cigarette wobbled between his lips as he spoke. "Claude has become a protegé of his."

"Of those who might have betrayed the Englishwoman," said a white-haired man called Le Chou-fleur, the Cauliflower, "the German does seem the most likely."

"Except that it couldn't have been," Le Concombre said sullenly.

"Why not?" asked Le Rasoir. "How can you know?"

Le Concombre stood up. Irritably, he swept his hand across before his face to clear the tobacco smoke. *"Simple,"* he said. "Simple enough. Colonel Heinrici could not have sent the Gestapo to the house on rue St. Vincent because he didn't know about it. We never told him about that place."

"Oh, really," scoffed Le Docteur. "You think he—"

"A *point* was made," Adriana interrupted. "A distinct point was made that Heinrici should not know about Sybil and the house on rue St. Vincent. Our radio. Our contact with London. It might be important that he not know how we communicate with London."

"Then he—" Le Capitaine began.

"He could not *possibly* have betrayed our radio operator," she said. "It's out of the question."

"Then who?" Le Chou-fleur demanded. "If you say it could not have been the Boche, then who?"

"When I was in England," Adriana said, "I had many idle days, and I read all the stories about the English detective, Sherlock Holmes. The writer has him say, when you have eliminated the impossible, whatever remains, however improbable, must be the truth. Colonel Heinrici has been eliminated."

"Théo is eliminated," said Le Concombre, nodding toward Le Capitaine. "He was never told about the house on rue St. Vincent."

"Then I am eliminated," said Le Rasoir. "For the same reason."

"That is correct, Raymond. You are. Our English friends have always been most secretive about their radio operators—who they are, where they are. They have always insisted we tell no one—except those who definitely had to know."

"But of course *you* knew," said Le Docteur.

Le Concombre nodded. "I was the leader here. I was the contact with the English. Then, of course, when you appeared, you insisted on being told everything—even, I might say, what there was no need for you to know."

"No need for me to know?" scoffed Le Docteur. "Who are you to decide what I need to know, Claude? Am I not the leader?" He turned to Le Chou-fleur. "Was I not appointed?"

Le Chou-fleur's face was flushed, and he grimaced wrathfully. "You were," he muttered. "But—"

"I am eliminated," growled Le Concombre. "The Gestapo was waiting for me, and if I had not been stopped by Théo, they would have arrested me when I came to the house."

"I was there trying to stop you, too," said Le Docteur.

Le Concombre settled a scornful stare on him. "But would you have stopped me?" he asked curtly.

Le Docteur turned to Le Chou-fleur and shrugged.

"Either of you would have liked to be rid of the other," said Le Rasoir to Le Docteur and Le Concombre. "But, as Claude has said, it was he who was almost arrested last night—not you, Robert."

"I was there trying to prevent it," insisted Le Docteur. He tossed down his cigarette butt and ground it out under his foot. "What am I hearing? An accusation?"

"I accuse you," declared Le Capitaine. "Yes, you were there last night—but only because Raymond and I told you we were going whether you did or not. You said we should not go."

Le Docteur swung around to face Le Capitaine. "And we should not have gone!" he yelled. "We might *all* have been taken. I said the risk was too great. And it was."

"I accuse you," Théo repeated sullenly.

"I accuse you," said Le Rasoir.

Le Docteur, alarmed, glared at Le Concombre, then at Adriana. "And I suppose *you* do. Ah . . . well. What none of you know—but *she* knows—is the real reason why the English are here, why they have allied themselves with such a clever Boche colonel, and why they have recruited a collection of dull-witted

Frenchmen to risk their lives. For the Jew, you think? Do you believe them, that they want to save the Jew?" He shook with a grotesque, high-pitched laugh. "It's the Jew's *money* they want! The Jew has money! That's what they're after! Ask her. Listen to her deny it."

"What money are you talking about?" she asked coldly.

"Ah, the Jew has money, all right." Le Docteur laughed. "Think about it, my friends. Did the English come here to rescue any *other* Jew? No. Just this Mercier. Rich as any Jews in Paris. Richer. They didn't tell you, did they? No. They didn't tell you."

Adriana glanced into the somber faces of Le Chou-fleur, Le Rasoir, and Le Capitaine. "That explains a great deal, doesn't it?" she said. "He thinks there is money. He wants it. Claude is an honest fellow, a naive fellow who might want to put the money to good purpose. So Robert wants to get rid of him."

Le Docteur shrieked with nervous laughter. "She's been in England a long time. Learned to lie like the English."

"Did you tell the Gestapo about this money?" Le Concombre asked.

Color faded from Le Docteur's face. "You don't believe me about the money," he said. "It is known. It is known that the Jew Mercier had money. A lot of money. It is hidden somewhere. The Germans don't know. But they're the only ones in Paris who don't."

"Who told you they don't know?" asked Le Chou-fleur.

Le Docteur reached inside his pocket and pulled out a bent cigarette. His hands trembled as he struck a match and lit the cigarette. "A figure of speech," he muttered. "I guess they don't know." He drew in smoke. "If they knew," he said, encouraged, "they would have seized the money and shipped Mercier to Germany. Yes. If they knew—"

"Who does know?" asked Le Chou-fleur. "You say the English know. Then you say everyone in Paris knows—everyone but the Germans. Who knows, Robert? What money is this they know about?"

"The Jew had money," Le Docteur insisted. "Everyone knows. He owned a big store. He hid money. What money? The money he—he didn't pay taxes. He is a *Jew!*"

"I want a direct answer to one question, Robert," said Le Chou-fleur dispassionately. "You are accused. Do you admit, or do you not admit, that you betrayed Claude and the English radio operator to the Germans?"

"Hah! Of course I don't admit . . . But suppose I did? Are we to die so these English swindlers can get their hands on the Jew's gold? *He* doesn't care—" He pointed at Le Concombre. "He has fallen for their lies."

Claude settled a cold stare on Le Chou-fleur. "You sent him to us and said, 'Let him lead.' He is a paid informer of the Gestapo."

Le Chou-fleur ignored Le Concombre's indictment. "Robert," he said to Le Docteur. "Who besides you could have done it?"

Le Docteur pressed the cigarette hard between his lips. His cheeks were sucked in as he drew smoke into his lungs. "Anyone," he mumbled. He drew himself erect. "You have no evidence against me. And you had better be careful. All of you. *You had better be careful.*"

"The evidence is, uh . . . not entirely conclusive," said Le Chou-fleur, frowning.

Adriana drew the silenced Belgian automatic from her purse. "The evidence is enough," she said. She aimed the pistol at Le Docteur. "You murdered Sybil," she said to him. "You betrayed Claude. Left alive, you would betray us all."

She pulled the trigger, and the little automatic bucked and spat a 7.65 mm slug into Le Docteur's chest. The sound was a distinct burp, not a loud report. Le Docteur clutched at the wound and shook his head at her. She pulled the trigger again. The second bullet crashed through his interlaced fingers. He choked, dropped first to his knees, then sprawled face-down on the stone floor.

In his suite in the Royal Monceau, Heinrici wandered from room to room. Wearing only his field-gray breeches and boots, he stalked the floors with a glass of champagne from a bottle brought up an hour ago. Adriana had not returned, and if she did not return within the next quarter of an hour, curfew would prevent her.

After meeting Baldwin in the railroad station, Heinrici had returned to Marcel Ange's flat and spent half an hour with Papa and Marie. Again he had Papa's assurance about the cars to be used in the escapes, but Papa reported that his contacts were asking for money in advance. The English would have to provide the money, and Heinrici wondered if the loss of Sybil meant they had lost all contact with Colonel Harding. He needed to know. He needed to know a hundred other things.

Some of Adriana's clothes lay about in the living room of the suite—the room where she slept. A blouse lay on a table, a skirt on the couch. He picked them up in turn, idly examining them. He could smell in the blouse the faint scent of the French soap she used with such pleasure. He was surprised at how that casual, innocent aroma aroused him. He had determined to deny himself the pleasure of her, even though she was extraordinarily beautiful and ingenuously enticing. Anyway, it seemed unlikely she would test his resolution. She had ceased to exhibit resentment for having to work with him; she had, unless he was wrong, even begun to show a measured, grudging esteem for him, but her bitterness persisted as a barrier.

He was annoyed with her for not returning, for not, at least, getting word to him. At the same time his concern for her was deepening. If anything had happened to her . . . He stalked to the window and stared down on the street. He began to wonder if he should not leave the Royal Monceau and go to Montmartre, to stay with Papa and Marie Ange until he could be sure Adriana was not under arrest and talking.

She arrived at five minutes before twelve.

"The last train on the Métro," she said weakly. "I was afraid I . . . Konrad . . . I killed Le Docteur." She staggered into a chair, sobbing.

"*You* killed him? Why couldn't Claude have done it? Or one of the others?"

She shook her head. "They don't carry weapons," she mumbled. "Besides, they wanted to talk about it more—and talk about it, and talk about it, endlessly. They were angry with me. But Le Docteur *was* the one who betrayed Sybil! He all but admitted it. And he threatened us, as if . . . Konrad, I don't think I had any choice."

"If you hadn't killed him, I would have," Heinrici said. "As soon as I could find him."

Adriana loked up into Heinrici's face. "This has been a horrible day for me . . . Sybil . . . I killed a man. And, Konrad—" She sobbed. "Konrad . . . this morning I learned that my husband is dead."

Heinrici reached out and stroked her cheek. "Oh, I am sorry, Adriana," he whispered. "I regret this news more than I possibly can tell you."

She closed her eyes and forced back her sobs. "I've known, of course. It was unrealistic to suppose he might still be alive."

Heinrici knelt down next to the chair and spoke softly. "You have great courage, Adriana," he said. "You are a brave, beautiful woman."

She nodded. "Oh, yes," she said dully. "Brave . . . What choice have I had? Be brave or—"

He suddenly drew her to him and kissed her on the cheek. For a moment Adriana stiffened, prompted by instinct to jerk away from him, but then she slackened and released her breath and let herself fall forward into his arms. He kissed her forehead, then her eyes, and again her cheeks. Aroused, and beyond fighting it, she lifted her face and offered her mouth. He kissed her passionately, until she slipped her face away and buried it against his neck, smearing it with her tears.

He lifted her to her feet, clutching her as tightly as he could. He kissed her gently on the mouth. She returned his kiss. In her confustion of grief and regret, she saw no reason not to acquiesce.

"Adriana . . . ?" he whispered. He nodded toward the bedroom.

She ran the back of her hand across her cheek, wiping away tears. Then she nodded. "Why not?" she muttered.

SATURDAY, JULY 15, 1944

THE sun rose early on a July morning. They had left the windows open, and a warm breeze billowed the curtains and filled their bedroom with dry summer smells. When the sunlight struck Heinrici's eyes, he awoke to find Adriana sitting up, propped against the headboard and two pillows, looking at him.

She smiled. "I was thinking of how you looked when I first saw you," she said.

"Quite naked," he laughed, and he reached over and pulled the sheet away from her hips and legs. "And chained."

Her smile widened. "I didn't notice that," she said. She lifted his penis gently and tilted her head. "I was looking at this. It wasn't quite as big then as it is now. Somehow..." Adriana bent over, slipped the tip of his shaft between her lips, and caressed it with her tongue. He cupped a hand under one of her breasts and raised it as if testing its weight. "I've never known a woman as nearly perfect as you are," he said.

"Nearly?" She sat up. "What defect do you find?"

Heinrici grinned. "Well, let me see," he mused. "What could be more perfect than these?" He ran his hand over each of her breasts. "White and smooth. And these—pink and smooth until they're touched, then wrinkled and hard. They like to be kissed, don't they? And this down here—so warm. And the hair is soft. Most

124

girls, you know, that's coarse. So warm. Wet and warm. Uh—defect . . . ? I don't
know. Ah! This little mole under the right one here. Is that a defect? Or a beauty
mark?"

"Kiss it," she said. "Maybe you'll find out if you kiss it."

He bent over, lifted her breast, and kissed it underneath, pausing for a moment after to nibble tenderly on her nipple.

"Kiss," she said, spreading her legs.

He dropped his face into her lap and kissed her, momentarily thrusting his
tongue inside her.

She rolled over, and they were lovers again.

At ten Adriana met Le Concombre on a bench in the Tuileries Garden. She
had brought a bag of pastries and a thermos of coffee from the hotel. They sat in
the shadow of the Jeu de Pomme, he eating the pastries hungrily, she taking an
occasional sip of the coffee but leaving most of that, too, for him. Le Concombre looked strained, weary.

"He said one thing that was right," Adriana told him. "When Le Docteur said
there was money, he was right. I don't think he *knew*, actually. I think he was
guessing. But he was right, Claude. Henri Mercier has access to a large amount
of money, in gold, hidden somewhere."

Le Concombre frowned. "What is it for?" he asked.

"It is money that was to have been used to save Jews from deportation.
Hundreds of lives, maybe thousands, could be saved by that money."

"Bribe money." Le Concombre nodded. "I understand."

"The other question he asked, Why *this* Jew, this one Jew? Because Mercier
knows where the money is and knows how to use it. If we can rescue him, we
may save the lives of—"

"—hundreds."

"And the daughter," Adriana said. "Because we are afraid Henri Mercier will
be unable to function if his daughter remains in a Gestapo prison. She would be
a hostage."

"Jews . . . ," murmured Le Concombre thoughtfully.

"Heinrici has reviewed the list of those who would have gone on the train
yesterday if we had not blown up the bridge. Résistants. Only a few Jews. Ten were
shot in reprisal for the two German soldiers killed in the explosion. Fifty or a
hundred Résistants remain in their cells. The war may end before they are shipped to
Germany."

"French Jews are Frenchmen, as much as I am."

She nodded. "And Dutch Jews are Dutchmen, German Jews Germans. But,
Claude—the colonel does not know about the money. Our orders, Baldwin's
and mine, were not to tell him."

* * *

In the cinema in Montparnasse, the afternoon picture had just begun—*Bel Ami,* a two-year-old romance made under the auspices of Goebbels's Department of Propaganda. Based on the novel by Guy de Maupassant, it attracted crowds in spite of its origin. The theater was half-filled, with a few uniformed German soldiers in the seats. Heinrici, dressed in his gray suit and gray hat, and carrying a walking stick, entered the theater after the doors were closed and the film was on the screen. He spotted Le Capitaine, who expected him, and he followed him down the steps to the cellar room under the screen.

Le Faussaire was at work at his bench. Baldwin sat in the junked theater seat against the wall. The air in the room was heavy with cigarette smoke, and a bottle of calvados stood open at the forger's side.

For a moment Heinrici thought he recognized Le Faussaire and that maybe Le Faussaire recognized him. How many skilled forgers were there in Paris, after all? But when their eyes met, the notion vanished; the jowly, florid man showed no sign of recognition, not even curiosity.

Lying at hand on the workbench was a dirty rag. Le Faussaire picked up a forged SS identification book With the rag and handed it, rag and all, to Heinrici. "Handle it with that," he said. "No fingerprints."

Heinrici took the rag reluctantly. He knew what it was. It was saturated with oil from the forger's unwashed hair, also with sweat from his body; whenever he felt sweaty and dirty he rubbed himself with the rag, which he then used to rub his forgeries to give them a long-carried, body-soiled look. The identification book was realistically soiled, a little discolored, a little oily.

"Hmm?" asked Le Faussaire.

Heinrici squinted at the document. "Excellent," he said. "Except that the stamps are too good. Smudge some of them a little. A hurried clerk doesn't press the stamps cleanly—he bangs them down on a hundred documents an hour, carelessly."

"Mmm," grunted Le Faussaire. "We learn something new every day."

"*I* do," Heinrici said. "And since I expect to risk my life on one of these, you may not mind the suggestion."

"May I examine your identification as colonel of the Abwehr?" Le Faussaire asked. "It bears the most recent stamps, does it not?"

Heinrici handed him his identification card and paybook. "Is everything ready?" he asked.

"Except for the photographs and signatures," said the forger.

"I will need one more," said Heinrici. "Blitzmädchen. Attached to SS headquarters, rue des Saussaies." He turned to Baldwin. "She insists she will go along. *Insists.*"

Baldwin shrugged. "You are surprised?"

Le Faussaire examined Heinrici's papers under a big magnifying glass. "This was prepared in Paris?" he asked.

"Berlin," said Heinrici.

"Ah," said Le Faussaire. "It makes a difference."

"You are going to make my photograph now?" Heinrici asked.

The forger nodded. "In uniform and in your civilian clothes," he said. "Let us review what we need. You are going to darken your hair a bit? Eyebrows too?"

"Write down these names and ranks," said Heinrici. "Oberführer Ulrich von Strauch, SD. That will be my name and rank. Obersturmbannführer Waldemar Heiden. That will be Baldwin. Hauptsturmführer Karl Forster. That will be Théo, Le Capitaine. Hauptsturmführer Franz Hanke. That will be Claude, Le Concombre. Untersturmführer Paul Sprenger. That will be Raymond, Le Rasoir. And a Blitzmädchen named Ilse Severing. That will be Adriana."

"I must have the photographs immediately," said Le Faussaire.

"You have three of us here now," Heinrici said. "The others—"

"I can't photograph you now," said Le Faussaire. "We don't have the uniforms."

"They will be provided," said Le Capitaine. "You know we had to give up one of our safe flats. We—"

"I heard the Englishwoman killed Le Docteur," Le Faussaire said blandly, his eyes fixed on a document under his magnifying glass.

"He was a traitor," said Le Capitaine.

"I need some additional documents," Heinrici said. He took from his pocket three sheets of the stationery provided by the Royal Monceau, on which he had written three letters. "These must be typed on the letterhead of the RSHA, Berlin, and signed Ernst Kaltenbrunner, Oberstgruppenführer SS."

Le Faussaire threw up his hands. "Where is a sample of the letterhead? Of the signature? I have never seen—"

"Neither have the people who will receive the documents," said Heinrici. "Fake them."

"When are all these documents to be used?" Le Faussaire asked with a loud sigh.

"In two days," said Heinrici. "Or three. I will need them Monday."

They had avoided meeting together, and had done so only once before. This had been stressed by Colonel Harding: Baldwin, Adriana, and Heinrici should not meet together. One sudden descent by the Gestapo could terminate the mission. Even so, Heinrici had suggested they meet in his bedroom over the Montmartre butcher shop. It was essential they review his plan for the deliverance of the Merciers.

Communication was not always easy. He went to the suite in the Royal Monceau, left a note for Adriana, then went to Papa's home to change into workingman's clothes, and arrived at the bedroom to find Baldwin, to whom he had lent a key, waiting for him.

In the heat of the closed-up room, Baldwin sat on the brass bed in his underpants and massaged his scarred leg.

"Konrad . . . ," Baldwin said quietly when Heinrici was inside and had moved to the window to see if anyone was on the street. "We have run out of time."

"We have four or five days," Heinrici said. He opened the window to let air into the room, and he took off his jacket and shirt. "Not much time, but—"

Baldwin shook his head. "Our Frenchmen are going to abandon us," he said.

Heinrici shook his head. "Le Concombre—"

"He's a good man," Baldwin interrupted. "I'm not worried about him, or maybe even about Le Capitaine and Le Rasoir—they will follow Le Concombre. But there are others. Outside our group. I know Adriana had to kill Le Docteur, but—"

"But there are all kinds of men in the Résistance," said Heinrici. "Not all of them are patriots."

"You told them that General Koenig ordered them to help us. Now they know he didn't."

"Often," Heinrici said, "men are led by lies."

"It can be dangerous when they learn the truth. And Le Docteur was not the only one who suspects our mission is going to cost the Résistance more than they want to invest."

Heinrici sat down on the bed beside Baldwin and glanced at his scarred leg, which Baldwin continued to rub and manipulate as if it ached. "Without Sybil, do we have any contact with London?" he asked.

Baldwin nodded. "My orders forbid me telling you how."

"Does Colonel Harding know what is going on? That Adriana killed Le Docteur? That our Frenchmen may abandon us?"

"Not yet. I am trying to get that word through."

"We need the weapons now, Len," Heinrici said. "Four Schmeisser submachine guns with three magazines for each. I have my sidearm, but the others will need officers' sidearms—Lugers or Walthers. We should have some grenades in the cars."

"We can't provide Schmeissers," Baldwin said. "We'll have three Mauser machine pistols with twenty-round magazines. Three is all I can get. Plus extra magazines. What about the cars?"

"I have those arranged. I need five hundred thousand francs for the cars. I need that now. Are you sure you can get it?"

"The guns and money are arranged," Baldwin said stiffly. "As we discussed. You can count on me for that much anyway." He winced as he massaged his leg. "About all you can count on me for, I'm afraid."

Heinrici smiled and slapped Baldwin lightly on the shoulder. "If you're looking for a chance to get killed," he said, "you are going to have it. You command the operation at Romainville."

Baldwin shook his head. "I'm not looking for a chance to get killed," he said quietly. "In fact, I . . ." He sighed despondently. "Adriana has had to risk herself, more than she should be asked to do, because I—"

"That's the way the team was put together," said Heinrici. "Everyone understood what you could do and couldn't. You haven't failed at anything."

"The truth," Baldwin said, "is that I'm constantly afraid, and I wish I hadn't come on this mission."

"I'm hardly a volunteer myself, you remember," said Heinrici. "You may be sure that *I'd* rather be somewhere else. And if you think I'm not afraid—"

"I'm not afraid of getting killed, actually," said Baldwin thoughtfully. "I'm afraid of another wound. And I'm afraid I'll be unable to do my part and be responsible for—"

"You'll win a medal, Len," Heinrici interrupted. He grinned. "I'm not worried about you."

Baldwin's mouth twisted in a bitter smile. "It was a mistake for them to have sent me." His chin fell to his chest.

Heinrici put his hands on Baldwin's shoulders and gripped him hard. "I'm not complaining," he said firmly. "Adriana is not complaining."

Baldwin put his hand on Heinrici's. "You are a complete surprise to us, you know."

Heinrici smiled. "Surprise is my metier." he said.

"Adriana and I were given an unqualified license to kill you."

"If I betrayed you," Heinrici said.

Baldwin shrugged. "No one would have questioned our judgment."

"Then—"

Baldwin shook his head. "At first I resented being dependent on you. I mean, apart from the fact that you are an enemy officer. And Adriana hated you."

"For good reason."

"For excellent reason," Baldwin agreed. "Anyway . . . We don't hate you anymore. It's hard to go on thinking of you as an enemy. I've never deceived myself about the effectiveness of the Radio Heinrici threat. It would have been good for a while, but this operation has taken longer than we supposed, and I have little doubt that a man as clever as you can find some way to defuse that threat. In fact—tell me frankly, Konrad—you *have* defused it, haven't you?"

"As a matter of fact, I haven't."

Baldwin smiled skeptically. "Well, anyway . . . You've defused my hostility toward you. I can work with you. It doesn't vex me now. Not anymore."

"Do you trust me?" Heinrici asked bluntly.

"I'm not deceived that you've totally switched sides," said Baldwin. "When opportunity affords, I think you'll return to your own side. And I am curious as to what motivates you. But I would very much like to think we can be friends for the time being—and maybe again when the war is over."

Heinrici grinned and took his hands off Baldwin's shoulders. "Good enough," he said. "Friends while we can be. And—who knows?—maybe it will be permanent."

"Maybe even more than friends," Baldwin said. "While we can be. You know what I mean, of course."

Heinrici frowned. "No . . . I'm not sure."

"They didn't tell you? No, I suppose they didn't. And they didn't tell Adriana, then. No. Boys don't tattle. And old boys don't either. That's the code. But you went to university, and you've been in the army a long time—you know what sometimes develops between men."

Heinrici drew a deep breath. He had no idea how to react.

"Do I disgust you?" Baldwin asked quietly.

Heinrici shook his head. "No . . . No, you don't disgust me."

"I'm attracted to you," Baldwin went on. "Physically we are not dissimilar, except for my wound. I'm as virile as you, Konrad." He sighed sharply. "Would I be introducing you to something you've never experienced?"

"Yes. You would."

"Well . . . Say no if you want to. I don't insist that you reciprocate."

Heinrici drew a deep breath. "Adriana will be here any minute," he said.

Baldwin grinned. "All right. I understand. Maybe sometime. But . . . don't suppose I can't do my part at Romainville," he said. "I won't muck up. I didn't at Dieppe."

"I've known brave men who are what you are," said Heinrici. "I'm not worried about your courage."

When their meeting was over, Baldwin left first, then Adriana, and finally Heinrici, who locked the room and now carried both the keys. As he walked down the steep slope of Montmartre in the red light of a low sun, he reviewed in his mind all the things they had discussed.

His plan was complex, as Adriana had complained; it would require precise timing. But it would appeal to the Frenchmen when he explained it to them—which he did not plan to do until the last moment—because it could be carried off without any loss of life.

They did have to think about reprisals. There was risk of reprisals even with this plan, but a plan not calculated to avoid killing Germans might cost many more lives—many French hostages chosen at random. Adriana assumed that any Germans killed would be SS or Gestapo brutes, but it wasn't necessarily so.

He looked around to see if Baldwin or Adriana had followed him, and when he was sure neither of them had, he turned into the street where Papa Ange lived, where he had to return to change into his uniform and where tonight he would make with Papa their final arrangements for Papa's part in the plan.

"Philippe!"

It was Sidonie. She was there, sitting in the little parlor with Marie. They were sipping red wine and nibbling on yellow cheese.

"The wine you brought us," Mama said, laughing. "And here we sit drinking it from ordinary glasses." They were drinking from small tumblers. "Wait. I'll fetch the Jew cups."

"Not necessary," Heinrici said with a grin. "I'll drink from the bottle."

Marie slapped at his hand. "No. I'll bring out the Jew cups. Papa would want you to drink from the Jew cups. Real silver, Sidonie. Heavy silver. Papa did the Jew a favor, and the Jew gave Papa these cups."

Mama rushed into the kitchen and was back in a moment with the silver cups Heinrici had seen before. She poured wine for Heinrici. Then she picked up Sidonie's glass and poured the wine into a cup. For herself, she tipped back her glass and emptied it.

"I'm going to do you two a favor," said Mama. "Papa won't be home for half an hour. I'll go out . . . So you can have the couch for a screw."

Sidonie laughed. "Ah, Marie!"

"Papa has business with Philippe," she said. "He can't do it with a horny man. Half an hour. No more. Papa will be back in half an hour."

Her corpulent body shaking with laughter, Mama grabbed her purse and went out.

Heinrici lifted the silver cup and drank the good red wine he had brought from the hotel. Sidonie was undressing.

"A week, Philippe," she said. "More. Papa tells me you are a very busy man."

"Busy—yes, I suppose so."

Sidonie had uncovered her breasts and now lifted them toward him. "Put your face between those like you used to do," she said, "and I am going to tell you something."

Smiling, he pressed his face between her big, soft breasts and nuzzled her moist skin, his nose filling with the mingled odors of sweat and cheap perfume. Frenchwoman that she was, she bathed less often than she dabbed on scent; and the smell was strong and sensual. Her voice was muffled by her flesh as she pushed her breasts against his ears, but he heard her—

"Papa trusts me. He has told me about the money. I am going to help you."

Heinrici drew back. "What do you mean?"

"I know about the Jew and the gold," she said. "You are going to need help, you know. Papa doesn't trust many people, not with word of a fortune in gold. But he trusts me. And you do. Don't you?"

He put his face between her breasts again, to hide whatever showed on his face of the dismay he felt. He nodded.

Sidonie chuckled deep in her throat and stroked the back of his neck and his ears and cheeks. "So screw me now, Philippe, before the old people come back."

Papa arrived laughing, having met Mama on the street and heard what was going on in his parlor. He was carrying a fat loaf of bread.

"Bread, huh? Look—"

Holding the loaf by both ends, he bent it in the middle until it broke. It was hollow. He pulled a wad of waxed paper out of the loaf; and, unfolding it on the table, uncovered a blue-green American passport.

"Hah! Look at that! Did you ever see anything so good?"

Heinrici examined the passport. It bore his photograph and all the correct-looking seals and stamps, on the laid and watermarked paper the Americans used. He had never given more than casual attention to an American passport before, but this one looked authentic.

"All you have to do is sign it. Look at the name."

Heinrici smiled—Henry Conrad.

"See the date. 1947. It's good until 1947. We can figure out something else in three years."

"Optimism here," said Heinrici pointing at a stamp on the second page. The stamp indicated that Henry Conrad had entered France on September 3, 1944, at Le Havre. Other stamps indicated he had been in England for three weeks before coming to France.

"So . . . ," Papa said, shrugging. "You come to France. You take up residence with a Frenchwoman. You are lovers. You have much money. An American in Paris. What could be more natural?"

"All this assumes the German army will be out of France before September," said Heinrici.

Papa's visage darkened. "You know more than I," he said. "Do you doubt it?"

"Le Havre is taken already," Heinrici said. "Paris"—he turned up the palms of his hands and turned down the corners of his mouth; he had long shared his countrymen's pride in holding Paris a captive city—"maybe. Maybe that soon."

Sidonie, who had only now finished refastening her clothes, put her hand on Heinrici's. "We lost the war in 1940," she said. She smiled. "And here we are. So you lose the war in 1944." She shrugged. *"Plus ça change, plus c'est la même chose.* For people like us, anyway."

Heinrici reached for the bottle and refilled his silver cup with dark red wine. "I think we must go on Tuesday night, Papa," he said. "Will you be ready?"

Marcel Ange nodded, but he frowned. "I must raise the question of money, Philippe," he said. "For the cars. For the men."

"Suppose I provide four hundred thousand francs on Monday," said Heinrici.

"Then I can provide the cars," said Papa.

"Where are you getting four hundred thousand francs, Philippe?" asked Sidonie. She, too, poured herself more wine. "Not printing it, I hope."

"No," Heinrici said curtly. Then to Papa, "And the safe flat?"

"For the Jew?"

"And his daughter. Two rooms. But safe, Papa. Absolutely safe. Every policeman in Paris, French or German, will be looking for them."

"A loft on avenue Junot," said Papa. "Not luxurious but suitable. People coming and going will be nothing new. Even German officers."

Sidonie snickered. "Where did you move the poor girl?"

"Madame has owed us a favor for a long time," said Papa solemnly. "Anyway, she needs a few weeks rest."

Heinrici raised his cup. "Papa. Mama." He drew a breath. "Sidonie. To the old times. And to the better ones that are coming."

Heinrici sat across the table from Oberleutnant Dietrich Krueger in the dining room of the Hotel George V, where they had first met at noon on Friday. It was Monday, July 17.

"I hope you enjoyed your Sunday in Paris," Heinrici said to Krueger when their appetizers had been set before them. "You are sufficiently apprised of the situation to know that I am not expressing defeatism when I say we may not enjoy many more lazy Sunday afternoons in Paris."

Krueger glanced around at the self-satisfied officers sitting at adjoining tables. "One hundred kilometers," he said under his breath. "One hundred kilometers from here. The fighting. The English and the Americans. And every day more thousands of their troops come ashore in Normandy." He glanced around again. "Herr Oberst," he said in an even lower voice, "how *can* we throw them back?"

"Our problem is a very different one," said Heinrici. "You did excellent work Friday. They had already identified their traitor, however—and shot him. In case you are asked. They identified him through his stupidity in giving the Gestapo information only one man could have had at that hour."

Krueger's mouth twitched. "But . . . it happened otherwise—through what I learned and reported. The Frenchman—"

"—would have compromised our mission, Oberleutnant, if he had continued to talk to the Gestapo. You *do* understand what we are doing? And why?"

The young man nodded emphatically. *"Jawohl, Herr Oberst."*

Heinrici picked up his glass and sniffed at the wine. "Are you a married man, Oberleutnant?"

Krueger shook his head. "No, Herr Oberst. I was a student at Heidelberg when the war came."

"Heidelberg. My university! I studied there. It seems a long time ago now."

"What did you study, Herr Oberst?"

"Languages," Heinrici said. "My father believed I should earn my living in international trade." He chuckled sardonically. "By the time I earned my diploma, we *had* no international trade."

"How did you happen to enter military intelligence work, Herr Oberst?"

"Krueger," said Heinrici, "would you believe it is because I am a scoundrel?"

"I would find that difficult to believe, Herr Oberst."

Heinrici smiled and rubbed his chin. "After the war—the other war—we Germans were unpopular in France and Italy, not to mention in England. I wanted to see Italy and France. I spoke their languages. But everywhere you went, showing a German passport made you a *Hun,* one of the old enemy." He grinned. "So . . . If the passport was the problem, why not go with a *Swiss* passport? Was it so difficult to forge a Swiss passport? Let me tell you, Krueger, it was not. Students . . . One of us had a Swiss passport, and we worked in the labs and print shops. I volunteered to test what we had made. I came here, to Paris, in 1930, on my second visit, and it was far more pleasurable than my first. Henri Morteau was far more welcome in Paris than Konrad Heinrici."

"And did you do espionage work?"

"Not then," said Heinrici. "I was arrested in Amsterdam in 1932—again traveling as the Swiss Henri Morteau. The Dutch were more amused than out-raged. They deported me. So died Henri Morteau. His passport was a crude forgery—as the first officer who really examined it discovered. My father told me I had disgraced the name Heinrici. But I was called to Berlin. Military intelligence was a small business then. I was asked if I was interested in serving my country. I was a linguist and something of a forger. Would I . . . Hell, Krueger, I was unemployed."

Oberleutnant Krueger dared to smile.

"I took a very small job in a very small agency. And then—" An expansive gesture. "Then the Führer came to power."

"To our very great benefit," Krueger said dutifully.

"To mine, I must admit," Heinrici said. "Shortly, I had my choice between working for Heydrich and the SD or Canaris and the Abwehr." He took a sip of his wine.

"And you chose—"

Henrici interrupted as he put down the glass. "I suppose I make a decent spy, Oberleutnant. I think I would make a very bad policeman."

Krueger stared for a moment at his plate, then raised his eyes. "As would I, Herr Oberst," he said gravely.

Now it was Heinrici's turn to glance around and be sure that no one was listening. "Tomorrow night, Krueger," he said, "I am going to try to steal two prisoners from the SS. I know General Hausser has told you why."

"In fact, he hasn't," said Krueger. "I understand that the Jew Mercier has access to a vast fortune in gold—which we would very much like to take from him. But I understand there is another reason, which the General has not seen fit to tell me."

"I am not at liberty to tell you either," said Heinrici. "But it need not concern you, Krueger."

The young lieutenant nodded. "My orders from General Hausser are to assist you in any way I can, Herr Oberst. What is my role on Tuesday night?"

Heinrici fixed a stare on Krueger as he chewed and swallowed a bite of the appetizer. Then he sipped wine. "Tell me, Oberleutnant," he said, "have you a great desire to expose yourself to danger, perhaps to get killed?"

Krueger was not intimidated by the question. "No, Herr Oberst," he said. "Not unnecessarily, anyway."

"Good. There is no reason for you to be with me Tuesday night. My plan was complete before I learned I would have your services at my disposal. I want you to play a little charade for me Tuesday night."

"I will try, Herr Oberst."

"An easy one," said Heinrici. "You will enjoy it. I want you to report to me in my suite at the Royal Monceau late Tuesday afternoon. Just before I go out, I will order dinner from room service. When it is delivered, you will be out of sight. The wiater will see only me. Immediately then, I will leave the hotel. I want you to remain in the suite, eat the food and drink the wine, and—no earlier than midnight—put the room-service table in the hall to be picked up. Hotel personnel and German officers on the floor will pass my door constantly, seeing no table, and then, at midnight, they will see a table." He shrugged and smiled. "Do you think they will believe I have been in my suite all evening?"

"It is possible, Herr Oberst."

"Well. Since I have no other assignment for you Tuesday night . . ."

"Perhaps I should also play the radio," Krueger said.

"Good."

Tuesday morning. From a telephone in the lobby of the Hotel George V, Heinrici and Adriana placed a call to the office of SS Oberführer Erhard Franck.

Adriana took the receiver first. "I have a call from the Reich Main Security Office in Berlin for the adjutant to Herr Oberführer Franck. It is Standartenführer Grothman calling. Yes. Standartenführer Grothmann is adjutant to Reichsführer Himmler. Thank you." She handed the phone to Heinrici.

"Sturmbannführer Heiden? Grothmann here. The Reichsführer will be telephoning officers in Paris and other cities during the evening. I need to know where Oberführer Franck is to be reached at, say, twenty-one hundred hours this evening. No, he need not remain in his office. In fact, the reichsführer would prefer the privacy of a call to his quarters. I believe I have the number, but just to be certain . . . Ah, yes. Thank you. Tell the Oberführer to expect a call from Berlin. The reichsführer will be communicating some instructions. Very well, Heiden. Is the weather good in Paris? Good. I hope to come there soon. Very good. Until then, Heiden."

XI

TUESDAY EVENING, JULY 18, 1944

THE prison at Fresnes, twelve kilometers south of the center of Paris, was a fortress, long since used to house prisoners of the French state. It was a ramshackle block of stone buildings around a central court, situated on low-lying land in a shallow valley in the village.

In July 1944 Fresnes Prison housed some prominent members of the Résistance, a few French criminals, and—ironically—a substantial number of German soldiers, serving sentences for violations of military law. Few prisoners were there only because they were Jews. Jews arrested just for deportation were confined in a concentration camp at Drancy, just northwest of Pantin station. Henri Mercier had originally been arrested because his son was a member of the Résistance—and later because Kriminalinspektor Gebel had ordered him held for interrogation.

Henri Mercier lay on his back on the stone floor of his cell. As the sunlight faded and another night fell over the prison, his cell, where little light penetrated at midday, became almost totally dark. Though he had lost track of the days, he thought that with the setting of the sun it was shabbat. But he would not pray. He never had, and surely, he thought, it would offend God if a man who had never prayed in prosperity suddenly began to in adversity.

It was ironic. The Nazis, by their hatred and abuse, had made him more of a Jew than he had ever been in his life. In the community of Jews before the war he had been condemned as an unbeliever, a despicable traitor to the synagogue. The observant Jews had come with ashes in their mouths when they came to ask *his* help. Some of them had openly scorned him, had avoided his society for many years.

He was not even a nonbeliever. He believed, he had told them, there was something somewhere, a force, an idea, that made the universe rational. What he did not believe was that the governing force of the universe heard prayers or noticed rituals—or that it prospered those who prayed with the proper words and postures and spitefully denied prosperity to those who didn't.

Then how can you call yourself a Jew? they had asked in 1923 when they left him to a civil marriage, denying him a religious ceremony. I don't, he had then defiantly replied.

He considered himself a Jew, just the same. He knew the history of his people, and he shared their deep sense of tragedy. He wanted his people to have their homeland, even though he himself would never go there. He felt kinship with the Jews suffering in Germany. Since 1935 he had been in contact with other Jewish businessmen, in France and elsewhere, looking for ways to help.

Everything he had done had been summed up for him one winter day in 1942. Two Jews from Amiens, a man of forty and his ten-year-old son who had escaped deportation, had arrived in Paris on their way toward the Spanish border. Someone insisted they should meet the man who had arranged their rescue, and the man and his son were brought to Magasin Mercier on rue du Faubourg de Saint Honoré.

The man had been limitlessly grateful; yet, he had been unable to conceal his curiosity as to why a man who was not himself an observant Jew would constantly risk his life to save the lives of Jews. Mercier had refused to satisfy his curiosity.

The son had been a beautiful child: innocent and wide-eyed, wearing short pants, his thin little legs unsteady from hunger and cold. Henri Mercier would never forget that little boy—the wool cap that was too big for him, the short coat with sleeves so long they covered his hands, the socks fallen halfway to his ankles—the prey of men who senselessly hated him, who were obsessed with tracking him down and killing him. It was enough to have saved that child. That was the sum of everything he had done.

They didn't kill that one. No, nor several hundred others. But for each one saved, how many were killed? He didn't know. He did not know much at all anymore, he realized bitterly. A man confined alone in a tiny stone cell cannot know much.

He did not know why his interrogations had stopped. He had to think that was ominous. Kriminalinspektor Gebel had not called on him for a week. Anyway, the Gestapo agent had never come to the point. He had never asked what officials had taken money, or why. He had never asked how many people had been saved. He never mentioned the British agents who had been saved the same way. Strange. Even more strange, he had never asked where the money came from, or if there was any left, or where it was. Henri Mercier could not guess why.

As days went by with no interrogation, he began to dread what would come next. As he saw it, there were three possibilities: excruciating torture that would force him to tell them everything they wanted to know, a noose or firing squad, or deportation to a death camp somewhere in the east. Each time the sun went down, he had survived another day. But what good were they?

The same white twilight that vanished from Henri Mercier's cell faded over Paris as a military truck sped through the Nineteenth Arrondissement toward the Pantin Gate, Pre–St. Gervais, and Romainville. Under that flat twilight, the city was sullenly silent. Silent bicycles, silent vélopèdes, silent pedestrians hurried through the streets. Chickens clucked. Goats bawled. Now and again an engine howled—a German motorcycle speeding on some urgent errand. From a bar here and there, sounds of tinny music cut through the silence: old musicians straining to lift the mood of the morose customers who sipped sour wartime wine or flat, muddy beer.

Twelve girls huddled on the floor in the back of the open truck, under the muzzle of the soldier who sat on the only bench. All were naked. All had shaven heads. One was as young as sixteen. The eldest was twenty-three. All of them were Parisiennes, all of them the daughters of families who had been solidly prosperous. Seven were Jews. Three were pregnant. Three suspected they were.

Jeanne Mercier sat with her arms crossed over her firm breasts, her dark eyes fixed glumly on her feet. Her head was smooth; it had been reshaved only this afternoon. A slight girl, she was barely five feet tall. She had been in training for the ballet, and in spite of beatings, hunger, dysentery, and long, cramped confinement in a tiny stone-floored cell she shared with five other girls, she still had the lithe body of the dancer she wanted to be.

The twelve girls had served as naked serving wenches for a dinner party for German officers, in an elegant home on boulevard Suchet, on the edge of the beautiful Bois de Boulogne. Tonight, oddly, the officers had wanted their dinner very early, and not long after eight o'clock the girls were loaded again on the truck and started on the long drive across the city and back to Romainville. For Jeanne Mercier this was the eleventh time she had been to the house on boulevard Suchet; it was the first time she had been returned to the prison before three in the morning. It was also the first time she had not been defiled.

Tonight she had been doubly lucky. Not only had she not been forced to submit to the usual coarse physical abuse, she had managed to eat enough to relieve her hunger for a few hours.

All of them succeeded in getting something to eat. They always did. None of them dreaded the trips to the house on beoulevard Suchet; they lay in their cells and dreamed of them, hoped for them, for the scraps of food they would get. The German cooks watched the naked girls to be sure they ate nothing from the plates they carried to the tables, but they tolerated the girls' snatching scraps off plates they carried *from* the tables. No one had to scrape the plates the Romainville girls carried into the kitchen—they bolted down every morsel they found, even half-chewed-and-spat-out chunks of gristle; they licked the plates and silverware for the last mite of nourishment. Given a moment, they would tear into the garbage cans to retrieve handfuls of potato peelings and apple cores.

Sometimes an officer, especially the SS general who was living in this requisitioned house, would order two or three of the girls to kneel by his chair and, saying he was going to feed them like the Jew bitches they were, would toss chunks of bread at them—which they were allowed to eat if they caught them in their mouths. The starving girls would lunge and snap at the bread while the Germans roared with laughter.

They had played that game for a few minutes this evening, and Jeanne had cursed her luck when she was not among those chosen for it. A few minutes later, though, a tense and half-drunk officer had shoved toward her a plate on which half a veal chop remained uneaten, together with a blob of mashed potatoes and some carrots. As soon as she was through the kitchen door, she shoved everything on the plate into her mouth. It was delicious.

A little later, carrying the sugar bowl and cream pitcher from one table, she had poured sugar into the cream that was left and gulped it down. Seeing this, the cook cuffed her on the head, but the mouthful of sugary white cream was well worth the punishment.

Romainville Prison was full of rumors. Rumor this morning had placed American tanks in the streets of Chartres, only sixty-five kilometers away, and the naked girls on the truck whispered about it now—quietly so the guard would not hear. Another rumor said the American tanks were at Soissons and racing for the Rhine, leaving Paris behind. Still another rumor held that the Résistance had seized control of all of central Paris—which they now knew was not true, for they had driven through it twice this evening. And, as every day, the rumor persisted that on the approach of liberating forces the Germans would shoot the entire prison population.

Though they did not mention it now, among the girls and women most of the rumors touched sooner or later on the name Ravensbrück. Ravensbrück was the concentration camp for women, somewhere in Germany or Poland. If you went there, you resigned all hope: no one ever came back alive from Ravensbrück. Everyone hoped to be spared, and they talked about it endlessly. How did the

Germans choose the ones who went? The ones who did not?

There was little point in speculating if you were a Jew. If you were a Jew, they would almost certainly send you to Ravensbrück, sooner or later. Jeanne knew her mother had gone. She knew she would go, too, as soon as the officers tired of her as a plaything for their dinner parties. Like the others, she had pretended to enjoy their abuse, even to lust for it, to keep the brutes satisfied. Crawling naked among their feet beneath their dinner table, hugging their legs and begging to be allowed to do what in truth she could hardly do without gagging, she had totally and unalterably degraded herself—but she was alive and still in Paris one more day, and tonight she had eaten meat and potatoes and sugar and cream!

XII

TUESDAY EVENING, JULY 18, 1944

BURN your headlamps. And drive faster."

Le Rasoir was driving. Obedient to Heinrici's order, he switched on the bright headlamps of the black Mercedes and pressed the accelerator. The car picked up speed and roared toward the unlighted Arc de Triomphe, visible only as a looming shadow ahead of them.

Sweat gleamed on Le Rasoir's forehead. He wore the black uniform of an untersturmführer SS, and he carried a document identifying him as Paul Sprenger. But he did not speak German.

"Checkpoint," said Le Capitaine. He spoke good German, and for tonight he was Hauptsturmführer Karl Forster, also in the black uniform of the SS. He sat beside Le Rasoir in the front seat. "Easy. I'll talk. Or the colonel will."

The checkpoint stood at the intersection of avenue Friedland and L'Etoile: half a dozen German soldiers and a dozen French gendarmes. They were stopping every vehicle.

"Sound your horn," Heinrici said. "Flash your lights."

Le Rasoir obeyed. Miraculously—as he saw it—two cars and a truck ahead of them edged to the side to make way for the Mercedes. Le Rasoir swerved around them and moved to the head of the line. Two soldiers, an officer, and a gendarme strode up to the Mercedes. Two soldiers lowered the muzzles of their Schmeissers, and the officer rapped on the window. Startled, Le Rasoir realized he had neglected to roll down the window. He grabbed at the crank.

"Guten abend," the officer said crisply. *"Papiere, bitte."*

Heinrici, who was wearing civilian clothes, leaned forward from the rear seat and offered his identification. The photograph on his identification book matched his present appearance: brown hair darkened almost to black, eyebrows darkened to match. He had refused to follow Le Faussaire's suggestion that he wear eyeglasses and perhaps attach a false mustache to his upper lip. He did not want to risk anything that had the appearance of a disguise. *"Schnell, bitte, Hauptmann,"* he said. Quickly, please, Captain.

The captain frowned over the passbook and handed it back. *"Danke, Herr Oberführer,"* he grunted, snapping to attention. *"Heil Hitler!"*

Heinrici slapped Le Rasoir on the shoulder, and Le Rasoir put the car in gear and drove into L'Etoile, the great round plaza and traffic circle around the arch. He accelerated to what he considered a high speed and turned west on avenue Foch.

In the rear seat, Heinrici ran the back of his right hand over his mouth and quietly released the breath that was inside him. He pushed his passbook down into his inside pocket and once again checked his pistol. It was a Walther P-38, the pistol most favored by knowledgeable officers: the personal sidearm issued to him on his return to Paris. Le Capitaine carried a Luger in his holster. Le Rasoir had no sidearm but would carry one of the Mauser machine pistols, a source of some concern to Heinrici—Raymond, Le Rasoir, had never fired a machine pistol.

The team headed for Fresnes Prison consisted of Heinrici, Le Capitaine, and Le Rasoir. In another car just now leaving a Montparnasse garage, Baldwin, Adriana, and Le Concombre made up the rescue team for Romainville. Heinrici glanced at his watch. Yes, the great old Daimler carrying the Romainville team would just now be starting north on boulevard Raspail.

They had to achieve two bold, simultaneous deceptions, since they could not assault the prisons and they could not risk occasioning scores of reprisal executions. He had hoped for a simpler plan, one with fewer risks, but with the resources at his command the scheme they were following had been the best he could devise. From this minute forward, every element of the plan had to proceed as scheduled. More than a few minutes deviation could be disastrous.

He was confident of his people. Le Capitaine looked Teutonic and spoke fluent German. Le Rasoir was strong and silent and would do what he had to do. Le Concombre had already proven himself; he was shrewd and fearless.

Len Baldwin . . . What he had said to Baldwin was true; he had known brave men who made love to other men. There were regiments in the Wehrmacht in which pederasty was a centuries-old tradition, and he understood the English had a like tradition. He had told Baldwin it did not disgust him, and that was true, too. Still, he wondered about the man's temperament. Baldwin was not rock-steady. If anyone failed, it would be Baldwin.

That was why he'd had to send Adriana with Baldwin.

Adriana . . . Heinrici smiled inwardly. He was carrying in his mind a new image of her: ardent, yet ingenuous, unsure of everything about her sensuality except her drive to satisfy it. In this as in everything else, she was anything but temperate. Tonight . . . She would do whatever she had to do.

Prompted by Heinrici, Le Rasoir drove the Mercedes past a police check where the street was not blocked. Brazenly flashing his lights and sounding his horn, he sped by without a glance at the soldiers who stepped out and held up their arms to signal a stop. No one pursued. Heinrici was confident they wouldn't.

Le Rasoir knew the way. He needed no prompting about that. He turned left off avenue Foch into boulevard Lannes, then drove south on the boulevard, across the Place de Colombie, and into boulevard Suchet.

Like most of the luxurious homes along the boulevard, this one was shielded from the street by a tall hedge. Le Rasoir pulled the Mercedes to the curb, switched off the headlamps, but left the running lights burning. The three men pushed open the wrought-iron gate in the gap in the hedge and walked to the main entrance door of the tall, elegant stone mansion.

The house was guarded by two SS soldiers in black uniforms and helmets and armed with Schmeisser submachine guns. They were visible through the etched glass of the doors: a corporal standing, smoking a cigarette, a sergeant sitting on a cushioned bench. Heinrici rapped imperiously. The seated one rose and came to the doors. Heinrici pressed his identification book against the glass.

The sergeant stared at the book, which identified Heinrici as an oberführer of the SS and a kommandeure of the SD. He stiffened to attention and opened the door.

The two soldiers lowered their Schmeissers and stood awed as Heinrici stalked into the foyer, followed by Le Capitaine and Le Rasoir. Both stood rigidly at attention.

"Where is Franck?" Heinrici demanded.

"Upstairs, Herr Oberführer," said the sergeant. "I can telephone him—"

"*No*. I am here to arrest him. He is to have no warning. Come with us. Show us his door. In the event of resistance, you will help us to effect the arrest."

The two soldiers led the way through a foyer to a wide, curving marble staircase. Le Rasoir, before he followed, knelt by the telephone stand and, underneath in an inconspicuous place, cut the wires.

At the top of the stairs, where Le Rasoir caught up, the sergeant pointed to a pair of paneled doors.

"Break them open," Heinrici said curtly.

"But Herr Oberführer," the sergeant protested hoarsely. "If we knock—"

"Break them down!"

The sergeant glanced at the corporal, then beckoned him forward, and the two threw their shoulders against the doors. The doors splintered and swung open.

The room inside was a dining room, lighted by small, dim bulbs burning in crystal chandeliers. A clutter of plates and silver and ashtrays and glasses and bottles had not yet been taken away from the table. Crumbs of bread littered the floor. Under the remnant of cigar smoke that hung in the air, the room had the sharp, uniquely Gallic odor of oiled wood and old dust.

Another set of double doors slammed back, and a heavy man in a maroon silk dressing gown confronted Heinrici with a small automatic pistol.

"Oberführer Erhard Franck?" Heinrici asked coldly.

"I am Oberführer Franck. Who are you?"

Heinrici forced a thin smile. "I am Oberführer Ulrich von Strauch, Kommandeure SD, from Berlin. I am here to place you under arrest and return you to Berlin. Put down the pistol, Herr Oberführer, or you will be shot."

Le Rasoir held the long barrel of his Mauser leveled directly at Franck's belly; Le Capitaine had drawn his Luger and held it, too, on the flushed, angry SS general.

Franck lowered his automatic. "On whose authority do you dare this outrage?" he asked.

Heinrici withdrew from his inner pocket the letter Le Faussaire had prepared. "On the authority of Oberstgruppenführer Kaltenbrunner, whose signature you will see. These are specific orders to return you to Berlin to answer to the charge of treason."

Franck gasped at the letter, stunned and disbelieving. Kaltenbrunner was the successor to Reinhard Heydrich; he was second only to Reichsführer Himmler himself in the Reichssicherheitshauptamt; he was chief of the SD and chief of the Gestapo.

Heinrici glanced at Le Capitaine, then at Le Rasoir. If Franck saw through the forgery, they would have to disable the two SS noncoms while he himself moved to subdue Franck. A man accustomed to receiving orders from the RSHA might see immediately that this letter was on spurious stationery. Also, had he ever seen the genuine signature of Ernst Kaltenbrunner? But, as Heinrici watched, springtight, the color drained from Franck's cheeks, and he dropped his little pistol into the pocket of his dressing gown.

"I wish to telephone Berlin," Franck said quietly. "In fact, I am under specific orders to await a telephone call from Reichsführer Himmler."

Heinrici smiled. "I know. A small deception of mine, to be sure you would be here when I came for you," he said. He glanced at his watch. "In a few hours you will *be* in Berlin, Herr Oberführer. We have no time to wait for a call to be put through. At dawn the skies will be full of Spitfires again, and I do not intend to be in the air in a vulnerable little Heinkel. I must require you to dress immediately."

"I will need time to pack a few things. And I must take my adjutant with me."

"*Herr Oberführer.* You are under *arrest*. You are fortunate that I let you dress at all and don't simply take you as you are."

Waving his pistol, Heinrici ordered the confused officer to move, and he followed him to the bedroom suite. Franck put aside his dressing gown and drew on field-gray breeches and tunic, then his varnished black boots. When he picked up his belt, Heinrici ordered him to remove his holster and pistol.

Le Capitaine instructed the two SS officers to wait in the dining room. While they waited, Le Rasoir explored the house, finding and cutting telephone wires.

With the corpulent Oberführer Franck now in uniform, complete with cap, Heinrici ordered Hauptsturmführer Forster—Le Capitaine—to handcuff him. Franck protested weakly in a frightened voice as Heinrici led him to the stairs. The two SS soldiers, shocked to see the oberführer in handcuffs, stood aside gaping.

Le Capitaine stopped to speak to them. "What you have seen and heard is confidential. It is not to be reported to anyone," he said. "Switch off the lights, return to your posts in the foyer, and remain there until you are relieved. That will be at midnight, I assume?"

"*Jawohl, Herr Hauptsturmführer.*"

"Very well. By that time we will be well on our way to Berlin. When you are relieved, you may inform your commanding officer that Herr Oberführer Franck has been called suddenly to Berlin. I suggest you do not describe his arrest to anyone. He *may* return."

Slumped in the rear seat of the Mercedes, Oberführer Franck was not so unobservant as to realize very quickly that they were not heading for Le Bourget. "Where are we going?" he demanded.

"Fresnes Prison," Heinrici said.

"Not Berlin?"

"Of course Berlin. We are picking up another prisoner."

As Le Rasoir sped east through Montparnasse, Heinrici wondered what kind of man Franck was. Was he sitting there in helpless anguish? Or would he, before they reached Fresnes, recover sufficient presence of mind to become dangerous? He looked like a fat pig of an SS bureaucrat, but he had not attained his rank by being a fool. If he was sitting there thinking, and not just trembling, he might assert authority at Fresnes. And who would the soldiers at Fresnes obey: the SD kommandeure from Berlin, or the officer whose orders they were accustomed to taking?

* * *

As Heinrici had ordered, Le Concombre drove the Daimler fast, with headlights blazing, on the most prominent boulevards. As expected, they were
stopped, once on the bridge over the Seine, once before the Gare de L'Est.

Each time, Baldwin carried off the bluff with aplomb that half surprised
Adriana. He was Obersturmbannführer Waldemar Heiden, of the SD, from the
Reichssicherheitshauptampt. He wore a field-gray uniform, and he barked
orders in German as though he had been doing it all his life. Le Concombre was
Haupsturmführer Franz Hanke, who glared impatiently at the men who examined the documents thrust through the window by Baldwin. Sitting unexplained
beside Le Concombre, Adriana was Ilse Severing, blitzmädchen.

A Mauser machine pistol lay on the front seat beside Le Concombre. A
second one was on the floor between Adriana's legs. She and Baldwin were
satisfied with the plan Heinrici had devised. They found it rather too compli-
cated but admired its insolent boldness. They had agreed it was more likely to
succeed than something less inventive, anything more conservative. The only
defect in it was that it required careful timing, and the second identity check, at
Le Gare de l'Est, took too much time.

"I have no interest," she had said earlier to Baldwin, "in committing suicide.
I wouldn't attempt this if I didn't think—"

"God knows how many lives are at stake," Baldwin had said. His mind was
on the same thing as hers, but his thoughts had taken a different turn. "When
they finish repairing that bridge, they'll start the deportations again. If Mercier
really has access to the money and remains in condition to function, this may be
a humanitarian mission almost without equal in this war."

"Pantin . . . ," grunted Claude.

The station and railroad yards were to their left, as was the canal, and the
railroad bridge they had blown was just ahead. Claude turned right, into Romainville and toward the fort.

South of the Porte d'Orleans, Le Capitaine nudged Le Rasoir and pointed at
his watch. They were slightly ahead of schedule, and Le Rasoir eased off on the
accelerator. They were to reach the prison fort at precisely 2145 hours. Heinrici
expected to effect the release of Henri Mercier and be away again in no more
than fifteen minutes.

At 2145 exactly, Le Rasoir drove up to the main gate of Fresnes Prison and
sounded his horn.

"*Schnell! Schnell!*" Heinrici demanded of the officer who finally came out to
see his documents. Hurry! Hurry!

Within five minutes, two bewildered junior officers escorted the short-tem-
pered SD kommandeure from Berlin and—to their dismay and astonishment—
a *handcuffed* Oberführer Franck into the office of the governor of the prison. It

was a snug little old room, once the office of the military governor of the fort, for decades the office of the French superintendent of the prison Fresnes had become. The ceiling was low. There was a fireplace, though tonight an oscillating electric fan whirred on a table before a window, bringing in cooler night air. Some rather worn oriental carpets covered part of the stone floor.

Erich Langbehn, governor of Fresnes Prison, was an honorary obersturmbannführer of the SS. When he saw Oberführer Franck in ignominious custody, he clutched his jaw in his right hand and drew his cheeks down with his fingers as if trying to waken himself.

"Herr Langbehn? I am Oberführer Ulrich von Strauch, kommandeure SD, from Berlin. Here are my papers. Here also is an order from Oberstgruppenführer Kaltenbrunner. I want you to take this prisoner off my hands for a short time, while you and I transact our business. We have not had time to strip and search him. Hauptsturmführer Forster will accompany your men to witness this procedure."

Langbehn glanced back and forth between the swelling red face of Franck and the documents he had been handed by Heinrici. He studied Heinrici's identify book and the letter ostensibly from Kaltenbrunner ordering him to turn over Mercier. At the same time he searched for some signal from the handcuffed officer he had held in awe ever since he arrived in Paris. Finally the perplexed Langbehn turned to Franck. "Herr—"

"There will be no conversation with my prisoner, Herr Langbehn," Heinrici snapped. He pointed a finger at one of the officers who had led the way from the gate to this office. "Be certain there is a thorough *anal* search as well as the rest of it," he said. "I do not want to take this man aboard an aircraft unless he has been *thoroughly* searched."

Le Capitaine seized Franck's arm and pushed him toward the door. At the door he stopped and looked back at the two junior officers. Langbehn nodded at one of them, and that one followed Théo.

Heinrici sat down. Le Rasoir stood behind him, with the Mauser cradled in the crook of his arm.

"This is amazing, Herr Oberführer," said Langbehn. "I hope you won't mind if I telephone Berlin for confirmation. I—"

"Herr Langbehn," said Heinrici firmly, "I have a lot of work to do tonight— plus a return flight to Berlin before morning light and a sky filled with Allied fighter planes. You have your order from Herr Oberstgruppenführer Kaltenbrunner. If there is any irregularity in the way I carry out my orders, the responsibility is mine."

Langbehn sat down behind his desk. "The Jew..." He shrugged. "That, of course, is—I mean, I see no difficulty. But... the arrest of a man of the rank and position of Herr Oberführer Franck! Well, I—"

"Herr Langbehn," Heinrici said as if restraining his anger, "as a concession to you, I will show you my order for the arrest of Franck, signed by the oberst-gruppenführer just as is the order to hand over the Jew. When you have perused my order, I suggest you subdue your astonishment. You can imagine the seriousness of what is developing here. I do not think a man of your rank and position wants to become a complicating factor."

Langbehn took the second forged letter and peered hard at it. "Go get the Jew," he said to the remaining officer with a flutter of his hand. His lips moved as he read the letter. He handed it back to Heinrici. "As you say, this originates at a level far higher than mine."

"It does indeed, Herr Langbehn," said Heinrici. "You may be glad you are mystified by it. If you were not, you might be in very deep trouble."

"I had supposed Mercier was an ordinary sort of prisoner. Kriminalinspektor Gebel interrogated him for some time, then he released him for deportation. He would have gone on an early transport."

"A Zionist, Herr Langbehn," Heinrici said casually. "And he would not have gone on an early transport. Herr Oberführer Franck would have seen to that."

Langbehn took a pack of cigarettes from the pocket of his jacket, offered them to Heinrici, who shook his head; Langbehn lit one with a match. "I have made it a point," he said, "to carry out my orders, never to question or criticize. I hope you will not think I have been impertinent."

Heinrici smiled. "Not at all, Herr Langbehn."

"Well, I—"

The telephone rang. Langbehn glanced at Heinrici for permission to answer. Heinrici nodded.

"Langbehn here. Yes. Yes. Excuse me for a moment. I will ask." He put the telephone down and spoke to Heinrici. "It is the governor of Romainville Prison. A subordinate of yours is there to pick up another prisoner. What may I tell him?"

"Tell him the truth," said Heinrici.

"Including...? Including the fact that you have arrested Herr Oberführer Franck?"

"Including that," said Heinrici.

The severe and doubting face of Walter Kleist, governor of Romainville, paled and weakened as he listened to Langbehn on the telephone. Baldwin watched intently, his apprehension diminishing. This man Kleist—who was no fool—was hearing straight from Langbehn that an SD general from Berlin had flown into Paris tonight, arrested SS general Franck, and was returning him to Berlin—together with two Jews, one from Fresnes and one from Romainville.

"You have *seen* the oberführer?" Kleist asked Langbehn. As he listened to the answer to this question, he pulled a shocked breath. "An *anal* search? Surely..."

Baldwin glanced at Adriana. Her relief was visible. What Kleist was hearing meant that Heinrici was still at Fresnes, still in command of the situation, and still had Franck in custody. Heinrici's plan had been that the handcuffed ober-führer would be more convincing evidence of his authority than any document they could forge. Since they could hardly kidnap *two* high-ranking officers of the Paris SS, the team at Romainville would benefit from the one they had by demanding that the governor of Romainville telephone the governor of Fresnes and hear his personal confirmation that Oberführer Franck was indeed an SD prisoner, under arrest, manacled, and even being subjected to an anal search.

Kleist put down the telephone. "Well, Herr Obersturmbannführer," he said. "It appears your story is accurate."

"I shall," Baldwin said calmly, "overlook the implication that I lied to you."

Walter Kleist was not fazed. He was a scarred political infighter with an ingrained hostility to what he thought he saw in Baldwin: a son of privilege with rank not justified by his age and wound.

"Why does Berlin want this Jew girl?" Kleist asked.

"Surely you don't expect me to answer," said Baldwin.

"No, Herr Obersturmbannführer Heiden, I don't expect you to answer," said Kleist. He removed his thick, round, steel-rimmed spectacles and rubbed at them with a white handkerchief. "Just curiosity."

In fact, Kleist felt more than curiosity. The Jew girl, Jeanne Mercier, had remained in Romainville Prison long after she might have been sent to Ra-vensbsbrück—except that Herr Oberführer Franck had ordered her retained here. Kleist had thought he understood—she was not the only girl the oberführer had ordered retained—but now he decided he had not understood. It could not be coincidence that the oberführer was under arrest and that an SD officer had been sent to take custody of the Jew girl. He pondered on the connection. He wondered if he had any reason to be concerned about the fact that he himself had twice brought her to this office and for a scrap of bread and an apple had enjoyed an erotic experience unique in his life.

Adriana was sweating heavily inside the field-gray uniform. Her impression of Baldwin's performance was not too far different from Kleist's: that the son of English wealth and privilege was quite comfortable snapping out orders and confidently expecting them to be obeyed. Thank God.

The light from Kleist's gooseneck lamp glared on the white papers in the file on his desk and reflected up into his face; the chiaroscuro shadows and bright reflections in his eyeglasses lent him something of a Mephistophelian aspect. She tried to shrug off the disturbing sense that he was suspicious of them and was searching for a way to delay their departure long enough for him to check on them in another way.

"You say you flew here from Berlin?" Kleist asked Baldwin. He had ignored Adriana and Claude. "This evening?"

"Yes," said Baldwin. "And twice we saw flights of Allied fighters. That is why Oberführer von Strauch insists we must be back to Tempelhof before sunrise."

"And you are carrying back the two Jews as well as Oberführer Franck?"

"Such are our orders," Baldwin said stiffly. "And I would be grateful if you would expedite the delivery of the girl. Oberführer von Strauch will be most upset if he has to wait at the airport for us."

Kleist picked up the telephone. "I will see what is delaying us," he said.

Two guards led Henri Mercier into the office of the prison governor. Le Rasoir stepped forward immediately and locked Mercier into heavy handcuffs.

Heinrici could not help but stare at the man for whom he was risking so much. Henri Mercier returned his stare: curious and apprehensive. He was hunched, emaciated, bruised. His blue eyes were watery and seemed to focus only intermittently. He ran out his tongue and licked his thin white lips. His long face was bristly with whiskers, as white as his long hair. He wore filthy, tattered clothes: a once-white shirt, the torn and crumpled remains of a blue double-breasted suit.

Le Capitaine returned, leading Oberführer Franck by the arm. The SS general blinked and squinted, unsteady on hs feet. The guards who had stripped him and subjected him to the anal search had taken his eyeglasses. Also his boots. His tunic was open, but he let his manacled hands hang and made no effort to rebutton it.

"Very well, Herr Langbehn," Heinrici said crisply. "We have our prisoners. We will go."

Le Rasoir seized Henri Mercier's arm and shoved him toward the door. Le Capitaine pushed Franck after them. Langbehn extended his hand, and Heinrici shook it before he followed the others out of the office.

Without words, the five walked down the steps and out into the courtyard where the Mercedes waited. Mercier and Franck were hurried into the rear seat, where Heinrici joined them. Le Rasoir took the wheel. Le Capitaine sat beside him. Le Rasoir started the engine and wheeled the car sharply around the court-yard and toward the gate, their last possible impediment to getting out of Fresnes Prison.

The guards there caused no delay. Le Rasoir pulled out, turned right, and sped toward the highway to Paris.

Five minutes later, on the highway, Heinrici ordered Le Rasoir to pull to the side and stop. Le Rasoir pulled off the pavement. Heinrici got out, came around the car, and opened the door on the right.

"All right, Herr Oberführer. Out!"

"No!" Franck cried.

Heinrici grabbed him by his tunic and jerked him out of the car. Franck dropped to his knees, whimpering.

"I'm not going to shoot you, you fool," Heinrici said. He strode back to the left side of the car and got in again. "All right, Raymond," he said. "To the rendezvous."

Le Capitaine had already turned, reached over the seat and pulled up Henri Mercier's handcuffs. He unlocked them and tossed them on the floor.

"Monsieur Mercier," Heinrici said. *"Nous sommes votre amis. Vous êtes libre."*

Mercier's lips trembled as he muttered, *"Personne n'est libre."* No one is free.

Oberleutnant Dietrich Krueger, driving an open Audi two-seater, had braked and stopped a hundred meters behind the Mercedes when it suddenly swerved to the side of the road and stopped. Now, as the Mercedes raced north again, toward the Porte d' Orleans apparently, Krueger accelerated and tried to maintain the hundred-meter separation. He was driving without lights, and it was not easy to keep to the highway. All he could do was follow the distant red taillight of the Mercedes.

He saw the shadow of a man at the side of the road as he passed the point where the Mercedes has stopped. The man was waving and screaming, but Krueger could not stop; if he did he would surely lose the Mercedes. He guessed the man was some sort of hostage Heinrici and his Frenchmen had seized, but whoever it was would have to fend for himself for a while longer.

Following the orders of General Hausser, Krueger had left the Royal Monceau Hotel shortly after Heinrici. He had driven to Fresnes and waited outside the prison until he saw the Mercedes arrive. He could not be absolutely certain the Mercedes was driven by Heinrici and his Frenchmen, but it seemed a reasonable assumption. Anyway, no other vehicle had arrived at the prison during Krueger's long wait there. He might be following the wrong automobile, but he didn't think he was. His orders were to discover where Heinrici took the French Jew.

In his office, Erich Langbehn tore furiously through the files in a four-drawer wooden filing cabinet, tossing some folders on the floor, riffling with nervous fingers through others. He had actually begun to shudder.

Here it was! Here . . . An order from the RSHA in Berlin. He stared at it. The paper was *not* the same. Not the same! My God!

XIII

TUESDAY NIGHT, JULY 18, 1944

BALDWIN gasped. The wraith they led into the office could not weigh more than 90 pounds. She would have been tiny at best, but now, starved and abused, she was but a specter of the nineteen-year-old girl he had been told to expect. Her round dark eyes were hollow, and they focused on him with apprehension. Her lips were cracked. Some kind of sore lay red and swollen on her jawline just ahead of her right ear. Her head was shaved; she hadn't a bristle of hair. Her clothing was nothing but a loose gray cotton dress, far too large for her—perhaps a prison uniform, perhaps just a rag that had been thrown at her sometime. Compassion stirred painfully in Baldwin. He ached to draw the girl into his arms and shelter her.

"So, the fourth Mercier. Maybe I should have interrogated her. It might have been more amusing than trying to thrash something out of her dried-up old father."

Baldwin glanced angrily at the man who had so callously spoken. He was a complicating factor. It was unhappy coincidence that he had been at Romainville tonight, interrogating a woman accused of Résistance activities. Kriminalinspektor Hans Gebel had also interrogated Henri Mercier for several weeks and was curious about the sudden interest the RSHA was taking in the family Mercier.

Kriminalinspektor Gebel, as he had often told Henri Mercier during their hours together, was a professional policeman; he had been transferred to the Geheime Staatspolizei, Gestapo, from the Prussian State Police shortly after the Gestapo was organized—and solely because it needed experienced professional investigators. Tonight he had stopped by this office before leaving the prison for two reasons: first, to notify the governor that he would arrange immediate execution for the woman he had been interrogating, second to have a glass of schnapps with Kleist, who seemed somehow to use his position to obtain some good things—like decent schnapps. He had been annoyed to find this gimpy obersturmbannführer from Berlin, with his oafish hauptsturmführer assistant and the vapid, busty blitzmädchen whose reason for being with them was unsubtly apparent.

The blitzmädchen was putting handcuffs on the Mercier girl, and she was awkward at even so simple a function as that.

They had brought the girl in just as Kleist was telling him about the inexplicable arrest of Oberführer Franck. That was beyond comprehension—beyond belief except that the word had been confirmed by Langbehn, who actually had Franck in custody at Fresnes and was subjecting him to routine processing into the status of prisoner. Something was strange about the whole business, Gebel thought.

"I suppose you can tell us nothing, Herr Obersturmbannführer."

Baldwin shook his head. "Nothing, Herr Kriminalinspektor."

"Von Strauch . . . ," Gebel said thoughtfully. "Oberführer von Strauch. The name is not familiar to me."

Adriana stiffened. It would be a serious error for Baldwin to try to invent an identity for Heinrici's Oberführer von Strauch.

Baldwin settled a condescending look on Gebel and faintly shrugged.

"Well, uh . . . Your prisoner, Herr Obersturmbannführer," said Kleist.

Baldwin nodded at the governor of the prison. "Thank you, Herr Kleist. We will be going then. Oberführer von Strauch was most emphatic about our returning to Le Bourget as soon as possible." He nodded then to Gebel. "A pleasure to meet you, Herr Kriminalinspektor."

Adriana took Jeanne Mercier by the arm and led her out of the office. Baldwin and Le Concombre followed. Adriana put her mouth close to the girl's ear and whispered in French—"We are from British Special Operations Executive. Keep quiet and keep walking."

The girl stiffened, glanced up at Adriana for an instant, then walked down the stairs with a resolute step.

They entered the prison yard. The old stone wall here did not surround the

prison. The missing parts of the circumference had been replaced with barbed
wire. The gate itself was of barbed wire, with a wooden guard tower to one
side. The Daimler was parked facing the gate.

Back in the office, Kriminalinspektor Gebel tapped his foot impatiently as the
telephone at his ear rang and rang.

"No answer," he said. "Not even from the guards who *must* be on duty." He
put down the telephone. "Now that is very strange."

"You can understand my reluctance to refuse to hand over the Jew girl," said
Kleist. "I suppose, after all, she couldn't be very important. If Oberführer
Franck had been brought into my office, I—"

The telephone rang.

"Kleist. Ah, yes, Langbehn." He listened. "You—are you *sure,* Langbehn?
Are you certain? *My God!"*

"What is it?" Gebel asked as Kleist put down the telephone.

"Langbehn compared his order from the RSHA with another recent order he
received from there. The paper is not the same. Not at all alike. He telephoned
Le Bourget Airport. The security officers on duty insist no SD officers arrived
there this evening, and there is no airplane waiting on the airport to take any SD
officers back to Berlin."

Gebel drew a small pistol from under his jacket. "They are still inside the
gate," he said. "Call your guards! I—" Without taking the time to finish, Gebel
turned and ran down the stairs.

The Daimler was moving toward the gate. Gebel shouted. Then he leveled
his pistol on the back of the car and fired. He was something of a marksman
with a pistol, always had been, and he noted with satisfaction that he had hit the
Daimler—the glass in the rear window shattered.

He took aim to fire again as the Daimler spun around. Good. He would fire at
the driver. But then he saw a Mauser machine pistol in the hands of Obersturmbannführer Heiden—or whoever he was—and he saw the Mauser jump and
spurt flame. His agony was brief.

The bullet that hit the Daimler had passed all the way through the car and
shattered the windshield as well—without hitting anyone. Le Concombre had
turned the car to give Baldwin his chance to shoot down the Gestapo man, and
now he swerved the other way, to give Baldwin and Adriana a clear shot at the
guard tower beside the gate.

Adriana shoved Jeanne Mercier to the floor. Now she thrust the second
Mauser through the window in the rear door and fired on the guard tower.
Baldwin fired a burst at the tower, too; splinters of wood flew from the flimsy
structure. No one moved in the tower. No fire was returned. Maybe there was
no guard there.

Le Concombre roared toward the gate. The big Daimler plowed into the asymmetrical structure, tore it loose from its posts, and reduced it to a tangled mass of wood and steel and barbed wire; but the car could not make it through the wreckage. Though Claude spun the wheels and threw dust and gravel back into the prison forecourt, the Daimler would not move forward. He jammed the car into reverse and backed away for another lunge.

The guard force had come to life. Bullets punched into the steel of the fenders and doors of the Daimler.

"Claude!" yelled Baldwin.

Le Concombre was slumped over the wheel. Hit by a bullet that had come through the left window, he gasped, gurgled, and fell silent.

"I can't drive," Baldwin shrieked.

Adriana was shoving a mew magazine into her Mauser. She set it on semi-automatic fire, shoved open the door, and rolled out onto the ground, muzzle up and firing single shots at the growing crowd of guards. Baldwin continued to fire bursts. She could see guards drop. They fell back. These were not German soldiers; they were SS prison guards, beer-gut bully boys, not used to shooting at people who shot back.

Adriana circled the car to the front and came up to the driver's-side door. Baldwin was pulling Claude over from behind the steering wheel. She stood erect and fired five quick shots toward the confusion of guards, then scrambled behind the wheel.

Throwing the car into first gear, Adriana shoved the accelerator to the floor. The Daimler leaped forward, tires screeching, and hit the tangled wreckage of the gate with all its mass. It broke through.

A car pulled out ahead of them. Baldwin fired a burst, and it swerved aside and crashed into a curb.

Hearing the crack of a pistol, Adriana looked around. The tiny French girl, though still handcuffed, had somehow gotten her hands on a pistol—maybe Claude's—and was firing through the rear window.

Adriana switched on the headlights. One of them was shot out. As she sped out of Romainville, she began to appraise their chances. Driving a—

"Claude is dead," said Baldwin.

The rendezvous point was the little Cimetière St. Vincent, on the north slope of Montmartre. Le Rasoir stopped to let them out—Heinrici, Henri Mercier, and Le Capitaine—and drove off with the Mercedes, to abandon it some distance away. Heinrici used a small tool to open the lock on the cemetery gate, and he led Henri Mercier inside, into the darkness of the old burial ground. The team from Romainville was not yet there, so Heinrici used the tool to open the wrought-iron gate of a small nineteenth-century mausoleum. The three men stooped to enter the square stone building. Heinrici closed the gate, and they descended four stone steps into the little burial chamber littered with leaves that had blown in on winter winds.

"My apologies for the accommodations," Monsieur Heinrici said. "I hope we don't have to wait here long."

Henri Mercier looked around the chamber. Even in the darkness he could see the stone shelves projecting from the walls, where once a family had placed vases of flowers. The burials were under the stone floors, under the leaves and a layer of dried mud. "I have come from a worse place," he said.

In spite of what he had suffered in the past two months, Henri Mercier had already begun to show his strength of character. In the car on the way from Fresnes he had been like a piece of crumpled paper unfolding of its own resiliency.

"It is like a dream," he had said to Heinrici as they sped north through Montparnasse. "It is like returning from a journey to a distant place. Already it is as though I had never been there but only dreamed of it. Except of course for..."

Heinrici silently completed the thought: that he had left his wife and son in that distant place.

In the shadows across the street Oberleutnant Dietrich Krueger peered into the darkness of the cemetery. He did not think he was wrong. No, three of the men from the Mercedes had entered the cemetery. Unless they had passed through it and out the opposite side, to Caulaincourt, they were still in there, and unless they were crouching among the stones, almost certainly they were inside one of the little mausoleums. He would wait. He had no choice. If they had left the cemetery, he had lost them.

On her hands and knees, Adriana crept along the wall, feeling the bricks, searching for the one that was loose, that she could pull out. The Daimler was behind her. Baldwin and Jeanne Mercier remained inside, anxiously staring into the darkness of the alley. In the rear seat with Jeanne, Baldwin had removed her handcuffs, and he was whispering to her a quick explanation of the Mauser machine pistols. The body of Claude, Le Concombre, lay on the front seat.

From Romainville Adriana had driven—at a normal speed, hoping not to attract attention—into the Nineteenth Arrondissement, the quarter called La Villette, through the dark, deserted streets of warehouses and small factories. After making two wrong turns, she had finally found the right street and had pulled the Daimler into the dark narrow alley that led to the loading dock at Galien et Fils. Now she was searching for the loose brick behind which Heinrici had left the key to the printing plant.

She was not sure what they could do if they got inside, but it was a refuge.

Certainly they could not remain on the streets: a blitzmädchen in a uniform soaked with blood, a crippled man in the uniform of the SS, and a tiny girl with no hair on her head. Certainly they could go no farther in the bullet-holed Daimler with a corpse in the front seat. Inside, they might not be much better off, but outside they were doomed.

Pushing brick after brick, she crawled along in the mud of the alley. God! How many bricks were there in twenty meters of wall? And in what course was the one brick she must find? The lowest? The second? The third? Already her fingertips were raw from pressing against rough bricks.

Baldwin had suggested she abandon him. Perhaps she would have to, later. But for now he was no impediment, no more than her own blood-soaked clothes, no more than the girl who was so conspicuously an escaped prisoner. None of them could pass a checkpoint. By now a description of them had been communicated to every security officer in the city, and since their operation had included the kidnapping of an SS general, the search was undoubtedly frenzied.

Jeanne Mercier knelt beside her. "Can I help?"

"Yes, you—Wait."

Adriana had found the loose brick. She tugged it out and thrust her hand eagerly into the hole. The key was there. She jerked it out with a triumphant snort and rose to her feet.

They left the body of Claude in the car; they had no choice. They carried their weapons, though, into the printing plant. Inside, they were confronted immediately with the glaring electric torch of the German guard. Adriana shot him. That was something else about which she had no choice. The shot rang through the building, but it raised no alarm. She took the guard's electric torch and still another Mauser machine pistol.

She led Baldwin and Jeanne into one of the offices and told them to sit down and wait while she explored the building.

Krueger took a chance. He walked around into Caulaincourt and found a telephone kiosk from which he could call General Hausser.

"It went very differently at Romainville," the general told him after he listened to his report. "They shot their way out of there, killed a Gestapo agent and three SS guards. I had Hals out there, doing the same thing you were doing. They fired on him, damaged his car, and he was not able to follow them. Right now I have a hell of a job in front of me—explaining what Leutnant Hals was doing at Romainville tonight. Oberführer Franck is back in the city, deranged with anger, and he has alerted the whole police appartatus. Frankly, Krueger, we don't dare let anyone suspect we know anything about this."

"My orders, Herr General?"

"Stay where you are. I'll send two men to support you. Don't tell them

anything, just that we want to follow the men who are hiding in that cemetery
—*may* be hiding in that cemetery—and don't want to lose them. Don't let
Heinrici see you."

In the gloom of the little mausoleum, Heinrici sat beside Henri Mercier in the
dry leaves on the floor. They had talked for some time and had left unspoken
the thought that dominated their minds: that the team from Romainville was
long overdue and had probably failed. Heinrici told Mercier of the Allied invasion of Normandy, of which Mercier had heard nothing. He explained to him
that he himself was an Abwehr officer who was now working for Special Operations Executive. He mentioned the name of Colonel Sir Henry Harding, which
meant nothing to Mercier.

"My wife . . . ," said Mercier. "Is there any possibility she could be returned?"

"We did not feel we could undertake an effort to free her until we had accomplished your own rescue. Now . . ." He shrugged. "Now it may be possible
to—well, to try, anyway."

"And my daughter," said Mercier glumly. "How long do we wait here, Monsieur?"

"For myself, I will wait all night," Heinrici said. "As for you, we have a
refuge waiting for you. It might be well if you go there now, before curfew."

"I would rather wait here," said Mercier.

"No," said Adriana firmly. "We don't dare carry weapons."

"And we have no papers," said Baldwin pessimistically. "Without papers,
without weapons . . . on the streets of Paris on a night when their patrols must be
fanatically alert—"

"Have you a better idea?" Adriana demanded.

Baldwin shook his head.

Adriana had discovered that Galien et Fils kept a washing and dressing room,
where the printers took off their ink-stained work clothes, washed up, and
dressed in their street clothes. Two dozen suits of inky blue coveralls hung from
pegs. Two dozen odd-shaped workingmen's caps, also stained with ink, were
scattered on the benches in the room. She used shears from one of the press
rooms to cut short the legs and arms of one suit of coveralls, so they would not
hang beyond Jean's hands and feet. An inky cap covered Jeanne's bald head.
Adriana had tucked her own hair up into a cap. Now, as they were about to
leave, she was smudging their faces with an inky rag.

"Something else," she said. She had found a half-empty bottle of red wine in
the biggest pressroom. "We may want to look a little drunk."

It would have been pointless to lock the entrance doors to Galien et Fils, though Adriana did take the time to run around into the alley to hide the key once again.

For a moment she stopped beside the Daimler and stared at the body of Claude. Her eyes filled with tears, and she choked. "God rest you, Claude." For a moment she leaned against the car and fought for control. She had no time. She had to move.

They had three quarters of an hour, a little less, to reach the Cimetière St. Vincent before curfew. Fortunately, it was only a few meters from the Caulaincourt Métro Station. It had been part of the plan from the beginning that they might have to travel by Métro. They had seen a station as she drove around looking for the printing plant. It was not far to walk, and they set out.

The station, they found, was called Crimée. It was all but deserted, and they were able to take the time to study the system map on the wall. They would have to change trains twice to reach the Caulaincourt station, they found. But what else could they do?

A couple of half-asleep German guards paid no one any attention in the Crimée station, and they boarded the train without difficulty. In the pre-curfew hours, no one but weary, half-sodden workers dozed in the cars on the Porte-de-la-Villette Line. They rode just two stations, changed without incident to a train on the Porte-Dauphine Line, and rode in a somewhat more crowded car to the Pigalle station.

The dimly lighted Pigalle station was crowded with people hurrying to reach home before the curfew. Many of them had remained at work or at their revels until the last possible moment, and their anxiety was multiplied when they entered the station and found it tightly controlled by a score of black-uniformed SS soldiers and a dozen harried gendarmes—plus God-knew-how-many alert plainclothesmen. Although they were not examining the documents of everyone who boarded or left a train, they were scrutinizing everyone and calling many aside for identity checks. Harried, fretful people jostled for access to the platforms.

Baldwin grabbed Adriana's arm. "They will be looking for a man who walks with a cane!"

She seized his cane and shoved it into the corner between a wall and a trash bin. "Then you won't walk with one."

"Adriana!" he gasped.

He had begun already to stumble, and she thrust her shoulder under his arm and supported him. Jeanne, seeing the idea, pressed against him from the other side.

"The wine, Len!"

He pulled the half-empty bottle from the deep pocket of his blue coveralls, tossed away the cork, and threw himself into the role of the drunken workingman. Exaggerating his limp, he let the two young women lead him through the throngs in the station and into the swarm of SS soldiers and gendarmes.

Adriana glanced up into Baldwin's face. In spite of her support under his arm, he was compelled to put more weight on his damaged leg than it was accustomed to bear; with each lurching step he winced visibly. Beads of sweat appeared on his forehead. Still, he played the drunk bravely, swaying, muttering, brandishing his bottle. Jeanne, conscious of his pain, tried to carry more of his weight. She was not tall enough or strong enough to carry much; she stumbled and was little help, and they staggered forward, in hazard of sprawling on the station floor.

"*Sing!*" Adriana hissed.

Baldwin nodded, hesitated for a moment, then in a mockery of drunken bravado, he sang gutturally,

Rule, Britannia!
Britannia, rule the waves!

The SS soldiers in black uniforms observed the drunken Frenchman with Teutonic contempt. The French policemen watched him with some suspicion but accepted the Germans' judgment. At pains to mime the tolerant apprentice helping the journeyman, Adriana could not search the faces of the perhaps-Gestapo men who watched the swaying trio reel through the station. Her own legs were almost as weak as Baldwin's, and she marveled at the courage of Jeanne Mercier, who had to be weak from hunger and abuse.

Jeanne knew the Métro. She had been riding it all her life. She knew how to find the platform. She nudged them between two Schmeisser-armed SS sergeants and onto the platform marked *Pte. de la Chapelle.*

"*Trunken Französich Schwein,*" grunted one of the sergeants. Baldwin belched and mimed the iminence of an eruption of vomit. "*Schnell!*" the German growled. Hurry up!

Baldwin groaned as they made their way down the platform. It was agony for him to put down most of his weight on the leg—which he had to do, in spite of Adriana's best efforts. He gasped and wiped sweat from his face with the sleeve of his coveralls.

"Almost, Len," Adriana whispered to him. "A few minutes more."

Jeanne wiped his forehead with the tips of her fingers. "A few more minutes," she repeated.

The northbound train rumbled into the station. It was twelve minutes until the curfew. People rushed the doors, but, as people will, they shrunk away from the ink-stained, reeling drunk. They let his two dirty apprentices steer him onto the train.

* * *

"Silence!"

The two young officers sent by General Hausser were altogether too eager, and Oberleutnant Krueger had to restrain them. "Keep quiet. We are dealing with people who have repeatedly eluded surveillance, and it is not impossible that those are the English operatives."

Three Frenchmen, clad in baggy blue workingmen's coveralls, staggered around the corner from the Caulaincourt station and into Rue St. Vincent. They were drunk—or pretending to be—and they were within three minutes of being curfew violators. There were no patrols around here, Krueger had observed during his hours of waiting; if these Frenchmen lived nearby they would reach home after curfew, without being arrested.

"Even if they are English," Krueger whispered to his two young officers, "we let them go on with what they are doing. We are looking for a particular Frenchman, and it is *him* we will follow if we see him and can identify him."

The three made it plain in a minute that they were not just three French workingmen. They stopped at the cemetery gate. As midnight arrived and the curfew settled on the city, they waited at the gate, in no hurry to move on, waiting for—waiting for what?

"Papa!"

Jeanne Mercier threw herself into her father's arms and wept like a child— like the child she really was, Baldwin thought as he dropped gratefully to the soft wet ground and relieved his leg of the torturing stress.

"Claude was killed," Adriana told Heinrici and Le Capitaine. "They started shooting at us just as we were leaving. Something happened. I don't know what. There was a Gestapo agent in the governor's office, and he ran after us and fired at the car with a pistol. Then all the guards started shooting."

"Where have you been?" Heinrici asked. "Where did . . . ?" He gestured at the coveralls.

"Galien et Fils," she said. "Your loose brick. The key. And we came here on the Métro."

"Resourceful," said Heinrici.

Adriana shrugged. Whatever had driven her had ebbed now, and she felt leaden. "Claude . . . ," she whispered. She sobbed.

Heinrici gestured toward Mercier. "A brave man, Adriana," he said. "I told him we could arrange to hide him in a safe home until the Allies come, or maybe he and his daughter could be taken to London until the war is over. He refuses anything like that. He says he has obligations in Paris and will not leave."

Adriana put her arms around Heinrici. "Of course," she said. "As soon as

I can, I will send word to Colonel Harding. You've done everything you committed yourself to do, Konrad. I know Len agrees. Radio Heinrici . . . is dead."

Heinrici held her close to him. "We can begin to think about our own lives now," he said.

"Soon," she said. "We've got to help Henri Mercier— Anyway, Len and I do. Then I have no more obligation—"

He kissed her. "I was afraid I had lost you," he said. Then he glanced at the Merciers. "We must get them to the flat in rue Cortot. Then—" He paused, smiled wryly. "I can hardly take you back to the Royal Monceau dressed like that. But my room over the butcher shop . . ."

She nodded. "It's after midnight. Get them to rue Cortot—"

"Yes," he said. He turned and walked back to the Merciers. "Monsieur, Mademoiselle. We have a safe place for you. It is nearby."

Henri Mercier held his daughter close, bud at Heinrici. "We will be grateful to be taken there."

Le Capitaine approached Adriana. "Claude . . . ?"

She sighed. "He died well, Théo. And quickly."

"And how many Boches?"

"I don't know," she whispered, shaking her head. "Two for certain. Probably more."

Le Capitaine drew a deep breath and looked at the Merciers, father and daughter. "I hope they are worth what they have cost and are going to cost," he said bitterly.

"It is possible," she said, "that Henri Mercier will be able to save hundreds of lives."

With a hand on his arm, Heinrici led Henri Mercier toward the gate onto rue St. Vincent. Jeanne clung to her father and walked with him.

"Adriana and I will take Monsieur and Mademoiselle Mercier to the house on rue Cortot," he said to Le Capitaine. "You help Len. Since it's after curfew, and he's without his walking stick, it might be well if you wait in the mausoleum until morning. No one is going to move far tonight without meeting a patrol."

Le Capitaine nodded. "We're safe enough here—if one doesn't mind sleeping in a tomb."

"*Bonne chance,* Théo," Heinrici said. Then he squatted beside Baldwin. "Well done, Len. I suggest you stay off the streets for a couple of days at least. Your SOE contacts will arrange your return to London now. Right?"

Baldwin shook his head. "We are ordered to stay in Paris until it is liberated. We are to do whatever we can to help Henri Mercier save lives."

Heinrici sighed and stood. "I am sure the liberation will come soon."

With Adriana and Henri Mercier and Jeanne, Heinrici stepped through the
gate and onto Rue St. Vincent.

Oberleutnant Krueger nudged one of his young officers. "We follow. But
carefully. They must not suspect."

He recognized Oberst Heinrici leading the group. The white-haired man behind him had to be Henri Mercier. The two smaller figures in workingmen's
coveralls . . . Well, possibly they were the Mercier daughter and the Dutchwoman. Heinrici led them along the fence toward the intersection of rue des
Saules.

"'*Alt!*'"

A black-uniformed patrol came trotting out of the darkness of rue des Saules.
An officer and three helmeted soldiers, they wore rubber-soled boots that had
allowed them to march quietly down the hill toward the Cimetière St. Vincent.
Their short, ugly weapons—Schmeisser submachine guns—were leveled on
Heinrici and his group.

Krueger seized the younger of his two officers by the sleeve and jerked him
into the cover of a doorway. The Heinrici connection would be bad enough;
General Hausser should not have to explain the presence of three more Abwehr
officers at the periphery of whatever Heinrici was doing.

The SS patrol lined up facing Heinrici, weapons aimed at him. An officer
stepped boldly forward. "I am Oberführer Ulrich von Strauch," Krueger heard
Heinrici say to the SS officer. Then his voice dropped to conversational level as
he stood and talked with the SS officer, and Krueger could not hear what was
said. The exchange seemed to be angry.

"*Herr Oberleutnant!*" hissed one of the junior officers behind Krueger. He
was pointing at the fence of the Cimetière St. Vincent, where two of Heinrici's
group had begun to edge away. With the attention of the patrol focused on
Heinrici's confrontation with the SS officer, the two used the darkness to their
advantage; they slipped along the fence and turned the corner into rue des
Saules, all but invisible dark figures against the dark background of the fence
and cemetery.

Krueger stiffened with anger. He could not run after the two—and he had no
doubt they were the Merciers. The clumsy SS patrol had interfered at the wrong
moment. Even Heinrici seemed unaware that the two Jews he had rescued were
escaping him.

The third figure left at the fence became aware of it. That one—the second
of the overall-clad figures—tried to follow, but . . .

"'*Alt!*'"

The third figure stopped, hands up. And in the confusion the first two ran
across rue des Saules and into another street. The SS officer yelled, two soldiers

of the patrol ran off after the Merciers, and the officer and Heinrici began shouting at each other.

Krueger listened for bursts of fire. When he heard none, he concluded that the two soldiers had run down the old man and the girl and recaptured them. The officer in command of the patrol swung abruptly away from Heinrici and the Dutchwoman and led the rest of his patrol at a trot into the street where his two soldiers had run.

XIV

WEDNESDAY, JULY 19,1944

ADRIANA lay on her back on the great brass bed in Heinrici's room above the butcher shop.

"It's all gone to hell," she grieved. "Claude . . . Why *Claude,* of all of us? And for *nothing,* from the look of it. That goddamned patrol! The Merciers . . . After all—"

"We don't know they caught them, Adriana," Heinrici said gently. "In fact, I don't think they did."

He had gone along the hall to the bathroom for a basin of water—cold water, it had to be—and was washing the ink off her face. The smudges were indistinct in the faint moonlight that had broken through murky clouds and was filtering into the room, but with his right hand he dabbed gently at the shadows around her face, while with the left he caressed her naked breasts and legs.

"Do you really think there's a chance they got away? Even if they did . . . On the streets . . . After curfew . . . " She shook her head. "What chance could they have?"

Heinrici shrugged. "Very little, I suppose."

Adriana sighed. "That tiny girl," she said. "So hurt! So abused . . . She told me on the Métro she's probably pregnant. And do you realize that Len may have reinjured his leg? So much courage from everyone. And then . . . Mercier. Why did he have to run? Couldn't he see you had the situation under control? *Why did he have to run?"*

"Simple enough," Heinrici said. "He thought he would be rearrested. He would rather die than go back to a Gestapo prison. He would rather take any chance than face that. And he made the same decision for his daughter."

"We weren't arrested. We—Konrad, what in God's name did you *say* to that SS officer?"

Heinrici kissed her cheek and ear. "When I was at university I took a little training in dramatics. I lie well."

"I know you do. But what did you say to him?"

"I told him he was interfering with an SD operation. The character of Ober-führer von Strauch served us one last time. When the Merciers walked away, I told him he was a stupid, meddling fool, that he was letting my prisoners escape. I really *was* angry. I frightened him. And he really was a fool. Before I could stop him, he set out to recapture my prisoners for me."

"And he probably did, too," she said dejectedly.

"In fact, he probably didn't," Heinrici said. "He would have brought them back. I think the Merciers got away from him."

"Suppose that's true. Then where would they go?"

"I don't know," he said. "They are lifelong residents of Paris. Maybe they knew where to go. Maybe they knew of a refuge for Jews, somewhere not far from where we were."

"We must find out, Konrad," she whispered hoarsely. "Tomorrow you must find out if they are in a Gestapo prison again. If they are . . ." She shook her head. "If they are, it has all been for nothing."

Adriana rose from the bed and stood at the window, looking out at the moon-lit city. Heinrici finished underessing and came to stand behind her, pressing his naked body against hers. She turned and raised her face to be kissed.

He kissed her, pushing his tongue through her lips and between her teeth. He was already erect, but now his shaft pulsed against her belly, where she could feel it: engorged and warm and wet. She reached down for it. She cupped his warm, rough scrotum in her hand, marveling again at its bulk. Her other hand pressed the back of his head, as if she were afraid he would stop kissing her.

"Konrad . . ."

"Adriana."

"Now, Konrad. Now and any time. Especially tonight! Make me feel a part of . . . Make me a part of life, not death. Bring me—"

He put his hand gently over her mouth and guided her toward the bed. She climbed onto it and stretched out on her back. He followed her and straddled her.

Adriana gasped as he entered her. "Konrad," she whispered. "No rubber sheath? You don't have any here?"

They had always used rubber sheaths when he entered her in the hotel room. Here he had none, and he shook his head.

Adriana moaned. "I don't care. Come into me, Konrad! Come into me! Do it! Do it all!"

"Rue Boulanger," said Sidonie. "Number 48, rue Boulanger, here on the Butte. I followed them. It was easy. Not far. He rapped on the door. Someone let him in."

Heinrici sat in the little parlor, nibbling on the bread and marmalade put on the table by Marie Ange. Papa smoked his pipe and sipped from the good Viennese coffee Mama had brewed.

"Your men did well, Papa," Heinrici said. "Did they have any idea why they were doing it?"

"None of them," mumbled Papa, his words broken by the pipestem resting on his lower lip. "They took their pay and asked no questions."

"You fox." Heinrici chuckled. "You said you could not get me Schmeissers."

"You want a Schmeisser?" Papa asked with a grin. "Mama. Bring Philippe a machine gun."

Marie did not have to leave the room. She squatted behind the couch and pulled out a Schmeisser submachine gun—made of wood. Papa laughed.

Heinrici laughed, too. "Don't do it in daylight, Papa," he said. "The stupidest flic would have seen the uniforms were fake—even if the wooden Schmeissers were good enough to fool me."

"You had other guests on rue St. Vincent, Philippe," Papa said. "Three of them. Boches, wearing gray uniforms. Watching from doorways across the street."

"Did they see where the Merciers went?" Heinrici asked.

Papa shook his head. "Your Jews ran through rue Paul Feval, then up the steps. They know the area, you can be sure."

Heinrici nodded. "The gold can't be far away," he said. "Montmartre must be their headquarters."

"How lucky," said Sidonie. "And how lucky you were last night. If they had not run, then what?"

"Then Papa's men would have arrested them," said Heinrici. "And shortly we would have faked an escape. I really did plan on their spending a night in the flat in the rue Cortot. That the old man ran was a piece of good luck."

"It was lucky I was waiting to follow them," said Sidonie.

"I would not have had it otherwise," said Heinrici. "You were an essential element of the plan, Sidonie."

"Just what I always wanted to be," she said. "An essential part of a plan."

"The time has come," said Heinrici, "to concentrate on the gold. No one but us. The four of us. I don't trust anyone else. The three of you must watch the house at 48 rue Boulanger. Who comes? Who goes? How do a man and woman who have no ration cards get their food?"

"We divide—" Sidonie began.

"We," snapped Heinrici firmly. "However much there is. Or if there is none."

"What about the woman who's asleep in your bed?"

Heinrici laughed. "I want your clothes, Sidonie," he said with a grin. "Now. For her. So I can take her back to the Royal Monceau."

"Leaving me sitting here naked?" Sidonie scoffed. "Anyway, I paid—"

"You'll be paid ten thousand times over," said Heinrici. "If we get our hands on the gold."

"If . . . ?"

"We'll get it," Heinrici said firmly. "Right now, we have an insuperable advantage. We know where the Merciers are. The SOE doesn't know. The Résistance doesn't know. The Gestapo doesn't know. The Abwehr doesn't know. But *we* know. You have someone watching 48 rue Boulanger?"

Papa puffed on his pipe. "Of course. And this morning I am going to rent a little flat across the street, the one at 53 rue Boulanger. The family who lived there has been deported. Sidonie will move in. From her window she can see the door at 48. I will sit in her window sometimes. Mama will sit. Maybe sometimes even you, Philippe. The house at 48 is owned, incidentally, by a family named Pascin. Jews. But they have been exempted from the Jew laws."

"I am going to go and visit Monsieur Mercier," Heinrici said. "He and I have much to discuss."

General Hausser offered a cigar. Heinrici, in uniform, with his Iron Cross at his throat, crossed his legs. If the general offered a cigar, then maybe the interview would not be as severe as Heinrici had feared.

"So. Henri Mercier. Where is he, Konrad?"

"I'm afraid I don't know at the moment, Herr General. Just as I was about to take him to a flat I had prepared for him and his daughter, an SS patrol appeared, and while I was engaged in ridding myself of an interfering fool of an untersturmführer the Merciers slipped away into the night."

"Then we have lost Mercier and we've lost the gold," said the general calmly. "Have we not?" It was apparent to Heinrici that General Hausser already knew about the encounter with the SS patrol and suspected nothing.

"Not necessarily," Heinrici said. "I may be able to find them. After all, how far can they have run?"

"You will be lucky if the Gestappo doesn't find them first," said General Hausser. "The search is . . . Heinrici, I have never seen one more intense. I am appalled, frankly, by how bloody your escape plot turned out to be. A senior kriminalinspektor of the Gestapo was killed at Romainville—together with four SS guards. Eight more were wounded. The automobile used by the escape gang was found abandoned in an alley in the La Villette quarter, with a dead Frenchman in it. The gang broke into a printing plant there and killed the German soldier who was guarding the plant. And . . . Well, I suppose I'm telling you nothing."

"That was the SOE group, Herr General. No one was killed at Fresnes, where I was in command."

"So—" The General stopped and grinned. "So *you* were Oberführer Ulrich von Strauch!"

Heinrici nodded.

General Hausser laughed as he paused to light his cigar and then to hand the lighter to Heinrici. Quickly he suppressed his laugh. "You should have killed Franck," he said. "Better than to risk his identifying you."

"I could make you a little wager, Herr General," said Heinrici. "We won't, of course, take the risk, but I would wager that if Franck walked into this office right now, he would not recognize me. He would sit down and smoke a cigar with us, and he would not make the connection between Heinrici and Strauch."

"Were you wearing some sort of disguise?"

Heinrici shrugged. "I darkened my hair a bit. That's all. Even without that, he still wouldn't know me. I've had the experience more than once."

"I wouldn't risk it," the general said glumly. "In fact, Heinrici, I think you should leave Paris. I will have you transferred. Perhaps to Berlin."

"May I suggest, Herr General, that you don't do that until the English have agreed not to compromise me through Radio Heinrici."

General Hausser drew on his cigar, frowned, and pondered this for a moment. "So. Have you spoken to them about that?"

"They are not satisfied. They want my help in finding the Merciers."

"They want the gold."

"I am sure they do. Of course, they haven't mentioned it to me."

"Don't risk an encounter with Oberführer Franck, Heinrici," said the general. "Stay away from places where he might be. Also Langbehn. What is more, you have very little time. Things are going badly. Rommel has been severely injured—his car was strafed, and it went in a ditch. He will not be able to return to command for months. The English have broken through our lines east of Caen. Until now we had held the Allied armies rather close to the Channel, in spite of the fact that they must have forty divisions ashore. Now they have bombed Caen out of existence. We've taken heavy casualties, lost hundreds of tanks. It is doubtful our armies can continue to hold. Once the English or Americans break out . . ." The general shook his head. "Paris . . . They could be here within days."

* * *

In the house at 48 rue Boulanger, Henri Mercier sat at a round table covered with a fringed red cloth, in a conspicuously bourgeois parlor—overstuffed chairs and sofa upholstered in red plush, cane-bottom chairs around the table, polished wooden floor scattered with worn rugs, red-flowered wallpaper above gray wainscoting. The fringed red drapes pulled across the tall window to shut off any view by the neighbors across the street also out shut out most of the daylight, leaving the room quite dim. Mercier noted that anything that might have suggested the family were Jews—the Menorah that had always sat on the mantel above the little fireplace, books, even the silver wine cups—had been removed.

He munched on bread and cheese and sipped red wine. He had eaten twice already today, but the hunger would not go away. He had bathed and shaved, and his hair had been clipped, somewhat inexpertly, by Louise Pascin. Jacob Pascin had offered him clothes from his own closet: underwear, shirt, socks, shoes, a gray suit. Nothing was quite big enough, but the clothes were intact and clean, and they made him feel like a person again.

Jeanne sat across the table from him, also hungrily eating bread and cheese. Louise had taken care of her: bathed her, put a healing salve on the sore on the side of her face, dressed her in the only clothes in the house that would fit her—a boy's white shirt and a pair of green corduroy trousers that had been their son's. Louise had offered a wool cap for her head, but Jeanne shook her head and said no; everyone knew she was bald, and she saw no point in hiding it.

"We know you are making a great sacrifice to supply us so generously with food," Mercier said to Jacob Pascin.

"Eat all you want," Pascin said. "It is the least we can do for you. And don't worry. One has resources."

Before the occupation Jacob Pascin had been a diamond cutter for Van Cleef & Arpels; he was also a designer and fabricator of custom-made jewelry. His skills were esteemed by the Germans, and they had exempted him from most of the ordeal of being a Jew in Paris during the occupation. He was not required to wear the yellow star. He could buy in any store, even eat in a restaurant if he could afford it. So could his wife and son. They lived, of course, at the whim of the functionaries who had given them their exemptions and who could withdraw them at any time. Even so, Jacob Pascin had involved himself in the effort to save Jews from deportation. What was more, he had opened his door last night.

"I never thought to see a decent home again," said Mercier. "Kindly people . . ." He lost his voice for an instant and looked at his daughter. "I am afraid to ask what abuses she suffered."

"Don't think about it, Papa," Jeanne said quietly.

"My son . . . ," Mercier whispered. He shook his head. "And my wife. It is better to think of him. He is dead. She is . . ." He sobbed.

Jeanne began to cry quietly. Louise stepped behind her and embraced her. Pascin went to Mercier and put a hand on his shoulder.

"I would not want," said Pascin, "to offer you any false hope, but I can tell you the news is good. The Nazis' world is falling down around them—at long last. For a while we were afraid the Allies had been stopped in Normandy and would never break out—that it might become trench war, like before. But the English and Americans have broken the line. They may come as fast as the Germans did in 1940. Also, the Allies are bombing unmercifully. They even managed to kill Feldmarschall Rommel. It could be that the war will end soon and—"

"And prisoners will be freed," said Mercier. "Or all will be killed."

Pascin shook his head. "Big transports," he said. "Mass deportations. Last week someone blew up the bridge over the canal by the Pantin Station and delayed the trains. But what we feared—"

Jacob Pascin sighed. He removed his round, gold-rimmed glasses, breathed on them, and began to rub them with a white handkerchief. His complexion was pink and shiny, his yellowish gray hair wavy, his face habitually long and solemn. Mercier was accustomed to think of him as unimaginative, though he had learned to respect his courage. Louise Pascin was a stylish, dark-haired woman, often outspoken, possibly the source of Jacob's courage. Mercier had guessed in the past that a man would regret disappointing Louise.

Henri Mercier stuffed a bite of cheese into his mouth, recovering as Heinrici had seen him recover last night. "The fund?" he asked.

"Intact," Pascin said. "We have used a little. But only a little. We didn't know where to go."

"I confess my error, Jacob," said Mercier. "I should have confided more. It was arrogant of me to keep everything to myself."

"We have little time," said Jacob Pascin. "There are rumors that every Jew in SS custody will be deported before the city falls to the Allied armies. Besides, there are new arrests every day. Even people who have been left alone are afraid. I myself . . ."

"You are of the exempt class."

Pascin shrugged. "Who cares about precious stones today? I split a fantastic diamond last week. Who knows when I'll see another one?"

"He created a magnificent bracelet for the wife of a German general," Louise said. "Based on that diamond. Designed the setting. Surrounded the diamond with emeralds. The woman was ecstatic."

"Yes," said Pascin. "They think I serve better splitting small precious stones than splitting big ones in a concentration camp. At least for now."

"Who blew out the bridge at Pantin?" asked Mercier.

"God knows. No one who communicates with us."

"When will another train go?"

"One would have gone Friday. Because of the bridge, that one didn't go. And the cars have been moved away. Maybe they are hauling troops. This Friday? Likely. And next. They are moving Résistants, too. Hundreds of them. But worse—children, Henri. There are maybe two hundred children in their custody—children whose parents are dead or . . . worse. There is a rumor that they are going to deport those children. All of them."

"Soulange," Mercier said decisively. "We must contact Soulange."

"Soulange is dead," said Madame Pascin.

"Sybil?"

"Sybil is dead."

Mercier glanced at his daughter, who regarded him with wide eyes.

Until last night, Jeanne had not known that her father was involved in saving Jews from deportation. She had thought of her brother as a hero of the Résistance, her father as a prosaic man whose principles extended only to honesty in business, care in accumulating money, and supporting his family in comfort.

For the moment Henri Mercier disregarded his daughter's newfound admiration. His glance at her had been one of anxiety and sympathy.

"The English contact," said Pascin. "We have not been able to —"

"Without Sybil . . ." Mercier interrupted. He shrugged. "Without Soulange. Of course we can reestablish, but it will take time. I can't go out. It must be done by you and others. And we have little time."

"The SOE team that achieved the prison break last night," said Pascin. "Surely they—"

"They were under the guns of an SS patrol when Jeanne and I were able to break away," said Mercier.

"That was unbelievably good fortune," said Pascin.

"You have used a good word, Jacob," said Mercier. "A good word. 'Unbelievable.' I have thought about it. It is difficult to think it was an accident. The coincidence was somehow . . . *too much* good fortune. Two of us escaped. Two did not. It had about it an element of . . . efficiency. Cleverness. Just as did the ruse at Fresnes. That man—the one who commanded. German, he said he was. Clever. Efficient. He put a mark on his work. I hazard a guess that we will see him again."

Baldwin lay on a cot in Le Faussaire's little shop under the cinema in Montparnasse. Upstairs, a movie was running. At his bench, Le Faussaire squinted over a document and experimented with techniques for duplicating it.

Le Capitaine had brought Baldwin here when at last they thought it safe to emerge from the little mausoleum. Baldwin was still dressed as an ink-stained printer, Le Capitaine still as an SS hauptsturmführer. Le Capitaine had put handcuffs on Baldwin and moved him from Montmartre to Montparnasse as an injured prisoner, in a vélo-taxi. They had passed through a security check without difficulty.

It was true, though, that Baldwin's leg had been injured. One of the deep scars had begun to bleed, and when Le Capitaine and Le Faussaire split his coveralls, they saw blood, both fresh and dried. Le Faussaire had sent for a doctor. Le Capitaine went out on some mission of his own, and Baldwin remained alone with the forger, lying on the narrow, lumpy cot, leg throbbing, weak from pain, afraid of infection. Le Faussaire had offered him calvados. The strong apple brandy had not relieved the pain, but it had eased Baldwin's anxiety a little.

"The German colonel," Le Faussaire said casually, as if only to make conversation. "I knew him. Years ago."

"You knew Heinrici?" Baldwin asked. "When? Where?"

"I thought I recognized him at first. Then I decided I didn't. Finally I realized I had been right the first time." Le Faussaire crushed a cigarette in the pan on his workbench. "He's a forger, like me."

"What do you mean?"

"Before the war," Le Faussaire said. "He was playing the Frenchman then. I can't remember what name he used. I suppose he was a German spy, now that I think of it. He worked for a printing company, one that printed government documents. He stole official paper."

"Of course," Baldwin said, staring at the grimy ceiling where pipes and wires were festooned with cobwebs. "He was a spy. Documents—"

"Documents the Germans couldn't have used," said Le Faussaire. "He was in it for profit. He was good, too. There aren't very many of us. Good forgers, I mean. That's why I'm sure. Remember, he told me to smudge my stamps. A nice touch, that."

"In the service of his country . . ."

Le Faussaire shook his head. "Maybe. But in his own service, too. We were called gangsters in the thirties. Before the other war, they called us apaches. Our kind always find ways to survive, to make money, to live better than other people. Always."

"Your documents worked perfectly last night," said Baldwin. "And if you are being paid for them, I don't know it. You can take credit for saving many lives."

Le Faussaire shrugged. "The Boches are shooting hostages all over town. I'm glad I'm down here. I don't know if I'd want to go on the street."

Baldwin closed his eyes. The room turned and swayed. Le Faussaire went on talking, but his words came from a distance: as vivid as before, each one, but no longer connected into meaning.

"Len!"

He looked up into the face of Adriana.

"A doctor will be here shortly. Le Capitaine will be back. I've seen Raymond. He got rid of the Mercedes. Everything is all right except . . . Do you know?"

"Know what?"

"The Merciers disappeared last night. After we left the cemetery, we ran into an SS patrol. While Konrad was arguing with the SS officer and getting rid of him, the Merciers slipped away in the darkness. We have no idea where they are."

"God . . . ," he murmured. "Recaptured."

"Maybe not," she said. "Konrad thinks not."

"If they were, everything was for nothing," he said weakly.

Adriana sighed and nodded.

"And if they weren't, we've got to find them. We've got to be sure they make contact with the people who need that gold. That was our whole purpose in coming here. Our job is not finished until—" He settled back, exhausted. "Not just two . . . ," he gasped. *"Many . . ."*

"Len," said Adriana, "I think we have an obligation to see to it that Konrad is released from Colonel Harding's threat."

"I've been watching for treachery," said Baldwin. "Haven't you? If it's there, I'm missing it somewhere."

"We've put our lives in his hands, Len," Adriana said soberly. "In his hands . . . If he wanted to—"

"No," Baldwin interrupted. "He doesn't want to. He has passed up every chance."

"I want to send the signal, Len. As soon as possible. Can you make the necessary contact?"

He nodded. "The people who supplied the money and the Mausers."

"They have a radio?"

"Yes. And an operator."

She seized his arm. "We have to send the signal," she said. "Today if possible, Len. If you can't, then you must let me do it."

"Tomorrow maybe," he said. "Soon enough."

Adriana tightened her grip on his arm. "No. Today. God knows what Colonel Harding is hearing. I don't trust him, Len. I mean, I don't trust his judgment. Given some odd signal from some source not well informed, he might . . . Len, we can't risk Konrad's life."

Baldwin looked up, frowning. "You love the man, don't you?" he said.

She lowered her eyes, then raised them directly to his. "Yes. Yes, I do. Can you understand?"

Baldwin smiled. "Entirely," he murmured.

"Who do I contact? How do I signal Colonel Harding?"

Baldwin glanced at Le Faussaire, who was bent over his workbench, making a determined effort not to pay attention to them. "Lean down." She bent over Baldwin. "Within two blocks of Gestapo headquarters on avenue Foch. On rue Guillaume. Number 12. Ring the bell marked 'Flandrine.' The man who comes to the door, a white-haired old man, is Monsieur Martin. Tell him you are David Bradford. Don't say David sent you or anything like that—say you *are* David Bradford. He will question you—who you are, where you were trained, and so on. Once he is satisfied, he will accept a message for transmission to London. Another test is that it will be correctly coded. Ask Le Faussaire for paper."

"Monsieur," she said to the forger. "A piece of paper, please. And a pen."

She sat hunched over Baldwin, conscious of his pain, while he told her how to code the message to London. They agreed on the text:

45-45-2030. MISSION HAS HALF FAILED. BETRAYED BY AMERICAN SERGEANT. URGE HE BE HANGED. PRIEST AND SON WITH US, BUT KNOW WHERE IRON IS, HOWEVER, SO IMPOSSIBLE OVERALL PURPOSE CAN BE ACHIEVED. EXPECT ARREST. DAVID. BATHSHEBA. 2030-45-45. ZQACTRD

Translated, it meant—"The mission is a partial success. The German colonel was loyal to us, and we recommend that he be released from his obligation. Henri Mercier and his daughter are missing. We do not know where the gold is but it is possible Mercier will use it for the purpose we had in mind. We are in no imminent danger of arrest. Baldwin and Kip."

Adriana smiled. "So. My code name is 'Bathsheba.' "

"I chose it, when they gave me 'David,' " said Baldwin. "It seemed to fit."

"I'll carry the message to rue Guillaume," she said.

"Not if there's the slightest chance you are being followed," Baldwin said urgently. "We lost Sybil. If we lose the group on rue Guillaume, we have no further contact."

Adriana glanced around the room. "Theo assured me the doctor will be here this afternoon."

"How did he contact you?"

"He did something rather foolish, as a matter of fact," she said. "He telephoned me at the Royal Monceau. Anyway, you should stay here until you are strong enough to walk. Raymond is bringing your clothes and identity papers from your flat."

"Paris is a dangerous city today," said Baldwin.

She nodded.

*　*　*

Adriana marveled at the translucent white and blue skin of the aged Monsieur Martin. Shrunken with age, he walked hunched over, shuffling across the oiled parquet floors of his living room and leading her to a seat on a Louis XV settee. His white hair was wispy, his eyes watery, his gentle smile fixed, his voice soft. Surrounded by antiques and art, he lived in luxurious rooms that seemed untouched by five years of war.

"Ah, Mademoiselle," he said. "May I offer you a glass of wine?"

"No, thank you, Monsieur. I suspect it is better that I stay only as long as we need to transact our business."

"And what business is that, Mademoiselle?"

He asked the question as ingenuously as if he had not admitted her to his apartment as David Bradford. He smiled as if he were addled.

"I wish to send a signal to London, Monsieur."

"London? To whom in London, Mademoiselle?"

"Colonel Sir Henry Harding."

"Harding . . . ? Harding?" He shook his head. "What sort of message do you wish to send to this man Harding?"

She took the coded message from inside her blouse, where she had tucked the folded paper into her brassière. The old man accepted it with a momentarily broadened smile. Slowly he extracted a pair of glasses from his vest pocket, and he put them on and peered at the message. She watched him nervously, unsure once again of the entire SOE operation.

"Umm," he said. "So."

"Can you send it, Monsieur?"

"It is rather long."

"It is rather important."

"Ah, but so are they all. A sudden burst of electromagnetic energy from somewhere near avenue Foch. The Boches are listening, you may be certain. I have lived in this apartment since 1910, Mademoiselle. I am too old to be afraid of death. I shoud hate, though, to see the precious things I have collected through a lifetime scattered through Germany because of the loquaciousness of two young agents who want to send a long message to Colonel Harding."

"Are you asking me to change the message, Monsieur?"

"No. Only to simplify the next one."

The old man rose slowly from the chair where he sat facing her. He shuffled to a delicate antique writing desk and sat down. From his vest pocket he extracted a small key and unlocked the desk, lowering the front to expose a writing surface and a number of tiny drawers and pigeonholes. Apparently a radio transmitter had been built into the complex of drawers, some parts in one, some in another. Continuing to move with the drawn-out, almost ritualistic motions of advanced age, Monsieur Martin opened one of the drawers and pulled out a set of headphones. From another he took a transmitting key. He put the headphones over his head and set the key exactly where he wanted it on the writing surface.

He turned and nodded at Adriana. He squinted at the message again, smoothing the paper out beside the key. "So," he said.

He touched the transmitting key with his fingertips: a staccato burst of dots and dashes from fingers that were suddenly amazingly nimble. Then he sat waiting, nervously tapping his fingers—waiting for London to acknowledge his call.

"So," he said again. He had heard the acknowledgement. His arm seemed to vibrate as his fingers sent another rapid stream of dots and dashes; she had never seen an operator send so rapidly. London must be recording him; few operators could transcribe at the speed he transmitted. In less than a minute he stopped and put the key back in the drawer.

For a while he sat with the earphones in place, frowning, listening, again drumming his fingers as if could not stop the burst of energy that had sustained the transmission. Then he began to nod his head, glancing at her, turning down the corners of his mouth. After a minute or so, he took off the earphones, replaced them, and closed and locked the desk.

"So," he said. "Colonel Harding says you should continue with your mission. He says he notes your recommendation about the American sergeant and will rely on your judgment about that matter."

Adriana drew a deep breath. "Very well, Monsieur," she said. "I cannot thank you enough."

"No," he said. "You really can't, can you? I suppose if I survive they will give me a medal."

"We must put in an appearance in the dining room," Heinrici said to Adriana. She had returned from her visit to Monsieur Martin and found him in the suite, brushing his gray wool uniform.

"I have news for you, Konrad," she said.

"Oh?" He turned away from his brushing. "What could it be?"

"I made contact this afternoon with Colonel Harding. I sent him a signal that Len and I urged your release from any further obligation to our mission. He signaled back that he will rely on our judgment. I think you may regard the threat of Radio Heinrici as dead."

He strode across the room to her and took her in his arms. He kissed her and held her.

"Now we can begin to think about lives for ourselves." he said.

Her mouth was pressed against his throat. "Yes," she murmured. "Somewhere. Not in Paris, I'm afraid. God knows what will happen when the armies come. Street-to-street fighting . . . And after . . . They'll kill you if they catch you — the French."

He led her by the arm to the window, and they looked out on the tree-shaded street. An elderly French woman, in fur-trimmed black coat even in mid-July, walked slowly along with a cane, making her way home in early evening. The words he was about to say caught in his throat as he watched her.

"Together, Konrad . . ." Adriana whispered. "We will be together. Somewhere."

He turned his eyes down into her uplifted face. If I can in any way contrive it, he thought.

THURSDAY, JULY 20, 1944

THE Führer's daily military conference, in his woodland command compound in East Prussia, ordinarily began at 1300 hours. Today, because Mussolini was scheduled to arrive shortly after lunch, the military conference had been advanced to 1230. The Führer was prompt, and when he walked across the path to the big wooden conference hut, some twenty officers summoned for the conference were waiting inside, sweating in the heat. Every window and door had been thrown open.

Among the officers gathered around the long conference table were Generalfeldmarschall Wilhelm Keitel, Chief of OKW (Oberkommando Wehrmacht); Generaloberst Alfred Jodl, Chief of Staff, OKW; General Adolf Heusinger, Deputy Chief of Staff; and Oberst Klaus Schenck Graf von Stauffenberg—Colonel Count von Stauffenberg—an aristocratic officer come to report to the Führer on the training of new Volksgrenadier divisions.

Oberst von Stauffenberg had been grievously wounded in North Africa. He had lost one arm entirely—plus two fingers from his remaining hand. He wore a patch over one eye. As the conference opened he placed a bulging yellow briefcase under the table, near the Führer.

Hitler drew up a high wicker stool. He sat down and faced a situation map of the central Russian front, picking up a magnifying glass so he could read the print on the map without his eyeglasses, and clutching a collection of pencils in various colors, which he would use to mark the situation map.

As the conference opened, Generalfeldmarschall Keitel pointed out Oberst von Stauffenberg to the Führer, saying the colonel would have an interesting report later. Hitler nodded a perfunctory greeting to Von Stauffenberg. His attention was already on the map.

General Heusinger began to deliver a report on activity on the Central Russian Front. The Führer leaned over the map, squinting at it through the magnifying glass so he could follow General Heusinger's report.

Oberst von Stauffenberg touched the arm of Oberst Heinz Brandt, who was standing next to him. He whispered to Brandt that he had to go out to take an important telephone call from Berlin. Would Brandt keep an eye on his briefcase? It contained secret documents. Brandt nodded. Von Stauffenberg left the hut.

General Heusinger continued. Oberst Brandt moved in closer, so he could learn over the map, too. The yellow briefcase, he discovered, was in the way of his foot, so he reached under the table and moved it—away from the Führer and beyond one of the heavy supports that held up the table.

"If our army group around Lake Peipus is not immediately withdrawn," General Heusinger was saying, "a catastrophe—"

The bomb in the yellow briefcase went off.

Oberst von Stauffenberg was waiting outside. He saw the wooden conference hut fly apart in an eruption of flame and smoke. He saw bodies flung in the air. Oddly, a geyser of flaming papers rose higher than the trees and began to flutter back down, driven toward the woods by the summer breeze. The broken remains of the conference hut collapsed on the dead and wounded.

Oberst von Stauffenberg hurried to his car and ordered his driver to take him immediately to the airport. On their way out of the command compound, they were stopped at three checkpoints, but Von Stauffenberg bluffed his way through. He was anxious to reach Berlin as soon as possible—to report the death of Adolf Hitler.

If he had remained in the compound a minute longer, he would have seen the Führer stagger out of the wreckage of the conference hut—burned and injured but alive.

Adriana returned to the suite in the Royal Monceau about five o'clock. She found Heinrici soaking in the bathtub.

"I'm sorry," he called out to her, "but I've got bad news for you."

She had come with bad news for him, but she decided to hear his first. She walked into the bathroom, sat down on the stool by the tub, and began to wash his back with a fat sponge.

"It seems we were noticed in the dining room last night by Gruppenführer Schenck," he said. "A very kind note has been delivered. We are invited—no, I should say summoned—to have dinner with him and his charming friend Martine. Our absence on several evenings has been noticed. We are going to have to think up some story to explain where we were Tuesday night."

"Let's hope he does not also invite Oberführer Franck," said Adriana wryly.

"Unlikely," Heinrici said. "Franck has become something of a joke in Paris. The anal search . . ."

"Konrad . . . ?

"Huh?"

"I went to see Len this afternoon." She dropped the sponge into the soapy water. "He's had a message from Colonel Harding."

"Is the English colonel reneging?"

She shook her head. "No. But he wants us to find the Merciers. If we can't find them, at least he wants us to find out what Henri Mercier is doing. He was involved, you know, in the Zionist effort to save Jews from deportation. Though you were not supposed to be told, there is a fund for the purpose. In gold. Quite a lot of gold, I understand. The British government hopes Henri Mercier will use that gold to delay as many deportations from Paris as possible—Résistants as well as Jews."

"A fund for paying bribes?"

"Yes. I suppose so. For saving lives, actually."

Heinrici turned around in the tub, so he could see Adriana's face. "Am I to understand you have received *orders* from Colonel Harding?"

She nodded.

"For me, too?"

"No. Len and I are ordered to try to persuade you to continue with the mission. There is no suggestion of renewing the threat about Radio Heinrici."

"But the two of you are ordered to risk your lives to find Mercier. Are you going to carry out that order?"

"You know Len will," she said quietly. "As for me"—she paused and shrugged—"I *am* subject to SOE orders. I took an oath. Of course . . . they *would* have to find me."

Heinrici hooked his toes in the chain on the rubber stopper, pulled, and let the bath water begin to run down the drain. "I am under some threat of being transferred," he said. "Perhaps to Berlin. If I receive such an order, I may desert." He looked up at her. "Does that surprise you?"

"No."

"It surprises *me*. I've thought about it, but the sound of the words coming out of my mouth surprises me."

"Konrad. We won't have to risk our lives again. I mean, to find Henri Mercier and the girl. It's a matter of ingenuity and maybe of your resources."

Heinrici stood and reached for a towel, but Adriana took the towel from him and began to dry him.

"I'll help you," he said.

He stretched out on the bed, wondering how exactly he was going to deal with the fact that he knew where Mercier was and was not going to tell her. She was undressing in the bathroom; he could hear her humming to herself. She was content with his promise to help in the search for Henri Mercier. A secret had never laid so heavily on him before.

Someone knocked on the door. Heinrici rose reluctantly, walked from the bedroom to the foyer of the suite, and stood close to the door.

"Who is it?"

It occurred to him that he had not carried his pistol, that maybe he had become too confident, but the voice from outside was assuring: "Oberleutnant Krueger, Herr Oberst."

A robe had been omitted from the items he had been supplied on his arrival in Paris, but he did not object to being seen in his underwear by Oberleutnant Krueger, and he opened the door.

Krueger pushed into the foyer and closed the door behind him. He was carrying a Schmeisser submachine gun. "Are you alone?" he asked hoarsely. His youthful face was flushed and glistening with sweat.

Heinrici glanced toward the bedroom. "Mademoiselle, uh . . . Clement is in the bathroom."

Krueger kept his voice low. "General Hausser ordered me to come directly to you. The Führer is dead! Apparently the SS has effected a putsch at the headquarters in East Prussia. The army is in control in Berlin. They've thrown the Nazis out. Generaloberst von Stülpnagel has taken command in Paris. Obergruppenführer Oberg has been arrested. So has Gruppenführer Schenck. And Oberführer Franck. All the senior SS and SD officers. General Hausser orders you to report to his headquarters at once."

Heinrici glanced once more toward the bedroom. "Are we firmly in control?" he asked in a low voice.

Krueger nodded. "The army has the city under control. The SS troops are confined to barracks. The army has seized control of SS, SD, and Gestapo headquarters."

"I'll dress," said Heinrici. "Wait for me here."

"Be sure to carry your sidearm."

Heinrici returned through the parlor to the bedroom, conscious of the ludicrous figure he made at such a time—clad in his skimpy summer underwear, without shoes. He closed the door between the bedroom and the parlor.

Could it be? And if it had . . . ? Who *was* he now? How did he live with some confused new order of things? What would these army officers do? To him? He was no more one of them than he was one of Hitler's Nazi zealots. How—

"Konrad . . . ?"

Adriana had come out of the bathroom. Finding him nervously pulling on his clothes, she smiled and turned up the palms of her hands in an inquiring gesture.

He turned to her. "Adriana. Something has happened. I'm not sure what. I want you to promise me something—that you won't leave these rooms until I return."

"Konrad, what's happened? I have to know."

"Nothing to do with us personally. It's something political."

"Konrad, I have to know," she insisted firmly.

He seized her by both arms. "Something that . . . Adriana, you must promise me you won't try to send word of this to England. I'll tell you if you'll promise me that."

She looked away from him for a moment. Then she drew a deep breath and nodded.

"All right," he said, lowering his voice. "There is a report that Hitler is dead. The army has taken power. Here in Paris, the chief officers of the SS and SD are under arrest, and all SS troops are confined to barracks. I'm ordered to report to Abwehr headquarters."

"It's good news, isn't it?" she asked uncertainly. "I mean, if the Nazis are forced out of power . . . I mean, for us."

"I don't know," he said. "I don't even know it's all true. But you must not leave these rooms." He tightened his grip on her arms. "There may be shooting in the streets. Oberleutnant Krueger is waiting in the foyer with a Schmeisser in his hands. Out there, there may be Germans shooting at Germans. And the French—" He shook his head. "If they see Germans shooting at Germans . . . Adriana, you must not go out."

"I—"

The telephone rang. Heinrici answered. General Hausser was on the line.

"Heinrici, I want you to take Krueger and go to the rue des Saussaies. Immediately. I'm getting conflicting signals from Berlin, and I want confirmation of what is going on. They say the army has taken over SS and Gestapo headquarters and arrested the chief officers. I have to know the truth. Find out as much as you can and telephone me."

"Very well, Herr General. Have you any further news?"

"Not on the telephone, Heinrici. There is a rumor that the Führer is dead. I don't even want to *think* of what that might mean. Find out for me what is going on at rue des Saussaies. Report as quickly as you can."

Heinrici put down the telephone. "I am ordered to go to SS headquarters," he said. "Adriana, *promise me* you will wait for me here."

She nodded. "I promise, Konrad. And you . . . You be careful."

* * *

Their transportation to the rue des Saussaies was ridiculous: an open Audi
two-seater sports car, which drew amused stares from Frenchmen on the streets
as it roared by carrying a lieutenant armed with a Schmeisser submachine gun
awkwardly stowed behind him and a colonel sitting stiffly in the passenger seat.

Krueger sped along the rue du Faubourg St. Honoré, and as they approached
SS headquarters it became apparent to Heinrici that at least part of Krueger's
story was true. The building was surrounded by gray-uniformed Wehrmacht
soldiers, all in battle gear, many with strings of grenades hung around their
shoulders. They stopped the Audi at the edge of Place Beauvau.

A sergeant saluted smartly. "The building is closed, Herr Oberst. I cannot
allow you to pass."

Heinrici climbed out of the car. "Your commanding officer, Sergeant," he
said curtly.

The sergeant saluted again and walked away to find his commanding officer.

"I wonder what the civilian population of Paris thinks of this," Heinrici muttered to Krueger, nodding toward the former Ministry building, which was
conspicuously under the guard of combat soldiers. A half-track sat before the
main entrance, with two machine guns commanding the square and the street.

"Herr Oberst? I am Hauptmann Best."

Heinrici turned to face a young captain, red in the face and puffing, carrying
a Mauser machine pistol fitted with a stock.

"Heinrici. Abwehr. My orders from General Hausser are to enter the building."

"May I see identification, please, Herr Oberst?"

"Of course."

After two more identity checks, Heinrici and Krueger entered the building.

When Heinrici had come there as Standartenführer Brunner a little more than
a week ago, SS headquarters had bustled with official activity. Black-uniformed
functionaries had scurried through the building on ten thousand errands. Now
only a few gray-uniformed officers strode through the long corridors.

"Herr Oberst," Krueger said quietly, nodding toward two officers who hurried past.

The two army officers were carrying armloads of files. It took a moment for
the significance of this to hit Heinrici—it explained the odor of smoke that
sharpened the air in the building. They were burning dossiers—dangerous SS,
SD, and Gestapo records. Not knowing which ones might contain their names,
they were burning them wholesale. It was partly a matter of precaution, but it
was more a matter of rage and frustration: burning the mysterious accumulation
of paper that had so long hung as a threat over them.

The building stood around a large courtyard. Heinrici and Krueger stepped
inside an abandoned office and looked down into the courtyard. Large fires

were burning, and officers were throwing file after file into the flames.

Heinrici picked up a telephone on one of the desks in the abandoned office. It was dead. "Find a live telephone, Krueger," he said. "Report to General Hausser. When you have finished, return here. I'm going to look around. I will meet you here."

Krueger looked hesitant, but he left the office on his errand.

It was not difficult to find the file rooms. Heinrici simply followed the hurrying officers. When he reached the main file room, where perhaps his own SD dossier was kept, he saw there was no reason to look for it: in the company of hundreds of other dossiers it had already gone to the courtyard and onto one of the fires.

Heinrici pushed his way past a score of officers, beyond the army files. The oaken cabinets of civilian dossiers stood side by side along the brick walls and in ranks through the center of the room: hundreds of cabinets, containing thousands of drawers, scores of thousands of dossiers. The civilian dossiers had been kept by the French, over decades, and had been inherited by the SD and Gestapo and supplemented energetically since 1940.

Neatly printed signs in German sat atop the cabinets to guide searchers to the dossiers they wanted. Clarity of organization was an element of German efficiency, Heinrici thought. It made it easy to find the files he wanted—Marcel Ange, Marie Ange, Jacob Pascin, Sidonie Cardin, and Philippe Valence.

Carrying these five dossiers, he hurried along to the cabinet where he thought he would find the dossiers for the family Mercier. They were out; cards stood in their place noting that these files had been removed to the office of Gruppenführer Karl Oberg or of his deputy Oberführer Erhard Franck.

The files on foreign intelligence operatives possibly active in France were in a separate room. The door was locked, but it was a simple wooden door; he kicked it open. He switched on the lights in that small room and glanced over the directory signs.

Kip. Adriana Kip. The SD had a dossier on her. It was thick with pictures clipped from magazines and newspapers.

He put that dossier under his arm with the others and opened another drawer, looking for a dossier on William Leonard Baldwin. None. He was unknown to the SD. Out of curiosity he checked his own name in the file of foreign intelligence operatives. Of course there was no dossier there. If there had been, he would have been long since dead.

"Herr Oberst?"

He swung around to find another captain in battle gear. This one stank of smoke. A litter of paper ash lay on his shoulders.

"I must ask you not to interfere with these files, Herr Oberst."

Heinrici produced him identity papers. "Abwehr," he said. "I am specifically authorized, Hauptmann."

The captain looked suspiciously at the dossiers under Heinrici's arm. He licked his lips and pondered.

"Which ones were betraying the armed forces, Hauptmann?" Heinrici asked. "Which ones were involved in the murder of the Führer?"

"Those dossiers tell you?" the captain asked.

"No," said Heinrici. "But they give some useful hints."

The captain drew a weary breath. "Very well, Herr Oberst," he said.

Carrying the six dossiers, Heinrici left the file rooms and, as soon as he was sure the captain was not watching him, joined the stream of officers carrying dossiers to the bonfires in the courtyard.

Half a dozen fires burned, each one tended by officers with broomhandles, with which they poked at the burning paper, making sure that every sheet was consumed in the smoky red blazes. Surrounded by the high walls of the building, the courtyard was filled with ash-filled smoke, white against the sunlit blue sky.

Heinrici sat down on a stone bench near one of the fires and read the files he had brought to the courtyard.

He looked first into the dossier on Adriana. She was identified as a Dutchwoman recruited by the English as an agent of SOE. Her last known whereabouts was Brussels, in December 1943, where she was responsible for the murder of a trusted and respected leader of the Belgian Nazi party, after which she had eluded capture and presumably returned to England. It was to be assumed, the dossier said, that she had returned to the Continent and was probably in France, possibly Paris. She was under sentence of death in Holland, for treason, and in Belgium, for murder. If arrested she was to be transported immediately and under the tightest security to Berlin, for severe interrogation. The order for transportation to Berlin was signed . . . Kaltenbrunner.

Heinrici rose and tossed the file into the flames, and he stood and watched it until he was certain it was burning. Then he sat down again and opened another file.

Marcel Ange. This was a thick dossier, with yellowed paper at least twenty years old. Papa was, so far as the SD and Gestapo were concerned, just an old Paris gangster, too old for labor service. He was suspected of black marketeering and of receiving stolen goods, but not of affiliation with any element of the Résistance.

Marie Ange. The dossier was thin. She had been a prostitute—a surprise to Heinrici—and since her marriage to Papa, a housewife without further entries in her file.

Jacob Pascin. A thin dossier, opened only in 1940 by the Race and Resettlement Office. Pascin was a Jew, exempt from the disabling laws as Papa had said, because he was a diamond cutter. There was no mention in the dossier of any connection between Jacob Pascin and Henri Mercier.

Philippe Valence. A thick dossier with no recent entries. He flipped through the sheets. It was frightening to discover how much the French police had known about him in the thirties—and encouraging to see that they had never suspected that the forger and counterfeiter Phillipe Valence was in fact Konrad Heinrici, agent of the Abwehr. They had no photograph of him, no fingerprints, because they had never arrested him. He was listed as a fugitive, supposedly in hiding somewhere in France. The dossier had been active as recently as April 1940. They had still been looking for him.

Sidonie Cardin. This dossier, too, was old. The police had identified her as a prostitute as long ago as 1931. She had been involved also in cocaine trafficking, and—something he had never known—she had served two years in prison: 1933 and 1934. She held a prostitute's identity card. This dossier too, he supposed, would end with the spring of 1940, but as he flipped over the pages he found it didn't. The Gestapo had added four sheets to the dossier since 1940, one as recently as May 1944.

Heinrici frowned over the Gestapo sheets. The top sheet was a list of some her clients. They included German officers. The next sheet was a report written by an agent of the Gestapo:

Mademoiselle Cardin has acted faithfully according to her instructions. Taking full advantage of the skills she has acquired through long experience, she has, as we might say, enslaved the subject Mandel. He has confided to her exactly what we expected.

On 14 February, Jacques Mandel confided to Mademoiselle Cardin that he is a maquisard, that he is the leader of a group, and that he has access to a store of weapons. (He wished to impress her, it seems, with the idea that he is not just an aging lawyer but is a brave man of action.)

On 18 February, Mandel confided further in Mademoiselle Cardin, giving her the names that will be found in my report of this date in the Mandel dossier.

As authorized, I have released to Mademoiselle Cardin the funds reserved for her. Also, as an additional incentive for her to seek more useful contacts, I recommend we give the young lady access to the reserved food stores for the month of March, so she may have somewhere to spend her francs.

Heinrici grabbed at the next sheet. It too was a Gestapo report and very similar. The final sheet was dated June 3, 1944:

It is strongly recommended that for the time being we discontinue the services of Mademoiselle Sidonie Cardin. She is too valuable a resource to be wasted, and I would respectfully point out that she has been a subject of too many "coincidences." If her affiliation with us is even suspected in certain quarters, we will lose her services permanently. I urge that she be "retired" for now and kept in reserve for the important investigation where her special skills may be highly valuable.

As authorized, I am continuing to pay her a "pension" of 20,000 francs per month.

Sidonie! For a moment Heinrici considered tearing the Gestapo reports from the dossier and stuffing them in his pockets, to take to Papa. But he didn't. He rose, stepped to the fire, and tossed the files to the flames. As he stood watching them burn, he reached a decision.

"Herr Oberst! We've got to get out of here!"

Krueger had waited as ordered, but Heinrici could see that he was on the verge of hysteria.

"What's the matter, Krueger?"

"The Fürher is *not* dead! The news . . . the radio . . . We must be out of here before the SS returns."

"General Hausser?"

"I reached him. Besides what the radio says, he has a wire from Berlin. It was the army, not the SS, who attempted the putsch. The Fürher will speak on the radio later tonight."

They were standing inside the office where Heinrici had ordered Krueger to wait for him. Looking out into the corridor, they could see the army officers still carrying dossiers to the fires.

"What are General Hausser's orders?" Heinrici asked.

"His orders are to get away from here, not to be identified with this," said Krueger. "I waited for you—"

"Yes. Thank you, Krueger. Well then, let's move."

Outside, army troops still surrounded the Ministry building. They ignored the two Abwehr officers striding across the square. Heinrici wondered if the combat captains in command of these units had heard that Hitler was alive.

Krueger regained his calm as he reached the Audi and sat down to start the engine. "Did you burn my dossier too, by any chance?" he asked.

Heinrici chuckled. "I didn't have to. The gentlemen of the Wehrmacht are taking care of all that for us."

"Where may I take you, Herr Oberst? Back to your hotel?"

"No, Krueger. I think not. Drive me up to Montmartre, to the Place du Tertre. I'll buy you a drink."

They chose a café and sat down. Heinrici went inside and telephoned Adriana. He told her he was safe but that it was not safe for her to go out. He said he would return in a little while.

It was one of the days when wine was not available to the civilian population, but a bottle could always be found for an officer with Heinrici's rank. They sat outdoors, under the resentful stares of passersby, and enjoyed a bottle of Bordeaux.

"The situation must be quite dangerous," said Krueger.

"If you have a decent suit of civilian clothes, I suggest you wear them tomorrow," said Heinrici.

"It seems strange to be sitting here drinking wine."

"Let us hope there are Gestapo agents among the civilians walking by," said Heinrici. "While other army officers are in SS headquarters burning dossiers, here we are, calmly drinking wine. It may be remembered."

"Your calm amazes me," said Krueger.

"Actually," said Heinrici, "I am trying to *become* calm."

He declined a second time to be driven back to the Royal Monceau. He dismissed Krueger, urging him to take the remainder of the wine with him; and for a while he sat with his last glass, watching Krueger walk away, glance back, and walk on down the hillside to where he had parked the Audi. Only when he was certain that Krueger was gone, had driven down from Montmartre, did Heinrici gulp his last swallow and rise from the table.

He walked down the stone steps behind the Place du Tertre, to rue St. Vincent, then around two corners and into rue Boulanger. Yesterday Papa had rented a flat across the street, as he had said he would, and moved Sidonie in, where she would have a view of 48 rue Boulanger from the parlor window. They had established a schedule. Sidonie should be there now.

He tried the door at 53. It was not locked. He walked in and up the narrow stairs to the flat. Sidonie was sitting in the parlor, near the window as she was supposed to be, though she was reading a magazine and giving the flat across the street little apparent attention. She was wearing an orange and yellow silk dressing gown.

"Get dressed," he said to her. "I'll take you out for a drink."

She glanced at the window.

"Mama will be along in a few minutes," he said.

"Well, then . . . ," she said. She smiled. "I guess in that uniform you can get a drink, even if we Parisians can't."

While she dressed in the bedroom, Heinrici stood at the window and stared thoughtfully at 48 rue Boulanger. The curtains were closed.

"Where will we go?" Sidonie asked when she returned. She had put on a dark blue dress and a little white straw hat. "Someplace nice? It's been a long time since you've taken me out for a drink."

"Someplace nice," he said. "We'll walk down to Pigalle."

They went out on the street—the tall, handsome decorated German officer and the cute little tart. She linked arms with him and walked with a bouncy gait.

"Where are we going, Philippe?" she asked when he turned toward the summit of Montmartre.

"I want to go in the church," he said.

"For God's sake, why?"

"Impulse," he said. He shrugged. "Five minutes. Then down to Pigalle or boulevard de Clichy."

The great white-domed basilica had been damaged by an American or English bomb, dropped in April. A part of it was closed. A part of it was boarded up. Even so, he led her to the terrace and up the steps and into the cavernous, mosaic-adorned sanctuary. A priest came in and began to tell them that the church was closed now except for confession or prayer, but when he saw the uniform he turned and scurried away.

Sidonie resisted the idea of strolling through the basilica. She tugged gently on Heinrici's arm, silently urging him to have done with this impulse and return into the pleasant evening sunlight. But he walked on, among the columns, looking around him.

The basilica was not deserted, but there were few worshipers there—as he had anticipated. Shortly, in the ambulatory behind the chancel, they were alone.

He stopped before a small altar. A few candles burned. "You should say a prayer while we're here," he said to Sidonie. "You're Catholic."

Sidonie smiled as if shy.

"People like us can hardly say too many prayers. Here. Put in this coin and light a candle."

Uncertain, maybe even apprehensive—What did she see in his face, hear in his voice?—she dropped the coin in the box, took an unlighted taper, touched it to another burning taper, and put it in place. She knelt on the kneeling bench and crossed herself. She lowered her face and began to murmur a prayer.

Heinrici glanced all around. His face hardened and twisted into a misshapen mask as he braced himself; then with his left hand he grabbed her by the hair, and instantly, with all the force he could bring, he chopped her across the back of her neck with the heel of his right hand. The blow would have knocked her forward into the candles if he had not been holding her by the hair. Stunned, maybe even paralyzed, she made no sound, not even a moan or cough. Seizing her head in both hands, he wrenched it back until he heard her neck break with a distressingly loud crack. He held her for a moment, until he was sure she was not breathing, then he propped her against the altar. On her knees and slumped forward, she would look as if she were praying—until someone came close.

Heinrici walked back the way he had come, out of the ambulatory, through the nave, and into the long-shadowed evening sunlight. He stood for a long moment on the damaged terrace before the basilica, suppressing a shudder that had begun in his back and now caused his hands to tremble. Sidonie . . . He shook his head. She had represented a risk he could not accept.

* * *

Gruppenführer Schenck raised his glass of champagne. "Let it not be imagined," he said with a broad smile, "that a small, ludicrous incident could ruin a pleasant dinner. A little late, but . . . Anyway—to the Führer! Providence has once again preserved him. May Providence grant him victory!"

"To the Führer and victory," echoed Heinrici.

Adriana—Jacqueline Clement in this company—drank silently; Martine Paul murmured a concurrence in the toast and sipped delicately.

As recently as an hour ago Schenck had been held in custody in the Hotel Continental, together with the other senior officers of the SS and SD, with their staffs. On arriving at the Royal Monceau, he had telephoned up to Heinrici's suite to announce that he was there and that their dinner was ready to be served. Heinrici had returned from Sacré Coeur an hour ago, and he had to cancel a room-service order when Schenck called.

"We will hear the Führer speak," said Schenck. "I have ordered his speech piped into the dining room."

The hour was late for the Monceau dining room. Only a few diners remained, and white-jacketed staff stood around the walls, trying to conceal their impatience. Schenck had demanded caviar, and the hotel had somehow managed to produce it. The champagne was excellent. A captain worked over filets of sole in a chafing dish. The candles smoked. Silver gleamed. The dinner was as serene as it might have been on a July evening a year ago.

"Stülpnagel and Oberg are at dinner, too," said Schenck. "I would not wish to be Generaloberst Stülpnagel tomorrow, though. And Franck . . ." He laughed. "He went home to soak his sore backside in a tub of hot bathwater. The entire episode has been a comedy."

"Except, I should think, for the attempt to assassinate the Führer," said Martine Paul.

"Except for that," said Schenck.

"Except also that they are burning dossiers in the rue des Saussaies," said Heinrici.

"Really?" asked Schenck, troubled. "I didn't know that."

"I walked past," said Heinrici. "You could see the smoke rising above the roof of the Ministry."

"Fools," said Schenck. His face darkened. "Our offices? Looted?"

Heinrici shrugged. "The Wehrmacht had the building surrounded."

"Where were you while all this was happening?" Schenck asked.

Heinrici glanced at Adriana, their eyes meeting. "I was here most of the afternoon, with Jacqueline," he said. "General Hausser called and asked me to go to rue des Saussaies, see what was going on there, and report to him— which I did. Otherwise, it has been an uneventful day for me."

The broadcast began after midnight. Speakers in the corners of the dining room amplified the words of Adolf Hitler, and the diners and staff fell silent and listened:

> A miniscule clique of ambitious, unscrupulous officers of criminal stupidity has been plotting to get rid of me and to liquidate virtually the entire German Wehrmacht command staff at the same time. The bomb was placed by Oberst Graf von Stauffenberg and exploded two meters away to my right. Several of my dear colleagues were gravely injured, one has died. I myself am completely uninjured apart from a few minor scratches, bruises, and burns. I regard this as a fresh confirmation of the mission given me by Providence to continue toward my goal.

Gruppenführer Schenck closed his eyes while Hitler spoke, and when the speech was over and the speakers fell silent, he opened his eyes and said, "May God bless and prosper him!"

TUESDAY, JULY 25, 1944

PAPA and Marie assured him that Henri Mercier remained in the house at 48 rue Boulanger. Even though Sidonie had for some reason disappeared and failed to do her part in keeping a watch on the house, they were sure that Mercier was still there. He told them he would sit in the parlor at 53 this morning. He would watch 48, and they need not come to relieve him until noon.

He sat and watched for a while, saw a man leave 48. About ten o'clock he walked out of 53, crossed the street, and knocked on the door. He moved quickly, to surprise the people inside and give them no time to escape. Surely they were cautious, probably watching the street. How would they react when a uniformed German officer crossed the street and knocked on their door?

He had intended to visit Henri Mercier three or four days ago. It had not been possible. General Hausser had summoned him to Abwehr headquarters in the Hotel Lutétia, and he had been compelled to remain there, a reluctant participant in General Hausser's nervous alert.

Although everyone heard the Führer's speech Thursday night, the army did not withdraw from rue des Saussaies until late the next day. Generaloberst Stülpnagel was called to Berlin. He set out in a car, but a few kilometers out of

Paris he was attacked and wounded by Résistants, or he attempted suicide, depending on whose story one chose to believe. In any event, he was blinded and had to be carried on to Berlin in an ambulance. Obergruppenführer Oberg returned to his headquarters and recovered police control of the city.

Surrounded by his officers, General Hausser sat in his headquarters, receiving a stream of messages from rue des Saussaies and from Berlin. On Sunday, Admiral Canaris was arrested and charged with having been a leading participant in the plot to assassinate the Führer. For several months he had no longer been chief of the Abwehr, but many officers who had been his protégés had to wonder how Reichsführer Himmler and Oberstgruppenführer Kaltenbrunner would look upon a man's record of long friendship with Canaris. General Hausser wondered if his own arrest was not imminent. On Monday he was summoned to Berlin. Terrified, unsure if he would ever return, he left Monday afternoon—at last freeing Heinrici to go to rue Boulanger.

In bed last night Adriana had told him of a meeting with the Résistants. Le Chou-fleur, one of their important leaders, had met with her and Baldwin. Le Capitaine and Le Rasoir were present. Le Chou-fleur, she said, was angry. Although she and Baldwin had insisted that the rescue of the Merciers had been carefully planned and executed so as to avoid killing any Germans and the firefight at Romainville had been an inexplicable accident, twenty-two French citizens had already been shot in reprisal, and there was a promise that at least as many more would be shot. Le Chou-fleur demanded to know where Henri Mercier was. He could not accept anyone's word that she and Baldwin—if not in fact Le Capitaine and La Rasoir—did not know where the Merciers were. It was true, Le Chou-fleur said, that Henri Mercier had access to a great deal of money, and he demanded that at least a good part of it be used to attempt to secure the release of Résistants. "They are as valuable as Jews," he said. "Since we the French have paid the price of this rescue, we insist that we receive part of the benefit."

Henri Mercier, Le Chou-fleur had said, could not hide long in Paris. If the Boches didn't find him, the Résistance would. If he did not come forward and volunteer a part of his gold, they might decide to take it all when they found him.

He strode across the street and knocked on the door at 48 rue Boulanger.

Louise Pascin opened the door.

"Good afternoon, Madame. I wish to speak with Monsieur Mercier."

The woman attempted to smile. "Ah, Monsieur," she said. "You have the wrong address. In fact, I don't know of a family by that name on this street."

Heinrici smiled and nodded. "I am sorry to contradict you, Madame," he said quietly, "but I *know* Henri Mercier and his daughter Jeanne are living with you.

You need not be afraid. Monsieur Mercier knows me. I am a friend. My visit is no threat to anyone."

"But, Monsieur—"

"Madame," he said firmly. "I will come in, if you don't mind. Tell Monsieur Mercier that Oberführer von Strauch is here. I know he will want to see me."

The woman retreated, and he entered the house. As she hurried up the stairs to another floor, nervously saying something about how she would ask Monsieur if he would see him, Heinrici stood in the parlor, politely holding his cap under his left arm, and looked at the comfortable home this family of Jews had managed to save. It was very much like his own home in Speyer. His mother had furnished her parlor very much like this, and after her death his father had changed nothing. He had to shrug off the memory; it troubled him.

"Von Strauch . . . ?" Henri Mercier asked apprehensively. He had come silently down the stairs and stood in the doorway. "Oberführer von Strauch?"

Heinrici turned, bowed slightly, and smiled. "Not really, of course. None of us were who we said we were. You do recognize me?"

"Of course . . ."

Heinrici bowed again. "Oberst Konrad Heinrici, Abwehr."

Mercier stood open-mouthed, frowning. "Do you mean to tell me it was the Abwehr that—"

"No," said Heinrici. "Well, actually . . . yes and no. It is a long story, Monsieur—which you must be told in full, sooner or later. For now . . . May we sit down and talk?"

Mercier nodded toward a chair. "Of course," he said.

Heinrici put his cap on the table and sat down in one of the overstuffed chairs. Madame Pascin had returned, and Heinrici looked up at her and smiled. He was reluctant to talk in her presence.

"Some coffee, Monsieur?" she asked. "I am afraid it is wartime coffee."

"No thank you, Madame. When I next visit, I will bring you some real coffee."

"Thank you, Monsieur," she said. She looked to Mercier for a signal, got one, and returned upstairs.

In the daylight Heinrici had another look at Henri Mercier. Fed and washed and wearing clothes that were intact, the man had recovered quickly from some of the outward manifestations of his ordeal. But not all. The flesh around his jaw was pale and loose. His eyes seemed to have drawn back into his skull; though they were animated and alert, they seemed to peer out from sheltering holes.

"How did you find me?"

Heinrici smiled. "Don't ask me to reveal all my professional secrets, Monsieur," he said. "I have known where you are for a week, since the night we rescued you from Fresnes Prison. I would have come to see you sooner, but you may know that we have experienced a little problem among ourselves lately. I mean, we Germans have had a little problem."

"Who are you, Herr Oberst?" asked Mercier directly.

"That depends on when you ask me, Monsieur," said Heinrici. "If, however, you were to inquire of Abwehr headquarters in the Hotel Lutétia, they could confirm that Oberst Heinrici is one of their officers, temporarily assigned to Paris. The question you really want answered is, who arranged to rescue you and your daughter from two prisons—not long, incidentally, before you were to be deported."

"Very well," said Mercier. "That *is* the question."

"The answer is that it was a joint operation, a cooperative venture involving Special Operations Executive, the Résistance, and the Abwehr. The Abwehr's role was unofficial, of course."

"Why the Abwehr?" asked Mercier.

"Not all Germans," Heinrici said, "believe in transporting people like cattle, to God knows where, to suffer God knows what. If you are dubious of my humanitarian motive, then think of this—that my country has lost the war and one day soon will have to pay for the crimes of our Führer and his fanatics. The SOE identifies you as a man who can do something to hinder the mass deportation of Jews from Paris. The Abwehr would like to hinder it, too—if for no better reason than that transport used to deport Jews could be carrying war materiel."

"Where are the others?" Mercier asked. "The SOE agents and the Résistants who took part in our liberation?"

"We need to discuss that." Heinrici clasped his hands before his chest. "The Résistance believes that you have access to a great deal of money, which they expect you will use to hinder the deportation of Jews. They want that money, to use for their own purposes. They do not know where you are. But they are looking for you. I must suggest, Monsieur, that you be very careful in your contacts, in whom you place your trust. The Résistance is not a homogeneous organization. Many of its members are communists. Some are just old-time French gangsters. Some are idealists. Some are thugs. They—"

"I am aware of this," Mercier said. "My contacts with the Résistance have been very limited."

"Some of them are anti-Semitic."

"Some of them are. I know that. But the SOE. Were there not two SOE agents in your group?"

"Yes. A man and a woman."

"And where are they?"

Heinrici shrugged. "Hiding. Maybe on their way back to England. They never trusted me entirely."

"You have kept to yourself the knowledge of my whereabouts," said Mercier.

"I thought it wise. The more people know—"

"—the more dangerous. Very well."

Mercier rose from his chair and walked restlessly around the room, pausing to look out the windows at the street, pausing again at the door as if he thought Madame Pascin might be on the stairs eavesdropping. Heinrici kept silent, waiting to see where Mercier would now lead the conversation.

"It is entirely coincidence that I am in this house," said Mercier. "If we had been in some other quarter when that patrol arrived, I don't know where I would have fled. I have other friends. There are other houses to which I could have gone. But after curfew, dressed as prisoners . . ." He shook his head. "We would almost certainly been arrested by another patrol before we could have reached safety."

"That patrol was under my command," said Heinrici. "You would have been arrested, taken beyond the view of the Résistants, and released in my custody. I had a flat waiting for you, not very far from here. When you ran, you surprised me. But it worked out well. My soldiers did not follow you far. But someone else did."

"Then someone else does know where I am."

"Two trustworthy friends," said Heinrici.

Mercier returned to his chair and sat down wearily. "So why have you come, Herr Oberst?"

"To make a proposition."

Mercier nodded. "Yes. I might have guessed."

"Nothing that will distress you, Monsieur," said Heinrici. "I may be able to do an important service for you. I say, I *may* be able. I can make no promise."

"What service?"

"Monsieur Mercier," Heinrici said slowly, as if cautious in his choice of words, "I regret your loss of your son. I regret the deportation of Madame Mercier. It is possible—just possible—that I might be able to secure her release and her return to Paris."

Henri Mercier lowered his face into his hands. He shook his head. "Do not raise false hope," he whispered.

"No, Monsieur," said Heinrici quietly. "I am saying to you that it is a possibility. Perhaps a remote possibility. I will remind you, however, that I did manage to achieve *your* liberation."

Mercier looked up. "How would you do it?" he asked gravely.

"The same way you save Jews from deportation. By paying one or more substantial bribes."

"What makes you think you could succeed?"

"I know where she was taken," said Heinrici. "To Ravensbrück, in East Prussia. I can go there. You can't. Indeed, I may soon be sent to Berlin, and from there I can reach Ravensbrück very readily. If I could offer—"

"How much?"

"I don't know. Obviously, the more the better."

"The money is not mine, Herr Oberst. It is true I have access to certain funds, but the money is not mine."

"I think no one would deny you the money necessary to save Madame Mercier if there is a possibility of saving her," said Heinrici. "Your risks and sacrifices—"

"You propose to carry the money to Germany?" Mercier asked, abruptly stiffening.

Heinrici smiled wryly. "You are thinking that once I have the money in hand I will disappear into Germany and you will never see me again. No. We would have to arrange some sort of transfer. You must have satisfactory evidence of your wife's release before you hand over the money."

"The details—"

"—will be difficult to arrange, Monsieur. Every element of the process will be difficult. And it may fail entirely. On the other hand, you may think it is worth trying."

"I could possibly . . . obtain some money," said Mercier.

"And you are wondering about something else," said Heinrici. "Why would this German officer go to so much trouble, and possibly take some risk, to attempt to secure the liberation of Madame Mercier? What motivates him?"

"A percentage," said Mercier.

Heinrici nodded. "Can we call it a fee?"

"Very well, a fee. How much do you have in mind? I would pay anything, you understand, for even a remote chance of saving my wife from the hell she must be suffering in a concentration camp. But the money belongs to others, who must approve my withdrawing any of it. I will have to make a specific proposal."

"Let us not talk in terms of French francs, Monsieur," said Heinrici. "The franc is so unstable. Anyway, we are talking of payments in gold—the only money my contacts will accept, the only kind I can accept. . . . I might be able to secure Madame Mercier's release for, say, four thousand British pounds, twenty thousand American dollars. And for myself, I would like, let us say, two thousand pounds. Nothing becomes payable until results are achieved."

Mercier drew breath and sighed. "I can perhaps obtain that much," he said.

"Then, if you wish, I will set inquiries in motion," said Heinrici.

Mercier nodded. "Yes. Please."

Once again, an apprehensive Madame Pascin opened the door on the street in response to a firm knock. This time she relaxed when she saw the face of the man who stood there.

She glanced up and down the street, just the same. "Ah, Père Jean," she said. "Come in!"

A middle-aged man, dressed in the cassock of a priest, entered the room where Oberst Heinrici had met with Henri Mercier only a couple of hours ago. He was Isidore Natanson, not a priest at all, but in clerical guise and carrying papers that identified him as Père Jean Pecheur. A portly man with dark straight hair that ran loose in all directions and a short, bristly mustache as ill-trimmed as his hair, Natanson sweated from his walk in the July sunshine, and his face was flushed.

He was a Jew, and he was Père Jean through the courage and kindness of the priests of Sacré Coeur. Before 1940 he had been a banker and financial adviser to the chapter, shrugging off the fees he was entitled to take; when the Germans arrived the priests invited their widower Jewish friend to join them. Through four years of occupation, the Germans had never guessed that Père Jean was anything but a fat priest—though one whose duties, so far as they noticed, were administrative and not pastoral.

He had brought a bottle of wine from the basilica's cellars, and he handed it to Louise Pascin to open and serve while they talked.

Jeanne Mercier came down before her father did. A scant fuzz of hair had emerged, forming a shadow on her head. She wore clothes left behind by the Pascins' son, who was living with the master of his former boarding school in Villeneuve-St.-Georges, where, it was thought, he might be better situated in the event of disaster. In green corduroy pants and a white shirt, she looked very much like a teen-aged boy.

"What word of the woman who was killed in the basilica?" she asked Natanson. "Has it caused any problem for you?"

Natanson shook his head. "A prostitute. Killed by a German officer, it appears. The investigation was taken over by the Gestapo. We have been asked no more questions."

Jeanne walked into the kitchen and reappeared after a brief moment, carrying four glasses. She carried herself with grace, with the posture and control she had learned to practice during her ballet training. Watching her—so young, so delicate, so artlessly feminine—he could not imagine a man so depraved as to choose to hurt her. But she had been hurt, and he doubted that even her father knew how much.

Henri Mercier entered the room just as Jeanne was distributing the glasses. "Ah, Isidore," he said. "How fortunate you did not arrive here in the morning."

Natanson rose to shake hands with his old friend. "This morning?"

"We had a visitor," said Mercier. "A German officer. The one who commanded the small group that liberated me last week. A scoundrel, as it turns out. He knows about the gold. At least, he suspects. He is looking for a way to take it away from us—at least some of it."

"It is not quite that simple, I think," said Jeanne.

"My daughter learned something from her prison experience," said Mercier. "How to contradict her father."

"It might be possible," Jeanne said to Natanson. "He said that with a lot of money he might be able to save Mama. It might be possible."

Mercier nodded soberly. "I can't forswear the hope," he said.

Isidore Natanson accepted a glass of the rich red wine he had brought from the stores of the church. He clasped it between his hands. He had never felt at ease in the skirtlike cassock, and he sat awkwardly, at some pains to arrange it.

"The German is nonetheless a scoundrel," said Henri Mercier.

"Given a choice between a scoundrel and a fanatic, I will choose the scoundrel any time," said Natanson.

"We cannot spare any of the money," said Mercier. "Too much remains to be done with it."

"Perhaps not as much as you think," said Natanson. "The news this morning —I mean, the news from our radio in the campanile—indicates that the war is taking a new turn. The Americans have broken the German line at Saint-Lô. At long last they have broken out of the beachhead. They could reach Paris in . . . in two weeks."

"And what will the Germans do?"

"Try to destroy the city maybe," Natanson said grimly. "At the very least they will empty the prisons and camps. They will deport as many prisoners as they can. And maybe they will kill the rest. General Stülpnagel is gone. The German army tried to assassinate Hitler last week. It failed, and now the fanatics are more firmly in control than ever. A momentary delay was achieved two weeks ago when someone destroyed a bridge near the Pantin Station, but that has been repaired, and we have to anticipate wholesale deportations."

"Then money cannot be spared," Mercier said glumly. "How much gold is left?"

Natanson clasped his hands before him, intertwining his fingers and pressing, his knuckles whitening. "A little less than a hundred kilos," he said. "Worth, say, twenty thousand pounds sterling—maybe twenty-five—about twenty million French francs. Judiciously used, it may prove enough to save hundreds of lives."

"But not enough to save thousands," said Mercier bitterly. "And thousands are at stake."

"We do what we can," Natanson said quietly. He sighed. "Besides money, there are other problems."

"The problems are—"

"Time," said Natanson, "and finding the people to pay off. It is with respect to the latter that we have been ineffective since you were away. We didn't know who to approach and were afraid we'd approach the wrong people. We risked a few timid actions and saved a few people. The son of François Herval, we saved him. And Yvonne Fleury. But"—he shrugged—"the trains, the shipments of people, packed in cars like pigs . . . those we could not stop. We did not know how."

"That is my fault," said Mercier. "I should have trusted you with the names of the Germans I dealt with."

"You were wise not to trust anyone," said Natanson. "You could not have anticipated your arrest."

"Some of my old contacts are afraid of me now," said Mercier. "I—"

"Henri," Natanson interrupted. "Draw from the fund whatever money you need for an effort to save your wife. She is as deserving as anyone we have saved."

"Thank you, Isidore," said Mercier. Jeanne, too, murmured her thanks.

"And now, Henri," said Natanson, "let me report to you some developments that have occurred since you were arrested. We have two new allies. First, the consul-general of Sweden has offered his help in preventing deportations. As the representative of a neutral nation, he can go anywhere with his diplomatic pass, see anyone. His name is Nordling, Raoul Nordling. And, strange to relate, he has recruited a high-ranking German to our cause. His name is Bender, Emil Bender. He is an agent of the Abwehr."

"Abwehr? The man who came here this morning, Oberst Heinrici, calls himself an officer of the Abwehr. Could it be that—"

"It is possible," interrupted Natanson, "that a uniformed officer working out of Abwehr headquarters in the Hotel Lutétia would not even know about Bender. He operates out of uniform. He has lived in Paris as a sybarite, a playboy—and an effective undercover agent. Consul Nordling believes Bender is a dedicated opponent of the fanatic elements among the Nazis. Specifically, he is opposed to deportations, for humanitarian reasons."

"Is it not possible," Mercier speculated, "that Bender and Heinrici are motivated by the same thing, a desire to get their hands on our fund? Is it not possible they are working together?"

"Is it not possible," Natanson responded, "that we can gain an advantage from them, whatever their motive? If they can help us, let us give them some money. A lot of money."

Mercier frowned. "It may be a fraud. It may be an effort to take money from us and do nothing for us in return. How can we trust these Germans?"

"My friend," said Natanson with a smile, "every German you have worked with, every French collaborator, has been venal and greedy. Who else takes bribes, except venal and greedy people?"

"We cannot, I suppose, be fussy about who we deal with, especially if time is running short."

Natanson sighed. "Yes. There is reason to believe a train will leave for Germany on Friday. A message smuggled out of the camp at Drancy tells of a selection in progress. As many as a thousand men and women may be going— almost all of them Jews. What is more, this may be only a small shipment, only a fraction of the size of deportations to come. Besides, there are two hundred children at Drancy. Rumor has it that they are to be deported, too."

"Then every risk must be taken," said Mercier.

"And every resource utilized," added Natanson.

"I will look for Gabrielle tomorrow."

Gabrielle. A woman of inflexible habits. How very fortunate, thought Mercier. She sat as she did every sunny weekday at noon on a bench in the Jardin des Tuileries, munching on a bit of bread and cheese, sipping an undistinguished wine, her feet up on a second chair which she had dragged around in front of her, apparently studying the toes of her shoes with absorbing interest. Tonight at Shéhérazade she would dance, almost nude: a glamorous, provocative figure to the German officers who would ogle her from the tables. But at noon, sitting in the park without her makeup, without her rhinestoned costume, in sunlight instead of stagelight, she was an ordinary looking, dark-haired, thirty-three-year-old woman who would not be recognized by a single officer who had seen her dance last night.

"Mercier! My God, don't sit by me!"

He pulled a chair closer and sat down anyway.

"I don't dare talk to you," she said, looking away, pretending she was not talking to him.

"I must see Rascher," he said. "The usual place, at three this afternoon. You must be there. You will receive your usual fee."

"Doubled," she snapped. "The risk—"

"Very well, doubled," he said. "And Rascher may expect to be very generously paid."

She glanced at him. "To be seen with you—"

"In a public place. They will hardly be looking for me there."

"How do you know he won't betray you? Or that I won't?"

Mercier shook his head. "I don't fear that, Gabrielle," he said. "Neither you nor Rascher will send the Gestapo. If I were arrested again, they would of course interrogate me before they shot me, and—"

"And we don't dare let that happen."

"On the other hand, Gabrielle," he said, "you may note that I did not give your names to the Gestapo during all the weeks I was in prison and under severe interrogation. Apart from the money, I think you and the sturmbannführer may regard that as worth something."

"We lived in terror," she said.

"So did I."

* * *

Sturmbannführer Hermann Rascher was prompt. When Mercier arrived at Le Colisée, the famous restaurant on the Champs Elysées, the German was already there, sitting at a sidewalk table with Gabrielle, drinking a beer, smoking his pipe. He was the achetypal *bitte:* solid, phlegmatic, pink, with his hair clipped off the sides of his head. He spoke no language but German. Which was why Gabrielle was there—Mercier was insufficiently comfortable with his German to carry on a complex conversation, and he wanted an interpreter.

Rascher spoke in German to Gabrielle as Mercier sat down, and she translated: "Your willingness to take risks may be acceptable to you, but you have involved us as well."

"Nothing ventured, nothing gained," said Mercier.

A waiter came, and Rascher, without consulting Mercier, ordered a beer for him.

Rascher was one of the lowest-ranking officers at the tables. Mercier was surprised at the number of officers who still sat here, as they had for the past four years, while a critical battle was raging only two hundred kilometers away. He was not surprised that Rascher would not be called to the front: Rascher was a glorified file clerk, second- or third-highest officer in the Race and Resettlement Office, on the rue des Saussaies.

"I suppose you want to buy some Jews again," Rascher said.

"More than that," said Mercier. "I want to buy *all* the Jews, all the ones scheduled to be deported Friday."

"That is impossible."

Though the dialogue was slowed by the necessity of Gabrielle's translation, it was bold and sharp on Mercier's part, nervous and rushed on Rascher's.

"Nothing is impossible. I want the train delayed. Surely there is reason to delay a deportation, when the transport demands of the armies to the west must be overwhelming."

Rascher shook his head as he heard the translation. "Even if I could delay it, the train would go in a few days anyway."

"In a few days many things may happen," said Mercier. "The war in Normandy had been almost static since the sixth of June. It isn't anymore. The Americans have broken loose. Their tanks are just as capable of running wild across France as yours were in 1940. You may not be in Paris much longer."

"Longer than you may think," said Rascher.

"Railroads are being bombed constantly," Mercier continued. "The Résistance may rise. The next attempt to overthrow your government may succeed."

"In any event, it is impossible," Rascher repeated firmly. "I cannot delay a train."

"Orders become confused sometimes," said Mercier. "Papers are lost. Equipment is sent to the wrong place. With the situation in Normandy deteriorating, transport must be urgently in demand, and there must be confusion. Even the German army becomes less than perfectly efficient in times of stress. Suppose you received an order from Berlin, telling you to release the locomotive and cars now standing in Pantin Station to, say, Rennes for vital military transport?"

"I have no such order. I will not receive such an order. In any event, I have no authority to send a train anywhere."

"Herr Sturmbannführer. I am prepared to deliver into your hands, let us say, ten kilos of gold. With such an incentive, I feel sure you can discover a way to send the train to Rennes."

"And risk getting shot," said Rascher.

"If there were no risk, I wouldn't offer you ten kilos of gold," said Mercier blandly.

"You *are* a Jew, aren't you?" Rascher muttered.

Mercier understood that without translation. "If such an order arrived from Berlin, what would you do? Suppose it were directed to your superior officer, the head of the Race and Resettlement Office, but came while he was away from the office. Would you not do two things? Would you not, first, telephone the appropriate transport office and tell them the SS has been ordered to release this train for military service, and then, second, file the order? The army would be glad enough to have the train and would quickly send it off to wherever it had to go. And who would question you? If someone did, you would refer to the order from Berlin, neatly filed. If someone actually doubted your word in the matter—a most unlikely prospect, you will admit—then you would refer to the filed order."

"Which no one would find," Rascher grunted as Gabrielle finished the translation.

Mercier shrugged. "Has no one ever misfiled a paper before? Never, in your office? Not even in these days when dossiers are being burnt in the courtyard at rue des Saussaies?"

"You know too much."

"I know you can send the train away from Pantin Station. I know you can do it with minimal risk to yourself. I know you would very much like to have ten kilos in gold—Swiss gold coins, let us say."

"Twenty kilos," said Rascher.

"Fifteen. Ten years' income. When you go back home, life is going to be hard. A man with fifteen kilos of gold hidden away—fifteen, did I say? fifteen —plus all that I paid you in the past. Perhaps you've spent that."

"You are asking us to risk our lives," Gabrielle said without translating.

"Be sure you get part of the money," Mercier said to her in French so rapid that he doubted Rascher would even catch the sense of it. "You are going to need it. What will happen to collaborationist women after the war will not be pretty."

"I will look to you," she said.

"And to him. I will give you something beyond your usual fee if this succeeds. But ask him for two or three of his fifteen kilos. He couldn't have earned it without you."

"He went out," said Papa Ange to Heinrici. "I don't know where. I don't have the people to follow him. He was gone from eleven in the morning until five in the afternoon."

"Just walked out?"

"Just walked out. Out the front door. Down the street."

Papa Ange had placed the call at a telephone kiosk on Montmartre, to a telephone in the lobby of the Hotel George V, where Heinrici had responded to a page for "Oberst Mayer."

"Papa . . . You must follow him. Or Mama must follow him. He may have gone to where he hides the gold."

"Phillipe—"

"And there's something else Papa," Heinrici interrupted. "I want a woman. Unless Sidonie returns, I want the woman who lives with me in the Royal Monceau. I want an American passport for her, like the one you had made for me. I'll bring you her photograph. Let her be named on it as my wife."

"Philippe . . . I know where Sidonie is."

"Well, where is she? About time that she returned to duty."

"She is dead, Philippe. They found her body in the basilica last Thursday evening. The Gestapo is investigating."

"Sidonie . . . ," Heinrici mumbled hoarsely. "Dead?"

"I could have happened many ways, Philippe," said Papa. "She was most vulnerable."

Heinrici glanced around the lobby of the hotel as he delayed speaking, as though he were too shocked to speak. An officer who supposed he recognized him nodded and smiled. Heinrici smiled back. "Well . . . That's a tragedy, Papa," he said softly. "We will miss her."

XVII

MONDAY, JULY 31, 1944

O N Thursday night a locomotive pulling twenty cattle cars left Pantin Station for Rennes. Sergeant Willi Weibel, summoned from his quarters, mounted his motorcycle and carried to the camp at Drancy an order canceling the Friday-morning transfer of Jews to the station. At one in the morning, many of them were already lined up, to be ready to climb into the trucks at first light of dawn. Cursing guards herded them back into their barracks.

Sergeant Weibel was allowed to return to his bed for a few hours and, at seven, was sent to Fresnes. Governor Erich Langbehn had his prisoners already loaded on trucks. He refused to return them to their cells until he could confirm the order by telephone to rue des Saussaies. When the order was confirmed, he sent thirty-two men and eight women—Résistants—back into the stone cell blocks.

On Friday afternoon the postponement of the deportation came to the attention of Sturmbannführer Rascher's chief in the Race and Resettlement Office. Angry at this interference by the army in an operation sanctioned and required by Reichsführer Himmler himself—and presumably therefore by the Führer—he complained to Oberführer Franck and asked him to take the matter up with the Militärbefehlshaber in Frankreich. Since July 20 that headquarters had been in panic and confusion, and the duty officer responded to Oberführer Franck that no one there, to his knowledge, had asked for the train. The order must have come from Soissons, that is, from the headquarters of Oberbefehlshaber West—Commander-in-Chief West—if not in fact from OKW itself, with the Führer in East Prussia. Oberführer Franck wrathfully ordered the transport office to ignore any further military requisitions of transport required by the SS for deportations. ("Since July 20 we don't obey generals," he said. "Not even field marshals.") Also, he put through an order for another train.

On Friday, Baldwin limped out of his squalid room for the last time and moved to a tiny flat on the Ile de la Cité. In the one-time atelier of half a dozen artists of small renown, he had a skylighted bedroom-parlor-studio with the rudiments of a kitchen in one end. The change had been arranged for him by the SOE, dissatisfied with the signals it was receiving from the Résistance. Fearing betrayal, however remote the possibility, London ordered Captain Baldwin moved into a hideout unknown to anyone but his SOE contact in Paris and Miss Kip.

The order had originated with a man neither Baldwin or Adriana had ever heard of or would ever meet—Colonel Claude Ollivier, code-named Jade Amicol, the chief of all British intelligence operations in France. It was emphatic that Baldwin's whereabouts were to be communicated to *no one* but those specifically authorized.

Adriana helped Baldwin move. When he was in place and could wipe from his forehead the sweat that riding across town in a vélo-taxi had produced, they reviewed their situation. They concluded that they had no chance of discovering the whereabouts of Henri Mercier and would have to call once more on the resources of Konrad Heinrici. Adriana confided in Baldwin that when their work was completed, or when they had to acknowledge they could do no more, she did not intend to return to England. Somehow, she told him, she and Konrad were going to find new lives. Baldwin wished her success.

"Even so," he said, "we must tell Konrad a lie. Tell him the French doctor has moved me to a private clinic for treatment of my leg."

Adriana frowned. "That's what I'll tell him," she said quietly.

For Adriana, Monday began the way she hoped every day could begin for the rest of her life. She awoke in a sunlit bedroom—wakened perhaps by the aroma of the coffee a room-service waiter had quietly left on a table in the sitting room of the suite. A warm breeze billowed the sheer curtains hanging in the tall open windows. Konrad lay beside her, tranquilly snoring. The good ache of their lovemaking lingered in her loins.

She went to the bathroom, relieved herself and washed herself on the bidet; then she brought their breakfast tray to the bed. He had wakened. They sat together, nude, and shared a breakfast of French bread and marmalade with coffee. There was no butter. Butter had disappeared from Paris, even for high-ranking officers billeted in the luxury hotels.

Though her contentment was complete, she knew it was momentary. Konrad had spent much of Sunday at the Hotel Lutétia, in company with other officers reading intelligence dispatches from the Normandy front. General Patton was now in action. His tanks had advanced forty kilometers on Sunday and had captured the town of Avranches. This meant, Konrad said, that Patton's armored divisions were now entirely outside the German defense perimeter, out of Normandy actually, and were charging into Brittany, from where they would be free to turn toward Paris. She knew they were rapidly running out of peaceful mornings when they would waken in this lovely bedroom in this fine old hotel. She did not conceal from Konrad her joy at the imminent defeat of Nazism, but neither did she conceal from him her wistful delight in these July days.

After they ate they drew the curtain around the great bathtub and stood together in a stream of steaming water that poured from the shower: another luxury denied to nearly everyone else in Paris. She luxuriated in the hot water and rich soap, letting Konrad wash her, then washing him, until they were sweating from the heat. He then added cold water to the mixture so they would emerge from their shower invigorated and cool.

They were accustomed to the discreet hotel personnel coming and going quietly, even when they were not dressed, so they were not alarmed when they heard the door to their sitting room open. It was, they supposed, the waiter come for their tray. Only when someone knocked firmly on the door between the sitting room and bedroom were they startled. Konrad pulled his pistol from the holster hanging over a chair.

"Entrez."

The door opened.

"Théo!"

It was Le Capitaine, dressed in the white uniform of a hotel waiter.

"Théo. Why have you come here? What's going on?"

Le Capitaine closed the bedroom door and sat down, spent, in an armchair. "I had to come," he said. "I didn't know how else to reach you. Raymond is dead. Le Rasoir. He threw himself off a station platform in front of a Métro train rather than let himself be taken."

"Taken by . . . ?"

"The SD. They identified him. And me."

"How?"

The blond young man glanced at the bottle of cognac sitting by the bedside table, and Adriana poured a glassful of it and handed it to him.

"I'm not sure," he said. "I think I know, but I'm not sure. They identified Claude's body—Le Concombre. I suspect that when Le Docteur was playing traitor, he identified Claude and Raymond and me. Probably others. Le Chou-fleur... They could have arrested us anytime, probably, but they were waiting for us to do something, waiting for the opportunity to force us to lead them to someone more important. This is my guess."

"All right," Heinrici said brusquely. He was buttoning his tunic. "Raymond could have identified Adriana and me, but he is dead. You can, and you are here. Le Chou-fleur—where is Le Chou-fleur?"

"Hiding," said Le Capitaine, swallowing a mouthful of the cognac.

"Where?"

"Can I tell you?"

"If you don't, I can hardly help him. Is he safe? Is he where they can't find him?"

"He fled into the Church of St. Gervais. There is a priest there who will hide him. But he can't stay there. Today ... not longer."

Heinrici buckled his belt and replaced his pistol in the holster. "Who else?" he asked Le Capitaine. "Who else could identify us?"

Le Capitaine shook his head. "No one, I think. The prison governors. The Gestapo agent who got a good look at us is dead. Oberführer Franck."

"And two SS noncoms at the house on boulevard Suchet," said Heinrici. "But we don't need to worry about those. In fact, the only one we need worry about is Le Chou-fleur. And you. I have a safe place for you, Théo." He glanced at Adriana. "The room over the butcher shop," he said—and she nodded. "But tell me something about Le Chou-fleur. Who is he, really?"

"His name is Georges Militiades," said Le Capitaine. "He is a professor of ancient languages at the Sorbonne. He has been a Résistant since the first days of the occupation. He established a clandestine newspaper at first, then was recruited to more dangerous work. He is, I might tell you, a communist. He expects to be a commissar when the war is over."

"Will he cooperate if I find him a place to hide?"

"I am sure he will. He is terrified right now. If he does not survive the next few weeks, he will not become a commissar," Le Capitaine said sarcastically.

Heinrici turned to Adriana. "First, we must get Théo to the room over the butcher shop. Then we must get Le Chou-fleur out of the Church of St. Gervais and to some other safe place. I think I know where I can put him." He smiled wryly. "I still have a friend or two in the La Villette quarter. I am going to ask you, Adriana, to go to the Church of St. Gervais. Speak to this priest. Théo will give you his name. Tell him a German officer—me—will appear later today. Tell him to trust me. Tell him I will take Le Chou-fleur to a safe place."

Adriana nodded. "We've almost overlooked the official investigation, haven't we? I mean, the SS and Gestapo must be furious—"

"I can promise you," said Heinrici, "that they will not trace us through the cars. What we are countering now may be the only lead they have."

"Every German in Paris—the flics as well—must be looking for me," Le Capitaine said miserably.

"So it always seems," said Heinrici. "I've spent half my life being the subject of intense manhuts, and only once, in England, did they catch me. Policemen are occupationally stupid, Théo. It is one of their qualifications. If they were anything but half-witted, there would be no crime, no revolutions. Don't be afraid of them."

Heinrici picked up the telephone. He called Oberleutnant Krueger at Abwehr headquarters and ordered him to drop the Audi two-seater in front of the hotel; he, Heinrici, wanted to use it.

Adriana walked up the few steps to the Church of St. Gervais. She took no notice of the somewhat confused architecture of the façade but hurried into the flamboyant sixteenth-century interior.

"Père Philippe?" she asked the first priest she saw.

"Père Philippe is attending a very ill lady," said the priest. "Perhaps I can help you."

"I must see Père Philippe," she said. "I have a message for Professor Militiades."

The priest drew a breath. "The name is not familiar to me," he said. "Please be seated. I will see if I can learn where Père Philippe may be found."

She sat down on one of the chairs that stood in ranks in the nave. Looking around, she had to acknowledge the beauty of the eclectic architecture. Vaultings, carvings, paintings, the font—it was all heterogeneous, yet somehow in harmony. It was easy, here, to comprehend the solace troubled spirits found in these serene and timeless buildings.

"Mademoiselle?"

"Père Philippe?"

The priest nodded.

"I have a message for Georges Militiades," she said. "Le Chou-fleur."

"I know no such person," the priest said gently.

"No. Of course not. But if you should encounter such a man, give him this message, please. A German officer will call here later today. He is, right now, driving Le Capitaine to a safe place. When he comes, he will drive Professor Militiades to a safe house, where he can remain until the Allies come. He should trust this German. Tell him the message is from Adriana. Remind him it was Adriana who shot the traitor."

The priest's eyes narrowed. "What was the name of the traitor?" he asked.

"Robert. Le Docteur. He was responsible for the death of Sybil."

The old priest nodded. "All this is quite mysterious to me. But if the man you are looking for appears, I will give him the message."

Heinrici's confidence with the Audi increased as he whipped it through the
narrow streets of Montmartre. Le Capitaine sat beside him, frightened by the
attention the car itself might draw, not to mention the attention Heinrici's incautious driving might attract. An oberst with an Iron Cross, a waiter in white
uniform: they must be a spectacle.

With the basilica of Sacré Coeur looming above them in the twisting streets,
Heinrici handed him a key.

"You are not to go out, remember," Heinrici said. "You have the food from
the hotel. I will arrange more food for you in a day or so. And clothes. And
maybe new papers. Stay in the room, Théo. Don't leave, no matter what. There
will be another stage in this, some further element of your escape. But don't
force me to worry about you when I am trying to cope with the rest of it."

Le Capitaine nodded. Heinrici dropped him before the butcher shop, and
Théo mounted the steps, unlocked the door, and entered the small room.

"Père Philippe? I am the officer sent by Adriana."

"I know no one named Adriana," said the priest.

"I will sit down and rest, then," said Heinrici. "It is permitted?"

"You are more than welcome to rest," the priest said quietly.

In two minutes Le Chou-fleur appeared—Georges Militiades, sixty years old,
a vigilant, animated man in a characteristically Gallic double-breasted blue suit.
"Herr Oberst," he said.

"I have taken Le Capitaine to a place I consider safe," said Heinrici. "I can
do the same for you."

"I hardly dare leave the church."

"With a German officer of my rank? In his personal automobile? No one will
challenge us."

Militiades nodded. "I will come with you."

Heinrici drove south through Montparnasse and on south on the road to
Fresnes.

"Out of the city?" Militiades asked.

"A country refuge," said Heinrici. "Temporarily."

He turned west off the southbound avenue, into the area of wooded country
homes south of Versailles.

"They tell me you are really a German officer," said Militiades. "Yet, you
were the leader of the rescue of the Jews. It is inconsistent."

"Let us say," suggested Heinrici, "that I am a realist. The war is almost over.
I may ask for your testimony if I am brought to trial as an enemy of France."

"When the war is over," said Militiades, "we will be more interested in who
are friends and enemies of the people than who are friends and enemies of
nations."

Heinrici glanced at him and nodded.

"A different world," said Militiades. "Under the aegis of Comrade Stalin, the victor in this war."

"The victor . . . in this war."

"After Lenin, the one great man this century has produced."

Heinrici turned right on a narrow road marked with a sign: CHARTRES. The road descended into a wooded valley, shaded by trees. They were following a small stream bordered by fields of corn and small pastures where a few old cows grazed. Stone farmhouses and barns stood along the road, two hundred meters or so apart. The fields were not well weeded, and big insects buzzed among the blossoms on the tall weeds. The heat was oppressive. The air was dusty.

Heinrici pulled to the side of the road and stopped. "Here, Monsieur," he said.

Militiades looked at him skeptically.

"Up through the woods," said Heinrici. "A small house. You will see. *We* will see. I will lead you up the hillside."

Militiades opened the door and climbed out of the low car. He stood at the side of the road, looking around . . . fearful. Heinrici drew his Walther and stood in the car.

"So," said Militiades. "Why didn't I know? Actually, I *did* know. Hun! Pig!"

Heinrici leveled his pistol and squeezed the trigger. The muzzle blast was astonishingly loud in the open summer air. Militiades, struck square in the chest, flopped back into the heavy grass and weeds at the roadside. Heinrici aimed another shot and fired into the recumbent body.

"Another time, it will not be so easy," said Henri Mercier. "This time it was too childishly easy, too simple. The next time . . ." He shook his head. "Also, they will be alert."

Being Friday evening, it was shabbat, but the Pascin family did not observe it. The only sign of it in their house was the quiet way in which Louise laid their simple meal on the table. She did not speak of it. Jacob did not speak of it. Only Jeanne understood why: they were afraid. As the symbols had been removed from the house, so were the observances banished—but remorsefully, with a sense of betrayal.

Jeanne was wearing a skirt. During the day Louise had made it from an old brown corduroy jacket—cutting the fabric to a rudimentary pattern, then fitting it to her, sewing with needle and thread, without a machine. Though Jeanne had not complained at wearing boy's clothes—because truly she didn't mind— Louise had supposed it must embarrass her.

Her father and the two Pascins smothered her with sympathy for the trivial— the boy's clothes she had to wear, her bald head. She knew why: they didn't want to think or talk of what had happened to her. Her father knew—he guessed, anyway—that she had been raped, yes, raped repeatedly. He didn't want to talk about that. It horrified him, of course, but besides that he was ashamed of it. Try as he might not to be, he was ashamed that his daughter had been defiled. He couldn't help himself.

Nor could the Pascins. They felt it, too: alienation from this girl who had endured what they did not want even to think of. She was contaminated. It was not her fault, but she was unclean. Their minds—and her father's—were filled like old attics with the accumulated litter of lifetimes, and reason could not sweep out what feeling and habit sealed in, no matter that they genuinely wanted it to.

Her own mind turned too often to something she wished she could banish: the other girls, left behind because no one had staged a daring rescue for them. She thought of two or three of them. She could not rid herself of the thought that her liberation had been a gross injustice to them, for which she could never atone. What right had she to sit here in this comfortable parlor, about to eat a warm, savory meal, while they lay on the stone floors of their cells, in their own filth, tormented by hunger?

"I wish," said Henri, "there were some way to reestablish contact with the two SOE operatives who took part in our liberation. The German colonel says they are probably on their way back to London, but—"

"I know how to contact the woman," Jeanne interrupted.

Her father's eyes hardened for a moment. He would never accustom himself to interruption by his daughter. But he nodded at her and listened.

"The Englishwoman—who, I think, is not really English—was living with the German colonel. I heard the colonel speak to her of the impossibility of her returning to the hotel that night. And when he was here, didn't he say he could be reached at the Hotel Royal Monceau? If she is still in Paris, then perhaps—"

"Perhaps she still lives with him," said Henri. "But . . . Can we trust this woman? If she is sharing a hotel room with the German colonel, is she not his confederate?"

"I trust her," Jeanne said simply. "That night—" She stopped, shook her head. "The woman was brave. The English officer let her lead. *He* trusted her. The Frenchman who was killed . . . He trusted her. She could have abandoned the crippled officer—and for that matter, she could have abandoned me—to save herself. And she didn't. I—"

"Very well," said Henri Mercier. "You trust her. I suppose then *we* can trust her. Even so, how can we contact her? None of us would dare go to the Royal Monceau."

"Suppose we telephoned the hotel and asked to speak to Colonel Heinrici," she said. "Maybe she will answer."

"A possibility," said Henri thoughtfully.

"A risk," said Jacob Pascin. "What if *he* answers?"

"Hang up," said Jeanne.

"Could such a telephone call not be traced?"

"We must place it from a kiosk," she said. *"I* must place it."

"You? Why you?"

"She will know my voice. If she wants to ask questions to establish that I am who I say I am, I can answer her."

"You, of all of us, dare not go on the streets," said Louise. "With your shaved head—" She sighed. "No, child. The first flic who saw you would know you have been in prison and would stop you."

"No," said Jeanne. "I dress like a boy. With a cap. After dark. Before curfew. A few streets. No one will notice me."

"An unacceptable risk," said her father flatly.

"Perhaps one we must take," she said. "Otherwise we and everything we are trying to do are at the mercy of the German colonel."

"I will go," he said.

"She saw you only for a few minutes, Papa, heard you speak only a few words."

"It would be foolish."

She heard in his voice the ebbing of his resolve. "Papa! What am I to do? Hide here until my hair grows out? Or the Allies come? Who knows what is going to happen in the next few weeks? We are talking about saving hundreds of lives, and you call it foolish for me to take a few minutes' small risk! You—"

"Very well," he interrupted gruffly. "Let it become a little darker."

She dressed again in boy's clothes—black trousers, a white shirt, a dark-blue beret covering her head. Louise used eyebrow pencil and darkened her head below the edge of the beret. Also, Louise bound her chest with a strip of cloth to flatten her breasts. Just at sunset, when the light was deceiving, as she said, Jeanne left the house and walked out onto rue Boulanger. She carried a loaf of bread under her arm, to suggest she was a boy sent out on an early-evening errand. She carried tokens for the telephone, three of which Jacob fortunately had been carrying in a pocket in his business suit. They had looked up the number. The nearest kiosk, Jacob said, was on rue Caulaincourt, four blocks away.

No one paid her the slightest attention. Anyone who noticed her took her for a thirteen- or fourteen-year-old boy. She passed under the eyes of scores of people. On a hot July evening many sat on their doorstoops, while others hurried on the varied and mysterious business of all city crowds. It was as it had been in the old times, before the Germans came—except that the omnipresent *bittes* were everywhere: promenading with girls on their arms, peering into shop windows—intent probably on buying what little merchandise Paris still had to offer—sitting in cafés, and, of course, walking casually through the streets in armed patrols, lazily aware of the futility of patrolling.

A *bitte* corporal jostled her and apologized in rough, accented French.

She was afraid. But it was different from fear she had known before: a high, nervous apprehension, colored with exhilaration, not the dull dread of her weeks of imprisonment nor the overpowering terror of the night of the escape. This was controllable fear. She mimed the carefree boy on his errand and tried not to walk too briskly, not to peer around her too intently.

The kiosk was vacant. She walked toward it quickly.

"Entshuldigen Sie."

A man in a black suit, black hat, had stepped between her and the kiosk. Jeanne froze.

"Haben Sie das Kleingeld für ein hundert francs?"

What was he saying? *Kleingeld?* She had heard more German than she ever wanted to hear for the rest of her life, but this word—*Hundert francs? "Pardonnez-mois, Monseiur?"* she mumbled.

"Uh . . . *avez-vous le monnaie de cent francs?"*

He held the hundred-franc note out to her. He wanted change. She stiffened and took control of her voice.

"Non, Monsieur. Je le regrette."

The German shrugged and walked away.

Her hand trembled as she lifted the telephone instrument and inserted her token. She had memorized the number, and suddenly it was gone. She focused, and it returned. She dialed. The telephone rang.

"Hotel Royal Monceau."

"Je voudrais parler avec Colonel Konrad Heinrici, s'il vous plaît."

"Ne quittez pas."

She heard the ring in his room.

"Heinrici hier."

She hung up.

Heinrici put down the telephone. Then he picked it up again and waited for the hotel operator.

"Monsieur?"

"Did we lose the connection, or did my party hang up?"

"I believe your party hung up, Monsieur."

"Who was it, do you have any idea?"

"No, Monsieur. From the voice I believe it was a young lady."

"Speaking French?"

"Yes, Monsieur. She asked for you by name."

Adriana came out of the bathroom. They were dressing for dinner, and she was almost ready.

"Anything important?"

"A young woman, the operator said. She hung up." He frowned. "You know, I don't like that sort of thing. A lifetime of expecting the worst, I guess."

Adriana nodded. "I've moved out of quarters after receiving a call like that."

Heinrici buttoned his gray tunic. "Well, I'm not moving out of these—not until I'm forced out, which will be soon enough."

A fiacre summoned by the hotel was waiting when they came down, and comfortably seated in it they rode behind a single white horse, around the Arch and down the Champs Elysées on their way to Maxim's. Heinrici had booked a table.

It was something they should do while they had the chance, he had told Adriana. Who could say how much longer he would have any special status in Paris, or even be there? Who could say he and she would survive the fighting that would surely come? Who could say Maxim's would? Or even Paris? They did not exchange all these thoughts, but such thoughts were in both their minds as they entered the warmly lighted rooms of the world-famous restaurant.

They sat side by side facing the room, at a table laid with white linen and with polished silver that reflected the points of flame from the four candles that burned in a silver candelabra. Half a dozen yellow roses lay in a silver dish under the candelabra.

The determined elegance that surrounded her was grotesque to Adriana. She felt as if she were on the stage where a bizarre farce was being played by a hundred crude and ungainly marionettes, all wooden-eyed, all wearing painted-on grins, none capable of a single realistic movement. German officers in uniforms of gray and black and sky blue, their sluts in silks and jewels, a few fat, flushed, be-ringed civilians, the usual corps of obsequious scurrying waiters, a sweating string quartet—all feigned gaiety and savoir faire in maladroit postures and movements, as if jerked on invisible strings.

"Don't they know?" Adriana asked Heinrici.

"A few days ago," said Heinrici, "Hitler told someone that the only fighting his Paris officers are doing is for choice tables in choice restaurants. But of course they know. They're here for the same reason we are. They thought they had plenty of time to experience Paris. A lifetime. Now . . . They know."

She glanced around and shook her head.

"Some of them will die in the next few weeks," he said. "Most of them will go home. Some would rather die than go home. And the women . . . They know what will happen to them." He too glanced around. "The most fortunate people here tonight are the waiters."

They ordered the best Maxim's had to offer. Heinrici had at last been able to draw almost all of his accumulated pay, which had been held for him during his long service in London, and he meant to spend his German marks while they could still buy something. Their waiter was pleased to serve a client who ordered what he wanted without so much as a glance at the price.

From somewhere, from cellars that had to be all but depleted, Maxim's brought out the same fine champagne that had always been served. There was still caviar. There was still squab, still pheasant, still everything, almost. Maxim's could do it, possibly because there were so very few who could afford it.

"It is possible," Heinrici said when their pheasant had been served and their Bordeaux poured, "that the city will be destroyed in the fighting. It was declared an open city by the French in 1940. I don't think the Befehlshaber Gross-Paris will do that. Even if he wanted to, Hitler would not allow it. But"
—he shook his head—"it seems inconceivable. And if it's not destroyed, it is where we should live."

"That will be impossible, Konrad," she said.

"Why impossible?" he asked. He put down his knife and fork and turned his head to face her directly. "Suppose you and I had two American passports, identifying us as a husband and wife from, say, Chicago. Suppose I had other papers identifying me as a wealthy American businessman with connections to some company that wants to resume doing business in France. Suppose—"

"Forged documents," she said. "Good until someone really looks at them."

"You remember the night I recovered paper and covers from the storeroom at Galien et Fils?" he asked. "I also took American passport paper and covers. Le Faussaire does good work. I do better. Anyway, when the war is over the French will be heartily tired of documents and stamps and all the rest of it. These passports will come with entry visas already in place. We can check into a hotel, later find a flat, as Mr. and Mrs. American. The French will note our presence in a file, as they do all visiting foreigners, but their action will be perfunctory. We speak English. We'll have to learn to speak it through our noses a little, to sound American. I see no difficulties."

"They will be obsessed with hunting down Germans," she said.

"*Some* Germans. Why me? I am not of the Gestapo, the SS. I was once a German spy in Paris, but they do not know my name, do not have my photograph, do not have my fingerprints. They were looking for me in 1940 but didn't know who they were looking for. Today"—he shrugged—"why would they be looking for me?"

"Better we leave here," said Adriana. "Go to a neutral country. Maybe to Spain."

"We should have alternatives," he said. "Did I not once hear that the SOE would provide us passes to let us through the Allied lines? We should have those documents. When the fighting begins, they may save our lives."

"I can get those documents," she said. "What about money? The SOE will provide me a little. But"—she shook her head—"we will have to eat."

"Let me tell you something," said Heinrici, lowering his voice a little. "The Abwehr maintains a secret fund, which is used for paying bribes and so on. It is in gold, in Swiss francs, much of it. I can get my hands on a substantial amount of that fund. It will be enough to take care of us for quite some time."

"Konrad, you . . . ?"

"I will have to desert. Once I have the gold in hand, I will have to disappear. I know Paris well, as you understand. I have friends here. We can hide here for a time, until the Allies come, then we can assume our American identities. On the other hand, if the city is bombed and shelled, we might want to get out. I have no problem with going through the German lines. I will still have the insignia and papers of an Abwehr colonel, and no little captain or lieutenant is going to ask many questions in the confusion of battle. Getting to the Allies' lines, your identity and your SOE passes would be our salvation."

Adriana put her hand on his. "It's a decision I've already made, you know," she said softly. "I mean, to stay with you, or to go with you—whatever happens, to be with you."

Heinrici nodded. "I know, Adriana," he said.

"I love you, Konrad," she said.

XVIII

THURSDAY, AUGUST 3, 1944

HENRI Mercier rose to speak. He glanced around the Pascin's parlor. The others—Jacob and Louise Pascin; Isidore Natanson, Pére Jean; Rabbi Benjamin Gardier, once leader of a large and prosperous congregation, now an emaciated, hollow-eyed man in hiding; Esther Baudin, widow of Jerome Baudin, now also in hiding since the deportation of her husband—all looked up at him with a raptness of attention that disturbed him and caused him, at this very last instant before he spoke, to reconsider his words.

"Since we . . . began our modest effort to save as many of our people as we could," Mercier began, "we have, I believe, saved the lives of as many as three hundred." He drew a breath and sighed. "We must, therefore, account ourselves as failures, because as many as twenty-five *thousand* may have been deported from France—nearly all of them, surely, to their deaths." He lowered his head. "Now, as we anticipate the liberation of Paris, we must also anticipate mass deportations and executions. I paid more than three and a half million francs last week to delay the deportation scheduled for Friday. Now we have received the appalling news of a plan to deport two hundred children from the camp at Drancy. We have a little less than nineteen million francs in gold left. It may be enough to save those children. Rabbi Gardier will review what we know, so we all understand what is at stake."

The Rabbi rose to speak, and Henri Mercier sat down. Rabbi Benjamin Gardier was scarred. In September 1940, when the Occupation was only three months old, he had been seized by a gang of French toughs who wanted to prove their commitment to the New Order. As a crowd stood by in sullen silence, they sprinkled gasoline on his beard and set it on fire.

When he walked the streets today—which he, too, did without the yellow star inscribed JUIF—he was taken for a wounded veteran. He carried a certificate of Aryanship, not a forgery but one obtained for him by a high official of the Paris police, certifying that Benjamin Gardier was not a Jew but a Coptic Christian whose Egyptian family had lived in Paris since 1884.

"The trains will go again," he said. "We are not deceived about that. Thousands more will die. How many can we save?"

"How do we choose who we save?" asked Isidore Natanson.

"I don't know," said the rabbi. "That has been a problem from the beginning."

"With few exceptions, we saved who we *could*," said Henri Mercier. "We did not choose. Circumstances chose for us."

"We may suppose," said the rabbi, "that God chooses those He allows us to help."

"I don't think I like your God very much," said Jeanne. She had sat apart in the corner of the room, listening. Keeping her silence. "'Whom I will save, I will save.' Out of twenty-five thousand, one thousand. Not including my mother." She shook her head. "God of love!" she sneered. "God of justice!"

"Go to your room, Jeanne," said Henri Mercier.

"No, Papa."

"Go . . . to . . . your . . . room!"

"No, Papa."

Henri Mercier glanced around the circle of his friends. "What am I to do?" he asked in quiet, angry resignation. "Strike her?"

"Pity her," said Rabbi Gardier simply.

"Yes," Mercier said. "I do."

Jeanne returned their curious glances with a hard stare. She chose not to speak further.

The rabbi licked his lips and wiped them with the back of his hand, taking a moment to refocus himself. "I think our choice is dictated to us." He glanced at Jeanne. "Whether by God or otherwise. Until now we have only heard rumors that the children were to be deported. Now it is worse than a rumor—it is a fact. They mean to deport two hundred children from the camp at Drancy, to Poland, to the prison the Germans call Auschwitz. I need hardly say what will happen to them there."

"Whose children are they? Do we know?" asked Jacob Pascin.

Esther Baudin answered. She was a slight, short woman, blonde, pink of complexion, with large round blue eyes behind her gold rimmed over spectacles. Her husband had been deported in November, 1943. Her daughter was one of the Jews Henri Mercier had managed to get across the Spanish frontier and was living in Portugal. In the seven months Esther had spent in hiding in Paris —which she refused to leave on the faint hope her husband might return—she had served the humanitarian cause with an odd aptitude no one had suspected she had: the ability to commit to memory enormous quantities of information, names mostly, that no one dared commit to paper. She carried a cyanide ampule and was prepared to use it.

Esther Baudin had taken a serious risk in coming here. After her husband's deportation, she had torn from her clothes the yellow stars all Jews were required to wear, and on the infrequent occasions when she dared go on the streets, she went without the star. The first policeman who looked at her papers would see she was a Jew, and she would be subject to arrest.

"The children are Jews, most of them," she said. "But not all. Some are the children of Résistants. If we had a list of the names, it's likely we would know some of the families. Some are the children of parents who have been killed. Some are the children of parents who are in prison. Some are little children. Some are older. All are to be shipped by train to Auschwitz."

"How can they be saved?" asked Louise Pascin.

"I don't know," said the rabbi. "I feared there was no hope—until our valued friend Henri Mercier was restored to us. Now—"

"We can only try," said Henri Mercier. "It will not be easy, but maybe we can find a way. Do all agree that this is our next—perhaps our last—task?"

They nodded, all of them, as he glanced from one face to another.

"Then I will try," he said solemnly.

"I want to raise another point," said Jacob Pascin. "I want this committee to vote the release of money for Henri's effort to save his wife."

"Oh, no," said Mercier firmly. "All we have may not be enough to save the children."

"What kind of people would we be if we did not try to save Narcisse Mercier?" asked Jacob. "I propose that we simply set aside ten kilos of gold for the purpose."

"No," said Mercier.

"Yes," said Jacob, and he was echoed around the room.

Henri Mercier lowered his head. "Only if there is a strong chance of success," he said.

The meeting was over, and Louise passed around small glasses of wine.

As they sipped, Jeanne stepped close to Rabbi Gardier and spoke quietly. "I am sorry, Rabbi," she said. "Not for how I feel. For offending you."

The rabbi looked down into the calm eyes of the diminutive girl. "I under-stand," he said.

"Don't pity me," she said.

"I . . . meant it figuratively."

"Even figuratively. Anyway, I want to go with you when you leave. I have a telephone call to make. If we walk together—"

They walked down the north slope of Montmartre, miming a father and son, the son receiving instruction from the father in impatient words. The rabbi strode along beside her, frowning over their earnest talk.

"I am not bitter. Really, I'm not. I hate the people who did what they did to me. I'd like to watch their executions. But I don't hate the world. I don't hate life."

"I am glad to hear it."

"I'm not ashamed of myself, either." She looked up into his face, defiant. *"I survived."*

He nodded uncertainly. "Why do you tell me this?"

"You know why."

They had reached a telephone kiosk. He stood aside while she stepped in, put her token in the slot, and dialed the Royal Monceau once again.

"Hotel Royal Monceau."

"Je voudrais parler avec Colonel Heinrici, s'il vous plait."

"Ne quittez paz."

She allowed two rings, no more.

"'Allo."

"Colonel Heinrici, s'il vous plait."

"Il n'est pas ici. Qui est à l'appareil?"

"Adriana? Ici Jeanne Mercier."

"I tell you, Heinrici, they are insane!"

General Karl Hausser was talking to Heinrici about what he had seen and heard on his visit to Berlin. He no longer considered his office safe for confi-dential conversation; if it was not wired now, it might be soon. They sat at lunch in the dining room of the Hotel George V.

"The situation is desperate, Heinrici. Desperate. General Patton is back in action—the most dangerous general the Allies have. He has broken loose. His tanks are running everywhere—anywhere they want to go. Do you have any idea how they are making war? A *thousand* of their Flying Fortresses—I do not exaggerate, a thousand—fly over our positions and drop tens of thousands of bombs! In half an hour, a whole division may disappear off the order of battle! Tanks are overturned. Artillery positions are reduced to wreckage. Every road, bridge, and railroad track for miles simply ceases to exist. Men—those who survive—run in panic. Units dissolve. Organization collapses. And when the smoke clears a bit, the commanding officer is confronted with two things—onrushing Allied troops and tanks, *and* an order from Rastenburg to counterattack! The Führer has no realistic idea of what is going on at the battle front."

To Heinrici all this was almost irrelevant, though he was interested in observing to what a surprising extent General Hausser had disintegrated. He had returned from Berlin shattered in his confidence, frightened. His fleshy face sagged. His voice was weak and hoarse.

"This weekend," Hausser went on, "General von Kluge *will* counterattack. If by some miracle he could break through to the sea, he could cut Patton off from his supply lines, isolate him, and leave him to be chewed up at leisure—while Army Group B falls on the western flank of the Normandy beachheads. If he is favored with a miracle, he could drive the Allies off the Continent. But"—he shrugged—"this miracle must be achieved with divisions that exist on paper only, or exist with twenty percent of their strength. For air support, all he will be able to rely on is, I believe, *twenty-three* Luftwaffe fighters. Units move cross country at night, because there are no roads, bridges, or railroads, and in daylight they are bombed unmercifully. We estimate the Allies have a million and a half men ashore in Europe! The miracle the Führer demands—"

"What is our role?" Heinrici asked, fearful he was about to receive an order to leave Paris, perhaps for the front.

General Hausser sipped from a glass of crisp, chilled white wine. He took a moment to savor it, to get a grip on himself. "Perhaps . . . ," he said. "Perhaps our role is to pray for the miracle the army needs."

Heinrici smiled wryly. "I am afraid our prayers would be lost in the din of those going up from three million Parisians."

"Praying for a German catastrophe," said Hausser.

Heinrici nodded.

"What progress have you made toward finding those Jews?" the general asked, abruptly changing the subject and abruptly crisp.

Heinrici drew a breath. "I've reduced the number of possibilities," he said.

General Hausser shook his head disdainfully. "In other words, you haven't found them and haven't found the gold."

"I haven't found them," said Heinrici. "Not yet."

"Millions . . . ," mused the general. "Millions of marks in gold. Heinrici . . . I have never been naive enough to suppose you intended to turn all that gold over to the Abwehr. I ordered you to, but I've never been deceived about what you would really do when you got your hands on it. Now I am giving you another order, Herr Oberst. When you find the gold, *bring it to me*."

"And what will you do with it, Herr General?"

The general glanced around the room, at the other officers eating and drinking. He looked Heinrici straight in the eye. "I will share it with you. After all, there is more than either of us can use."

From the windows of Baldwin's flat Adriana could see little but walls and rooftops. The towers of Notre Dame stood so high above the streets that they were actually visible through the skylight, but nothing else of the great cathedral could be seen from here: neither could the river.

She sat at a little table and watched Baldwin burn slightly moistened sheets of newspaper in a little tin stove; he was frying the two eggs she had brought him from the hotel. The smoke rose to the skylight, which was partly open, and was sucked out by the breeze.

"I had a thousand questions," said Adriana. "I couldn't ask one. She was afraid to stay on the telephone. I didn't even get a chance to tell her the time she suggested was all but impossible."

"You could change the dinner arrangement," said Baldwin.

"I suppose so. But Konrad has decided to cultivate the friendship of Gruppenführer Schenck. Since July twentieth every army officer is suspect—Abwehr officers in particular—and Konrad wants to have a friend in the enemy camp. He arranged this dinner. I actually bought a dress for the occasion. He insisted."

"Have you told Heinrici about the call?"

"I haven't seen him. General Hausser returned from Berlin and called Konrad to the Hotel Lutétia."

"You have no doubt the voice on the telephone was that of Jeanne Mercier?"

"No doubt at all. Not from her voice, from what she said. I can tell you every word she said. 'Adriana, this is Jeanne. I was with you the night you found the key behind the brick. I want to see you again. At seven tomorrow evening I will be in the Jarden des Tuileries at the pond where they sail boats. Please be there. Alone. Don't tell anyone about this call. Don't tell Colonel Heinrici.' And she hung up."

"Someone may have had her at gunpoint. Or worse."

"So are we to ignore her?"

Baldwin looked away from his eggs. "Of course not. Though it's a risk."

"I am sorry to have to ask you to take it."

He looked again to his eggs. "If Colonel Harding knew about it, he would order me to take it. There may be a degree of safety in my going. If she is in Gestapo hands and they have set up a trap for you, they may overlook me."

"They are looking for a man who walks with a cane," she said.

"They won't see one," said Baldwin. He pointed toward a corner of the studio. "The doctor fetched me those nice crutches when he came here. I hobble around this room with a cane, but I'm to go on those if I go out."

She frowned. "They do add to your disguise."

"Yes. You could look at it that way."

"I'm sorry, Len. I don't mean to be flippant."

"And I don't mean to be cynical," he said. "After all, if I hadn't damned near lost my leg at Dieppe, chances are I'd have come ashore in Normandy on June sixth, still a commando, with the odds decidedly against my survival." He shrugged. "So—the doctor says I need to be in the hospital. If I could, I'd send a wire to Eisenhower—'Come quick to Paris, while I've still got two legs.'"

"You trust this doctor? I don't mean his medical judgment—"

"You mean, is he likely to betray me? Ask Théo. He sent him. Speaking of whom, how is he doing?"

"Still in Konrad's room over the butcher shop. Complaining that it's like solitary confinement. He's only a boy, you know. He was a student. I mean, he was a student until Monday. He was on the street Tuesday. Telephoned his parents. It was a stupid thing to do. Fortunately he didn't give them the least hint as to where he is. Anyway, he says he didn't."

Baldwin carried the frying pan to the table and began to salt and pepper his fried eggs. "I'm grateful to you for these," he said.

"The hotel believes they were broken into a glass of tomato juice and drunk as a cure for the morning-after nausea," she said. "If you are a German officer or his mistress, among your privileges are those of being able to drink too much, then of being able to obtain something to cure the hangover."

He began to eat. "I am going to make a suggestion," he said. "I know you are in love with Konrad. In fact, I hold him in high regard myself. Even so, I suggest you do what Jeanne Mercier asked and don't tell him about the call until we see what comes of it."

"Why?"

Baldwin raised his eyebrows high. "Well . . . You've been an intelligence operative longer than I have. Isn't it a rule that information is given only to those who must have it? We have no idea what the Mercier girl wants. She—"

"When she called, she asked for Konrad."

"But she didn't ask for him to meet her. She asked for you. Alone. Why alone?"

"Maybe she and her father are terrified of German officers—of all German officers, including the one who engineered their escapes."

"We can speculate," said Baldwin. "I suggest we find out if there was a reason why she said 'alone,' or if it was just a coincidence."

Adriana frowned and shook her head. "It wasn't a coincidence. Obviously she had rehearsed what she was going to say."

"I trust Konrad," said Baldwin. "But let's find out what she has in mind. When we're ready to tell him, we can say she contacted me, not you. We—"

"You're right, Len."

* * *

Friday, August 4 was a blustery day, with clusters of threatening clouds hurrying across the sky, west to east. Late-morning thunder stopped people on the streets all over Paris—French and Germans alike. They stood listening, tensely alert. They thought they might possibly, just possibly, be hearing the roar of artillery.

Rumor put General Patton's tanks at Le Mans, halfway from Normandy to Paris. Other rumors had the English across the Seine at Rouen and racing toward Paris from the northwest.

Abwehr headquarters refused to deny a rumor circulating among the German officers of the Kommandantur that an SS panzer division had retaken Avranches and isolated Patton from his supplies. Though General Hausser and all his officers knew the rumor was not true, they were afraid of being accused of defeatism if they denied it.

Adriana had spoken the truth when she told Baldwin that Heinrici had insisted she buy a new dress for the dinner party he was giving that night for Gruppenführer Schenck and Martine Paul. Many German marks, offered in a shop on the Place Vendome, had produced from the shop's depleted stock a few silk dresses, from which Heinrici had prompted her to make a choice: a simple tube of thin black silk that fell over her figure like oil, held up by thin black straps, with a hemline just above her knees. Except for a half-inch border of black lace around the neckline and hemline, it was without trim or ornament and must have been left over from the twenties, so far was it from the styles of recent years. Konrad thought it beautiful, and that was what mattered.

But she had to stay in the suite most of the day while a seamstress worked at fitting the dress to her. The old woman, who reeked of garlic, remained as silent as she could and by manner and expression declared her haughty contempt for a young woman who would prostitute herself to a *bitte*. Half a dozen times she stabbed Adriana with pins, and Adriana had no doubt it was deliberate.

Konrad arrived at six, carrying a small box. He handed it to her. She opened it and found within a jade necklace: ovals of pale jade and a darker jade pendant carved to form the delicate, intricate figure of a leering Chinese god.

"With your blond hair, your black dress . . ."

"Konrad!"

She threw her arms around Konrad and clung to him, pressing her face to his neck, to hide her flushed face and her tears—tears for Dirk, who used to come home with small gifts, surprises.

"Where in the world did you get it?" she asked later when she was dressed to go out and he was fastening the clasp for her.

"I had the help of a man you'll meet someday," he said. "I call him Papa."

She contemplated her image in the mirror. It was true that the jade lying on her pale skin was an interesting color contrast with the black dress. Her shoulders and arms were bare—as were her legs; no stockings they could find in Paris were sheer and flattering. Besides, garter clasps would have stood up as visible lumps under the black silk. She felt physically naked, but cloaked by a warm sense that more than compensated: the certainty that Konrad was going to be proud of her. It was an uncomplicated little feeling, a sentiment she had almost forgotten.

Gruppenführer Heinz Schenck wore that night the black uniform of the SS, silver insignia polished, black boots gleaming. Martine Paul was elegantly dressed in a flowing black skirt, white knit blouse, black jacket with padded shoulders; her hair was bound up in a black turban. Though her outfit was the height of Paris fashion, she attracted far less admiration than Adriana.

"The rain is oppressive," said Gruppenführer Schenck. "If it is raining like this in Normandy, Patton's tanks will burn all their petrol churning their tracks in the mud—and since they have been cut off from their supply of petrol, they will be immobilized."

"That is excellent news," said Martine Paul.

Schenck raised a glass of champagne. "The Allied invasion is at an end," he said. "That episode is over. Within a week the English and Americans will be driven back on their beachheads, and within two weeks they will have withdrawn what they can and will be gone, once and for all. To victory!"

All drank.

"This is marvelous news, Herr Gruppenführer," said Adriana.

Schenck nodded. "Then, with our victory weapons—rockets, rocket planes, other things the Führer has held in reserve for this hour—we will finish the war." He glanced around the table. "Let us," he said, "make ourselves a mutual pledge." He raised his glass. "To August 4, 1945, when we four will meet here again!"

As Adriana raised her glass for this toast, she glanced at Heinrici. He had warned her that Schenck was likely to propose that the two couples trade off tonight in the hotel, she sleeping with Schenck, Heinrici sleeping with the Schiaparelli model—and he had promised her that he would avoid it, no matter what reason he had to give.

Baldwin rode in a vélo-taxi to the Place de la Concorde, once again encountering a security check, but his ugly wound won quick acceptance of his identity as a French veteran crippled in 1940. Swinging along on his crutches, he reached the steps into the Jardin des Tuileries, climbed up, and then swung along one of the broad gravel paths between the Jeu de Paume and L'Orangerie.

This August evening, with rain threatening, Parisians still enjoyed their park. Where vendors would have sold ice cream, vendors now sold weakly flavored water, the best they could do in wartime. Young girls with their hair combed up

into untidy masses atop their heads, wearing short, bright-colored skirts, and
wooden-heeled shoes, ambled nonchalantly as though there were no war, no
Normandy front, no German soldiers ogling them. The soldiers followed the
girls, joking to each other in quiet German and breaking into laughter they tried
to subdue but could not. Children ran. Old people sat on the benches, some of
them clutching canes between their knees.

Within view, almost luminous against the darkening clouds, the red, white,
and black swastika flags whipped on staffs above the Louvre and the requisitioned hotels on the rue de Rivoli. Even the young German soldiers—boys,
most of them, probably passing through Paris on their way to the front and
having the experience of a lifetime, which they would describe in letters home
—seemed hardly to notice the flags, as if they were the most natural thing in the
world. Baldwin found it hard to see any menace in these children. It was a
measure of Germany's condition that these youths were in uniform and here in
Paris.

Near the pond, old women with square carts rented out toy sailboats as they
had done every year that Baldwin had been in Paris. Parents offered a few
francs, and their children carried the little boats—with their sails of red and
green and orange and blue—to the edge of the round pond, then sat on the
stone border and pushed them out into the water with sticks. This evening, in
the freshening wind of a summer storm, the boats sped into a cluster on the
northeast side of the pond, and the children gathered there, shrieking and pushing.

Jeanne Mercier. A slight girl, hollow-eyed, with a bald head. How could she
venture on the streets at all, much less to a crowded park where some of the
civilians sitting around were likely as not to be agents of one kind or another?
He worked his way around the pond.

"Jeanne?" he said to a slight girl. A wig? Could she be? "Jeanne?"

She ignored him and walked on, glancing back at the odd man who had
spoken.

A girl. A nineteen-year-old girl with no hair on her head. She had to be
somehow disguised. And she was looking for Adriana. He searched, staring
into the faces of a dozen girls and boys, meeting eyes and getting no reaction.

A boy in a dark-blue beret sat on one of the benches, closely studying his
sailboat and toying with the strings as if he were repairing something. Baldwin
stopped before him, stared, and met his eyes. The boy's eyes met his, then
turned down. Baldwin planted his crutches in the gravel and swung wearily
away. He had begun to believe he would not find Jeanne Mercier—or that
Gestapo agents were indeed here, watching for Adriana.

"Monsieur?"

He turned around. The boy with the sailboat was speaking to him.

The boy gestured toward the bench. "Would you like to sit down, Monsieur?"

Baldwin glanced at the bench, where an aged man and woman had sat beside the boy. "Yes, thank you," he said. He was in fact tired, and he sat down gratefully.

As he sat staring at the pond and the two-score children scampering around their boats, the first drops of rain fell. The old man and woman beside him rose immediately and hurried away. The children began to retrieve their boats—though most of them, he knew, would leave them on the water for the old woman who rented them to retrieve. The wind began to bend the trees. The crowd scattered.

He sat there. By the time he returned to the Place de la Concorde and found a vélo-taxi, which would not be easy now, he would be wet. He would be no wetter for sitting there. The rain broke in earnest, cold even on this hot August night.

"Monsieur?"

The boy who had given him the seat had come up behind him.

"Monsieur . . . Where is Adriana?"

Baldwin swung around. The boy was . . . "Jeanne!"

"Adriana?"

"She couldn't come. But you know me."

Jeanne nodded. "We must talk." She looked up, silently saying that the rain thwarted them.

"I came in a vélo-taxi. I was going to find another if I could. Where can I take you?"

She shook her head. "Only to somewhere where we can talk."

"Somewhere safe and dry, hmm?"

She nodded.

"Are you willing to come to my flat?"

"Where is it?"

"On the Ile de la Cité."

"All right," she said quietly.

They could not, in the rain, find a vélo-taxi with a roof. They hired an open one, pedaled by a young woman soaked with rainwater, whose dripping clothes clung to her as she crossed the bridge onto the island. On the square before Notre Dame, Jeanne asked the young woman to stop for a moment while she made a telephone call. Baldwin waited while Jeanne called her father with reassurances—he supposed—and shortly, both of them drenched, they reached his flat. He paid the young woman twice her fare, plus a tip, and led Jeanne up the stairs to his studio.

He had no clothes to offer her. While he stood with his back to her, she took off her wet shirt and skirt, dried herself with a towel, and wrapped herself in the wool blanket from his cot. When he turned she stood in the middle of the room, half smiling.

"If you will do me the same favor, he said, I will change too."

He took off his own wet clothes and put on the only other shirt and pants he had. "I can make some hot tea," he said as he pulled up the dry pants. They spoke French; he discovered she did not speak English.

Jeanne nodded and sat down at his small table. She watched silently as he lit a fire and began to heat water. The stove sat on the table by the sink, and he leaned against the sink and balanced himself with a cane. Odd, she thought, that the English should send a man as badly crippled as this on a dangerous mission in an enemy-occupied city. Either they were stupid or he was an exceptionally brave and effective agent. He was handsome, anyway: handsome and virile. Except for his damaged leg, he could have been a powerful athlete or an agile dancer.

"I'm sorry I don't have clothes to offer you," he said.

"Two months ago I would have cared."

He turned to face her. "We learn to focus on things that really matter, don't we?"

She nodded. "I have moments when I think I've become very wise. I suppose I'm wrong."

"We share that," he said, turning again to the stove. He pushed in another scrap of newspaper. "You and I. Adriana. Many others."

"Adriana?"

"Her husband and child were killed in 1940."

Jeanne shook her head. "She seemed so—she seemed so assured, so . . ."

"She is," Baldwin said.

"The German. Is he *really* German?"

Baldwin picked up his teapot and spooned in two heaping spoons of dark tea that Adriana had brought him from the Royal Monceau. "He is really German."

"My father wants to know more about him."

"I can tell you a great deal more about him. He planned and led the operation to liberate you and your father. We could not have done it without him. He has been absolutely loyal to us."

"I am glad to hear that."

"We've learned to trust him," said Baldwin. "I was hostile and suspicious toward him at first. Adriana was determined to kill him when the mission ended—whether it was a success or a failure." Baldwin paused, smiled, shook his head. "Now . . . I have to acknowledge that the man has had a major impact on me. And Adriana has developed real affection for him."

Jeanne nodded and withheld the questions that were in her mind. She would save her questions for a while, until she gained better understanding of

Adriana's "affection" for Heinrici and the "impact" he'd had on Baldwin.

Baldwin poured boiling water over the tea leaves in the pot. "English tea," he said. "Good Ceylon tea, boiling water. Do you take sugar?"

"Do you?" she asked.

"No, in fact. No . . . I don't. And I can't offer you milk or lemon."

"I'll have it as you have it," she said.

"I've no proper cups either," he said. "Two mugs that don't match."

"What are you called?" she asked.

"Called? Oh. Len. My name is William Leonard Baldwin. I am called Len."

"I told my father on the telephone that I would very likely have to spend the night with you," she said. "I told him you are a very proper English gentleman, that he could rely on that."

Baldwin sucked in his breath. "He can rely on it, Jeanne. Absolutely. Beyond question."

"Your wound . . . ?"

"Oh, no. I'm not wounded that way."

She watched him pour their tea, his face dark, pensive, even gloomy over the two white mugs. He frowned over the tea, as if it somehow failed to satisfy him. Obviously he was engrossed in some private thought he did not want to impart. It had to do with her, she guessed—since he glanced nervously at her. Maybe he was judging her.

He could not carry two mugs of tea! She rose quickly and hurried to his side to take one. She was clumsy, trying to keep the blanket clutched around her as she reached past him and grabbed at a mug. The moment was wretchedly awkward: it was all too plain that she was trying to help the crippled man; he frowned and was anything but pleased. She understood—he was not resigned to his handicap; he still fought it.

"I was an athlete," he said as if he had read her thoughts.

He sat down at the table, and she drew her chair closer to his. She clasped her hands around her mug of tea and lifted it to her lips. She raised her dark, solemn eyes to his.

"I'm sorry," he said. "You see me feeling sorry for myself. And you were hurt as badly as I am. Worse."

"We survived," she said simply.

Baldwin ran his hand across her head, feeling the sparse bristle that had grown on her scalp.

She tipped her head back, as if to follow the touch of his fingers. She lifted her shoulders. "No one has dared touch me there," she said. "As if it would burn their hands."

"You are extraordinarily beautiful just as you are," he said. "If you were my wife, I would ask you to keep your head shaved. I'd buy you an assortment of wigs, but in private I would want you just as you are."

"You're trying to make me feel better."

He shook his head.

"Len . . ." She stopped. Her eyes filled with tears, her face turned red, and she sobbed. "What about . . . what they made me?"

"They made you a martyr," he said grimly. "That's supposed to be a good thing to be—though I doubt that you and I, who might be so defined, would ever have chosen it if we'd had the choice." He sighed. "I'm looking at a beautiful girl . . . who's been hurt."

"Not *hurt,* I suppose," she said softly.

He caressed her head gently. "Yes, hurt," he murmured.

"Can you imagine what they did to me?" she whispered. "Can you even *imagine?*"

He nodded.

She drew a deep breath and sighed. "I survived . . . I'm pregnant. Can you imagine? I'm carrying something put in me by one of those beasts."

"Are you sure?"

"A friend tried to tell me I can't be sure. Maybe I'm not. But I have the symptoms."

He cupped the back of her neck in his hand. "If I could draw it out of you, I would."

She essayed a weak smile. "Len . . ."

Baldwin covered what was for him a troubled, affected moment by lifting his mug and casting his eyes up to the rain still spattering hard on the skylight of his studio, to the last gray light of the day in the rain clouds above. The hours of electricity had not yet begun, and he struck a match to light the stub of a white candle stuck in a saucer on the table.

"What kind of pass do you carry?" he asked.

She shook her head "None."

"You cannot risk the streets tonight," he said.

"No."

"You must indeed stay with the . . . the 'proper English gentleman.'"

"I know."

"I won't touch you, Jeanne. You may be sure."

"Len . . . Why not?"

XIX

SATURDAY, AUGUST 5, 1944

THE sun rose early. It was on its way back to the long, gray winter, but still it rose early. Long before they wanted to wake it was high above, and its fierce white light was streaming through the skylight, etching everything in the little studio with hard lines of gleam and shadow. Jeanne had dreamed she was back in the dark cell at Romainville, and in the bright sunlight she woke exhilarated, confirmed in her escape.

The Englishman slept on. She frowned over his mangled leg. During the night, blood had oozed from one of the deep scars. He had said he was wounded in the Dieppe raid. It was difficult to belive the wound could be bleeding yet.

His penis lay limp on his right leg. For a while she lay and looked at it. He was not circumcised. In his soft condition, his foreskin looked like the tip of an elephant's trunk, like a rose about to open from bud to blossom, like a lip pursed to kiss, like the spout of an English teapot . . . She touched it lightly with the tip of a finger and smiled as the whole shaft began to pulse and swell, even though Len had not wakened. She stroked its underside and watched it grow.

His sympathy was different from her father's and from the Pascins'. It was sympathy, not pity. His concern was that she had been hurt, not that she had been diminished. He was anxious that she should not be hurt more, and he had allowed himself to come to her only very slowly last night, only reluctantly, only with constant assurances. He was a gentle man, a strangely complex man, self-assured and fulfilled in many ways, diffident and incomplete in others.

He had told her during the night that he made love with men. With a man, actually—one man, not a succession of them. He told her of the man's marvelous warmth and compassion. He even told her his name: David. He had spoken of this David's sensitivity and generosity, also of the anguish of the relationship he'd had with him: the constant fear of publicity, the persistent sense of guilt that would not subside. Len's life as an Englishman of good family had been a life circumscribed by the relentless expectations of his father and grandfather. They had scorned the career he had chosen—that of a research chemist who had elected to remain at university. What contempt they would have shown for him if they had suspected he took shelter from them in the arms of a man!

"Let me tell you what my father said of my wound," he whispered to her during the night. "That being wounded in the service of my country was the only thing I'd ever done that he was proud of. And of my medal. Yes, I've got a medal. He likes that."

Bitterness was supposed to be ugly. Somehow his wasn't. It didn't repel Jeanne; it drew her to him.

She closed her hand around his organ and kneaded it gently. It swelled even more, and he woke.

Adriana arrived at the studio about ten. She was anxious to see Baldwin and hear of his meeting with Jeanne. She was surprised to find Jeanne there, obviously having slept with Len.

She was pleased in a sense, too. She was pleased that this chronically solemn man had taken pleasure in the girl's company—even if that should prove to be a complicating factor in their relationship with her father.

"I brought two more eggs," she said. And with a sly smile she added, "I'd have brought four if I'd known there were two of you here."

She had also brought half a dozen skimpy newspapers for fuel. She sat down on the threadbare sofa that, besides the bed and the table and chairs, was the chief item of furniture in the flat. It was a warm morning. The streets were steaming after last night's hard rain. She was damp with perspiration.

Jeanne said she could cook the eggs, and Baldwin sat at the table, telling her how to fuel the stove.

"Jeanne tells me her father wants to try to save two hundred children from deportation," said Baldwin.

"My father delayed last Friday's deportation," said Jeanne. "He paid a German officer to send the locomotive and cars away, to pretend they had been commandeered for military purposes."

"But the train will go this week," Adriana said grimly. "Won't it?"

Jeanne nodded. "Probably. Unless . . . something else can be arranged. But that's not the train with the children. It may be scheduled for next week. Or even later. If it can be delayed long enough—"

"The Allies will come," said Adriana. She sighed. "Some people think they will be here tomorrow. Last night I heard a high-ranking German officer say they will never come. Sometime between tomorrow and never, I suppose they will come. A week's delay of a train—I don't know. It could be enough."

"What can anyone do but try?" asked Baldwin.

"My father will try," said Jeanne. "He and his friends will take any reasonable risk to save the children."

"Delay . . . ," said Adriana. "Even when we destroyed a bridge near Pantin Station, all we achieved was delay."

Jeanne puffed her cheeks and blew on the smoky newspaper fire. "I heard my father say he and his friends have managed to save almost three hundred people." She stopped to blow again. "I don't know how they did it. But three hundred—"

"I'm not saying it isn't worth trying," said Adriana. "I only wish there were some way we could *prevent* deportation, not just delay it. Does your father want our help? Is that why you contacted us?"

"Yes," said Jeanne. "That and for another reason. We wanted to talk with you about Colonel Heinrici. We wanted to know how far we could trust him. Len has said we can trust him completely."

Adriana smiled. *"We* have learned to. He'll be glad to know we've found you. He's been looking for you, trying every way he could think of to find you."

Jeanne turned from the stove to face Adriana. "What do you mean?" she said sharply. "Colonel Heinrici has always known where we were. He came to see my father ten days ago."

Adriana glanced at Baldwin. Color rose in her face, and she stiffened. "He *what?*"

"He has always known where we were," Jeanne repeated. "When he came to see us ten days ago, he said he had known where we were all along, since the night we ran away from the German patrol by the St. Vincent Cemetery. He said those soldiers were under his command. When we ran, he had someone follow us. He knew where we went."

Adriana bent forward and covered her face with her hands. *"Oh, no!"* she cried. "What did he . . . ?" she gasped, then shook her head, unable to continue, bending lower and moaning deep in her throat.

Baldwin lurched toward her without his cane and reached out to lay his hand on her head. Adriana wept.

"What did Heinrici want when he came to see you?" Baldwin asked Jeanne.

Jeanne abandoned the little tin stove and came to the couch. She crouched on her knees before Adriana. "He said he might be able to save my mother," she whispered. "For money. If we could pay enough money, he might be able to buy her release."

Baldwin took his hand from Adriana's head and put it on Jeanne's. "Your mother was transported to Ravensbrück," he said softly.

Jeanne nodded. "We know. But he said he might be able to get her out."

Adriana raised her face toward Jeanne's, then up toward Len's. Her cheeks glistened with streams of tears. She shook her head. "I'm going to kill him," she said through her sobs.

Jeanne was dumbstruck by Adriana's pain. She looked up at Baldwin, her mouth open, her lips trembling. "He lied to you, then," she said. "He told us he didn't know where either of you were. I knew that was a lie when Adriana answered the telephone in his hotel room. And he didn't tell you . . . ? Oh, no!"

"I swear I'll kill him!" Adriana sobbed.

Baldwin shook his head. "I can't understand him. Why would . . . ? He's risked his *life*. Repeatedly. And then . . . Why?"

Adriana drew successive deep breaths, heaving with each one. "The money . . . ," she mumbled. "The gold. He knows about it. He's known about it since . . . God knows when."

"You didn't tell him?"

"No," said Adriana emphatically. "But it's no very big secret. Colonel Harding knows. Le Docteur knew. And Konrad . . . He has his contacts, his own resources, his own people. Where did the cars come from? And that German patrol that happened on us just at the wrong moment that night—which you now say he commanded. Who were those men?" She took a breath. "He took the threat about Radio Heinrici seriously. He worked with us. But he found out about the gold and—"

"All of you know about that?" Jeanne asked. "The gold? The money?"

Len Baldwin could no longer stand without his cane. He dropped beside Adriana on the couch, his face pale and his forehead damp with perspiration brought out by his pain. "We knew . . . ," he said.

"And that is why my father and I—and not any of a thousand others—were rescued from Fresnes and Romainville," said Jeanne. "The gold—"   \

"Not the gold, Jeanne. Not you, either. Why did you suppose?" Adriana asked. *"Two hundred children!* The lives your father can save with the gold. That was our mission."

Jeanne rose from the floor. She returned to the little stove and frowned over the ashes of newspaper, the fire that had gone out without frying the eggs. "My father probably understands," she said.

Adriana walked to the window and looked down on the narrow, cobblestoned street. "Heinrici is a horrible threat to us," she said. "He knows where you are,

Jeanne, and where your father is." She turned toward Baldwin. "He doesn't know where you are, though. Does he?"

"Not unless you've told him," said Baldwin.

"What the hell does he want?" Adriana spat. "The gold . . . Yes, sure. The gold. Of course. That's what he's going to live on after the war. He talks about forged documents, living in Paris after the war . . . He's mentioned a secret Abwehr fund, in gold. That's not the gold he has in mind. He wants *this* gold!"

"He doesn't know where to find it, does he?" Baldwin asked Jeanne.

"My father is no fool," she said. "The gold is hidden."

"How much is there, Jeanne?" Adriana asked hoarsely.

Jeanne glanced once more at the black charred paper under the stove, then walked away from it. She shrugged. "Maybe seventy, eighty kilos. My father paid out fifteen kilos to delay last Friday's train. Say eighty kilos."

Adriana's face twisted into a grotesque grin. "Eighty kilos! Eighty! Colonel Harding thought there were hundreds of kilos! Half a million pounds Sterling? There is less than *twenty thousand* pounds! Hundreds of millions of francs? There is less than *twenty* million francs!"

"It may be enough to save two-hundred children," Jeanne said quietly.

Adriana nodded. "Maybe. Yes. And enough to fund Heinrici's survival. Not enough to live the rest of his life in luxury, but enough to survive on until—" She shivered. "Of course . . . What counts is not how much there really is but how much he thinks there is. He'll kill for it."

"He's a renegade," said Baldwin. "He's not working for the Germans either, obviously. If he were, we'd all be in a Gestapo prison."

"Unless he's still afraid that Colonel Harding would find out and start broadcasting on Radio Heinrici," Adriana said.

"He's looking for the gold," said Baldwin. "His offer to try to save Madame Mercier has to be a ploy. He thinks there are several hundred kilograms of it, and he knows very well it's not in the house where Jeanne and her father ran that night. He wants to encourage Henri Mercier to go to the cache—or send someone—so he can follow and learn where it is hidden."

Adriana nodded.

Baldwin spoke to Jeanne. "I don't want you to tell me where it is. But do you know?"

Jeanne shook her head.

"Has your father developed a specific plan to stop the deportation of the children?"

"I don't know. He's a very private man and hasn't told me."

"The house is not safe for him anymore," said Adriana. "God knows what Heinrici might decide to do."

Baldwin struggled up from the couch and hobbled to the table for his cane, then began to relight the newspapers under the stove. They watched in silence as he pulled away ash, stuffed in more paper, and struck a match.

"It is possible we're wrong about Konrad," he said quietly.

"I have more reason than anyone to wish we were," said Adriana.

Adriana walked along the quay, where even in this troubled August the book-sellers displayed their little stocks of books under wood and canvas. Old men and women, hunched and peering through their bifocal spectacles, browsed placidly. A few Germans examined books, too—though more hurriedly, as if German efficiency required them to look through so many books a minute. Most of the shops behind the quay were shuttered. She had heard this was where they had sold flowers and caged birds. The door to a stamp-collector's shop stood open; an old man with a magnifying glass examined a stamp with a happy smile, as if he had just found a treasure.

A pair of Germans smiled suggestively at her. Young soldiers, maybe only seventeen years old.

She would have to face him. Konrad. She would have to face him. And she would have to try to hide what she knew and what rage and hatred flamed inside her. She and Baldwin—with even Jeanne concurring—had agreed she must dissemble for a while. A confrontation would be dangerous. She must go on with Konrad, as if nothing had changed, at least until Henri Mercier could be warned. And Le Capitaine. Both of them had to move and do it without his knowledge, if possible without his discovering they were gone.

She and Baldwin had been stricken with a new awareness of how much they had relied on Konrad Heinrici. It was difficult to suppress the impulse to go to him with their new problems, to hand him the responsibility, to accept his judgment.

And she was empty. It was nothing like what she had suffered in 1940, when on one day she had lost everyone she cared for, who cared for her; still, a residuum of that bleak pain was renewed. She was alone again. She had lost her future again.

"I cannot believe it is safe for her to go out. She has no papers. If she encounters a routine police check—"

"I am well aware of the risk, Colonel Heinrici," said Henri Mercier. "More acutely aware than you are. More deeply concerned."

Because it was a Saturday morning, Jacob Pascin was at home. He had shaken the hand of the handsome German colonel, wondering if he had not seen him before—seen him, that is, buying jewelry. The man was smooth, charis-matic. He had brought with him two bottles of wine and a fist-sized cheese, which he as a German could still buy with his marks.

Henri was disinclined to trust the colonel; oberst, the Boches called the rank.

Henri's judgment was good. Neither he, Jacob, nor Henri placed much credence in the suggestion that Narcisse could be rescued from Ravensbrück. Still, Henri came back to the subject repeatedly. It preyed on him. The German colonel had, after all, saved him and Jeanne. Was it an impossible hope that he could achieve another miracle?

"I find it odd, Monsieur, that you would allow your daughter—"

"She is young. She is hurt. She is defiant," said Henri Mercier.

"But with her shaved head—"

"She goes as a boy," said Mercier.

"Then allow me to get her an identity card," said Heinrici. "You will have to provide a photograph—a photograph of her as she is now. Can you do that? I'll need twenty-four hours after I have the photograph. And one for yourself, perhaps. I suggest to you, Monsieur, it is not safe for either of you to go on the streets without papers. It will be hazardous enough *with* them."

"We will be grateful for cartes d'identité, Colonel."

Heinrici nodded. "Shall I call tomorrow for the photographs? And now— about the matter of the possible rescue of Madame Mercier. I am afraid it will require a great deal of money, Monsieur. I warned you of that. I have made inquiries, and I have learned that your wife is alive and that release from Ravensbrück is possible. I say possible. It will depend on some difficult negotiations and generous payments to those who will have to take grave risks."

"How much money are you talking about, Colonel?"

Heinrici glanced at Jacob Pascin, then turned his eyes back to Mercier. "If," he said, "you will authorize me to spend ten thousand pounds Sterling, I can virtually guarantee the release of Madame Mercier."

Henri Mercier shook his head sorrowfully. "I do not have so much money," he said in a hushed, sad voice. "I have no way to raise so much. If I sold everything I owned . . . But"—he shrugged—"I have nothing to sell. I dare not go near anything that was mine. Even the clothes you see me wearing are not mine."

"But you told me you have access to a fund," said Heinrici.

"I told you I do not control that fund. My friends have to authorize every expenditure from it. Ten thousand pounds . . . I could not even suggest it."

Heinrici appeared stunned. "There . . . there *is* much more than that in the fund. Of course. Isn't there?"

"Whatever there is," said Mercier solemnly, "I cannot take ten thousand pounds Sterling from it."

"Can you take five?"

Mercier shook his head. "My friends very generously offered me two million gold francs—say twenty-four hundred pounds—which I said I would use only if I felt certain it would produce results."

"Are you aware," Heinrici asked, "that men will be asked to risk their lives to achieve this release? All of these things are dangerous. We are dealing with fanatics."

"Fanaticism and venality," said Mercier.

"Yes. And . . . just twenty-four hundred pounds! Monsieur—"

"Look at it this way," said Mercier. "A family can live very comfortably for three or four years on two million francs. Very comfortably. Few families have so much income. This will be in gold, as good in Germany as in France. Ten kilos of gold. Difficult times are coming. A man with ten kilos of gold will be well off."

Heinrici nodded. "Yes. Yes, my contact in Berlin is being unrealistic. Have I your permission to offer ten kilos of gold?"

"I will need proof," said Henri Mercier.

"I will see what I can get," said Heinrici curtly. "Will you have the two photographs tomorrow?"

Mericer looked to Jacob Pascin, who nodded.

Papa puffed on his pipe, making so much heavy smoke that the room was filled with it; Heinrici brushed his hand before his face to get a half-clean breath of air. They sat near the window in the flat across the street from 48 rue Boulanger. Heinrici had entered the building from the rear so Mercier and his friends would not know he had gone directly from meeting them to a meeting with Papa Ange.

"Can we do it alone?" Heinrici asked. "I'd like to do it alone. I don't want to trust anyone else—or share with anyone else."

Papa shook his head. "There are too many of them. We can't follow them all. How can we know which one will go to get the gold?"

"Yes," Heinrici muttered. "He's talking about ten kilos now. Anyone can carry ten kilos."

"Marie followed one of them," said Papa. "He's a priest! A priest of Sacré Coeur. Can you imagine? He's come to see the Jews twice that we know about. Do you suppose they've got the gold in the crypt of the church?"

"Why would they limit me to two million francs, ten kilos?" Heinrici speculated.

"Jews," said Papa, stroking his unshaven chin.

"No. Don't be a fool. A Jew loves his wife, his children's mother, as much as anyone. He would—"

"Maybe that's all they've got," Papa interjected. "Maybe this fabulous fortune does not exist."

"No, he admits there's more. Much more. The answer, Papa, is that they are planning to use the rest of the gold for something else. More of their bribes. Another effort to—"

"This surprises you? That is why they *have* the gold."

Heinrici drove his right fist angrily into his left palm. "We must learn where it is hidden. Before they scatter the gold among half the bribable officers in the rue des Saussaies."

"I suggest," Papa Ange said in a firm voice, "that you take off the squarehead uniform, interrupt your enjoyment of your conquered city, and start following some of the people who go in and out over there. Mama and I can't follow them all. The daughter—"

"I know. She's gone."

"Yes. Left yesterday. And not back yet."

"She will come back," said Heinrici. "Or someone will go to meet her. They have to take her picture."

"Where did she spend the night?" asked Papa.

"When we know that, we may know something very important."

Papa Ange drew smoke deep into his lungs and pursed his lips as he blew it out, looking contemplatively at the sky above the street. "What if the Jews don't have the hundred million, Philippe?" he asked. "Who is going to pay your share of the expenses? The American passport? I paid good money for that job."

"The paper and covers I brought you are worth ten times the cost of that job," said Heinrici. "So don't worry about it. And don't worry about the gold, either. It's there. But we are going to need help. I know a young Frenchman I think we can trust. After him, a young German."

"I trust who you trust," said Papa. "But not to know who I am. Keep them away from me."

Reluctantly, Heinrici approached the butcher shop while still wearing his uniform. He had made it a fast rule not to visit the room over the butcher shop except in the shabby clothes of a working-class Frenchman. He was impatient today, though, and did not want to take the time and trouble to change.

Théo. Le Capitaine. What could he tell him to draw him into service for a few days? As he climbed the Montmartre slope, he turned over ideas, one after another. How would he explain the absence of Adriana and Baldwin?—for neither of them could play any role in the final act he had now to plot. Le Capitaine knew about the gold. He knew where to contact Adriana. If, on the other hand, he thought she had been taken by the Gestapo . . . He could tell Le Capitaine that he himself was a fugitive who dared not go near the Royal Monceau again. And Baldwin—for that matter, just where *was* Baldwin? Adriana didn't know either. What had . . . Was there any possibility he had been taken? He was not a tough man. Would—

Heinrici hurried up the wooden stairs toward the door of the room over the butcher shop.

He knocked on the door. "Théo! Théo, it is Heinrici!"

The knock seemed to echo within the room.

"Théo!"

He took out his key and opened the door.

Gone. Le Capitaine was not there. Scraps of food wrappers remained. Empty bottles. No sign of a struggle. The white waiter's jacket! He . . . *Damn!*

The Hotel Prince de Galles, on Avenue Georges V, had been requisitioned by the Lutwaffe early in the war. For three years, Luftwaffe officers sat under the palms in its comfortable dining room, telling their exploits with the gestures universally used by flyers, while dining elegantly from its excellent kitchens. In August 1944, very few Luftwaffe officers remained in Paris; very little of the German air force remained in action. The dining room of the Hotel Prince de Galles now served a hodgepodge of officers from all services—including officers wounded at the Normandy front, who had been returned to Paris for treatment and rest and were billeted in the hotel. Officers who showed any outward sign of their wounds—like bandages—were under orders not to leave their billets, not to be seen on the streets of Paris, so they took their dinners glumly in the dining room, some of them sullen, some of them drained and all but immobile in their exhaustion.

Sitting at a table among them, himself young, unmarked, and handsome, Oberleutnant Dietrich Krueger felt certain he was the focus of resentful stares. He crushed his cigarette in the ashtray. Herr Oberst Heinrici, sitting with him, wore the Iron Cross with oak leaves: evidence he had done something in this war but sit behind a desk. He was apprehensive, too, about Heinrici's purpose in inviting him to this dinner. On the telephone he had been emphatic: the oberleutnant must meet him for dinner.

"You were a student at Heidelberg," said Heinrici. "With good family connections, I imagine."

"I suppose they might be so described, Herr Oberst."

"My own father was a general in the other war," said Heinrici conversationally. "I can't say the connection was of any particular value to me—so far as advancement in the Abwehr was concerned. I will say, though, that when I met the Führer he mentioned my father, remembered him. He's been a schoolmaster for many years. Quite senile now. I wrote him a letter when I arrived in Paris. His housekeeper returned a note saying my father received my letter and was pleased—but couldn't answer personally because his eyesight is too weak to allow him to write. Your father—"

Krueger smiled: partly pride, partly diffidence. "You probably have on your person something manufactured by my family," he said.

"Ah? What?"

"The sidearm in your holster, Herr Oberst. Since 1938, Kruegerwerke in Düsseldorf has been manufacturing pistols and rifles under license from Walther and Mauser. Before 1938, our family manufactured small tools—hammers, axes, screwdrivers, pliers, wrenches, and so on."

"And there is a political connection," said Heinrici. "Yes?"

"My grandfather gave a great deal of money to the Party before it came to power. More than that. It was my grandfather who secured for the Führer an invitation to speak to a luncheon of the Industry League, in 1931."

Heinrici nodded.

Krueger understood the implication: that his family's excellent political connections had won him his commission as an officer and his assignment to the Abwehr. It was true—that plus his ability to speak French. He had served in Belgium, then in Lyon, now in Paris. He had never so much as heard the sounds of combat. When he was alone he congratulated himself on what his family influence had done for him; at all other times he felt constrained to show a modest embarrassment about it.

"Has your family's business been damaged by the bombing?"

"It has disappeared, Herr Oberst. Gone. There is nothing left of the Kruegerwerke but a tangle of rusting wreckage. My home also. Blasted into rubble. Fortunately my family was able to retreat into the countryside, where they live with cousins."

Heinrici pressed the palms of his hands together in front of his chin. "So . . . ," he said. "I am afraid you must anticipate hard times when you go home. The Rhineland was occupied by the French after the last war. This time" —he shook his head—"it will be worse."

Krueger nodded. "My grandfather has said we may even be imprisoned. Those who manufactured arms."

"I think that is possible," said Heinrici.

Krueger sighed. He glanced around the room. "It is absurd, what we are doing," he said quietly. "You and I should be at the front, fighting."

"Do you really think it would make any difference?"

The young man shook his head. His face flushed. "No," he said.

"But you are right," said Heinrici. "It *is* insane for us simply to sit here, as thousands of officers are doing, enjoying the last days of our brief glory—just waiting for annihilation. It is stupid."

"What are you driving at, Herr Oberst?"

"I am sure you've guessed," said Heinrici. He lifted his glass of Bordeaux. "Enjoy this wine. It is not inane to savor things like this while we have the chance."

Krueger sipped hesitantly.

"General Hausser assigned you to follow me, not to help me," said Heinrici brusquely. "He ordered you to watch what I did, listen to what I said, and report to him in detail. Which you tried to do."

"I tried to follow my orders, Herr Oberst."

"Of course I understood from the beginning what your orders were, Krueger. Consider what Hausser ordered you to do: try to follow a man who has spent the last ten years as a spy. Not very intelligent, hmm?"

"You were a very difficult man to trail, Herr Oberst," Krueger said stiffly.

Heinrici smiled. "Thank you. You did extremely well one night—up to a point. You should have followed the Merciers when they ran away from the SS patrol on rue St. Vincent. Then General Hausser would have known where they went, which was most important to him."

Krueger sighed. "I couldn't follow them without revealing myself to you. And to the SS patrol. My orders were to keep out of sight."

Heinrici nodded. "You know what I've been doing. You know *my* orders, don't you? To find a hundred million francs—five million marks—in gold. That is what Mercier is supposed to have hidden. That is why we liberated him and his daughter from SS prisons—to see if we could get our hands on the gold, for the Abwehr. That is why we worked in cooperation with the English. They want the gold, too. As does the Résistance."

"But Mercier ran away that night. The whole operation—"

"—failed," said Heinrici, using the word the young lieutenant was reluctant to use.

"And your present orders are to track down Mercier."

"Yes. But the situation has changed. Radically. Since July twentieth."

Krueger nodded. "I am not certain of my duty anymore."

Heinrici leaned back in his chair for a moment, holding his wine glass under his nose and savoring the clean bouquet of the Bordeaux. Then he leaned forward again, so he could speak quietly to Krueger over the table.

"General Hausser returned from Berlin convinced that the Führer has lost his mind, that the worst of the fanatics are in control of everything, and that we are heading into a debacle. A Götterdämmerung, Kreuger. A Götterdämmerung."

"I don't think the Führer can save the situation," said Krueger. "I don't think anyone can. We've been overpowered. Once the Americans came in against us—"

"General Hausser," Heinrici interrupted, "is no longer interested in getting the Mercier gold for the Abwehr. He wants it for himself. He has offered to give me a share."

Krueger frowned deeply. " '*Sauve qui peut*,' " he said bitterly.

Heinrici nodded. "Precisely. Let him save himself who can."

"A bureaucrat," muttered Krueger.

Heinrici smiled. "Yes. Not a bad fellow, actually. The problem is, he seems to think his rank gives him first claim on the gold. He'll give me a bit as a reward for finding it for him, but . . . Well. You see."

Krueger pressed his index fingers to his lips and frowned pensively. "Your question is, will I betray General Hausser and join you—in finding and sharing the gold?" He drew his shoulders up. "Have you found it?"

"Not yet. But I have a pretty good lead."

"What would be my role and my share?"

"To be there for the kill, as we might say—though I hope no one will be killed. On the other hand, we must anticipate that the Jews do not leave the gold unguarded. I expect to get it by surprise, deception, whatever—certainly not by a frontal attack. In any event, I will need help. I need some people followed. I can't do everything alone. Then—well, think of this, Krueger. A hundred million francs in gold will weigh over four hundred kilograms. We will have difficulty carrying it away. Think of that problem! More gold than we can carry."

"And my share?" Krueger persisted.

"I have to commit one third to—to certain French interests . . . that is, to people who have been essential to what I've accomplished so far and who would also be in a position to ruin everything if they were not participants. If the total amount of gold in the cache is in fact five million marks, my share will be more than three million. For your help I will give you twenty percent of my share—more than six hundred thousand marks in gold. Something good to take home. About as much as you can carry."

"How in fact am I to get it home?"

"In a few weeks—probably sooner, in fact—there is going to be a panic-stricken exodus from Paris like nothing ever before seen in the history of the world. Germans will be carrying everything they can. In the confusion . . . You will manage. Of course there will be risk. There is in everything worthwhile."

"General Hausser . . . ?"

"General Hausser has already assigned you to help me. I'll tell him I am working on leads and still need your help."

"Very well," said Krueger. He raised his glass in toast. "To our success, Herr Oberst."

"To our survival, Krueger. To our escape and survival."

When the electricity went off for the night, he had not returned. Alone in the suite, Adriana closed the blackout curtains, lighted a candle, and sat by the table to read by the yellow, flickering light. She could have slept, but it seemed incautious to be unaware when he came in. There was no way he could suspect she knew anything she had not known when he left this morning; yet, she could not shake off the idea that he was newly menacing.

She still had a small automatic pistol—the little Browning the SOE had provided—kept in a handbag in the armoire all this time, and immediately upon returning to the suite she had checked it, driven by the irrational idea that he might have found it and removed it. It would be foolish to hide the pistol within reach beneath the mattress on her side of the bed—What in God's name would she say if he discovered it?—yet, she had to suppress the impetus.

She had chained the door so he could not enter with his key, while she spent half an hour searching through everything he had in the suite: his uniform, his civilian clothes, his few simple toiletries, the few papers he had, including a curt letter from his father's housekeeper. The last had stopped her. So accustomed had she become to thinking of him as a man as alone in this world, as she was, she had been startled to find a personal letter containing word that he had *sent* a personal letter.

Then she had found the American passport.

He had spoken of the passport. She had been photographed, and hers was to be ready today or tomorrow. Still—there he was, in civilian clothes, Henry Conrad, staring blankly from the photograph affixed to the blue-green American passport. Stamps on the pages indicated that Henry Conrad had entered the United Kingdom through Croydon Airport on August 11 and entered France at Le Havre on September 3, 1944—almost a month from now. The passport naming her Betty Conrad would bear the same forged stamps. She had been tempted to tear it up, to flush the bits down the toliet, but she hadn't; she had put it back where she had found it.

Le Capitaine was now with Baldwin and Jeanne in the studio on the Ile de la Cité. She had hurried to him and rushed him back to the studio. Monday, Baldwin would go to Le Faussaire in the cellar under the cinema in Montparnasse and try to obtain forged identity cards for Jeanne and Le Capitaine. They had no photographs for them, so Baldwin would try to borrow a camera from the forger. Otherwise, one of them would have to try to buy one somewhere. Surely La Faussaire could at least develop the film. It was something else that Konrad had handled so effectively.

And food. Baldwin would try to buy ration stamps from Le Faussaire. She would carry every scrap she could from the hotel. It would be difficult. If Konrad noticed, he would wonder what mouths she was feeding. Again—

She heard his key in the lock.

"Adriana . . ."

"I'm here, Konrad."

He came into the bedroom, into the candlelight, and bent over to kiss her. He smelled of wine and of something sharper, perhaps calvados. He was not drunk—she had seen him drink a great deal without becoming in the least drunk—but he was warmly comfortable in what he had consumed. He began to remove his uniform.

"I am sorry to be so late. I had to have dinner with an officer from the Hotel Lutétia. Were you out all day?"

She nodded. "Still trying to locate Baldwin."

Heinrici drew a breath and released it loudly. "Uhh. I don't like it. Where—"

"In hospital," she interrupted. "Théo insists he must be all right, that he was taken by the doctor to a small private clinic where they could treat his leg and not have to make any kind of report."

"What clinic?"

"Théo doesn't know. He's been hiding in the place over the butcher shop since—"

"Did you see Théo today?"

She shook her head. "I took him food yesterday."

Heinrici sat on the edge of the bed as he pushed off his boots. Then he stood, pulled down his breeches and his underpants, and was naked. He picked up the candle to light another, then carried the second candle in the bathroom. She knew his routine—he was drying his damp body with a towel, after which he would dust himself all over with talcum powder and return to bed smelling faintly of the flowerly scent of the powder, expecting her to have undressed and be waiting for him in the bed.

And what choice did she have? She pulled off her clothes.

"Adriana," he said as he mounted the bed. "The way we made love last night . . . It was good, wasn't it? Let's do it like that."

"All right."

"I'm sorry. Are you tired? Would you rather just—"

"No," she said resolutely. No, she thought. Like last night. Then you'll go to sleep, and I won't have to talk to you. "Like last night . . ."

He sighed contentedly. He'd probably been thinking about it all the way to the hotel. "Good," he breathed.

Adriana rose on her knees, put her face down into the pillows—which *was* good, because he couldn't see her—and presented her backside to him. She looked back and watched him fumble with the rubber sheath she insisted he wear. Then chuckling, muttering under his breath, he slipped his penis into her. Adriana clenched her teeth and submitted.

WEDNESDAY, AUGUST 9, 1944

The outcome of the battle for France depends on the success of the attack on the southern wing of the Seventh Army. Commander-in-Chief West will have a unique and unrepeatable opportunity of thrusting into a region largely devoid of the enemy, and to change the whole situation thereby.

—ADOLF HITLER
August 6, 1944

The attack failed because Kluge wanted *it to fail.*
—ADOLF HITLER
August 8, 1944

THE battle will be fought somewhere else," Gruppenführer Heinz Schenck said to Heinrici and Adriana in the lobby of the Royal Monceau during a momentary encounter on Tuesday afternoon. "General von Kluge lost this opportunity, but the victory weapons will tip the balance somewhere else. In the meanwhile . . ."

SS headquarters staff had already packed important files for shipment to Germany. Other documents were burning in the courtyard where Heinrici had watched hundreds of dossiers burn. But Schenck was not leaving. Neither was Obergruppenführer Oberg. They would stay in Paris, confront the new military commander, rumored to be Generalmajor Dietrin von Choltitz, and defend the interests of the SS against the arrogant pretensions of the army. They would remain to see that the Führer's orders were carried out, that he was not again betrayed by cowardly generals.

But not all high SS officers would stay. Later that same Tuesday, in the evening, Oberführer Erhard Franck and his friends were served by naked girl prisoners for the last time. Oberführer Franck's household goods were packed —most of them, of course, the property of the French family whose house the SS had requisitioned—and in the after-midnight darkness he would leave for

Munich, driving at the head of a small convoy of trucks. The house on boulevard Suchet was left vacant.

The collapse of the Normandy front could no longer be concealed from the population of Paris. Trucks rolled in from the west, carrying thousands of wounded, thousands more of exhausted men. What Paris had known before, it had known from listening to the forbidden broadcasts of the BBC. Now the Germans confirmed what the BBC was saying by letting Paris see their retreat.

Suddenly there was less electricity. Less food. The faltering supply system, maintained with Teutonic determination and efficiency, was breaking down.

Suddenly Paris was less gray, less tired. What had been rumored forever, as it seemed, was about to happen.

Heinrici returned to the house at 48 rue Boulanger on Sunday, to pick up photographs of Henri Mercier and his daughter. The daughter had not returned. A roll of film with a picture of Mercier was ready, but he and his friends denied they knew where the daughter was. Heinrici did not believe them. If they had not known, they would have been more concerned, he thought. Why weren't they more visibly agitated?

Nevertheless, he had carried the photograph of Henri Mercier to the kommandatur and obtained for him a carte d'identité, naming him Jacques Duplessis, electrical engineer. Returning on Monday afternoon with the card, he found the daughter still had not returned. In fact, this time Henri Mercier had gone out. Louise Pascin accepted the card with thanks and said Monsieur Mercier had only stepped out for a short walk, to take some air, and would return shortly.

Now he knew they were lying to him. Mama Ange, watching from across the street, had seen Mercier leave the house Sunday evening. She had tried to follow him but could not keep up with his fast, purposeful stride. He had not returned.

Very well. They were lying. Why not? Heinrici had never expected they would trust him, never supposed they would innocently lead him to their treasure. He was glad they were lying. For a little while he had worried that Henri Mercier might possibly be telling the truth when he described the fund he and his friends controlled as very limited. It was reassuring to know they didn't trust him and were lying to him.

With General Hausser's amused approval, Oberleutnant Krueger was now wearing *bleu de travail*—and was spending his days in the neighborhood of rue Boulanger, helping Papa and Mama Ange. Mercier would return to Number 48, if for nothing else, to pick up his new *carte d'identité,* and when he did, Krueger would follow him. Krueger would not lose him the way Mama had. Henri Mercier could not outstride the young officer.

Papa had handed over the American passport for Adriana. It was in the armoire in their bedroom at the Royal Monceau, together with his. She was oddly apathetic about the passport. He had pointed out the excellent job of forgery someone had done, but her enthusiasm was lackluster. Indeed, Adriana was in a queer mood: withdrawn, preoccupied, severe.

He supposed it was because there was still no word from Baldwin. Also, when she went to take him food she, too, had discovered that Le Capitaine had abandoned the room over the butcher shop. Yes, the disappearance of both of them clearly troubled her. It disturbed him, too.

They were approaching the most dangerous days of their lives, and he disliked loose ends. He prided himself on a logical mind: perceptive and analytical; he liked to tie up everything he faced in an ordered, manageable package. But Baldwin was outside, and so was Le Capitaine. He hoped they had fled, because if that was not the explanation for their disappearance, then they were a threat.

General Hausser had lost his composure. Fearful that he would be arrested any day and would share the fate of Admiral Canaris—of whom the rumor was that he was dead—Hausser stalked around his office, smoking cigars, drinking brandy, turning over in his mind one fear after another. Heinrici rarely returned to the Royal Monceau without finding a message from General Hausser. He spent more time than he would have wished with the general. It was time he could have put to better purpose.

Henri Mercier opened the window in the bedroom of the little flat on rue du Mont. Looking down, he frowned over a narrow brick-walled shaft that fell to a brick-paved, littered square four floors below. Looking to his right, he saw the rude steel ladder Marie-Madeleine had described. Just beyond the window, and a few feet out, a thick rope hung down, punctuated by thick knots. It was beyond his reach. Marie-Madeleine stood in the doorway between the bedroom and the small living room of the flat.

"It is firmly attached?" he asked uncertainly.

"I have used it," she said. "It bears *my* weight."

He sat on the windowsill and, leaning out precariously, extended his right hand toward the ladder. If *she* . . . had used . . . He closed a tight grip around the ladder. If she . . .He leaned out until his balance shifted. Tightening his grip even more, he let his weight fall outward, and as his legs slipped from the window sill, he grabbed with his left hand. He swung for an instant above the long shaft. Then his left hand closed over a rung of the ladder, and he hung there, secure on the steel.

She leaned out and looked. She nodded. *"Bonne,"* she said.

"So," he muttered. "And how do I get back?"

"With the rope," she said. "You'll see."

He nodded skeptically and began to climb the ladder. He climbed past one more floor and stepped out onto the roof of the building. It was flat, except for the skylight of the studio flat on the top floor. The rope was tied around a vent pipe. If he pulled it up, someone in the apartment—a Gestapo agent, for example—would see no evidence that someone had escaped to the roof.

He crouched low and crossed to the front of the building, dropping to his knees and crawling as he approached the edge. Lying flat, he peered down at the street. No one appeared to be watching. No soldiers. No idle man whose presence could not be explained. Not now anyway.

Henri Mercier returned to the edge of the roof above the air shaft. So, at age sixty, he was now supposed to climb down a rope and swing through a window. Well . . . Marie-Madeleine had done it—or so she said. She was waiting below.

He tested the rope. It was securely tied. The knots afforded handholds at half-meter intervals. So . . . He gripped with both hands and rolled over the edge of the roof.

It was easier than coming out. He lowered himself faster than he had supposed he would, hand over hand, knot by knot, until he was hanging outside the window where Marie-Madeleine waited.

"Swing out," she said. "Then—"

He planted his feet against the brick wall beside the window, kicked, swung out, and swung toward the window.

"No, no, Henri! Feet up!"

His shins banged against the bricks. "Uhh!"

"Feet up! Feet up!" she cried. "And kick harder!"

For a moment he hung on the quivering rope, assuring himself of his grip. Then he planted his feet again against the wall and straightened his legs convulsively. The effort threw him out. He swung, it seemed, halfway across the shaft. Then he swung back, and this time he drew his legs up.

It was terrifying. He swung through the open window. She shrieked as his weight hit her and knocked her back, but she seized him and hung on. "Let go!" she yelled. He let go of the rope and dropped on his back on the bedroom floor.

"My God!" she exclaimed as they lay side by side, she with her skirt up around her hips. "I have known more graceful men."

Marie-Madeleine Lefevre was his own age, a handsome, aristocratic woman who, even in the midst of her misfortune, managed to maintain a subtle refinement that was the product of a lifetime comfortably spent. She wore understated cosmetics, graying hair gracefully coiffed, a gray-blue cashmere suit with two strands of pearls and a small gold-and-pearl pin. Her husband had died of a heart attack shortly after his shoe factory was seized by the Germans in 1941. Her home had been requisitioned as a residence for Gestapo officers. She was not a Jew, but she hated the occupiers as much as if she were, and since 1941 she had been involved in the struggle to save Jewish lives.

"You can cross the roofs," she said as she sat up and straightened her clothes, "and come down through the Fourcade flat, through their skylight, and out onto rue Paul Ferval."

"If I don't kill myself," he said.

"I have done it many times," she said calmly, "when I suspected the place might be watched. And I had no one to catch me when I swung back in."

"Théo is a fool," said Jeanne.

Baldwin reached for her, and she came into his arms. Once more he was surprised—he could not stop being surprised—by how small and delicate she was. He held her, and he ran his hand over her head, over her returning hair, which was growing out fine and light brown. He had learned that she loved his caresses there; even now she lifted her shoulders and breathed in, welcoming the gentle stroke of his palm across her scalp. He cupped one of her little breasts in his other hand.

"Len . . . He has taken an awful risk. Not just for him. For us. For Adriana."

Le Capitaine had stayed with them in the one-room studio since Saturday, when Adriana had brought him from the room over the butcher shop on Montmartre. Fretful and apprehensive, Le Capitaine had spent much of the five days pacing the floor, repeating his misgivings, arguing that he could wait no longer for Adriana to bring him a *carte d'identité* from Le Faussaire. Monday, Baldwin had traveled to Montparnasse in a vélo-taxi and borrowed a camera from the forger—not without some argument. Tuesday, he had returned to Le Faussaire with exposed film. Today, Adriana was to pick up identity cards and bring them to the Ile de la Cité. This morning Le Capitaine had declared himself incapable of waiting any longer and had bolted out of the studio.

Jeanne lifted her face to Baldwin's and kissed him.

Since the first night, when they had been alone together and had made love, Le Capitaine had been with them night and day. He had been intensely uncomfortable about it and had offered to go out walking and let them have some privacy, but they had insisted, as Adriana had insisted, that the risk was too great. They had been close, and they had slept together on Baldwin's narrow bed, but they had not coupled while Le Capitaine lay on the sofa not ten feet from them, even when he snored. Yet they had explored each other quietly in the night . . .

"He has risked all our lives," Jeanne whispered. "The fool! To go out . . . If he is arrested—"

"He is a brave young man," Baldwin said, aware how feeble his words were.

She shook her head. "No one is brave enough," she said. "If he is arrested and interrogated"—she sighed—"he'll tell where we are. Where Adriana is. Anything they ask."

"Raymond knew," said Baldwin. "Le Rasoir. He killed himself rather than face interrogation."

"Of course," she said simply. Her eyes were wet with tears. "Of course..." she whispered.

He took her head between his hands, holding her just behind her ears, and he brushed her lips, then her nose, then her eyes, with his lips. "They hurt you, didn't they?" he murmured. "More than you've told me."

She nodded.

He nuzzled her throat, intent on being gentle. He could not imagine how anyone could—or why anyone would—abuse this exquisite little creature.

"I was not interrogated," Jeanne said. "I knew girls who were. Their injuries were—" She shook her head.

"You don't have to talk about it."

"One morning they opened the cell door and pushed in a girl who had been interrogated all night. Two of the girls took off their clothes. When the rest of us understood what they were going to do, we took off ours too. They made a big wad of cloth. Two of them held her down, and two of them smothered her. I mean, they killed her."

"To stop her suffering?"

Jeanne nodded. "It was getting worse."

Baldwin held Jeanne more tightly. He pressed her face to his shoulder and stroked her head. He felt her shudder.

"I was never tortured," she said. "But within two hours after I was arrested, they—they held me down. I think there were eight of them, before it was over. I stopped screaming after the second one."

"That's not torture?"

She shook her head. "Not compared to... No. Not compared to what they did to others. They didn't make me want to die. I ate garbage to keep alive. And did other things. To survive."

"You don't ever have to talk about it again," he said.

"But I will," she said, raising her head from his shoulder. "A day is coming when I will talk about it. Loudly. When people start crying for peace, saying forgive them so we can have peace—then I'll have something to say. Something to *shout*, by God."

He kissed the top of her head, pressing his face into the light brown bristle that was already becoming soft. She was right that Le Capitaine was a fool. He had risked their safety. His reckless, self-indulgent bolt could send Jeanne back to a Gestapo prison. It would have been better to kill him than let him go.

"It is imperative, Madame. It is imperative. I must see Monsieur Mercier. When will he return?"

Heinrici stood just inside the door of the Pascins' house. Louise Pascin had just told him that Henri Mercier was once again away from the house, only for a short walk she believed, but she didn't know where he was or when he would return.

Heinrici would have been surprised to find him there; he knew that Mercier was not living there anymore. "Madame," he said, glancing at his watch. "I will return at five. Please tell Monsieur Mercier it is important I see him then."

She nodded. "I will tell him as soon as he returns."

Heinrici strode briskly down the hill, miming impatience since he was certain Louise Pascin was watching him from her window. He did not glance across rue Boulanger, where Oberleutnant Krueger, in his blue coveralls, lounged against a wheelbarrow full of sand and drank wine from a bottle. And Krueger did not look at him.

Three minutes after Heinrici disappeared around the corner, Louise Pascin left her house and hurried away up the street. Krueger left his wheelbarrow and, carrying his bottle of wine, ambled after her. He followed her into rue du Mont and identified the building where Henri Mercier was staying with Marie-Madeleine Lefevre. He returned to his wheelbarrow and wheeled it down the hill to where Heinrici sat in a café, watching for him. Heinrici ordered him to return to the address on rue du Mont at 4:45 to see if Henri Mercier came out to go to his 5 P.M. appointment at 48 rue Boulanger.

Heinrici did not keep the appointment. He decided it might be well to let Mercier fret a little. When Krueger called to report to him at the Royal Monceau, Heinrici was soaking in a tub of cool water. Mercier, Kreuger said, had left the building on rue du Mont at 4:50, had gone to 48 rue Boulanger, and left 48 rue Boulanger at 6:10 to return to rue du Mont.

"We have nowhere else to go," Adriana said to Baldwin. "We can't go to another flat—we don't have one." She sat down wearily at his table. "To be altogether frank, Len—and Jeanne—we are running out of resources."

"My father can provide a safe place," said Jeanne.

"I think we should keep the two of you apart," said Baldwin. "Your father is engaged in something dangerous, and if something happens to him, I would rather he didn't know where you are. I'm sure he would feel that way, too."

"Even so," said Jeanne. "We have to keep in contact with him."

Baldwin spoke quietly to Adriana. "Go see Martin," he said. "We need help." He glanced at Jeanne. "Excuse us for a minute," he said to her. "We have to code a message."

An hour later Adriana arrived at the house on rue Guillaume. "Do you remember me?" she asked. "I am David Bradford."

The fragile old man admitted her to his apartment without a word. When they were in his parlor and seated on his Louis XV settee, he offered her a glass of wine. She accepted.

"Another message for London?" he asked as he poured golden wine into tiny crystal glasses.

She nodded and pulled the paper from her blouse.

The old man did not look at it until he had handed her a glass and sipped a silent toast. It was an old, musty white Bordeaux—an excellent wine, she had no doubt, but an acquired taste. He put his glass aside and took her coded message in his white, blue-veined hands.

He read:

57–57–2130. JUST LEARNED AMERICAN SERGEANT TOTALLY LOYAL. HE HAS NOT LOCATED PRIEST AND IS NO THREAT TO HIM. SITUATION UNDER CONTROL. NO HELP NEEDED. DAVID. BATHSHEBA. 2130–57– 57. ZQACTRD.

"So . . . ," he murmured. "That bad?" He shook his head.

She nodded.

Once more she marveled at the speed with which the old man transmitted. As his fingers tapped the key in staccato bursts, she drank the rest of her wine. As before, he waited with the earphones over his white hair, and after what seemed like a long wait he began to write down the reply from London. He nodded, glanced at her, scribbled, and nodded again. When he was finished, he closed and locked the antique desk. Then he handed her the reply. It was not written in opposites. It meant just what it said:

GO TO GROUND. TAKE ORIGINAL SUBJECTS WITH YOU IF POSSIBLE. NOTHING MORE YOU CAN DO NOW. CANNOT OFFER HELP. SITUATION ABOUT TO CHANGE RADICALLY. GO TO GROUND AND WAIT. GOOD LUCK.

She scowled over the message. "Monsieur . . . ," she said hesitantly, "can you send another message to Colonel Harding?"

The old man, who had picked up his glass and was sipping appreciatively from the golden wine, shook his head. "An occasional brief transmission," he said. "That one alerted the Boches. If I were to transmit again today, the risk . . . Well. You understand, I have obligations."

"Monsieur," she said. "I am going to explain something to you. I don't know what contacts you have. I don't want to know. But you can perhaps communicate to someone who can help. At stake are the lives of two hundred children—"

"Jews," he interrupted.

"Yes. Mostly, I suppose."

The old man shrugged. "Yes. Well . . . their lives are as good as others'."

"Two hundred children, Monsieur," she said.

"I dare not transmit again today," he said. "But . . ." He shrugged.

The French could shrug more expressively than any other people in the world, she thought, imparting a world of thought and feeling in that simple gesture. "I rely on you, Monsieur," she said. "Perhaps you can give the word to someone. If you can get word to Colonel Harding, tell him Bathsheba will not abandon the mission—and she doubts that David will either."

The old man nodded. His weak lids fell down over his eyes for a moment. "I will do what I can, Mademoiselle Kip," he said. He smiled gently. "Oh, yes. I recognized you from the first moment. Have you any idea how fortunate you are that God-knows-who has not recognized you, too?"

He went to the priceless seventeenth-century cabinet where he kept his wines, and refilled their glases.

"Monsieur—"

"You are welcome to stay here," he said. "You can stay until the day when American tanks roll down the Champs Elysées. I know you won't. You have . . . friends. But you are welcome. I would be honored to give you refuge."

"It is you who honor me, Monsieur."

"And Dirk ter Horst? And the baby? Wilhelmina?"

"Dead, Monsieur," said Adriana. "The baby was killed in the bombing of Rotterdam, with her grandparents. Dirk was taken prisoner and died of his wounds."

The old man reached for her hands, took them in his—she found them oddly cold—raised them to his lips, and kissed them. "My dear," he murmured, "you must survive. You must live, Adriana. The world is going to need the like of you."

"I mean to survive," she said grimly.

He sighed, saliva bubbling in the corners of his mouth. "But you won't hide here with me until—"

"No. I am going to try to save those children. And some friends. If—"

"You will be welcome here."

She reached for his hands. "I won't bring the Gestapo," she said. "It is important that you survive, too."

"The risk was within acceptable limits," said Henri Mercier. "I'm carrying an authentic *carte d'identité*, issued by the Kommandantur."

Emil Bender, called Bobby by everyone who knew him, smiled and nodded. "You are a clever man, Monsieur Mercier. And a resourceful man. You always were."

Bender was an undercover Abwehr operative, ostensibly a Swiss civilian, sent to Paris in 1940 to ferret out resources the French business community might be holding out from official requisition, and also to find precious art and antiques that might be seized and sold in Switzerland to put hard money in Abwehr secret funds. It was part of his work to play the role of a wealthy sybarite, and he had lived for a long time in this luxurious apartment, enjoying the advantages of Paris in ways that few German officers knew how to do. He was a fervent anti-Nazi who held Hitler in contempt ("After all," he had said to Admiral Canaris, "What confidence can one put in a leader who does not know Burgundy from Bordeaux?") and was a leader of the anti-Nazi clique within the Abwehr. Although technically subordinate to General Hausser, he did not in fact report to him, and the general had only a vague idea about what he did.

Forty-five years old, Bender was blond, handsome, and self-possessed.

For fifteen months he had been involved in the process of saving people from deportation—Jews, Résistants, Gaullists, Communists... whoever. He was anxious to survive the war, to be identified as an anti-Nazi humanitarian, and to live afterward in reasonable comfort. His motives were mixed, but his contributions were undeniable.

"You are the second most-wanted man in Paris, Monsieur Mercier—the first most-wanted being the man who kidnapped Oberführer Franck to facilitate your escape. I am amazed that you dare walk the streets, with or without a *carte d'identité*."

"I come over the rooftops," Mercier said with a sly smile.

He had in fact left the flat on rue du Mont by way of the rooftops. Descending through the apartment of the Fourcade family, he had emerged on the street and walked down from Montmartre to Bender's apartment, not too far from his department store—still open and run by God-knew-who.

It had been emotionally difficult to walk through streets only two months ago his quiet home, where he had walked on summer evenings with his wife and children, year after year. The crickets still chirped, their shrill notes filling the quiet summer air as they had always done. The world continued, the crickets would live on and fill summer evenings with their eternal din no matter what men did to each other.

"I know of the deportation you have come to talk about, Monsieur Mercier. That of the children. It constitutes just two cars in a train that will carry hundreds of French men and women. Many Jews, yes, but also many others. It can't be stopped."

"The children. All I want is the children."

Bender had offered Napoleon brandy, pouring generous amounts of the precious amber liquid into two tulip glasses. "You are talking, I suppose, about money," he said.

"All that we have left," said Mercier.

"We have alternatives," said Bender. "An appeal to humanity through Consul Nordling—"

"My daughter and I have seen a bit of the humanity we can expect from the SS," Mercier interjected.

"—or a bribe carefully placed."

"I would have more confidence in the latter."

"And a third alternative. The new commanding general, von Choltitz. He is a soldier. A Prussian. He may not like the idea of deporting children. An appeal . . ."

"Two cars," said Mercier. "Out of a train that will consist of—what? Twenty? Two hundred children. Why does anyone want to deport *them?*"

"To be cruelly frank, Monsieur Mercier, it is simply because certain pencil pushers in the Race and Resettlement Office are troubled by the untidiness of having two hundred unattached children in the system. They can think of no way to classify them."

"And for that they will kill them," whispered Mercier. "What kind of monsters has your country produced?"

"They are true believers, Monsieur," Bender said. "If you believe in something strongly enough, then you don't have to think, you don't have to understand. The euphemism for that state of mind is faith. May God save the world from the faithful."

"Are you going to help us save these children?"

Bender drew a deep breath and for a moment paused. "I am leaving Paris very soon. I . . . I will go to the Swedish Consulate. Perhaps Consul Nordling can accomplish something by an appeal through the International Red Cross."

"I will be grateful for that," said Mercier. "I would be more grateful, though, for your help in finding someone whom we can bribe. I can offer about seventeen million francs. In gold. Surely there is someone who would be influenced by that."

Bender nodded. "Almost anyone would be influenced by that. Except the faithful. Unhappily the deportations are controlled by mindless fanatics—the Nazi faithful."

"I've had a bit of experience with the faithful, Nazis and others," said Mercier, "but I have encountered none who valued their faith at more than seventeen million gold francs."

Bender smiled. "You are as cynical as I am," he said.

"I need your help."

"Well . . . I'm not at all certain I can do anything," said Bender. "As I told you, I am leaving Paris in a couple of days."

"If we can save the children for less than the seventeen million, you are welcome to the balance."

"No. I want something more valuable than that," said Bender.

"What? What can I give you?"

"I want your written statement that I helped you. I have a few similar documents. They may be very important to me soon."

"I will write you one now," said Mercier. "If we succeed in stopping the deportation, I'll write you another."

After dinner, they returned to their suite. The war had at long last reached the privileged officers billeted in the Royal Monceau—dinner had been skimpy—and now they had to climb the stairs because there was no electricity to run the lift. In the suite they lit candles. Even candles, they had been warned, were in short supply.

Heinrici was troubled by a rumor he had heard at the Hotel Lutétia when he went there late in the afternoon to report to General Hausser. He had heard that the Abwehr would close its Paris headquarters within a few days and that all Abwehr officers in the city would either be sent to Berlin or assigned to the staff of the garrison commander. The incoming commander, von Choltitz, was rumored to be a stiff-necked Prussian, a relentless disciplinarian, and an officer absolutely loyal to Adolf Hitler.

"If such an order comes—either option—I will desert," Heinrici said to Adriana. He glanced around the candlelit suite. "The room over the butcher shop—the one Théo abandoned—may have to be our home for a while."

Adriana nodded.

Looking at her in the candlelight, he renewed his determination that she share with him the life he was going to make with the Jews' gold. A good life, that was what he wanted. And this exquisite creature would be an important element of that good life.

She stood at the window, with the blackout curtains parted, looking down on the moonlit street. He stepped up behind her and kissed the back of her neck. He put his hands under her breasts and lifted them, held them tightly. He had learned that she liked that. He began to unbutton her blouse.

Adriana tried not to tense. Every night she accepted him, determined tht he not detect in her anything that would kindle a suspicion. As he undressed her, she intensified her resolution.

Nothing she had ever been asked to do before had been so intrusive, so violative, as this. To have to allow him license with her body was bad enough. To have to seem to welcome it was worse. His hands were all over her: on her breasts, her belly, her hips, between her legs. She arched her back. He could not have guessed it was no longer a sign he was arousing her, but a spasm of revulsion.

"Adriana . . ."

He turned her around and held her at arm's length to look at her. Her breasts were modeled in soft contrasts of candlelight and shadow. Flickering yellow light gleamed on her nipples. He pushed her back on the bed and spread her legs so that the light would enter her cleft; he enjoyed looking at her fine hair and the shiny pink flesh of her most private part.

He sat down beside her and with a finger gently traced the contours within her. She was dry. The flesh was warm and smooth, but it was dry; she was not aroused. He pressed his finger deeper into her until he felt moisture. She was tense, her eyes fixed solemnly on his face. He stroked the inner flesh, and she closed her eyes and drew a deep breath.

"Adriana," he whispered. "We *will* marry. I mean, when we can. As soon as we can. You want that, don't you?"

He did not understand her tears. He misinterpreted them entirely. "I love you, Adriana," he said. He supposed that was what she wanted to hear.

XXI

SATURDAY, AUGUST 12, 1944

GRUPPENFÜHRER Schenck ate often in the dining room of the Royal Monceau because he lived in a requisitioned house only a few doors away and across the street on Avenue Hoche. There, late on Saturday afternoon, he met with Emil Bender and Henri Mercier.

He was out of uniform. He wore a painter's blue smock, for in fact he was painting a semi-nude portrait of the Schiaparelli model, Martine Paul. He was not without talent. Several pictures of Martine Paul, clothed and unclothed, hung in gilded frames around the room, and each one was a recognizable likeness; one or two of them even caught something of her personality.

Henri Mercier surveyed the sunlit room with detachment. He was little impressed with the comfortable furnishings, the valuable antiques. His chief thought was that the house was much like his own, and he wondered what had happened to the owner of this one.

He glanced casually at the model and then made it a point not to stare at her. She sat in a straight-backed armchair upholstered in peach-colored plush. She wore a black skirt and shoes and stockings but was naked above the waist—her white blouse and a brassière lay on a table nearby. Her breasts were small and firm and oddly slender—almost pointed, he thought. She had moved to cover

261

herself and abandon her pose when he and Bender entered the room, but Schenck had spoken sharply to her, and she had sat down again, faintly blushing. Her eyes were fixed on something outside the window—giving Schenck the profile he wanted—and she remained silent and unmoving.

"Pour us some brandy, if you will be so good, Bender. Four glasses. After we toast a pleasant day, I will ask Fräulein Paul to leave us while we discuss business."

Bender stepped to the array of bottles and glasses on a cabinet and poured four generous splashes of a superior Napoleon brandy. "Would you mind speaking French, Herr Gruppenführer?" he said. "Monsieur Mercier understands a little German but not much."

"Français . . . Commez vous voudrez."

Schenck's eye fluttered; it looked as if he had winked. Mercier was startled, then realized he had seen a nervous paroxysm. Everything about the SS general was a surprise: the tic, his interest in art and the talent he seemed to possess, the emaciated pale face, the watery pale-blue eyes.

Bender carried a brandy to the model, who accepted it with a quiet word of thanks, sipped, and turned her head back toward the window.

"Have you met the new commanding general of the Paris garrison?" Schenck asked. He held a sip of brandy between his lips and tongue, visibly savoring it. "Generalmajor von Choltitz?"

"I've not had the privilege," said Bender.

"I don't think you'll like him."

"I assume *you* don't," Bender said bluntly.

Schenck glanced at Martine Paul, then dabbed at his painting with his brush. "Not a cultured man," he said. "A family man, I understand. The Führer expects great things of him."

"Like defending the city against overwhelming force," said Bender.

Schenck cast a cynical eye on Bender. "Something like that," he said.

"I am afraid the Führer may be disappointed."

"Many officers have disappointed him." Schenck sighed and tossed back his brandy. "My dear . . . ," he said to the model.

Martine Paul rose, picked up her blouse, and left the room.

"Well, then," said Schenck. He continued to dab at his canvas with first one brush and then another. "What have we to discuss?"

"Have you confirmed the rumor?" Bender asked.

"It is as you say," Schenck mumbled, frowning intently over his painting.

"Two hundred children," said Mercier gravely.

"One hundred eighty-nine," Schenck said, glancing at Mercier.

"What will be required to save them?" Bender asked.

Schenck looked at Bender as if really seeing him for the first time—running his eyes up and down, appraising his handsomely tailored cream-colored summer suit. He shrugged. "My signature," he said.

"Then will you sign the order?"

"No. How can I? Why should I? If I canceled this deportation, sooner or later I would have to explain myself. To Berlin. And what would I say?" He turned away from his painting and turned up the palms of his hands. "Am I to say, 'I canceled the deportation of one hundred eighty-nine Jews because I was paid eight hundred thousand marks.'?"

"Herr Gruppenführer," Mercier said quietly. "Could you not say, 'I canceled it because two carloads of children were no threat to the Reich'? What possible reason is there for sending two hundred children to their deaths?"

"Only the philosophical one—that it rids Europe of a hundred eighty-nine more Jews," Schenck said, turning his attention once more to his painting. He glanced briefly at Mercier. "I should like to have your eight hundred thousand marks. I'll take them gladly. But I must have something more, something that will justify me when I am required to explain my action."

Henri Mercier shook his head despondently. "What could we possibly give you, Herr Gruppenführer?"

"There is no insuperable difficulty," said Schenck. "I will trade you the children for eight hundred thousand marks, in gold—*plus* the three English agents who arranged your escape and your daughter's escape from Fresnes and Romainville."

Henri Mercier shook his head. He closed his eyes. His face reddened. "I—"

Schenck cast a sidelong look at him. "It should be easy for you. Initially you will hesitate, as a matter of principle. But when you consider . . . One hundred eighty-nine children for three English agents. A better principle applies. Also, the quid pro quo justifies me very nicely. My superiors will be pleased with the trade."

Henri Mercier looked at Bender, who shook his head and lowered his eyes. "What I was about to say, Herr Gruppenführer," Mercier murmured in a throaty whisper, "is that in the first place, there were not three English agents, there were two, and anyway I don't know where they are."

"*Three,* Monsieur," said Schenck coldly.

"Two, Herr Gruppenführer," Mercier insisted. "The third agent was a German officer."

"Ah-hah! A renegade officer! As I have suspected, actually. His name, Mercier. What is his name?"

"Herr Gruppenführer . . . The children?"

Schenck put down his brushes and palette. "Mercier . . . Eight hundred thousand marks, in gold. The identity of this German officer. *And proof.* Some sort of evidence." He nodded. "For that, you can have your children."

* * *

Baldwin and Jeanne did not expect a visit from Adriana that Sunday. She had told them Saturday afternoon that Heinrici had made her a bizarre proposition: that they carry a picnic lunch from the hotel and go to the races at Auteuil. It was the first day of the three-day Assumption holiday in France, and in spite of everyone's dread of the coming battle, Parisians would spend their summer Sunday taking the sun in the parks and along the Seine, many of them swimming, others kicking at footballs, everyone eating outdoors the food and wine that had been hoarded for the holiday picnics. Even the *bittes,* Adriana had said, would be on holiday—most of them, anyway. Jeanne had nodded. It had been that way the past four summers. Even the squareheads took the holiday.

The weather was fine: a blue sky with only a few white clouds, a warm breeze, hot bright sunshine. Baldwin and Jeanne were tempted to go out. Everyone would be on the streets, Adriana had said—how could the *bittes* check everyone? By mid-morning, though, they decided not to venture out; the least mishap could bring calamity. They elected to remain in the studio and make as festive a meal as they could from what remained of the supplies Adriana had left. They were avowedly in love, and they could be as happy together in the confines of the shabby little studio as they could be at a picnic on the Seine.

They had lived together more than a week now. Her father knew where she was, though he could not reach her by telephone and she could not reach him. They had not spoken since she left the house at 48 rue Boulanger. They relied on Adriana as their contact. She had spoken with Henri Mercier twice on the telephone, and she had spoken twice more with Louise Pascin when she learned Mercier no longer stayed at 48 rue Boulanger. Jeanne's father asked for assurances that his daughter was living "respectably." Adriana had given them.

The studio had a private toilet, fortunately, enclosed in a tiny closet. They could not entirely close the closet door—there was no electricity in the daytime, and the closet was dark with the door closed. Late in the morning, while Baldwin was chopping the last of their raw vegetables into a salad, for which he expected to concoct a dressing of oil and red wine, Jeanne went inside the little closet. He pretended not to hear a sound from there. But today he did hear sounds. He heard her gasp, then sob.

"Jeanne!" He grabbed his cane and hobbled toward the door.

"Len! Len, it's all right. Don't come in."

He hesitated just outside the door. "Jeanne . . ."

"Hand me a towel," she said quietly. "A rag. Anything . . ."

"Jeanne?"

"Yes! Damnit!" she sobbed. "I'm bleeding. Either it's the normal thing coming back, or I'm losing what the Boches put in me."

He waited near the door until she came out. The bleeding was a measured, normal flow. She decided she was not pregnant, and she clung to him and wept joyfully.

They made the best of their meager rations. There were no more eggs, no meat, just some turnips and carrots and onions and a cabbage, which he had cut up for the salad, and some bread and cheese—with some wine. She was in a whimsical mood.

"What in the world is being celebrated on Assumption?" she asked. "Don't tell me; I don't want to know. My girlfriends and I used to play a little game, making up verses from the names of the odd holidays we didn't understand." She said in a singsong:

> *Annuncation, Maundy Thursday,*
> *Palm Sunday, Shrove Tuesday*
> *Ash Wednesday, Assumption someday.*

"When *I* was a child I was required to know the significance of every one of them," he said. "Michaelmas, Candelmas . . . Boxing Day."

"We were different," she said solemnly. "And our family was different in another way—we weren't observant Jews. But when I was very young my father told me about Alfred Dreyfus. I was supposed to understand a lot . . . because of the story of Dreyfus. What's more, I did understand it."

Baldwin nodded and opened his mouth to speak, but she continued, "Maybe someday I'll have a little girl. Maybe with you, Len. How will I explain to her that there are people in the world who will want to kill her just because her mother was born of parents who were born of parents who . . . were born of parents . . . How will I explain?"

He put his hand gently to her mouth and then took it away and kissed her. "What in God's name can I say?"

In the Bois de Boulogne, in one of the tribunes overlooking the race course of Auteuil, Adriana sat beside Heinrici. Their wicker hamper, packed for them by the hotel, sat between them, filled with bread and cheese, paté and sausages, fruit and wine. They were sharing hampers with two other couples: a young submarine commander named Kampmeier and his pudgy little wife, and a Hauptmann Ritter of the 12th SS Panzer Division and the voluptuous peasant girl he had brought from Brittany on her first visit to Paris.

Adriana found the two young women grotesque—both of them self-consciously certain they were models of fashion in their flowered summer dresses, high-heeled shoes, and broad-brimmed white straw hats. The panzer captain was a thick Bavarian whose French vocabulary probably did not exceed the minimum had needed to seduce the altogether-too-willing Breton maid. She spoke no German at all. The naval officer was a short, swarthy Mecklenburger in a stained, worn uniform. He spoke French, but his wife didn't, not a word. All four of these people were grateful to be accepted in the company of such a high-ranking officer of the Abwehr. They were deferential, too, toward the elegant dancer Jacqueline Clement—the role Adriana was playing for what she hoped would be the last time.

Although the section where they were seated was given over exclusively to German officers, other sections were filled by thousands of French civilians, all gaily dressed for the holiday, all carrying picnic hampers. In the judges' tribune high above, the race-course officials presided in formal clothes: gray top hats and white gloves. On the track the jockeys wore colorful silks and paraded horses that, though a little thin, were sleekly groomed and nervously ready to run.

Hauptmann Ritter had drunk a good deal of wine and was describing to Heinrici the tank battle in which his battalion had been wiped out. He was, he said, one of very few tank commanders who survived. "There are no roads left, Herr Oberst. No railroads. In some places the land looks like what the surface of the moon must look like—nothing but craters. We were short of petrol, short of ammunition, short of food. I hope you will not think I am a defeatist."

"No," Heinrici muttered. He had borrowed the naval officer's fine binoculars and was studying the horses, trying to select one on which to bet a few marks. In the years before the war he had come here often on summer days, sometimes with Sidonie, sometimes with Yvette. He glanced at Adriana. Neither of them had been as beautiful as she was. They would come here again—as Mr. and Mrs. Henry Conrad. He would abandon the field gray uniform, even the Iron Cross in which he took some pride, and at the Assumption holiday in 1945 they would sit together here, just as they were today, in the company of Frenchmen and Americans.

"Herr Oberst—"

Heinrici put down the binoculars. He too was aware that the vast crowd in the tribunes had suddenly fallen silent. Thousands of men and women, French and Germans, sat in perplexed silence, bewildered by a sound most of them had never heard before and could not identify, afraid to guess what it might be.

"Thunder?" whispered Frau Kampmeier.

The SS panzer captain stiffened and sat tall, listening to the distant low rumble from the south. He shook his head. "Artillery," he said quietly.

Terrified, Jeanne opened the door—expecting to see policemen or Gestapo agents. Instead, she confronted an excited Le Capitaine. He rushed past her, into the studio, and turned to close the door.

"Jeanne! Len! Thank God you're safe!"

"No thanks to you," Baldwin said, calmly reproachful. "You risked all our lives by running out of here."

"I've told no one where you are," he said. "But I've brought you things."

He was carrying a canvas bag, which he put down on the floor. He knelt beside it and opened it.

"I'm sorry I could only get one," he said as he pulled out an old nickel-plated revolver. "And no extra ammunition. It's loaded with five shots. It's an ugly thing. I—" He turned it over in his hands. The nickel plating was worn off around the cylinder. The black grip was round; the barrel, short. "It's deadly, though. I can tell you. It's been used."

Jeanne scowled at him. "Théo," she said quietly. "My brother and his friends are dead. My mother has been sent to Ravensbrück. I suffered. My father suffered. And do you know what started it all? My brother was carrying a pistol when he was stopped for a routine check." She shrugged. "Or so the *bittes* said when I was arrested."

"There are no routine checks today," Le Capitaine said with a grin. "You want to know why? The *bittes* are taking the flics' guns. All over the city! The new Kommandant Gross Paris ordered the army to disarm the Paris police. They're at it right now, gathering up and hauling away all the guns. The flics are submitting, but they're furious. It's the end of their cooperation. The Germans are right, actually, not to trust them anymore, because the police are about to join *us!*"

"Join who?" Baldwin asked as he examined the revolver Le Capitaine had handed him.

Le Capitaine grinned, his face bright with enthusiasm. "Us!" he said. "We are about to put an end to it. Patton's tanks are only a hundred kilometers away. From Montparnasse, they say, you can hear the roar of the guns. Tomorrow, or maybe Tuesday, there will be fighting in the streets. You may have to protect yourselves. Also, I've brought you some food—what I could get."

He began pulling small packages from the bag: black bread, a small piece of cheese, some beets, some rutabagas.

"You and the Résistance—"

"Yes! I could not sit here with you and wait for—for God knows what. I . . . I had other contacts. Students. The universities, you know, have always been Résistance centers. In fact—I don't suppose you know—Le Chou-fleur is Professor Militiades. It is because of him that I joined the cause originally."

"Has anyone heard from him?" Baldwin asked.

Le Capitaine shook his head.

"We entrusted his life to Heinrici," Baldwin said soberly.

"And where is that one? And Adriana?"

"At Auteuil, at the races," Jeanne said. She was gathering his offering of food into a pile on the table, where they would divide it into portions for an evening meal and tomorrow's meals. "Taking the holiday."

"I have word for your father," said Le Capitaine. "A train is definitely leaving Pantin Station on Tuesday. If he hasn't done whatever he has to do to save the children, it may be too late."

Monday Adriana found what she had been told she would find: a rope, securely tied to a vent pipe and hanging down the air shaft. It was conveniently knotted at intervals and would afford her a relatively easy descent to the window. If she could not get in as she had been told she could, she could climb back up.

She glanced around. No one was on any other roof within sight. No one was watching. Konrad had been suspicious of her this morning when she said she wanted to leave the hotel alone—to resume her effort to find Baldwin, she had told him. She had wondered if he might not try to follow her. He had begun to wonder, she knew, if she didn't in fact know where Baldwin was, if Baldwin had not elected an independent course.

She had found it difficult to make her way from the Royal Monceau to the Butte of Montmartre. For some odd reason, the new Kommandant Gross Paris had ordered a military parade for this Monday afternoon, the second day of the Assumption holiday. Even Heinrici had been ordered to report to the Hotel Lutétia, to take a seat in one of the armored cars that would roll through the streets—an order he neglected to obey, she knew. Streets were blocked for an hour as tanks, armored cars, trucks, and marching soldiers wound through the long parade route. It seemed that Generalmajor von Choltitz had decided to make a show of force.

Adriana hung her handbag around her neck, clutched the rope, and slipped over the edge of the roof. She let herself down, knot by knot, until she reached the window she had been told would be open. She doubled her knees, planted her feet against the brick sill, and thrust herself out. As she swung back, she extended her legs before her, swung through the open window, and dropped lightly on the floor of a bedroom.

A woman appeared immediately in the doorway. "We expected you much earlier, Mademoiselle."

Henri Mercier appeared behind the woman. "Did you have difficulty?" he asked anxiously.

"Only in getting past a parade," she said as she pulled her handbag from around her neck.

"None in climbing down?" he asked. "We would have been here to help you, but—"

"No difficulty," said Adriana.

"Good," said Mercier. "In that event, come with us and let us show you why we asked you to enter that way."

They walked into Marie-Madeleine Lefevre's small parlor and stood at a

window, where Mercier pointed down at the street. Adriana saw the man he
pointed at. She recognized him.

"Oberleutnant Dietrich Krueger," she said. "Abwehr. He belongs to
Heinrici."

"So. Then Heinrici knows where I am."

"But as of the moment, he apparently does not know you have an alternative
means of coming and going. I hope you do use the door sometimes."

"Well . . ."

"I suggest, Monsieur," Adriana said, "that you make a point of going out
occasionally. Let him follow you. He knows about 48 rue Boulanger. Go there.
Return. If he never sees you leave, he will begin looking for an alternative
way."

Mercier turned away from the window and sat down on Marie-Madeleine's
sofa. "I will not introduce my lovely hostess," he said. "It is better we do not
exchange names."

"I agree," said Adriana. She smiled at Marie-Madeleine and sat down facing
Mercier.

"My daughter—?"

"—is well, Monsieur. She had been afraid she might be pregnant. She knows
now that she is not."

Mercier nodded. "She is where it is safe? With the English captain?"

Adriana nodded. "As much safety as there is in Paris today. Anyway, Colonel
Heinrici doesn't know where they are."

"I accept your judgment that she should not be with me. I am involved in a
dangerous game."

"I came to talk to you, Monsieur, because there is a strong rumor in the
Résistance that a train will leave Pantin tomorrow. The children could be
going."

"I have news for you, too," said Mercier. "The children are not going tomorrow. I have been in contact with a German who can save them. Unless he is
deceiving me, the scheduled deportation of the children will be cancelled. For a
price."

"For a price . . ."

Mercier nodded. "He asked me for *you*, Mademoiselle. And Captain Baldwin. I said I had no idea where you might be. I did, though, offer him a
renegade German officer."

"Konrad."

"Colonel Heinrici. Deportation of the children will be cancelled *if* I pay over
the remainder of the gold in our fund, name the German officer who arranged
the escapes for me and Jeanne, *and* offer some convincing evidence of that
officer's disloyalty to the Reich. That is why I wanted to see you. Urgently.

What evidence can we supply? Are you willing to supply it?"

"I am," she said. "I can provide the evidence. I wonder how the SD would react to a forged American passport—that is to say, one forged for him by someone in Paris, not by his own government? I wonder also how the Germans would react if Radio Heinrici came back to life."

"Radio Heinrici?"

"I'll explain later," Adriana said. "Yes, I can provide evidence of Colonel Heinrici's double dealing." She paused. "But—consider something. He knows almost everything. He knows, for example, where you are living. Once he is in custody, they will force everything out of him." She nodded toward Marie-Madeleine. "You may not be giving me this lady's name, for example, but when he gives this address, she—"

"We will move," said Marie-Madeleine. "The Pascins too. We will have to hide until the Germans are driven out of Paris, but how much longer can that be?"

"May I ask what functionary promises to cancel the deportation?" Adriana asked.

Mercier nodded. "His name is Gruppenführer Heinz Schenck. Second only to Obergruppenführer Oberg, he is the chief of the SS, SD, and Gestapo in Paris. With a stroke of the pen, he can—"

"Schenck!"

"Schenck. Yes. Do you know of him?"

Adriana drew a deep breath. "Yes, I know him. What is more to the point, Heinrici knows him. Schenck thinks I'm an unclothed dancer at the Moulin Rouge. And—" She stopped, frowned, and considered for a moment. "And I'm sure he thinks Heinrici is a completely loyal officer."

"Maybe he is," said Mercier. "Maybe he has been deceiving us all along, for some larger purpose."

Adriana shook her head. "I don't think so. If so, why the American passport? Why would he provide one for *me?* No, Monsieur. I think Konrad Heinrici wants your gold."

"Schenck . . . ," mused Mercier. "Is it possible he really doesn't know—is it possible he really *does* want to trade the lives of the children for the life of Herr Oberst Heinrici?"

"I think it is entirely possible, Monsieur Mercier, that he and Heinrici are identically motivated. They want your gold. I think it is entirely possible that Schenck's promise to cancel the deportation order is no more valid than Konrad's promise to secure the release of your wife."

"The Boches . . . ," muttered Marie-Madeleine.

Adriana nodded. "They murdered my husband and baby, Madame."

"Oh!" exclaimed Henri Mercier. "My dear . . . I had no idea!"

Adriana changed the subject. "Tomorrow's train," she said. "What assurance do we have that the children will not be deported tomorrow—after which Schenck will take your money and laugh at you?"

Mercier rose and walked to the window. He looked down at Krueger, who was sitting on a wheelbarrow, miming the weary workman. "The arrangement is for the children to be delivered into the hands of the International Red Cross," he said. "In fact, Gruppenführer Schenck has insisted they must be handed over to a humanitarian organization that will take responsibility for them, not just released on the streets. We are dealing with Raoul Nordling, the Swedish consul. He promises to arrange for the children to be delivered into the custody of neutrals, after which they will be taken to a convent or monastery to remain until Paris is liberated."

"He speaks of Paris being liberated?"

"No. No, of course not. *My* word."

Adriana shook her head. "Oberleutnant Krueger is on the street. Heinrici knows you are here. God only can guess what Schenck knows or conjectures. I would like to be certain, Monsieur, that the children are not deported tomorrow."

"Other than by going to Pantin—which I think I dare not do—I don't know how I can be certain."

"Maybe I can find out," she said. "Maybe . . . Maybe Colonel Heinrici can find out for us."

General Hausser strode across the floor of his office, smiling, extending his hand. "Mademoiselle! A rare pleasure."

Martine Paul let him kiss her hand, then she sat down in one of the chairs facing his desk. "I've come on business, Herr General," she said. "I have something interesting to report. Also, I want my release."

Hausser frowned as he returned to his chair behind his desk. "Release?"

"You promised to pay me. If I lived with Gruppenführer Schenck and reported to you everything of value I heard—" She stopped, touched a tear in the corner of her eye, and took a breath. "I want to go home. I don't want to be in Paris when the Allies come."

Hausser nodded. "I can understand that. But—it won't be easy. It's Limoges, isn't it—where you want to go? I'm afraid that's quite impossible. There are American armored divisions between here and Limoges."

"I know," she said. "I know very well. But I can take a train to Lyon, and from there I can reach Limoges."

"Trains . . ." He shook his head. "There are hardly any. Besides, the tracks are bombed daily."

"General Hausser," she said firmly, "with the documents you can provide me, plus the money you promised to pay me, I can leave Paris. I can go somewhere"—she lowered her eyes—"anywhere. I don't *dare* stay here."

"I understand. I'm afraid a good many pretty French girls will be—How shall we say?—*abused,* when the Parisians recapture Paris."

"I was promised money and protection," she said.

"I keep my promises, Mademoiselle. When do you want to leave?"

"Today. This afternoon. I want to be out of Paris before Schenck returns to the house."

"I can give you half a million francs," he said. "And the necessary pass and travel authorization."

"Maybe when you hear what I have to tell you, you will give me a whole million."

"Is it that good?"

"Judge for yourself," she said. "Heinz had two interesting visitors Saturday afternoon. I was sent from the room, but I stayed near the door and listened. One of his visitors was an Abwehr officer—Herr Emil Bender. The other was the escaped Zionist, Henri Mercier."

"Mercier!"

"Mercier," she affirmed. "He wants to prevent the deportation of a large number of Jewish children, and Heinz has the power to cancel the deportation. He offered Heinz eight hundred thousand marks in gold for his signature on the paper canceling the deportation."

"Eight hundred thousand—"

"But Heinz wanted more," she interrupted. "He wanted the three English agents who arranged Mercier's escape. The Jew said there were only two English agents involved and that he has no contact with them. Then he said the third man involved was in fact a German officer. He *has* contact with him, apparently. He agreed to name him and provide evidence against him. Heinz is going to cancel the deportation—for eight hundred thousand marks and the name of this German officer."

Hausser was on his feet, and he began to pace the room. "Mademoiselle," he said. "You've earned your million francs. But you must not leave Paris today. I need one more bit of information. *When* is Gruppenführer Schenck to meet with Mercier to complete the transaction? Find out for me, and I will give you another half million! You'll have a million and a half, and I will have you driven to Limoges by an officer with authority to escort you there."

She licked her lips. "I have your . . . assurance, then? Maybe I will also be able to find out the name of the officer."

"Don't trouble yourself about that, Mademoiselle," said General Hausser. "I know the name of the officer."

"This is foolish, Adriana," Heinrici muttered. "A risk—"

"You've said it before, Konrad. A hundred times. But I *must* know."

"I could have found out otherwise."

"I wouldn't have been satisfied. They may not know his name. They might not have told you the truth."

They had returned to Pantin Station. It was Assumption Day, the fifteenth of August, and in the oppressive heat of a glaring sun they could see that the rumors were true: a train of cattle cars was being loaded to carry—how many? two thousand? three thousand?—prisoners away from Paris, out of France. The green buses lined up for hundreds of meters, bringing men and women from Fresnes, Romainville, and Drancy to this freight yard.

Adriana had told Heinrici there was a possibility Baldwin was being deported this morning. She had arranged for Louise Pascin to telephone her at the Royal Monceau after midnight. Startled by the call, Konrad had handed her the telephone, and she had pretended to listen to an urgent message from a woman saying the wounded English captain was among the political prisoners being deported this morning. They had argued most of the rest of the night, she and Konrad. She had told him she would come to Pantin without him if he would not bring her.

"They won't deport him, if they have him," Heinrici grumbled. "They'll shoot him. If he's lucky."

"Yes. You said that."

The scene was impossible to believe. The cars were strung out along a siding, some twenty cattle cars packed with human beings. The loading had begun before dawn apparently, for now, in the heat of mid-morning, few remained to be jammed inside the already obscenely crowded cars. Men and women inside clamored for air, for water, for room to sit—obviously they were so tightly packed that they lacked space even to relieve themselves except on the floor and on each other. Through the narrow gaps between the slats that made the sides of the cars Adriana could see naked flesh, men's and women's, crushed against those crude wooden walls and gleaming with stinking sweat.

"Wer sind diese Gefängeners?" Heinrici asked an SS sergeant. Who are these prisoners?

The sergeant's eyes flicked over Heinrici's insignia, and he raised an arm and called for a hauptsturmführer. Heinrici repeated the question to a puffing, sweating blond man.

"Saboteurs, Herr Oberst," the hauptsturmführer said. "Murderers, mostly."

"I am looking for an English agent who may be among them," said Heinrici. "A wounded man who walks with a cane."

The hauptsturmführer shook his head. "Not in this lot," he said. "I am sure, Herr Oberst. I know who is aboard this train. No foreign agents. All French."

"Jews?" Adriana asked. She glanced up and down the line of cars, trying to look casual.

"No," said the SS officer. "There were to have been five carloads of Jews this morning, but their buses haven't come, and we're not going to wait for them. We'll send them later."

"Children?" she asked.

The hauptsturmführer shook his head emphatically. "No, thank God! No children. Children are trouble. Difficult to handle. Always hysterical. No. No children today."

Adriana stared at the cars. All the doors were closed now, and the train was about to move. The moaning from the crammed cars was low and constant.

"It is this," she said quietly to Heinrici, "that Henri Mercier wanted to prevent."

"If he wanted to prevent it," Heinrici said coldly, "he should not have run away from us."

Adriana turned away from him and focused once again on the cattle cars crammed with suffering people. For a moment she had hoped he might, at the very least, evince some little scruple about diverting the gold that was intended to free hundreds of people—though he might not know it was children—from what he was standing here witnessing. But he was not moved.

He'd had his last chance.

XXII

THURSDAY, AUGUST 17, 1944

EMIL Bender settled gratefully into a comfortable leather-upholstered chair in Gruppenführer Schenck's parlor. He had already, at Schenck's invitation, poured himself a generous amount of brandy. Drinking before noon was a significant change in his life's habits. Drinking before ten in the morning was even more significant. It was significant too that at such an hour Gruppenführer Schenck was at home with his easel and model, not at his headquarters.

"You can talk in front of her," Schenck said, nodding toward Martine Paul, who was again posing semi-nude for the painting he had almost completed. "I didn't want her to hear what the Jew might say, but between you and me"—he shrugged—"we have no secrets from Martine."

Bender tipped his head as he looked at the bare-breasted model, who seemed more tense now, more embarrassed, than she had seemed when he saw her before on Saturday afternoon. He was exhausted. Working with Consul Nordling, he had struggled to stop the Annunciation Day deportation—and they had failed. The train had left for Germany carrying more than two thousand men and more than four hundred women—all of them Résistants; something had happened at Drancy to delay the thousand or so Jews scheduled to be deported

275

on that train, and they had not gone. The blow to the Résistance—to France, ultimately to Germany—was incalculable.

"I am surprised you are still here," said Schenck. "I had supposed that by now you would be long gone." He smiled wryly, looking away from his painting for a moment. "Where is it you are going? Switzerland?"

"Not while there is still the opportunity to do something important for the Fatherland," Bender said smoothly. He had it in mind that preventing the deportation of the Jewish children might lessen Germany's postwar punishment a measure—a motive in clear contrast with Schenck's reasons for remaining in Paris.

"The Red Cross?" asked Bender.

"Must have representatives at Drancy at fourteen hundred hours on Saturday," said Schenck. "I will be there. I will receive the eight hundred thousand marks in gold—*plus* proof that a German officer betrayed our country by contriving the escapes from Fresnes and Romainville."

Bender nodded. "Fourteen hundred hours," he said.

"And why should I not put an end to Mercier, once I have what I want from him?"

Bender shook his head. "I doubt he will come personally," he said. "I doubt that you will ever see him again, Heinz."

Schenck began to clean his brushes. Noticing that, Martine Paul picked up her blouse and pulled it on.

"Who will come to Drancy?" Schenck asked. "You?"

"I don't know."

"Be sure the Jews don't mean to play any sly tricks," said Schenck. "I want the renegade officer. I want proof. I won't sign the order until I have proof."

General Hausser rose and beckoned to Heinrici. He had summoned him to this meeting at a sidewalk table at Le Colisée. Heinrici was punctual and so arrived just as the daily noontime parade down the Champs Elysées passed by. Heinrici sat down. Talk would have to wait until the blaring military band had marched on a little distance and until the Frenchmen at nearby tables continued their interrupted conversations.

"Their resentment is palpable," said General Hausser quietly, as soon as he could.

Heinrici shrugged. "If a parade of *their* troops marched under the Brandenburger Tor every day—"

"We would resent it. We *will* resent it."

"Yes."

General Hausser sipped from his small glass of vermouth. "Our time in Paris is growing very short, Heinrici. A week . . . Two at the most. The situation in Normandy has deteriorated into an utter debacle. We are in danger of losing

Army Group B—I mean *all* of Army Group B—fifty-six divisions. Tuesday the Americans and French landed an army in the south. Army Group G is just retreating up the Rhine. Next month we will be fighting to hold the Allies west of the Rhine."

"'*Sauve qui peut*,'" Heinrici said dryly. He nodded toward the street, where, the ceremonial parade having passed, lines of trucks now filled the Champs Elysées. A German exodus had begun: hurried and disorderly. "'*Suave qui peut*,'" Heinrici repeated.

The general nodded. "And with that thought in mind, Heinrici, where is the Mercier gold?"

"I am not sure, Herr General."

"Where is Mercier?"

"I think I know, Herr General. I am waiting for him to visit his treasury, and when he does I will follow him—or Krueger will. I am going to see him this afternoon. I've been working on a means of getting him to go to his treasury."

"What means?"

"I told him I might be able to secure his wife's release from Ravensbrück, in return for a payment of money. He is a suspicious man. He wants evidence that his wife is alive and that her release can be secured. I have a letter from the camp commandant at Ravensbrück, indicating—"

"A letter. From—? What risk have you taken, Heinrici?"

"A *forged* letter, Herr General. No risk."

General Hausser shook his head. "Never mind the letter, then. I have something better. Mercier is going to pay a big bribe Saturday afternoon—eight hundred thousand marks, in gold, to save two hundred Jewish children from deportation. Unless he is keeping the gold in the flat where he lives, he has to go to his treasury. Saturday morning."

"Who gets this gold? And where?" asked Heinrici.

"I don't want to tell you who is taking the bribe. The gold is to be delivered to the camp at Drancy, where the children are, where they are to be released into the custody of the International Red Cross."

"Drancy."

"Yes. Heinrici . . . I want you to let the eight hundred thousand marks go. Do you understand? That is an order."

"May I ask why?"

"Why not? There are millions there. We can let eight hundred thousand go. And there are good reasons. In the first place, the man who is to receive the gold is a high-ranking political officer and very dangerous. If he had the slightest reason to suspect we are interfering . . . Well, Heinrici. Take my word. Besides, two hundred children . . ." The general shrugged. "I wouldn't want them on my conscience."

"Very well. Eight hundred thousand."

"Let Mercier take the eight hundred thousand and go to his appointment. As soon as he is away, we can move in and haul out the rest of the gold at our leisure." The general stroked his chin thoughtfully. "You will, I assume, station yourself early Saturday morning to watch for Mercier leaving his hideout. Do you need another man? Is Krueger enough?"

"Krueger is enough. In some respects, he is one too many."

General Hausser sighed and leaned back in his chair. He glanced around the sidewalk café at the Frenchmen sweating in the hot August sunshine. "Don't fail, Heinrici," he said. "We can't afford to fail. Neither of us."

Oberleutnant Dietrich Krueger saluted General Karl Hausser; then, realizing that a military salute from a man dressed in bleu de travail was incongruous, he slackened his shoulders, grinned, and shrugged. He had been summoned to the Hotel Lutétia by a young officer who had approached him on the street; there had been no time to return to his billet and change into uniform.

"You shrug like a Frenchman, Oberleutnant," said Hausser. "Sit down. Maybe you've played the Frenchman too long."

"The first hour of it was too long, Herr General," said Krueger.

General Hausser took a cigar from his box and pushed the box across the desk to Krueger. "We are in a highly fluid situation, Oberleutnant," he said. "Since you have been away from headquarters, pushing your barrow about the streets, you may have lost track of the situation. Do you know, for example, that General Patton's tanks entered Orléans this morning?"

"No, Herr General," Krueger said stiffly. The news did distress him. It meant that Paris was being encircled, that escape might soon become extremely difficult, if not impossible.

"A trifle," said Hausser with a flip of his hand. "What is far more important is the situation of the entire German army in France. It has been surrounded in Normandy, at Falaise, and our only hope lies with the stupidity and cowardice of that egomaniacal English general, Montgomery. If he closes the gap, we lose everything we have in France—except the insignificant Paris garrison. Paris"—he gestured scornfully—"is lost. It is of little strategic importance. Napoleon captured Moscow and lost an army. Hitler holds Paris. What good is it if we lose the army we need to defend the borders of the Fatherland?"

Krueger was absorbed in the lighting of his cigar: for him an awkward business at best.

"Krueger," said the general. "We have two weeks more at best—two weeks before we are compelled to abandon the city we said we would hold for a thousand years. If you were not standing around on Montmartre in your workman's coveralls, you would be rifling the files in this office, dividing our records into those that are to be burned and those that are to be carried home."

"Herr General—"

"Heinrici," the general interrupted firmly. "Do you understand what our Herr Oberst Heinrici is doing?"

"Trying to find the Jews' gold," said Krueger. "A vast fortune."

"Exactly," said Hausser. "Trying to find a vast fortune in gold. "And do you know why?"

"To get it out of the hands of the Jews," said Krueger, feigning naivete.

"And then what?" asked Hausser. "As we beat an ignominious retreat from Paris . . . What is to become of this gold?"

Krueger shook his head. He disliked the turn of the conversation. What did the general know?

"The gold, Oberleutnant, is supposed to be placed in a special Abwehr fund. As you know, we need money from time to time, for clandestine operations we do not wish to have to explain. Effective intelligence work costs money, and we don't always get enough from Berlin. Anyway, this is in gold, which makes it even more useful. The Jews' gold will do important work."

Krueger decided General Hausser was an unskilled liar. He decided he would rather believe Heinrici, who undoubtedly also lied—but who had sufficient respect for a young lieutenant to lie adroitly. He assumed an air of cautious interest and waited for the general to continue.

"Oberst Heinrici intends to take the gold for himself, of course," said General Hausser.

So that was it. He knew. Krueger tensed involuntarily and shuddered. He hoped the general didn't notice.

"There is a worse problem," the general went on. "In the course of his machinations to gain the release of the Merciers, then to find their treasury, he has brought himself to the attention of the SD. I would guess, Oberleutnant, that Heinrici is within a few days of arrest. Do you see the problem?"

"Under interrogation, he might accuse us," said Krueger.

"Yes, and if the matter is thoroughly investigated, our role will be discovered."

"Yes. That would be very dangerous."

"On Saturday morning," said the general, "Henri Mercier will go to the Jews' treasury and withdraw a large amount of gold. You and Heinrici will follow him. Having found the gold—more than one man can carry—Heinrici will want your assistance in moving it. So you will be with him. *I give you now a direct order, Oberleutnant Krueger. Once you have found the gold, you will kill Heinrici. Immediately.*"

General Hausser paused to judge the younger man's reaction.

Krueger was successful in concealing it.

"Then you will telephone me and tell me where you are. Are you capable of carrying out that order, Oberleutnant?"

"I am, sir."

"I can send help."

"I can do it, sir."

"There will be several millions in gold," said General Hausser. "No one will hold us to strict account, so we will be able to reward ourselves a bit from it. But killing Heinrici is imperative. If he is arrested, you and I may well be arrested, too, within hours. I do not want to take that chance."

"No, sir."

"He trusts you, doesn't he?"

"Yes, sir. I believe he does."

"Then it should not be difficult."

"No, sir. It will not be difficult. But why . . . why wait? Why not kill him now?"

"Because we need him, Oberleutnant. Heinrici is a wily and treacherous man. Unless I mistake him, he has kept to himself some vital scrap of information, his personal key to the Jews' treasury; and without him and that key, we may fail. Anyway, we need at least two men on the street, and if we don't use Heinrici we will have to trust another man. If we expect to reward ourselves from the treasury, we don't need another partner. Do you agree, Oberleutnant?"

"I agree, Herr General."

In the cellar of the Hotel Lutétia, in a stone-walled room that had been filled with fruit and vegetable bins before the war, the Abwehr had constructed four heavily barred cells. Military intelligence did keep prisoners temporarily from time to time. The cells had been empty for months now, but since late this morning one of them had held a prisoner. General Hausser had taken all the keys to that part of the cellar and had left orders that no one was to enter the room where the cells were, no one was to talk to the prisoner. No one was to enter, not for any reason.

Now, late in the afternoon, he had decided she should have something to eat. He had the tray brought to his office, and he carried it down himself.

"Liar!" she shrieked as soon as he entered the room.

Martine Paul gripped the bars of her cell and tried to rattle the heavy door. Her face was flushed from long weeping, now from fury.

"Liar! You promised—"

"My promise may be redeemed," said General Hausser. "But it will not be until I see if yours is. If what you told me proves true on Saturday afternoon, then—" He smiled. "Then we shall see what we can do for you. In the meantime, you stay here."

He put the tray of food on the floor just outside her door.

"I trusted you," she muttered hoarsely.

"Gruppenführer Schenck trusted *you*. And you called him a fool for trusting you. Anyone who trusts anyone else is a fool."

She sank down on her bunk and began to sob. "You made me a collaborationist," she whispered.

"Yes," he said. "You betrayed your country, too. How can you be surprised if I lie to you? Anyway, Mademoiselle, if your story proves true on Saturday, I will still help you escape the fury of the Parisians."

Back in his office, General Hausser read the dispatches and radio intercepts while a blitzmädchen laid out wine and cheese, some fruit and a few bits of vegetables. She murmured an apology that it had become difficult to buy food in Paris, even for a general.

The news from Normandy continued to be discouraging. General von Kluge had sent to the Führer an urgent appeal to be allowed to disengage and retreat. There was almost no chance the Führer would allow it.

A firm knock. The blitzmädchen hurried to open the door. A stout, sweating captain entered.

"Birkenfeld," said General Hausser. "Have some wine, some cheese. Would you prefer brandy?"

Birkenfeld snapped his heels together, saluted, and said, "Some wine, Herr General, with pleasure."

The general nodded a dismissal at the blitzmädchen, and she left the office. He poured two glasses of white wine.

"I am glad to see you again, Birkenfeld. I regret the circumstances that require you to return to Paris, but I am glad to see you again."

Since May, Hauptmann Joachim Birkenfeld had been attached as Abwehr liason officer to the headquarters of the Seventh Army, at Le Mans; now, with that headquarters compelled to retreat, many of its administrative and liason officers had hurried to Paris to avoid the risk of being sent into the line.

"I hope you haven't made yourself too comfortable in Paris," said the general.

The captain had cut himself a generous slice of white cheese, and he spoke with difficulty through a mouthful of it. "I am surprised we are still here," he said.

"A few more days," said General Hausser. "We are burning our papers."

"The Führer has ordered the Kommandant Gross Paris to hold the city at all costs," said Birkenfeld as he sipped wine.

"Street fighting," said the general. "I do not propose to remain to witness that. I'll be leaving no later than Sunday. I may tell you, however, that my orders are to transfer every officer and man who is fit for combat to the command of General von Choltitz—to remain here and fight in defense of the city."

"I see," the captain said uneasily.

General Hausser, who held his glass of wine in his right hand, used his left to pat his belly derisively. "You don't look quite fit for combat, Birkenfeld. I hear

Choltitz has ordered his headquarters staff to begin daily calisthenics."

"Distressing . . . ," mumbled Birkenfeld with a tentative smile, testing how serious the general was.

"I am also allowed to retain officers who are indispensable to me," said the general.

"I hope I am indispensable to you, Herr General."

"You can make yourself so."

"I hope I can, sir."

General Hausser refilled his own glass and Birkenfeld's. "Suppose," he said, "I asked you to kill a German officer. A traitor. Without trial—we haven't time for anything like that. An officer who is about to be arrested by the SD."

"I believe I understand, Herr General," Birkenfeld said crisply.

"I imagine you do," said the general.

"I am prepared to carry out your orders, Herr General."

"Saturday," said Papa Ange. "So. At last. None too soon, Philippe. None too soon."

"I understand your impatience," said Heinrici.

Papa Ange poked a finger into his pipe, frowning over the tobacco, that had lost its fire. "My impatience is a different subject," he said. "Are you blind, Philippe? Have you no idea what is going on in Paris? Or are you another stupid squarehead?"

"Papa . . . I know the Allied armies are—"

"Armies! Never mind armies. You *are* German. You *are* stupid, after all. Don't you see what is happening under your nose? Paris will free *itself* within a few days! Our new Kommandant Gross Paris disarmed the flics. Do you know what that means? That means that twenty thousand infuriated policemen have now picked up their own private weapons and are an army of twenty thousand to fight back against the *bittes*. But put them aside. Flics. What good have they ever been? They will fight for France now, to cover their collaboration over the past four years. They are not the point, Philippe. *Aux barricades!* How many times has Paris gone to the barricades? Our people will do it again! Tomorrow! Saturday! Sunday! When . . . ?" He shrugged. "Before any army comes. You may be sure of it. And then . . . Who knows? By this day next week, nothing will be as it has been the last four years."

"Nothing will be as it has been the last fifty years," said Mama Ange.

"And?" asked Heinrici.

Papa frowned and drew the flame of a wooden match into the cache of strong, black tobacco in the bowl of his pipe. "And . . . people . . . like . . . us"— he puffed—"will survive. As we always have. Even if the communists come."

"Exactly," said Heinrici. "With the aid of a hundred million francs in gold."

"On which we will put our hands on Saturday?"

"Saturday morning," said Heinrici. "Papa... You must put aside your long-time refusal to carry a gun."

Papa Ange laughed. "For a hundred million I would carry a sword."

"The Jew is leaving the building on rue du Mont by some other way than the street door," said Heinrici. "Over the roofs, most likely. Mama saw him at 48 rue Boulanger on Monday. My man on the street did not see him leave the building, and my man is faithful."

"You do not want to bring in more people?"

"Not if we can avoid it."

"Ah...," mused Papa. "Well, we know a family who live on rue Paul Ferval. From their roof you can see"—he shrugged—"many rooftops. If Mama were there, with a nice pair of binoculars—Hmm? Mama cannot chase through the streets after hurrying people, but she can watch... and signal."

"On the street," said Heinrici. "My young man. Oberleutant Dietrich Krueger. Look at his face, Papa. Know him."

"Because—?"

"Because I have promised him a share, Papa."

"Ah. Who kills him, then? You? Or me?"

"Whoever has the right opportunity," said Heinrici. "He'll have brought a car. It will be nearby. A hundred million francs in gold will weigh more than four hundred kilograms. Even with the car, we will have difficulty moving it."

"We come here," said Papa Ange firmly. "Here, in my house, we will sit down and divide it."

"Agreed," said Heinrici. "I trust you, Papa," he said with a smile. "And you trust me. We trust no one else."

"We have been in business a long time, Philippe. We know it is important to be able to trust somebody."

"And not to trust others," added Heinrici.

"So, this girl," said Mama. "You trust her?"

"You mean—"

"Betty Conrad," said Mama. "The blonde on the passport we had made for you."

"Mama...," said Heinrici quietly. "Why do you suppose I wanted the passport for her? She is part of my future."

"Who killed Sidonie?" Mama asked.

Heinrici shook his head. "I don't know. It could have been—"

"It could have been a lover who didn't want her anymore," Mama said indignantly.

"It could have been a man who learned she was betraying her friends to the Gestapo," said Heinrici.

"Could this be true?"

Heinrici nodded. "It could be true."

"And when we have the gold," said Papa. "What then?"

"No more a *bitte*," said Heinrici. "Henry Conrad. I'll want to hide somewhere while they fight. Then, when the Allies are here, the American couple registers at a hotel, stays a week or two, then leases a flat. The American and his wife."

"This girl," said Mama. "This English girl—"

"She is Dutch, Mama."

"You trust her?"

"She is in love with me."

"And you with her? Have you become a romantic?"

Heinrici shrugged. "*She's* in love, Mama. That's why I can trust her."

When he left the Anges, Heinrici walked to rue due Mont where he found Krueger wearily on watch. He did not speak to him but gave him a sign to follow. Krueger understood, waited until Heinrici was a block away, then abandoned his station. Heinrici led him to the St. Vincent Cemetery, where he walked inside and waited for Krueger to approach him.

"Saturday morning," said Heinrici. "Dressed as you are now. As I will be. Fully armed. They will go to the gold Saturday morning. They are paying out part of it Saturday afternoon. Have the car nearby—the Audi. We will *load it with gold*, Krueger!"

Krueger nodded. "He went out for an hour this morning. To 48 rue Boulanger."

"Even so, he is going out another way—over the rooftops, almost certainly. I will have someone watching the roof of his building on Saturday. In fact, she will begin watching from there tomorrow."

"She?" Krueger asked. "Oh, Mademoiselle Clement."

"Uh . . . Uh, yes," said Heinrici. Good. If Krueger thought it was Adriana who would be watching the rooftops, let him think so. Better he not know there was someone else. "Yes. You understand, Krueger, that she is a part of everything."

Krueger smiled. "She is beautiful."

"She will signal us from a rooftop. I will point her out to you, so you will know where to look. Mercier could come out on two streets, depending on where he leaves the roofs and goes down through a building. Her signal will tell us which street."

"Good."

"Well then. Everything—"

"No, Herr Oberst," said Krueger. "Everything is not in order. We have a serious problem. General Hausser knows your plans. He seems to know everything except that I am with you. He has ordered me to kill you Saturday morning."

Heinrici slapped Krueger's arm. "Of course," he said, feigning unconcern, though he was in fact stunned by the word. "We had to anticipate that."

"He offered to send another man to help me," said Krueger soberly. "I said I could do it alone, but obviously he *will* send another man."

"Yes. But the other man is no factor unless he follows us to the Jews' treasury. Unless he follows us, he won't know where to go."

"How do we rid ourselves of him—unless we kill him?"

"Are you willing to do that, Oberleutnant?"

"To kill a German . . .?"

"That German is willing to kill *me*," said Heinrici. "I am a German, too."

Krueger nodded slowly. "Something more. The general says the SD is about to arrest you."

"But not before Saturday?"

"No."

"No. Not before we lead General Hausser to the gold!" declared Heinrici. "I *told* you he wants it to himself. Did he offer you a share, Krueger?"

"Uh . . . Well, yes. A reward, he said. It may be possible for us to reward ourselves from the gold, he said."

"Yes. After Heinrici is dead. Of course! And maybe after Krueger is dead, too. Hey, Herr Oberleutnant? Huh? Do you still have any doubts?"

"I never did have any, Herr Oberst," said Krueger. "Not since you proposed I join with you. But all this of course means we must go into hiding. I want to go home with my share, and—"

"Possibly that will have to be deferred," said Heinrici. "But it will be no problem a little later. With a small amount of the gold, you can buy false papers. I know how to get them. I'll arrange that for you, just as I've arranged it for—for Mademoiselle Clement. One day, a month from now, two months from now, you will go home with your gold. Or, if things are too bad, you can go somewhere else with your gold. A man with gold can choose where he goes."

Krueger nodded unhappily. "It becomes more and more difficult," he said.

"If it were easy, you wouldn't be earning a fortune by doing it."

He had one final stop for the evening, before he returned to the hotel and joined Adriana for dinner. At 48 rue Boulanger he rapped firmly on the door. Louise Pascin opened it.

"Madam. Is Monsieur Mercier here?"

"I regret to say he is not, Monsieur."

Heinrici smiled inscrutably. "He seems to get about a good deal for a man in his situation. No matter. Please give him this envelope when he returns. In it he will find something of interest. Good evening, Madame."

*   *   *

"Saturday," Heinrici said to Adriana. "Saturday afternoon. Are you ready? Do you have any hesitation?"

She glanced over her shoulder at him. They had eaten a bland, skimpy dinner and were in the suite now, where they were undressing for bed. Keeping her back to him, she steadied herself and searched for a reply. "I . . . I'd like to find Len Baldwin before we do it," she said.

"So would I," he said. "But I'm afraid I'm running out of options."

"*Must* it be Saturday?"

"As of Saturday afternoon, I will be a thief," he said. "An embezzler, anyway. I can't come back to the hotel. This time the Gestapo will be looking for Oberst Heinrici, not for Oberführer von Strauch. They know where to find Heinrici. From Saturday afternoon on, I can no longer be Heinrici."

"How much money will we have, actually?" she asked him. She turned around. She had to face him; she couldn't avoid it. She couldn't avoid showing him her nakedness, either. "And in what form?"

"In gold, Adriana. As much as I can carry in two big satchels: maybe forty kilos, worth maybe ten thousand English pounds. Enough to live on until it is safe for us to reappear. As I told you, it's an Abwehr fund used to meet the extraordinary expenses of intelligence work: paying bribes, buying opium and cocaine, very often paying the fees of prostitutes. There has always been a big fund in the Paris headquarters. I have the combination to General Hausser's office safe. In his absence—and he will be absent Saturday afternoon—I am the ranking officer. I will take as much gold as I have the strength to carry."

He was a skillful liar. She had admired him for it before, when it had served their mission. Now it wrenched her to listen to him. He was handsome, personable . . . and despicable.

It was difficult not to cover herself and turn away from him. Baldwin had suggested she leave him, saying her continuing self-immolation in these rooms and on this bed were not indispensable to saving the Jewish children. But she wasn't sure: she knew little enough of what he had been doing the past days. To lose all contact with him could be fatal.

"You told me," he said, "that Baldwin had SOE documents that would pass us through the Allied lines. Did he leave those where we can get them?"

"No," she said. She went to the bed and began to turn down all the bedding but the sheets. "He was the SOE contact. He was in charge of the mission. After Sybil died—" She shook her head.

"Then our fate is locked to the fate of Paris," he said. "Let's hope the liberation is quick and easy."

XXIII

FRIDAY, AUGUST 18, 1944

THE morning dawned sunny, but within an hour Paris knew it was not just another hot summer day. Telephone lines were dead. The Métro was not running. No mail was delivered. No French policemen were at their stations on the streets. There were no newspapers on the kiosks. Overnight an almost total general strike had frozen civil functions in the city.

For Adriana, another bright summer morning was chiefly a reminder of the false hopes other sunny mornings had raised. She awoke. Heinrici still snored beside her in the bed. She rose and went into the bathroom, where she bathed in a tub of cold water. Hot water had completely disappeared.

He came in while she was in the tub. He shaved, soaped with cold water, reviewing with her as he ran his safety razor over his cheeks his plans for raiding the Abwehr's confidential fund. He begged her to take no chances today, either in her search for Baldwin or in trying to find Henri Mercier. Tonight they would sleep one last time in the Royal Monceau. Tomorrow night they would be in the home of friends. And then . . . Well, he would use their money to provide them the safest possible refuge during the coming battle.

An apologetic waiter brought their breakfast. There was no more coffee, he said, so he had brought tea. There were no eggs, no sausage, no bacon, only coarse bread, no butter of course, a dab of marmalade. He had brought two small apples. And wine. There was always wine, it seemed, and he asked if they by chance wanted it for breakfast. Konrad brought the tray into the bathroom and put it on the stool by the tub. She sat in the cold water, sipped lukewarm tea, and wondered how she would find food for Baldwin and Jeanne.

When Konrad was dressed he came in the bathroom again. "I will ask you to carry the passports," he said. "God forbid they should be found on either of us . . . but if I were caught with them, and the gold, I'd be hard put to explain what I was doing."

He apologized for being hurried and left the suite while she was still in the tub.

She dried herself and dressed, and examined the passports once again. She would have liked to take them with her this morning, to deliver them to Henri Mercier, but it was always possible Heinrici would want to look at them again tonight.

She knelt beside their bed and tugged the bedside radio away from the wall. Inside, tucked between the transformer and the cabinet, she had hidden the Belgian automatic she had used to kill Le Docteur; Heinrici believed she had thrown it away. She had a few extra cartridges for it, and she reloaded the clip—it was short the two shots she had fired into the body of the traitor—and dropped the pistol and extra ammunition into her handbag.

She left the hotel a little after ten, emerging onto streets eerily silent, sullen. Wanting to look inconspicuously Parisian, she wore a white cotton peasant blouse, a short black skirt, and sandals with wooden soles and heels.

With no Métro running, there was not a vélo-taxi to be found. She had no choice but to walk, and it was more than an hour before she reached the Montmartre rooftop from which she could lower herself to Marie-Madeleine Lefevre's flat.

They did not expect her; the window was not open. She hung on the rope, kicking the glass gently until the woman came and raised the sash.

"We are fortunate you are so young, so strong," said Mercier. "I— I would have fallen. In fact, each time I go out I fear . . . Well. Anyway, I am glad to see you. I have much to tell you."

"I have some things to tell you, Monsieur," said Adriana. She sat down and took her shoes from her handbag, where she had put them so she could cross the roofs without setting up a clatter. "Tomorrow—"

"Yes," he said. "If you can supply the passport you spoke of—"

"He knows," she said.

"Colonel Heinrici?"

"Yes. He told me he expects to come into possession of as much gold as he can carry. Tomorrow. He speaks of an Abwehr secret fund, but obviously the gold he's talking about is yours."

She went to the window and looked down. The young German officer was still there, dressed as a workman.

"Of course," sighed Mercier. "Look at this." He handed her the letter Heinrici had delivered to Louise Pascin. "He hasn't given up on this idea either. And if I went to get gold to pay him, he would follow—or the young fellow down there would."

"Or someone else," said Adriana. "There may be others."

Mercier nodded. "Maybe."

"Monsieur—"

"Tomorrow afternoon," said Mercier, "at Drancy, Gruppenführer Schenck will sign the order canceling the deportation of the children. The International Red Cross is taking custody of them and will move them into the countryside, to a convent where they will be cared for until the Germans are driven out of France. We hand over the gold and your document, and they will hand over the children."

"Will they indeed, Henri?" asked Marie-Madeleine. "If they are in good faith, then how does this Boche colonel know? Maybe the whole thing is a betrayal."

Adriana sighed heavily. "That thought has occurred to me, too."

"Then it is all a charade? No." He shook his head. "I was in Schenck's hands a week ago. If all he wanted was the gold, he could have arrested me."

"I suppose you're right. They couldn't be working together," Adriana said. "I mean, Schenck and Heinrici. They know each other. I might even call them friends, but—"

"If they are working together, one of them is withholding essential information from the other," said Marie-Madeleine. "If Schenck knows Heinrici was the man who led the group that rescued Henri from Fresnes, then why does he want documentary proof that Heinrici is a renegade? It makes no sense."

"There is risk," said Henri Mercier. "Tomorrow, I may be walking into some kind of elaborate trap. But it is a risk I am going to take. There are too many lives at stake."

"Why walk into a trap?" asked Adriana. "Why not outwit the trappers? Why not move the gold tonight? You could take it someplace Heinrici will not be watching tomorrow—perhaps to the studio where your daughter is living. What is more, you could stay there. With the gold. You could shift the whole operation to another part of the city."

Mercier shook his head. "I can't."

"Why not, Henri?" asked Marie-Madeleine.

He shrugged. "Very simply, because I don't know where the gold is," he said. "I've never known, not for a long time. I thought this was clear. As we organized our effort to save lives, I worked, as we say in the merchandising trade, on the floor. I was always exposed, to a degree. I might have been arrested and tortured, and we arranged things so that I could not ransom myself with a fund meant to save many lives. When I need money for some purpose, I send word. I know who I send word to, but I don't know who he sends it along to. I sent word yesterday. The gold won't be delivered until tomorrow morning."

"Where? Here?" Marie-Madeleine asked.

"No. Not here. Nor to the Pascins' house. To another place, not far from here." He smiled. "It's an interesting place. We've always used it as a stock room, as you might say. One or two of my friends actually think it is the warehouse. It never was."

"Couldn't you send word to have the gold delivered somewhere else?" Adriana asked.

"Only with the grave risk that a contradictory order would be taken as evidence that something was wrong—in which case they probably would not deliver the gold at all."

"Then," said Adriana, "why can't someone besides you go to get the gold? You could lead Heinrici and his friends off in the wrong direction, while someone else went to your . . . stock room."

Again Mercier shook his head. "The gold will not be lying unguarded. There will be a man there, maybe two, well armed. They will know me. Anyone else . . ." He shook his head still again.

"Well then," said Adriana, "at least you can leave here tonight and go to your warehouse in the morning from a place not known to Heinrici."

"I shall do better than that," said Mercier. "I will go in the morning, over the roof—"

"They may suspect that," Adriana interrupted.

"Only it will not be Henri," said Marie-Madeleine. "*I* will go out in the morning, over the roof—dressed in his clothes. Henri will watch from the window until the young officer moves to follow me. Then he will go out the door, dressed in *my* clothes."

"Suppose they are not watching the roof?" asked Adriana. "Suppose Krueger doesn't move?"

"Then we will know they are not watching the roof, and I will leave that way," said Mercier.

Adriana sighed. "I can't be confident," she said.

"I've another alternative," said Mercier. He stepped to a small writing desk, opened a drawer, and withdrew a muffler-equipped pistol. "I know Heinrici, and I know that young man down there. If one of them follows me, I will kill him. Once I am inside, I will have the help of the man who will be guarding the gold. We will kill both of them if necessary."

"Let me be with you," said Adriana.

"That is impossible," said Mercier. "If Heinrici or the young man saw you ... No."

"How is the gold being delivered to Schenck?"

"In a diplomatic car belonging to the Swedish government. Three of us are driving to Drancy—Herr Bender, Consul Nordling, and myself. We will carry the gold and the forged American passport."

"I don't have the passport with me," said Adriana. "I left it in the hotel. If he by some chance wants to look at it one more time tonight, it has to be there. Fortunately, he expects me to carry it for him tomorrow—together with the civilian clothes that go with it. I will have to bring it tomorrow."

"In that case, I am going to have to tell you where the warehouse is," said Mercier grimly. "Bring the passport to 112 rue Québec. The car flying the Swedish flag will be there at eleven o'clock. Consul Nordling is a plump man with a mustache. You can trust the document to him."

"Does Schenck know what kind of document he is getting?" Adriana asked.

"No."

"Can you get word to him?"

"Perhaps. Through Herr Bender."

"Send this word, if you possibly can," she said. "Tell Grupenführer Schenck to have Erich Langbehn with him at Drancy."

"Who is Erich Langbehn?"

"The governor of Fresnes Prison. He will vividly remember the night of your escape. When he sees Heinrici's picture on the American passport, he will remember him, too."

"I will try to get that word to Schenck."

"I'm going to do something more," said Adriana. "I'll send along *my* forged American passport. If Schenck could have Walter Kleist, governor of Romainville, there—"

"The risk," Mercier interrupted.

"I am named on the passport as Betty Conrad," she said, "wife of Henry Conrad—the name on Heinrici's passport. If Kleist can't be there, tell them to compare the photo of Betty Conrad to their file photos of Adriana Kip. They know me well, Monsieur."

"You are a gallant woman, Mademoiselle," said Marie-Madeleine.

"Can you really risk having the Gestapo know you are in Paris?" Mercier asked.

"Monsieur," said Adriana. "After tomorrow, we go to ground. Those are my orders from London. We must hide until the battle is over. I may ask you for help, in fact."

Trudging down from Montmartre in her uncomfortable wooden soled shoes, under a glaring August sun, Adriana hurried toward the Ile de la Cité, hoping to find Len and Jeanne keeping safely inside the studio flat.

The German retreat was more apparent. Open trucks—canvas covers removed to let sweltering men benefit from the air—bore wounded soldiers through the streets. They were no longer delivering their wounded to Paris hospitals but were moving them instead through the city and on to the northeast. Glimpses of these men revealed bloody bandages, missing limbs, blindness— suffering. Men groaned. Some screamed. And Paris was allowed to see.

She found tanks standing on the Place de la Concorde. Passing into the rue de Rivoli, she saw machine guns, behind sandbags, before the Hotel Meurice, headquarters of the Kommandant Gross Paris. The young soldiers manning those guns, like the ones sitting outside their tanks, grinned at the pretty girl who hurried by, her wooden soles clattering on the pavement. They had no idea that she fervently wished death to every one of them.

Perspiring and uncomfortable, Adriana made her way to the Pont Notre Dame and crossed to the Ile de la Cité. Passing directly east on the Quai de la Corse, she walked into the still-peaceful streets in the shadow of Notre Dame and climbed the wooden stairs to the door of the studio flat.

Jeanne came to the door. "He is out, Adriana," she said immediately. "With Théo. They went out to buy food. An hour ago."

"Why two of them?" asked Adriana. "If Théo—"

"Len insists he can walk," said Jeanne. "He thinks it's important to exercise his leg."

Adrianna crossed the room and dropped gratefully on the sofa. The studio felt cool after the heat of the streets.

"We had run out of food," Jeanne said, half-apologetically, as if they had been self-indulgent to try to stave off hunger.

She was exquisitely beautiful. A quarter-inch of light brown hair now covered her head, and Adriana wondered if she would be as delicately lovely when it was fully grown out. She had, apparently, taken the absence of Len and Le Capitaine as an opportunity to wash the single outfit of clothes she had, and her skirt and blouse hung drying on chairs; she wore a pair of white panties and a white vest undershirt.

"I'm sorry I couldn't bring food," said Adriana. "Even our hotel has run out."

"Len would have gone on the streets anyway," said Jeanne. "He insists his leg is improving. You should see him, Adriana—hobbling around here with such determination, exercising. I honestly believe he is gaining strength. Anyway, you know how he feels."

"He refuses to be a cripple," said Adriana.

Jeanne nodded.

"I've just come from your father. He is well. Tomorrow is the day they will stop the deportation."

"Théo says there won't be any tomorrow. I mean, not for the Germans. Tomorrow Paris will rise."

"Even so," said Adriana, "the SS gruppenführer must receive his bribe. The children are at Drancy. They could be taken away while the streets of Paris are in flames. Anyway, Théo may be wrong. And even if he is not, the Germans may crush an insurrection in one day."

"God forbid! What would happen to us all then?"

Adriana glanced around the large sunny room that was the studio. "This may be our refuge," she said. "Your father may have to come here. I may return here. Théo must not make this place look suspicious."

"Ile de la Cité," said Jeanne. "The great cathedral . . . Surely there will be no fighting here."

Even as they spoke, SS engineers were at work all over the Ile de la Cité, finishing the process of laying high-explosive mines, not only under the bridges between the island and the banks of the Seine, but also in the Préfecture de Police, in the courts of law and their magnificent medieval monument the Sainte Chapelle, and even in Notre Dame itself.

Baldwin returned in an hour, alone. He carried a small cotton bag, from which he pulled half a loaf of coarse bread and a few wilted vegetables. He had stood in line, he said, for these small provisions.

Adriana explained to him what was going to happen tomorrow. She would return here after she delivered the passports to Consul Nordling, she said.

"What is the address?" Baldwin asked.

"I am reluctant to tell you," said Adriana. "You must not come there. Neither of you."

"It is foolish not to tell us," said Baldwin. "A hundred things might happen."

"Well . . . The address is 112 rue Québec. I am to meet Consul Nordling at eleven o'clock. He has allowed plenty of extra time to get to Drancy, which is probably good judgment."

Jeanne was lighting newspaper under a small pot of water. They still had tea. "I have a terrible sense," she said, "that we are being drawn into a trap. You, my father . . . Why couldn't someone else go to 112 rue Québec?"

"I had the same idea," said Adriana, "but your father insists he has to go. I couldn't argue with his reasons—except by saying I doubted he was telling the entire truth, and of course I couldn't say that. He is a brave man, and he is determined. I *know* he suspects a trap. But he's going to risk it."

"For the lives involved," said Baldwin quietly.

"Our mission to Paris is more important than we ever expected, Len."

A few minutes after Adriana left the studio flat an exuberant Le Capitaine arrived, carrying bags of food.

"The bastards! The Milice—you know, the collaborationist militia—had storehouses of food! They meant to eat well, even if Paris starved. Well, no more. We've raided them. Our people stole everything! Here. Cheese. Dried eggs. Coffee. Sugar. Potatoes! I haven't seen a potato since—"

"Taken by force?" Baldwin asked.

"Taken by force," Le Capitaine confirmed.

"Weapons—?"

"*A chacun son Boche!*" cried Théo. To each one his German! "Each one we kill, we get his weapon. This morning two German trucks broke down on the road. Within minutes our people killed the drivers and seized . . . I don't know how much they seized. Machine guns! Rifles!"

"Théo," said Jeanne. She was drawing on her wet clothes, uncomfortable under his appreciative gaze. "Théo, tomorrow my father will carry a fortune in gold to Drancy, to stop the deportation of the children."

"Tomorrow," Le Capitaine said with a small frown.

"We may need help, Théo. Can you—"

"We can seize the camp and rescue the children."

"No," said Baldwin firmly. "The camp guards are SS men. They have machine guns, grenades . . . If the camp is attacked, they'll turn their weapons on the prisoners—including the children. The children are to be released into the custody of the Red Cross. Let it happen, Théo. Don't interfere."

Le Capitaine nodded thoughtfully as he continued to pull food from his bags and spread it on the table.

"But we must go to Montmartre tomorrow morning," said Jeanne. "To help my father. In case there's treachery."

"We can do as much damage interfering there," said Baldwin.

"I am going there, Len," she said resolutely. "Colonel Heinrici intends to surprise my father. Better that *he* should be surprised."

"If rue Québec is crowded with armed Résistants," Baldwin said sternly, "Consul Nordling will turn away. He represents a neutral nation, and he can't afford to become involved in a street fight. If the gold is not transferred into his automobile, the whole purpose—"

"Why must you assume we will do everything badly, Len?" Le Capitaine asked. "I will go with Jeanne, with maybe one more student. We can—"

"You will get her killed," Baldwin argued. "Or arrested, which is just as bad." He turned to speak directly at Jeanne. "If your father—"

"My father would say I must stay away," she interrupted. "My father thinks I'm a child and incapable of doing anything. *I am going, Len.*"

"Then I go, of course."

"No. There is no reason—"

"There is an overpowering reason," said Baldwin. "I love you, and I—"

"Len . . ."

"It would be better if neither of you went," said Le Capitaine.

The dining room of the Royal Monceau was lighted by candles. Electricity would be available only from 10:30 to midnight. Adriana entered on Konrad's arm. He wore his gray uniform with the Iron Cross—for the last time, almost, he had said in their suite. She was dressed as he had asked her, in the black silk dress he had bought her for the dinner with Gruppenführer Schenck. The tight, revealing dress seemed highly inappropriate for this final night in the hotel dining room, where austerity had at last caught up with the hotel's high-ranking residents, but she had not argued with him.

Only one other table was occupied when they arrived at the dining room: Gruppenführer Schenck, sitting alone. They could not refuse to join him.

"Ah, Heinrici," he said. "What keeps you in Paris, loyalty or profit?"

"I am afraid, Herr Gruppenführer, I reached the city too late to get a hand on any of its profits."

"You have found something more valuable," said Schenck, lifting Adriana's hand from the table and kissing it. "Mademoiselle Clement . . ."

"Where is—"

"Martine? Gone. I suppose she was afraid she would be caught by the Résistants and have her hair cut off. Let me suggest to you, Mademoiselle, that you go where you are not known and stay inside until the insanity subsides. If your neighbors know you have been living with a German officer, you may find yourself marching through the streets of your neighborhood, shorn and even naked."

His conversation was a relief. She had wondered if he could possibly suspect whose name and photograph he would be given tomorrow afternoon. Obviously he didn't. Obviously, too, Heinrici had no suspicion that it was to Gruppenführer Schenck that Henri Mercier was to deliver his gold. She was on treacherous ground: she knew what neither of them knew, and if either of them learned what she knew, she would die immediately.

"How much longer are you staying in Paris, Heinrici?" asked Schenck.

"Until General Hausser leaves, I suppose."

"Obergruppenführer Oberg left today," Schenck said. "Paris is left to von Choltitz."

"And you, Herr Gruppenführer?"

"Tomorrow, I think, Heinrici. I had wanted to stay, no matter what. But . . . orders from Berlin. My aides are packing my things tonight. The Führer's orders are clear—Paris is to be defended, destroyed if it cannot be held. But . . . you and I are not a part of that. We will fight somewhere else."

"Where, Herr Gruppenführer?" Adriana asked boldly.

Schenck waited until the waiter had finished pouring champagne for all of them, then answered, "In the streets of Berlin, Mademoiselle, if necessary."

"And may we expect to see you in Paris again?"

"Yes, I believe so," Schenck said solemnly. "In the end. Two or three years from now. Yes. I shall return."

Heinrici raised his glass. "To our return, Herr Gruppenführer!"

Schenck nodded curtly before he sipped. *"Heil Hitler!"* he snapped.

"Heil Hitler!" Heinrici joined.

Both of them turned to Adriana, holding their glasses ready, waiting. *"Heil Hitler,"* she murmured, and drank.

Striding about naked, he lit every candle in the suite. He had carried a bottle of champagne up from the dining room—it was warm, since the hotel could not make ice without electricity—and it popped and foamed out on the floor when he pulled the cork. He laughed and danced past her, carrying the dripping green bottle.

She undressed reluctantly, anticipating that tonight he would want celebratory sex. The little Belgian automatic was still in her handbag. If she just shot him now—

But she could not believe he had not established some shrewd strategem that would risk, if not cost, the lives of the children if he did not appear tomorrow morning at 112 rue Québec. Krueger was working with him. And someone besides, obviously—else, where had he gotten the forged passports, where had he gotten the cars they used the night of the escapes? All this time he had been building an elaborate scheme to gather the Mercier gold into his own hands. And it had become obvious to her that this had been his purpose from the beginning.

How had he learned about it? Had Colonel Harding won his cooperation by telling him about it? When Colonel Harding ordered her and Baldwin to 'go to ground,' had he been ordering them, actually, to stand aside and let Heinrici snatch his reward? He—

With his fingers Heinrici wet her nipples with champagne, then he bent down and sucked it off. His tongue circled her breasts, tasting of her after the champagne was gone from her skin. He misinterpreted her shudder.

"I love you! I love you, Adriana," he whispered.

The liar! She could not force out of herself the words he waited for. She *couldn't* say it! She could not match his gross lie.

He lifted her and carried her to the bed. He put her down and spread her legs. Her body gleamed in the light of a dozen candles. He knelt above her.

"The sheath!" she whispered. "The rubber, Konrad . . ."

He shook his head. "No . . . not this time. Let's have a baby, Adriana! Let's have a son. Or daughter. You and I!"

A child by him! In his callous arrogance, he failed to recognize revulsion. Desensitized by his excitement, her loathing was invisible to him. To carry his child! To rear it, knowing . . .

"Not now, Konrad," she whispered. "Not until . . . We can't go to a doctor, to a hospital, with a false passport. No yet. Not . . . not nine months from now."

He nodded. He slipped on the sheath and came to her. She submitted to him. For the last time.

XXIV

SATURDAY, AUGUST 19, 1944

AFTER a succession of sunny mornings with brilliant blue skies, Saturday dawned gray and leaden, with the threat of rain hanging darkly over the city. The grumble of artillery was regularly heard now, in every part of Paris—indistinguishable today from the roll of morning thunder out of the north.

Heinrici was awake. Gratefully, affectionately, he ran his hand over Adriana's warm, smooth bottom. His genitals still ached from what they had done last night. He kissed her shoulder, her back, then her bottom, and rolled off the bed. He went in the bathroom.

He was still in the bathroom, shaving, when the telephone rang.

"'Allo."

"Mademoiselle! You are still there? When will you be on the roof?"

Adriana licked her lips. "Uh . . . very soon. Very soon. Do you want to talk to Oberst Heinrici?"

"Has he any new instructions for me?"

Covering the mouthpiece with her hand, she called into the bathroom. "Konrad! Do you have any special orders for Oberleutnant Krueger?"

"No. Nothing different. Tell him yesterday's orders stand."

She spoke into the telephone. "Nothing new, Oberleutnant. We will see you shortly."

"Thank you, Mademoiselle."

On the roof . . . Someone was to be watching the rooftops. So . . . why did Krueger think *she* was to be there? No matter. *Someone* was watching. Mercier should know. Was there any way to get the word to him?

Konrad came out of the bathroom: naked, grinning, still yawning, dabbing at his face with a towel. His penis rose as he saw her, and she was glad he was in a hurry and would not suggest a quick repeat of last night's activities. He came to her and kissed her.

"Today," he said. "This is the day! Tonight you and I will sleep in a simpler bed—but with a little fortune of our own in two satchels of gold coins. I've written down"—he stepped to the little writing table and picked up a sheet of the hotel's note paper—"the address. Wait for me there. It's the home of a French couple—old friends. They are expecting you. They will help us hide until the battle for Paris is over."

He was pulling on his uniform. She looked at the address, then tore up the note.

"Be very careful, Adriana," he said. "Civil authority has broken down in Paris. There could be violence in the streets today. Plan to meet me about noon. Stay here as long as you can, then come directly to that address. Except for the passports, don't carry anything much." He paused and smiled. "You might fold the black dress in your bag and hide the passports under it. I'd like you to bring the black dress."

He checked his sidearm—the Walther hanging in his holster—something she had hardly ever seen him do. He kissed her once more, held her for a moment, then rushed out of the suite.

In the flat on rue du Mont, Henri Mercier had wakened early, as had Marie-Madeleine Lefevre. He slept in the living room, she in the bedroom. By eight she had been in the kitchen, lighting a newspaper fire to heat water for chestnut coffee. All they had to eat with the bitter brew was a hunk of coarse bread. This morning's adventure interfered with her morning routine. Usually she took her place in line before a bakery or grocery at this time of day. What they would eat tomorrow, she did not know.

As early as eight, Henri had looked down and spotted the young German lieutenant, already on watch on the street.

Oberleutnant Dietrich Krueger was painfully tired. No duty he had ever performed had proved as taxing to the legs and back as this constant watching from the street. Surely he had afforded someone a spectacle this morning. In his blue coveralls, he had driven to Montmartre in the Audi.

It was a bit of luck that he had been able to complete the call to Oberst Heinrici. The telephone service was not working well this morning. The exchanges were probably targets for the FFI, who seemed to be starting an insurrection.

A block away, Hauptmann Joachim Birkenfeld pounded a pick into the pavement of the street. He hoped he would not have to dig a deep hole before Oberleutnant Krueger moved.

On a rooftop directly above Birkenfeld, Mama Ange sat on a wooden kitchen chair and surveyed the area roofs through binoculars. Lying at her feet were green and red flags. She could signal Papa or Philippe—Heinrici—the moment she saw anyone on the roof of the building where the Jew was hiding. Papa was below and a hundred meters away. He was out of sight of Krueger or Birkenfeld, but he was perfectly positioned to see Mama wave her flag.

Karl Hausser finished a cup of genuine coffee—poured from his own thermos—at a table on the Place du Tertre. It was his guess that nothing much would happen before noon, and he had decided to let Birkenfeld keep watch alone for a time. Birkenfeld would make a *hell* of a hole in the street before anyone moved, he reflected with some amusement. He picked a bit of lint off the lapel of his dark blue suit. He had been reconsidering his decision not to tell Birkenfeld about Krueger or Krueger about Birkenfeld. When he went to see Birkenfeld he would at least tell the captain about the lieutenant. He was not going to tell the lieutenant about the captain, though. Birkenfeld would be his little secret.

Adriana pulled the two American passports from their hiding place in the armoire. She checked her pistol. Looking around the suite, she wondered if there was anything else she wanted to take, anything that would be of value to her. She found one thing. For a moment she hesitated, staring at it; then she picked up and shoved into her handbag the jade necklace Konrad had given her. She couldn't say why; for now she knew she wanted it, and that was enough.

She had not walked fifty meters from the hotel when she saw the poster:

MOBILISATION GENERALE!

The poster called on all citizens of Paris to rise, to fight, to kill German soldiers. *A chacun son Boche!* And, quite obviously, the city was responding. She could hear the angry popping of small-arms gunfire, coming intermittently from every direction. She hurried north on avenue Hoche to Parc Monceau. She planned her ascent of Montmartre—she would avoid the main streets and squares, the town halls of the arrondissements, and the schools: places where there might be fighting.

Len Baldwin was in the hold of powerful and conflicting emotions: he felt that two passionate children were leading him into peril neither could possibly justify; yet he could not let Jeanne venture onto the streets alone. And Jeanne was determined. She *would* go to Montmartre, to 112 rue Québec. She knew why she shouldn't go, but she was going anyway and she would not listen to argument.

Besides, his leg was bleeding. Le Capitaine had stolen a vélo-taxi. On the way down, Len had twisted his leg awkwardly, breaking open once more one of the deep seams that had never properly healed, and now his trousers were wet with a big stain of blood. Jeanne and Le Capitaine proposed to take him back up to the studio flat. On this point, *he* was adamant. If they must go to Montmartre, they would go together.

Le Capitaine pedaled the vélo-taxi. In one pocket of his jacket he carried a 9mm Luger. In the other he carried the white armband of the FFI. Jeanne was carrying the revolver Le Capitaine had brought to the studio. If they were stopped by a patrol, they would be taken directly to Fort Vincennes and shot—even if the Germans learned nothing more about them. In the circumstances, he had no choice but to carry his own pistol, the other of the two Belgian automatics the SOE had supplied him and Adriana. He had slipped it under his leg on the cushioned seat of the little vehicle.

As Le Capitaine pedaled into rue du Cloitre, they were shocked by a sound only Len had ever heard before: the distinctive angry crack of an 88mm gun. It was nearby. There had been small-arms firing around the Préfecture de Police for an hour or more, but this was the sound of artillery—almost certainly the turret gun of a tank. Le Capitaine spun the vélo-taxi around and pedaled fast for the Pont St. Louis. He crossed the bridge onto the Ile St. Louis and sped east on the center street of the small island, toward Pont Sully, the farthest bridge from the firing.

"They'll have all the bridges blocked," Len said.

"Maybe yes, maybe no," gasped Le Capitaine. "They have a lot of trouble this morning."

General Hausser heard the firing, including the brutal crack of 88mm guns. From his vantage point high on Montmartre, he could see smoke rising from the Ile de la Cité; he thought he understood what was happening—that Résistants were attacking the Préfecture de Police. He was wrong. The FFI had taken the Préfecture, and the loud cracks were the turret guns of tanks firing on the building. The noise troubled him, anyway, and he rose, carried his thermos to his car, and set out on foot for rue du Mont.

* * *

Heinrici used a key to let himself into the Anges' house. He went directly to the little spare bedroom he expected to share with Adriana, and there he quickly stripped off his uniform—for the last time almost certainly and not without a twinge of regret. In its place he put on bleu de travail. He folded the well-brushed gray wool carefully, deposited the Iron Cross in a tunic pocket, wrapped his breeches around his polished boots, stacked everything neatly, with his cap on top, and pushed the stack well back under the bed. He took the Walther from his holster and shoved it, together with an extra clip of cartridges, into the deep pockets of his coveralls. Settling an old black beret on his head, he returned to the street and set off for rue du Mont.

Marie-Madeleine Lefevre lunged for the ladder, caught it ungracefully but firmly, and hung breathing hard. After a moment she began to climb toward the roof.

She was dressed in a man's clothes, Jacob Pascin's in fact: gray suit, white shirt, blue necktie, gray hat. In a minute she clambered over the edge of the roof and stood there erect.

Three blocks away, Marie Ange stiffened and grabbed for her binoculars. Thank God, a man was on the roof at last! That rain might fall any minute and drench her was a matter of little moment to Mama Ange. That lightning might begin to flash in the low clouds above the Butte de Montmartre was something else again. A woman exposed on a roof, wet with rainwater, was a natural lightning rod! She pressed the binoculars to her eyes and studied the figure on the roof.

Marie-Medeleine had not spotted the woman with binoculars. She had little doubt, though, that she was being watched from somewhere. She crouched and scurried over the rooftops, playing a role she had rehearsed in her mind for two days.

Mama watched. So. North. He was hurrying north over the rooftops. She watched until the man in the gray suit and hat opened a door and descended into a flat below, then she knelt, picked up her green flag—a bit of faded curtain attached to a stick—and began to wave it back and forth.

Papa saw. Heinrici saw.

"Rue Paul Ferval," Heinrici said to Papa Ange. "He'll come out on rue Paul Ferval. I'll follow him from there. You go to Krueger on rue du Mont and tell him to climb the steps and turn into rue Cortot. If no one follows him, he can come around by rue St. Vincent and return to you. If someone follows him, he is to lead him away. You stay at his place on rue du Mont."

Papa nodded and hurried away without a word.

Striding into rue Paul Ferval, Heinrici was in time to see the figure in the gray suit come out onto the street. Marie-Madeleine suspected the man in bleu de travail was someone detailed to follow her, and she strode away toward the Cimitière St. Vincent as fast as she could.

Papa Ange reached Oberleutnant Krueger on rue du Mont. He gave him Heinrici's order, and Krueger turned away and began to climb the steps toward the basilica.

General Hausser was talking with Hauptmann Birkenfeld when both of them saw the old Frenchman approach Krueger. "Stay here," the general said to Birkenfeld. Birkenfeld sighed and pounded his pick once more into the hole he had dug knee-deep in the street; General Hausser strode off after Krueger.

Adriana reached rue Québec. No one was on the street, and she decided she could risk ambling by 112 just once. She entered the narrow, cobblestone-paved street, shadowed by the buildings that stood to three and four stories on either side of it.

The house at 112 rue Québec was a two-story building of time-softened pink brick. Oddly, there were no ground-floor windows, except for the stained-glass windows to each side of the door. The door was of polished oak, handsomely carved, with the number 112 on a brass plate. Oddly, too, the number 112 was worked into the patterns of the stained glass and at night would have glowed toward the street.

My God, it was a whorehouse! Beyond any doubt, 112 rue Québec was a brothel—and, from its appearance, a rich one, a maison d'illusion that attracted a prominent and monied clientèle. Adriana smiled. Henri Mercier and his friends were clever. They brought their gold here, where traffic in and out drew no attention.

She could not stand there and stare at it. She walked out of rue Québec, out of the street and around the corner.

Le Capitaine pedaled across the Pont Sully without incident. He had been right—the Boches were so busy with the uprising developing all over the city that they could not cover every bridge. Suspecting that the Place de la Bastille would be a focus of the rising, and of the German vigilance, he turned off boulevard Henri IV, into the smaller streets through which he could work his way toward Montmarte.

It was good judgment and yet it was not. Barricades had been thrown up, not on the Place de la Bastille itself but on the narrower streets leading into it. Better that he should have turned west on the quay. He carried Jeanne and Len directly into the fighting.

Turning into the rue St. Paul, Le Capitaine stopped abruptly. A hundred meters away, the street was blocked by a barricade, an immense, grotesque heap of debris: sandbags, stones, furniture, two cars, a pissoir, half a dozen vélo-taxis, crates and boxes, street signs, an uprooted telephone kiosk . . . A ragged hoard of armed men and women glared from behind the barricade, ready to shoot.

"*'Alt!*"

Six black-uniformed SS troopers trotted into the street, each one leveling a Schmeisser at the vélo-taxi.

For the moment, a standoff. Three of the SS men turned toward the barricade, menacing its defenders with their Schmeissers. Three bursts of 9mm slugs, chopping through the flimsy debris, would kill indiscriminately, and the FFI defenders knew it. A few well-aimed pistol shots from behind the barricade could drop three or four of the SS soldiers in an instant. Warily, the SS troopers aimed their Schmeissers at the vélo-taxi.

"*Papiere!*" barked the sergeant-leader.

"Sergeant!" yelled Len. "*Wo is der nächst Lazarett? Ich habe eine Wunde!*" He pointed at the wet blood on his pants leg. "*Gottverdammt Französich Schnepfer!*" Where is the nearest hospital? I have been wounded by a goddamned French sniper!

"*Sie sind Deutsch?*" asked the sergeant skeptically.

"*Ja! Ja! Ein Lazarett, Sergeant! Ich bin blutend.*" I am bleeding.

The SS sergeant glanced at the barricade, then back at the vélo-taxi. "*Papiere, bitte,*" he said coldly.

From a window in Marie-Madeleine's parlor, Henri Mercier had seen a shabby old Frenchman approach the German lieutenant and had seen the German lieutenant hurry purposefully away. But the old Frenchman had stayed, as if he were replacing the young German. Mercier had gone into Marie-Madeleine's bedroom and began—most reluctantly—to dress himself in her clothes: a violet and blue cotton dress, a dark blue linen jacket, low-heeled shoes, a blue straw hat with a veil that covered his upper face. Regarding himself in a mirror, he decided he looked bizarre. He had no choice but to apply red lipstick to his lips and rouge to his cheeks. He checked the time. It was 10:10. He would wait five minutes, then go out.

Heinrici had followed Marie-Madeleine Lefevre as far as rue Marcadet, on the north slope, but the determined pace of the figure ahead of him had begun to seem artificial. A person hurrying toward a fixed goal might walk this way but would walk more directly. This gray-clad person had taken odd turns. Also, if he thought he was being followed, how could he resist the temptation to glance behind him?

Heinrici's nerve failed. At the intersection of rue Marcadet and rue Carpeaux he ran forward and seized the gray-clad figure by the shoulder. If it were Mercier, he would force him to lead on. If not . . . *It was a woman!* She laughed at him. Heinrici swung around and ran back toward rue du Mont.

* * *

Papa Ange was following the woman who had emerged through the front door. She was in no hurry. Wearing a flowered blue-and-violet dress, she ambled along as though she had no particular purpose in the world. She climbed the shorter flight of steps on rue du Mont and, at the corner of rue St. Vincent, began to climb the longer flight toward the basilica.

Henri Mercier, well aware that he was being followed, could see no choice now but to go on to 112 rue Québec. Marie-Madeleine's deception had not worked. Or maybe it had, since there was no sign of Colonel Heinrici.

He was carrying an English Wembley revolver in his handbag. Whoever was guarding the gold would also be armed. If the threat were only Heinrici and this young officer, they would match them.

Heinrici ran all the way back to rue du Mont. Papa was gone. Krueger was gone. Mama was gone from the rooftop.

He glanced around. A workman in blue de travail was still digging in the street, as he had been all morning. Heinrici had been suspicious from the first, and now he was quite certain. The workman digging in the street was—was he a Jew, watching the street for Henri Mercier? Was he . . . Was he a German? If so—Gestapo? Or . . . Or Abwehr? Sent by Hausser? Very possible.

But Papa . . . Heinrici tightened, half-panicked. Being compelled to wait was the worst thing that could happen, but he had no option. Nervously, he felt the Walther in his pocket. He leaned against a wall near a doorway and shifted his focus back and forth from the digging workman to the streets abandoned by Krueger and Papa Ange.

The SS sergeant hesitated for a long time—conferring with one of his men, glancing at the barricade a hundred meters away, obviously uncertain, obviously bewildered as to how he was expected to cope with the unanticipated insurgency.

Le Capitaine's hand was in his pocket, on his pistol. So was Jeanne's. Baldwin could not imagine a more precarious situation: two armed children fingering their pistols, six Schmeisser-equipped SS thugs nervously wondering what to do.

"Sergeant! Der Lazarett, bitte."

"Ruhig," muttered the sergeant. Quiet.

That settled whatever question remained. The sergeant was not impressed with a bleeding man's claim that he was a German, of the Abwehr, and in immediate need of medical attention.

"Théo," Baldwin said quietly. "I'll take the sergeant and the two nearest him. You take the ones with their backs to us. Jeanne—The three nearest. Can you?"

Her eyes flared. "Can you?" she whispered angrily.

Baldwin drew the pistol from under his leg, took quick aim on the SS sergeant, and shot him dead. As the others swung around, he fired on them. The pop-popping of pistols was overcome by the roar of Schmeissers, and Baldwin supposed they had lost and were about to die. Then he saw that the automatic fire was the convulsive reaction of men falling with bullets in their bodies.

It was astounding. He could not believe it. Three people with pistols . . . Then he realized that heavy fire was coming from the barricade. Rifles had been aimed all along.

"Ahhh!"

Le Capitaine was hit.

Jeanne scrambled to her feet and threw herself across Le Capitaine as he slipped down from the seat of the vélo-taxi, to the pavement. Baldwin's eyes flicked to the fallen Germans, one and then another. He aimed his pistol to the one who was still trying to rise, but before he could squeeze off a shot the SS soldier flopped on his back, hit by three or four bullets from the barricade.

Le Capitaine screamed. Jeanne began tearing at his clothes to uncover his wound.

At the door of 112 rue Québec, Henri Mercier paused. He fought against turning to see if the unshaven Frenchman had followed him. It was pointless to turn and stare; he *knew* the man had followed him. He dared not try to kill him, either. A shot fired, a body left lying on the street, a crowd, police . . . Consul Nordling would not stop.

He turned the knob. The door was not locked. Good. He entered and hurried up the stairs.

"Monsieur." It was Aaron. They recognized each other. At the top of the stairs, they shook hands. "Not a believable woman, Monsieur," the young man said with a smile.

"I didn't deceive the Germans either, and I feel like a fool," Mercier said. "I hope I'll have time some way to change clothes before I go to Drancy."

"Germans?"

"Only thieves," said Mercier. "Not the Gestapo. Just two officers dressed like workmen. They want to steal the gold. Uh, it *is* here, I assume."

"Yes, it is here, Monsieur."

"Hidden?"

"Actually, no. It is on the table. Eighty kilos. Three of us brought it. The others—I ordered them to go."

"Aaron . . . within minutes at least two Germans are going to come in downstairs. One of them is very shrewd, a very experienced and capable intelligence agent, who survived years of spying in Paris and London and elsewhere. Another one is a young man, maybe not so shrewd and experienced but dangerous just the same. There is also a Frenchman who followed me. They are armed. And you—"

"I have a Boche pistol, Monsieur."

"Mine has a silencer," said Mercier. "I'm not sure how good that is. None of them really silence a pistol, I understand. Anyway, we cannot just shoot them down as they come in the door. We don't dare make a big noise, draw the police, draw a crowd. On the other hand, I see no option but to kill them."

"Two Boches. It's all right with me."

"All right. We have to let them in. They won't know where we are. We'll have an advantage. You say the gold is in here?"

"Yes. Madame's little parlor."

"I want to draw them into the house, well into the house, before we fire on them. We—"

"I understand, Monsieur. And...uh, happily, Madame left some men's clothes in her armoire. You can wipe off your makeup and change, Monsieur."

Krueger had led General Hausser on a hurried tour of the small, tangled streets of Montmartre. He had been surprised, actually, at how well the general managed to follow him; it had been difficult to outpace him, difficult finally to lose him. Lose him he did, though, on the southeast slope, and now he hurried back to the rue du Mont, breathless. He reached the street and saw Oberst Heinrici, just in time to hear his exchange with the shabby Frenchman.

"The bordel! The old maison d'illusion at 112 rue Québec! The Jew is smart. He's using the old bordel. Madame took her girls south in 1940, and the place has been vacant since."

"You are certain it was Mercier?" Heinrici asked. "I was following a woman."

"So was I." Papa laughed. "Only no woman. A man dressed as a woman. It was the Jew. I have no doubt of it."

Heinrici nodded and turned to Krueger. "Hausser?"

"He followed me. He recognized me, too. I'm sure he did."

"He'll come back here," said Heinrici. "What else can he do? He won't know where else to go."

"And we won't be here," said Krueger. "We move on to—"

"No," said Heinrici. "Don't look now, but you know there is a man digging in the street, a little way down."

"All morning," said Papa.

"And who else is digging up the pavements of Paris this morning?" asked Heinrici. "A general strike...Shooting, all over the city." He glanced at Hauptmann Birkenfeld, still busily digging. "Gestapo. Or someone from the Hotel Lutétia."

Papa Ange nodded. "Very likely. And he sees us here. He's been watching us all morning."

"The two of you take care of him," said Heinrici. "And when you're done, come to 112 rue Québec." He put a hand on Krueger's shoulder. "All right? You can do it?"

"Jawohl, Herr Oberst," Krueger said with stiff solemnity.

Heinrici nodded to Papa Ange. Papa returned his nod. The understanding between them was perfect.

Henri Mercier and Aaron went into the parlor to the left at the top of the stairway, the room where the madame of the house had once presided. She had sat there once, at the round .oak table covered with a red fringed cloth, and played cards with her girls as they waited for clients to be admitted by the maids who attended the front and rear doors. There now, on that red cloth, sat four large black leather valises, each one heavy with twenty kilos of gold coins.

Mercier opened each one and saw the golden hoard of Swiss francs, French francs, English guineas, German marks, Dutch gulden, and American double-eagles—many of which were long out of circulation but of course worth their weight in the gold from which they had been minted.

As Aaron had said, several men's suits hung in an oversized, ornate armoire in Madame's parlor. Henri Mercier had changed into a brown suit—though he had no shirt and was bare-chested under the brown wool jacket.

Aaron stood at the window, looking down at the street. He had noticed a young woman, a gorgeous blonde, on the street, at the corner, but no man in bleu de travail had appeared on the street. Not yet. Though now—

"Monsieur!"

Henri Mercier joined him at the window. He nodded. "Colonel Heinrici. That's the man. Look at him, Aaron. There is the enemy. Don't underestimate him."

Heinrici walked boldly up to the door. He tried the knob. It turned. He pushed the door back with his foot, looked, listened; then, cautiously, Walther ready in his hand, he stepped through the door and into the foyer of the brothel.

Adriana entered a tiny neighborhood café and bar, around the corner from 112 rue Québec. The proprietor, a man of perhaps sixty, heavy, lethargic, wearing a yellow-gray walrus moustache, stared at her and offered no welcome.

"Monsieur."

"Mademoiselle."

"The house at 112 rue Québec. A maison d'illusion, is it not?"

The man shrugged.

"Of the first class," she said. "And that means there was an entrance other than by the street door, so that gentlemen who valued their privacy could enter without notice."

Again, the man shrugged.

"I need to enter that house," she said. "I need to go in by that door."

"The house is closed," he said. "Come back in a few weeks. Madame may have returned by then. She might employ you. I wouldn't know."

"I want to go in now. And by the private door."

The man shrugged still again—and turned his back on her.

"Monsieur . . ."

He glanced contemptuously over his shoulder—and saw the Belgian automatic in her hand, aimed at his back.

"The door, Monsieur," she said.

Men and women, wearing the white armbands of the FFI dragged the vélo-taxi, the wounded Le Capitaine slumped beside Baldwin, behind the barricade. Tearing off his pants, they found that he had suffered two wounds to his left leg, apparently from two ricocheting rounds from a Schmeisser. One bullet had torn open a furrow in his thigh. The other, almost spent when it hit, was in the flesh below his knee. The men and women behind the barricade had expected to see wounds, but on Le Capitaine's leg they saw their first blood. A few of them wandered away.

They had no doctor, but one of the women was a trained surgical nurse. She took charge of Le Capitaine, cleaning and binding his wounds. After a few minutes she ordered two men to carry him away. They took him inside a bar, where they laid him on the zinc-topped counter. Someone ran for a doctor.

"We must go on to Montmartre," Jeanne pleaded with some of the FFI men. "It is urgent!"

After a few minutes, one of the young men volunteered to pedal the vélo-taxi, and they set out again. The young man wore the white armband and carried a rifle slung over his shoulder. Baldwin said they would never reach the Butte.

Heinrici could not but be struck by the mock elegance of the house. From the marble-floored foyer a broad, carpeted stairway led to an upper floor. On pedestals to either side of the stairway, stood polished black marble figures: nude Moors with gilded turbans. A cluster of frosted globes overhead would have lighted the foyer if there had been electricity. To the right of the stairs, a hallway led toward the back of the house. A heavy green curtain blocked any view along the hall.

Edging his way along the wall, past the staircase, he dropped to a squat and jerked back the curtain. The hall was partitioned by green curtians; another one hung five meters away. He understood: the curtains facilitated moving clients in and out without their meeting each other.

The hall was carpeted with a well-worn runner woven in an oriental pattern. Doors to either side of the hall were numbered with brass numbers.

He cautiously opened the door closest to him. The room inside was modestly furnished with a comfortable-looking brass bed, an armoire with mirrored doors, a chair upholstered in rose-colored plush—and a washbasin and bidet. The room looked as if it had been abandoned hastily: a flowered crepe wrapper hung from a knob on the armoire, and a flower, dry and brittle, stood in a little glass vase on the stand by the bed.

Heinrici quietly closed that door and turned and opened the one opposite. It was furnished the same.

Henri Mercier and Aaron knew Heinrici was downstairs. They whispered to each other. Would he check every room before he came up? When he reached the rear of the house, would he return to the front or come up the back stairs? They could not hear him. They talked about the best way to station themselves, to be ready for him whichever way he came.

At the top of the broad stairs, a short hall crossed the house, intersecting the main hall. From the short hall, one could enter the two big rooms at the front of the house: Madame's parlor, where the gold was, and opposite that a waiting room. The long hall, partitioned by heavy green curtains, ran to the back of the house and the narrow back stairs. Mercier and Aaron agreed to station themselves in the two ends of the cross hall. Whether Heinrici came up the back stairs and along the hall or up the broad front stairs, he would't be able to see them, and they could fire on him from both sides.

The sullen proprietor of the café had led Adriana to a door that opened onto a small brick-paved courtyard behind his café and the house at 112 rue Québec. He pointed to a door, then turned and retreated.

The upper half of the door was stained glass, the number 112 worked in the colorful pattern. The door was locked, of course. Her problem was somehow to get inside without making a noise that would alarm whoever was inside—either Henri Mercier or Heinrici.

She took a knife from her bag and set to work on one of the lead strips that held the colored glass in place. The lead was soft and yielded to her steel blade. In three or four minutes, she thought, she would be able to pull out a yellow pane. Then she could reach inside and unlock the door.

Dietrich Krueger was about to commit murder. That is, he was about to help this squalid old French gangster—called Papa—commit a murder. They didn't even know who the man in the blue coveralls was, but they were going to kill him. The Frenchman seemed to be utterly without conscience about it. Krueger had suggested that maybe Papa could lead the man away, while he, Krueger, hurried to 112 rue Québec to help Oberst Heinrici. Papa had shaken his head. Too much risk, he said. Too much at stake. That man—nodding toward the man knee-deep in the hole he had dug—could ruin everything. Anyway, he said, Philippe said we should take care of him. "Philippe" was his name for

Oberst Heinrici. As Krueger walked toward the man in the hole, he wondered miserably what kind of people these were, Heinrici and this Papa.

Papa walked ahead of him and passed by the man in blue coveralls. Now Krueger walked directly toward him.

"Monsieur..."

The man raised his eyes, somewhat startled. That was the point: to surprise him, distract him. He was a heavy man, soaked with sweat, and winded by his long labor with pick and shovel.

"Monsieur. Vous étes Allemand, n'est-ce pas?"

The man put down his shovel. "Ja, Herr Leutnant," he said coldly.

He never noticed that Papa had come up behind him. The shot that killed him was only a muffled pop, produced by a 7.65mm bullet at close range. Krueger had expected a dramatic bang, and could hardly believe it when the man crumpled and fell in the hole he had spent the morning digging.

Suddenly he heard a loud crack and the whine of a ricocheting bullet.

"Krueger!"

Krueger turned and saw General Hausser, fifty meters away and taking aim on him for a second shot. Papa Ange fired wildly at the general. Chips flew from the brick wall beside him, and General Hausser ducked into a doorway. Krueger drew his pistol and steadied himself. The general stepped out and leveled his Walther. Krueger fired. General Hausser dropped the Walther and for a long moment stood staring at Krueger as if he saw something amazing about him. He pitched forward.

"Mein Gott!" yelled Krueger. Stunned, he staggered toward the fallen general.

Papa followed him, close behind. The frightened young German knelt over the Abwehr general, his commanding officer, he had just shot to death. He didn't notice that Papa was just above and behind him. Papa's bullet entered his head just behind the left ear and blew off the front of his skull.

Papa stood erect and tucked his pistol into his pocket. He glanced around. No one had seen him. But as he climbed the stone steps toward rue St. Vincent, five German soldiers suddenly appeared at the top of the higher set of steps. They shouted an order to him to halt. He turned and ran down rue Becquerel. They fired at him, but their bullets missed widely. He yelled, though, as if he were hit. As he ran down the street and turned the corner, he could hear their hobnailed boots clattering down the steps. What he would do for Philippe and the gold right now was lead these clumsy squareheads away from rue Québec.

Somehow the young FFI man pedaling the vélo-taxi managed to reach the foot of the Butte. They could hear firing above. A German patrol ran past them, so intent on reaching the battle that seemed to have broken out somewhere on the Butte de Montmarte that they did not even notice that the young man on the vélo-taxi was wearing the armband of the FFI.

He could not pedal them up the steep streets. Baldwin could not walk, so the young man began to push the vélo-taxi up the hill. It was slow. Jeanne was impatient. Baldwin pleaded with her to stay with him, but she began to cry and ran up the hill alone, toward rue Québec.

For an unhappy moment Heinrici began to wonder if Papa had followed the wrong man or had made some mistake. Or could Mercier have come in, grabbed his gold, and left in the few minutes before he, Heinrici, got here? Or—if he was in the house, where was he?

He pondered the layout for a moment. Guests would have been received in the foyer. But it was ulikely that girls were displayed to them there, where the door opened directly on the street. So there had to be a room where the girls were shown to the men—and there had to be a room where they waited, where Madame held court. Upstairs. Of course. Up that broad staircase. There was nothing but more cribs along this ground-floor hall. Upstairs, maybe Madame had even had a safe!

Unless he had succeeded with some clever deception, Henri Mercier was upstairs—and so was the gold.

Heinrici returned to the foyer and slid along the wall until he could see up the stairs. No one. He opened the street door. No Krueger. No Papa. He could not wait long for them. Could they have had trouble?

It was quiet upstairs. He wondered if Mercier knew he was in the house. He wondered if Mercier was alone. Nervously, he checked the Walther once more. It was loaded. He cocked it. It was capable of firing double-action, without cocking, just by pulling the trigger, but it would be a split-second faster if it was cocked.

He looked up and down rue Québec one more time. Then he turned and began to climb the stairs.

The yellow pane cracked, but it did not fall noisily. Adriana reached inside the door and groped for the lock. She could not reach it. She would have to wrench out another pane, but that would go faster. In a minute she would be inside.

She wondered if Heinrici was in the house. She was sure he had set up a clever scheme for following Henri Mercier, but Mercier was clever, too, and he was determined not to be followed. If he had eluded Heinrici, everything would be very easy. She would help him protect the loading of the gold into Consul Nordling's car; then she would go to the studio flat on the Ile de la Cité and stay with Len and Jeanne until the Paris fighting subsided.

Heinrici crawled up the stairs, keeping absolutely quiet—and thinking what a fool he looked if there were no one above. He could see a green curtain, the same as the ones in the hall downstairs. But there was a hall running across the house, too. Behind the curtain would be more cribs. At the front of the house—

A face! To his right, at the corner of the cross hall, a man had poked his face out to have a look down the stairs. And what was more, unless Heinrici were grossly wrong, the man had not seen him.

All right. It was not Mercier. So there were two of them. Maybe more. But they wouldn't surprise him now. He knew where one of them was, and very likely another one—*the* other one?—was in the opposite end of the cross hall. And the one to his right was too nervous, or too impatient, to wait. He was a fool. He had thrown away his advantage.

If he was that nervous . . . Heinrici dug into the pockets of his coveralls. He found the extra clip for the Walther. The key to the Anges' house. It was a big key. Heavy. Heinrici stretched out on the carpeted stairs, aimed his pistol, and with his left hand tossed the key down to the parquet floor of the foyer. It made a better noise than he expected. It struck the floor with a bang and clattered across the floor.

The man peered around the corner as before. Again he didn't see Heinrici prone on the stairs below him, so he stepped out for a better look. Heinrici fired one shot. Hit in the upper belly, the man shrieked, dropped his Luger and clasped his wound, and fell first to his knees, then over on his back.

Heinrici took advantage of the surprise. He sprang forward and threw himself above Heinrici.

"Well, Monsieur."

The Walther was aimed at his belly, and Mercier surrendered. He lowered the gun and let it drop to the floor.

Adriana heard the shots inside the house. She smashed through the stained glass and unlocked the door.

Heinrici led Henri Mercier into the front room where the four valises of gold sat on the table. Holding his Walther in his right hand, with his left he opened one of the valises and stirred the gold coins inside. He lifted the valise, tried its weight. He lifted each of the others in turn.

"Where is the rest of it, Monsieur?"

Henri Mercier shook his head sadly. "That's all of it. It is to save the lives of nearly two hundred children."

"Do you think I am stupid?" Heinrici asked. "This couldn't be all of it."

"That's all there is, Colonel Heinrici. That's all the gold there is—except a small amount set aside for the unlikely chance you ever really were in communication with someone who could have freed my wife from Ravensbrück."

Heinrici lifted one of the valises a second time. "Monsieur, I do not believe you."

"So . . . ," murmured Henri Mercier. "If I agree to lead you to the rest of the gold, will you release this to save the children?"

"You do seem to think I'm a fool," said Heinrici.

Adriana jerked aside green curtains, recklessly hurrying along the ground-floor hall. She shoved open the doors of two of the cribs before she decided they were all alike. She reached the foyer. From there, at the bottom of the stairs, she could hear voices from above: Heinrici and Mercier, somewhere near but upstairs.

Where was Krueger? She clung to the walls of the foyer and circled it, looking for Krueger or someone else who might be guarding Heinrici's rear.

She pressed her face to the stained glass of the front door. My God! Through the colored, bubbly glass she could see a black car. Consul Nordling was here!

Carefully, quietly, she opened the door. There were three men in the car: a driver and two other men, probably the Consul and an aide. Adriana saluted them and forced a smile.

"*Un moment, Messieurs,*" she said softly.

Jeanne came running from across the street. Adriana put her finger to her mouth to signal silence, pointed back across the street, and locked and bolted the door.

Wherever Krueger was, she could not delay. She kicked off her shoes and trotted up the stairs, pistol in hand. The voices came from the room to the left. She flattened herself against the wall and moved to the door.

Heinrici was speaking—"If this is only a fraction of the gold, then I will release this for your children. All you have to do is show me the rest of it. Is it in the house?"

Adriana stepped into the doorway.

"*Adriana!*"

She held the Belgian automatic close to her body, aimed at Heinrici. "Consul Nordling is on the street outside, Monsieur," she said to Mercier. "Go out and speak to him. Have his driver come up and help you carry the gold. Also, Jeanne is out there. Don't let her come in the house."

Henri Mercier edged his way past Heinrici and rushed out and down the stairs.

Heinrici stared at the Belgian automatic. Involuntarily he let his eyes fall for an instant to his Walther. He had lowered it while he was talking to the unarmed Mercier, and its muzzle pointed at the floor. She saw his eyes drop. She read his thought. Her finger tightened on her trigger.

Heinrici sighed. "How much do you know?" he asked.

"Everything," she said. "Just about everything, I think."

He had spilled the contents of one of the valises on the red fringed tablecloth, and he put his hand now on the pile of gold coin. "It's ours, Adriana," he said. "This is the future we've talked about. And this is only a small part of it."

"No, Konrad," she said. "That's all there is. About seventy kilos of it. It will save two hundred children from deportation to a Nazi death camp."

"It is *ours,* Adriana," he said. "We've risked our lives for it."

"I don't want it," she said.

"He's lying about the children," said Heinrici. "He—"

"He is about to give it to Consul Nordling, the Swedish consul in Paris, who is outside waiting for it. Consul Nordling is delivering it to Gruppenführer Schenck, who will sign the order releasing the children into the custody of the International Red Cross."

"You are fools. Schenck will kill you all."

"We'll have died for something better than a scheme to make ourselves rich. All along, all the risks you took . . . that's all you had in mind, Konrad. That's all you cared about."

Heinrici shook his head. "I had something besides in mind," he said. "I love you, Adriana. I really do."

"You lie," she said coldly.

"Then can you kill me, Adriana?" he asked. A faint smile turned up the corners of his mouth, and he began very slowly to raise the muzzle of the Walther.

"Yes," she said. "Yes, I can, Konrad. Don't test me."

"I love you, Adriana," he said again—but the muzzle of his pistol steadily, slowly rose.

She fired.

The little bullet from the silenced pistol hit him low on the chest, shattered a rib, and plowed into his lung.

"*Adriana!*" he coughed. He shook his head, unbelieving. Then he stiffened and raised his shoulders. She aimed higher and fired twice more.

His knees buckled and he toppled over the table, then slid off and fell to the floor.

EPILOGUE

Adriana went to the street door, unlocked and opened it, and calmly told Henri Mercier he could take his gold now, Heinrici was dead. She handed him the two forged passports.

Emil Bender and Consul Nordling's driver carried the heavy valises of gold to the car. As they came down from upstairs the second time, Len Baldwin arrived. He clasped Jeanne to him, and together they went inside the house to comfort Adriana. She sat on the bed in the first crib behind the green curtain, numb and oddly silent.

The Swedish diplomat was impatient to move. The city was in chaos, he said, with heavy fighting at many points, and he was not sure they could reach Drancy. Before he entered the car, Henri Mercier told Jeanne to take their friends to the flat on rue du Mont. It still wasn't known and would be safe. Then he took his place in the front seat, and the black car, flying the Swedish flag from a fender, sped down from the Butte and set off across the city toward the prison camp at Drancy.

They were stopped repeatedly on the way, both by German roadblocks and by armed and angry young men and women of the FFI. Each time the Swedish flag and diplomatic passport—plus some firm words in German by Emil Bender and

316

others in French by Henri Mercier—got them through. They were able to keep the two o'clock appointment with Gruppenführer Schenck.

At first, Schenck was outraged by the accusation against Oberst Konrad Heinrici and refused to consider the bargain met, but Erich Langbehn, governor of Fresnes Prison, took one look at the photograph on the Henry Conrad passport—as Adriana had suggested—and he verified the charge against Heinrici: vehemently. They also studied the Betty Conrad passport. Schenck recognized the beautiful blonde of the photograph as the young woman he knew as Jacqueline Clement. Walter Kleist, governor of Romainville, recognized her as the blitzmädchen who had taken part in the assault on his prison.

Schenck radioed orders back to Paris for the arrest of Oberst Heinrici and the English spy Adriana Kip, both of whom would be found at the Royal Monceau Hotel. Henri Mercier saw no reason to tell him that neither Konrad Heinrici or Adriana Kip would be found at the Royal Monceau.

Schenck and his staff did not return to Paris. They set out immediately for the Rhine.

The number of children released was not 189 but 236—177 of them Jews, 59 the sons and daughters of Résistants. They ranged in age from four years to fifteen. The nuns of Montceleux acted as representatives of the International Red Cross. The children were loaded on trucks without incident and driven away to the convent, where they would remain until after the liberation of Paris the following week.

French armored divisions entered Paris on the following Friday, August 25.

Gruppenführer Heinz Schenck surrendered to British officers on May 23, 1945. He was returned to Paris, imprisoned, tried, and sentenced to death for crimes against the French people. On the basis of evidence of his role in the liberation of 236 children in August 1944, his sentence was commuted to life imprisonment. He was released from prison in 1953 and returned to Frankfurt, where he was admitted to partnership in his brother's retail shoe store.

The gold he carried away from Drancy was never recovered. He testified that it was stolen from him by SD investigators within a month after he returned to Germany.

Martine Paul was released from her cell within hours after the death of General Hausser. Having no place to go, she returned to her flat in Montparnasse. On Thursday, August 24, she was accused as a collaborator, tried on the street and found guilty. Her head was shaved, she was stripped to her underwear, and with several other women guilty of minor acts of collaboration, she was marched through the streets for several blocks, while crowds jeered and laughed. Even so, she was able to reestablish her career. Though never again employed by Schiaparelli, she was, through the 1950s, a successful and highly paid fashion model. She married a physician in 1962 and retired from modeling.

In January, 1946, Oberführer Erhard Franck was hanged at Fort Vincennes. Included in the evidence agaist him was the testimony of six of the young women who had been abused in his house on boulevard Suchet. One of the witnesses was Jeanne Mercier.

When the prewar madame failed to return, Marcel and Marie Ange reopened the house at 112 rue Québec and operated it as a highly successful brothel until the National Assembly enacted the 1947 law prohibiting open and notorious houses of prostitution. After that, they retired. Papa said a man could always find a way to earn a few thousand francs, if he needed them.

Théo, whose full name was Théodore Vaubin, recovered so quickly from his wounds that he was on the barricades during the final days of the fighting. He returned to his studies in the winter, and ultimately became a lawyer. In 1950 he was elected to the Paris city council, as a Communist. He served one term. In 1964 he was elected again, this time as a Gaullist. In both election campaigns he used his wartime pseudonym, Le Capitaine.

Narcisse Mercier died at Ravensbrück on January 12, 1945, of pneumonia and dysentery. Word of her death did not reach Henri Mercier until June. By then he had recovered his store and his home. In March, 1946 he married Marie-Madeleine Lefevre.

Through the fall and winter of 1944–45, Len Baldwin underwent a series of operations on his leg, which made it possible for him eventually to walk without a cane. Jeanne came to London and lived in a cold flat near the hospital, so she could be with him. In April 1945 they were married in Westminster Abbey— both having curtly dismissed the objections of their fathers.

They moved to Cambridge, where Len returned to his chemistry laboratory. He and Jeanne became the parents of two sons and two daughters. In the 1960s Doctor William Leonard Baldwin was internationally honored for his work in organic chemistry. Eventually he would share a Nobel Prize.

Adriana . . .

In London in May, 1945, Adriana Kip Ter Horst was summoned to Buckingham Palace, where, in the presence of Winston Churchill, the King invested her with the insignia of the order of the British Empire. In The Hague the next month, Queen Wilhelmina admitted her to the Order of the Netherlands Lion.

Then she went to Paris for the ceremonies of her induction into the Legion of Honor.

For a few weeks she almost heard the cries again: "Adriana! Adriana!" It was almost the way it had been eight or nine years before.

And yet, of course, it wasn't. It couldn't be.

Sir Henry Harding arranged for her to be offered a job as swimming instructor at a school just outside London. But for Adriana London was a foreign city, as ever. Except for Len and Jeanne, she had no friends in England and, except for the teaching, no reason to stay in an alien land.

She went home, only to find that The Netherlands was not her home anymore either. She had no family. Of her friends, some had collaborated during the war and were half afraid to see her. Even those who hadn't were uncomfortable with her. They didn't know how to talk to her. They didn't know what to say to a one-time friend they had not seen for years and had supposed was dead: who had lost as much as she had lost and who, as they had heard, had more than once killed, with her own hands.

Perhaps inevitably, she returned to Paris, in mid-summer 1945. She rambled through the streets, from avenue Hoche to rue Québec, from Les Halles to Romainville. It wasn't the same. The city was intent on clearing its memory as fast as it could, hurrying resolutely into its future. It was pleasant to be able to amble here and there, along the river and in the neighborhoods, without fear. But it was lonely, too, and the street-wandering was frivolous.

One day she turned a corner, glanced into a courtyard, and was shocked to see the red-white-black swastika flag hanging above a doorway guarded by two soldiers in field-gray, Schmeissers on their hips. She gasped before she noticed the camera and the lights. They were making a film. Already everything that had happened last summer had become unreal, the stuff of make-believe.

She was short of money. She moved into a pension not far from Les Halles. And from there, one morning early in November, 1945, the police took her, first to jail, and then once she was identified as Adriana Kip, to a hospital. She was suffering from malnutrition and alcohol poisoning.

For twenty-four hours it was not certain she would live. When she regained the ability to recognize people and hear their words, she saw Henri Mercier at her bedside. Then Théo came. And the next day an engraved card was brought to her. The nurse told her the gentleman whose name was on the card wanted to see her.

The name was Maurice Martin Charles Gabriel de Fransac-Rochefort. He was the elderly man she had known as Monsieur Martin, the radio operator who had transmitted her messages from Paris to London. He renewed his invitation to her to move into his elegant apartment on rue Guillaume. Very gently he suggested that she was in need, and he said he would be honored to help her.

Adriana wept. The old man rose and stood behind her chair, gently rubbing her shoulders and the back of her neck, and she covered her face in her hands and wept for her losses, for her loneliness, for her life. She admitted to him that she had no money and no place to go. She accepted his offer.

She lived with Monsieur Martin, as she continued to call him, all that winter, and in the spring she moved with him when he went south to open his villa on the Riviera. He was infinitely kind, and he enjoyed sharing reminiscences of the war years. They were real to him, as they were to her. He shared her sense that they had been years of purpose; and, though he hated what those years had done as much as she did, he understood, as almost no one else did, the void left in her life by the disappearance of purpose.

He loved to entertain. Rarely were he and she alone for dinner. His guests included such diverse characters as Ernest Hemingway and the Duke of Windsor, Gertrude Stein and Josephine Baker, Maurice Chevalier and Henri Matisse.

Monsieur Martin was a second father to her. She was not in his bedroom when he died. His servant woke her on a late-spring morning in 1946 and told her he had died in his sleep overnight. Adriana went down to breakfast with Ernest Hemingway, who happened to be in the villa that morning, having been the guest of honor at a quiet dinner the night before. They talked for an hour. No one knows what they said. Hemingway told investigators that afterward Adriana said she believed she would go for a swim.

She was never seen again after she plunged into the gentle Mediterranean surf that morning. Her body was never recovered. For a long time it was assumed that Adriana Kip could not have drowned, that she was alive somewhere; and tabloid newspapers reported her appearance in places as widely separated as Havana and Bangkok. By his will, Monsieur Martin left her a wealthy woman. She never claimed the legacy.